Notorious, fabulously rich,

Spendi  Italian

One night in
MILAN

Three wonderful, passionate and
intense bestselling novels

One night in
MILAN

MICHELLE REID · INDIA GREY · KATE HEWITT

One night in
RIO

ANNE MATHER · JENNIE LUCAS · OLIVIA GATES

One night in
BUENOS AIRES

MAGGIE COX · CHANTELLE SHAW · SARAH MORGAN

One night in
MADRID

KATE WALKER · JENNIE LUCAS · ABBY GREEN

One night in MILAN

MICHELLE REID

KATE HEWITT

INDIA GREY

MILLS & BOON

Harlequin Mills & Boon Limited, Eton House,
18-24 Paradise Road, Richmond, Surrey TW9 1SR

ONE NIGHT IN MILAN © Harlequin Enterprises II B.V./S.à.r.l. 2011

The Italian's Future Bride © Michelle Reid 2006
The Italian's Chosen Wife © Kate Hewitt 2007
The Italian's Captive Virgin © India Grey 2007

ISBN: 978 0 263 88535 4

009-0311

Harlequin Mills & Boon policy is to use papers that are
natural, renewable and recyclable products and made from
wood grown in sustainable forests. The logging and
manufacturing processes conform to the legal environmental
regulations of the country of origin.

Printed and bound in Spain
by Litografia Rosés S.A., Barcelona

The Italian's Future Bride

MICHELLE REID

Michelle Reid grew up on the southern edges of Manchester, the youngest in a family of five lively children. Now she lives in the beautiful county of Cheshire, with her busy executive husband and two grown-up daughters. She loves reading, the ballet, and playing tennis when she gets the chance. She hates cooking, cleaning, and despises ironing! Sleep she can do without and produces some of her best written work during the early hours of the morning.

Don't miss Michelle Reid's exciting new novel,
After Their Vows, **out in April from**
Mills & Boon® Modern™.

CHAPTER ONE

IT WAS like playing Russian roulette with your sex life: place a loaded invitation in the barrel, then shoot and see if you scored a hit.

Everyone was doing it, Raffaelle Villani observed cynically—the young and nubile, complete with breast implants and carefully straightened and dyed blonde hair. They circled the room eyeing up likely victims, picked the richest man they could find, then primed him and fired their lucky shot.

Or unlucky, depending from which side of the fence you viewed it.

Some you win, some you lose, he mused as one eager player tried the deal on him only to be rewarded with the sight of his back.

Contempt twisting his lean golden features, he beat a retreat to the furthest corner of the room where the bar was situated. Discarding his untouched glass of champagne, he ordered a glass of full-blooded red wine to take its place.

Functions like this were the pits and he would not have come but for his stepsister twisting his arm. He owed Daniella a favour for pulling him out of a tricky situation recently with a woman who had been about to become his latest lover—until Daniella had whispered in his ear that the woman was married with a small son.

It turned out that she had even lied to him about her name. Discovering that she was actually the ex-catwalk model Elise Castle, now married to the heavyweight Greek Leo Savakis, had not made Raffaelle feel good about himself.

Married women were not his bag. Married women with small children were an even bigger turn-off. As were neat little liars who pretended to be someone they were not. Elise Castle ticked the boxes in all three categories and the hardest part of it all had been accepting how thoroughly he had been duped by a pair of innocent blue eyes and a set of good breasts that had been her own.

Or maybe not, Raffaelle then contended. Perhaps the breasts and the blue eyes had been just more lies the beautiful Elise had fed to him. Fortunately he had not managed to get close enough to find out.

But he still owed it to Daniella that he'd managed to get out of a potentially scandal-spinning tangle before it had exploded in his face.

He was into gun metaphors, he noticed. What a great way to spend a Saturday night.

Where was Daniella—?

Straightening his six-foot-four-inch frame up from its bored languid slouch against the bar, Raffaelle began scanning the sea of bodies milling about in front of him for a glimpse of the sylphlike figure belonging to his beautiful stepsister.

He found her almost instantly. Her glossy mane of black hair and the red dress she was wearing made her virtually impossible to miss. She was standing with some smooth-looking guy over by a wall on the other side of the room, and it came as a shock to Raffaelle to see that she was playing the game like all the rest!

She was pouting, her pose distinctly saucy, her breasts pushed up almost against the guy's chest while he looked down at her with one of those lazy I'm-interested-smiles on his handsome face.

Were Daniella's breasts her own—?

The question hit Raffaelle's brain and made him curse softly because he didn't care what Daniella's breasts were made of. She was not and never had been his type. And anyway, as his stepsister, she was and always had been off limits.

She was also getting married in two months, to one of his closest friends. But there she stood, coming on to another man!

Annoyance launched him away from the bar with the grim intention of going over there and hauling her away before one of the other kind of circling vultures here—the press—noticed her and ruined the foolish creature's life.

'Mr Villani?' a husky female voice spoke to him. 'I'm really sorry to bother you but...'

Raffaelle spun on his heel to find himself staring down at yet another nubile young thing with the requisite blonde hair and good breasts. His expression turned to ice as he looked down at her, though the way she was looking up at him through tense, apprehensive, big blue eyes almost made him think twice about turning his back.

More so when the pink tip of her tongue arrived to nervously calm the little tremor he could see happening with her lips.

Nice lips, he noticed. Full, very pink, very lush lips.

'Do you think I could h-have a word with you?' she requested nervously. 'It's really important,' she added quickly. 'I need to ask you a big favour...'

A favour? Well, that was a novel approach. Raffaelle felt the corner of his mouth give a twitch—and thereby did the worst thing he could have done, by allowing a chink of interest to stop him from walking away.

Her silky hair hung dead straight to her slender shoulders and she possessed the most amazing pearly-white skin. He sent his eyes skimming down her front to her cleavage where two firm, plump very white breasts balanced precariously inside the tiny bodice of the short and skimpy pale turquoise silk thing he supposed he should call a dress. She wasn't tall by his standards, but she had a pair of legs on her that did not need the four inch heels she was wearing to extend their fabulous length.

Cosmetically enhanced or not, this one was probably the most appealing package in the room tonight, he accepted as he lifted his eyes back to the pair of pink lips to watch them tremble some more as she waited for his response.

When he still did not give one, she took a step closer, her too-blue eyes lighting up with appeal. 'You see I have this— problem…'

She was going to touch him. His stupid hesitation had given her encouragement to believe that he was interested.

Raffaelle stiffened, each well toned muscle in his long lean framework abruptly tightening up.

'No,' he iced out.

Then turned on his heel and strode off.

Cold, rude, arrogant swine, Rachel mentally tossed after him in stinging frustration. Did the too-tall, dark and disgustingly handsome devil think he was so special that he didn't need to be polite to a woman?

Well, you're not my type, Mr Villani, she told the long length of his retreating figure. Especially if *his* type was the kind of women doing the rounds here tonight.

Rachel's blue eyes turned bitter as she flicked them round the gathered assembly of the famously rich and beautiful—in that order, money being the biggest attraction here tonight. It was a trade fair for the beautiful people to ply their wares in front of London's wealthiest, though it hid under the more respectable title of a Charity Fundraising Event.

She should not have come here. If Elise hadn't convinced

her it was the only way to get close to a man like Raffaelle Villani, she would not have been seen dead at a do like this.

'He likes them blonde and slinky,' Elise had said. 'Notoriously can't keep his hands off. You only have to read down the list of his last fifteen girlfriends to know the man has no control when he's faced with blonde hair and a great pair of legs.'

Well, not in my case, Rachel thought heavily as she gave a grim tug at the hem of the dress Elise had made her wear. 'You have to look the part,' her half-sister had insisted. 'When you pay the extortionate price for tickets like these it means you have to look as if you can afford to throw good money away.'

The silly price of the tickets was one thing, but a five figure sum dress only earned its price tag if it looked good on the wearer.

Rachel felt as if she looked like a very cheap tart.

'Hello, beautiful…' The unremarkable hit line arrived as a hand squeezed around her waist at the same time and a pair of lips arrived at one of the straps which held up the dress. 'Having trouble with the dress? Can I help?'

His teeth nipped at the shoulder strap. Rachel heaved in a thick breath of disgust. 'Take your hands and your teeth off me,' she iced out, then broke free and walked off without giving the guy a single glance.

She'd taken about five steps before she realised she'd inadvertently walked in the same direction as Raffaelle Villani.

And there he was.

She stopped dead.

He was in the process of disentangling a lovely young thing wearing red from the possessive clutches of another man. The vision in red turned to pout a protest at him, then flung her arms around his neck and kissed him full on the mouth.

So much for him preferring them blonde, Rachel thought cynically. The creature he'd just claimed and was now kissing was hot-lipped, glossy and black-haired.

Oh, God, she thought helplessly, what was she going to do if she did not manage to pull this off?

'You're drunk,' Raffaelle informed Daniella.

'Tiddly,' his half-English stepsister insisted with a smile gauged to melt his irritation away.

It did not succeed. 'Admit to being drunk, *cara*,' he advised as he grabbed both of her hands and dragged them down from around his neck. 'It is the only excuse Gino will accept for what you have just been doing.'

'I haven't been doing anything—!' Eyes the colour of warm dark chocolate opened wide and tried their best to look innocent.

'You were hitting on that guy,' Raffaelle accused her.

'We were flirting, that's all! And what do you think you're doing, Raffaelle?' she protested when he took hold of her hand and turned towards the exit.

'Taking you home,' he clipped out. 'I don't know why I let you talk me into bringing you here in the first place.'

'For some fun?' Daniella offered up.

'I don't do this kind of fun.'

'That's your big problem, Raffaelle,' she informed him as he trailed her behind him. 'You don't *do* anything these days other than work yourself into the ground.'

'My choice.'

'To be a grouch.'

A nerve ticked at the corner of his mouth because she was right: he was becoming grouch—a bitter and cynical grouch.

'All because one woman managed to con you into believing she was pure sweetness and light...'

'As you try to do, you mean?'

'I *am* all sweetness and light!' Daniella insisted. 'And that wasn't very nice,' she complained. 'Nor do I lie or cheat.'

'Tell that to Gino not to me,' Raffaelle countered. 'If he had seen the way you were preparing to wrap yourself around that guy, he would call the wedding off.'

'But Gino isn't here because he prefers to be halfway across the world playing the hot shot tycoon.'

'However, the press *is* here—'

Raffaelle stopped walking as a sudden thought hit him. He swung round to pierce her with a hard stare.

'Is that what this is about?' he demanded. 'Did you drag me out to this thing—which is nothing more than an overpriced knocking shop,' he said with contempt, 'so that you would be caught on camera playing the vamp with some other guy just to punish Gino, knowing that *I* would be on hand to haul you out of trouble before you got yourself in too deep?'

'I hate him,' Daniella announced. 'I might even decide not to marry him. I'm supposed to be the love of his life yet I haven't set eyes on him in two wh-whole weeks!'

The small break in her voice did it. Raffaelle heard the fight with tears and released a sigh. 'Come here, you idiot.' He pulled her into his arms. 'You know Gino worships the ground you walk upon but he is busy trying to free himself up for that long glorious honeymoon he has planned for you both.'

'He even sounds like he would rather be doing something else when he rings me,' she sniffed into his shirt front. 'I'm not a doormat. I refuse to let him wipe his feet on me!'

Raffaelle shifted his stance.

'You're laughing at me!' Daniella choked out.

'No, I am not.'

What he was actually doing was staring over Daniella's glossy dark head into the cynical blue eyes of the blonde who had approached him a few minutes ago. She was now standing about ten feet away being buffeted by the milling crowd but not noticing because she was too busy looking at him as if he was a snake.

A sting injected itself down the front of his body. The con-

fusing signals she was giving off dressed—or *un*dressed—
like she was, while glaring at him like that, were setting his
senses on edge.

Who the hell was she, anyway? Why had he not hung
around long enough to find out?

Did he want to know?

His eyes cooled and hardened. No, he didn't, he answered
his own question. Expensive tarts in expensive dresses were
ten-a-Euro to buy in this room. He did not need to buy his
women. And this one was more the type for the guy who was
approaching her from behind right now and eyeing her up and
down as if she was his next tasty snack.

And tasty said it, he found himself reluctantly admitting as
he ran a glance down her front until he reached the place
where those two fabulous legs came together.

Was the hair at her crotch the same pale gold colour as the
hair on her head?

He shifted again, was vaguely aware of Daniella talking into
his shirt but didn't hear what she said. That damn inconven-
ient thing called sexual curiosity was trying to take him over,
heating him up like a pot coming to the boil.

The blonde stiffened, tugging his gaze back to her face to
clash with the shocked look in her eyes. He realised then that
she knew what he had been thinking, her pearly-white skin
suffused with heat.

Feeling the spark too, *cara*? his glinting eyes mocked her.
Well hard damn luck because I am not buying.

The approaching man had reached her—a tall fair haired
good-looking guy who stepped right in behind her and ran his
fingers up her bare arms to her shoulders, then bent to murmur
something in her ear.

She quivered—Raffaelle saw it happen. As she slowly
blinked her eyes and turned her head sideways so she was no

longer looking at him, he watched her sumptuous pink mouth tilt into a smile.

She turns on for any man, he observed grimly.

'Hi,' Rachel said, still stinging at the way Raffaelle Villani had just looked at her as if she was a sex object put on show to be bought.

'Hi to you too,' Mark returned. 'No luck with the appeal approach?'

'Look at him,' she sighed, glancing back at Mr Villani who was now in the process of curving the clinging dark-haired woman beneath the crook of his arm.

What was he, six-three—six four? Rachel found herself giving him a thorough once-over. He had a great pair of shoulders inside the black dinner suit he was wearing, and a mean pair of long powerful legs. His bright white dress shirt gave the honey-gold tones of his skin at his throat a warm, tight, healthy glow that annoyingly made the tip of her tongue grow moist.

He was supposed to be a fantastic athlete, so Elise had said. Watching him as he began guiding the dark-haired woman through the doors which led to the hotel foyer, Rachel could see why. He moved with loose-limbed grace, languid and supple but firm. If you stripped him down to a pair of running shorts she would be prepared to bet you wouldn't see a single ripple of unwanted flesh.

Marital status: single. Age: thirty three. Loves snow-skiing and water-skiing. Owns his own sexy powerboat which he races at the weekend when he has the time. Owns homes in London, Paris, Monaco and, of course, his native Milan. Plus a huge private skiing lodge inside the very prestigious Gigante Park, where he likes to his spend part of his winters refining his no doubt amazing skills on the ski slopes. Inherited his wealth from his heavyweight banking family, then went on to triple that fortune with shrewd investments which pushed him and the Villani name right to the top of the rich list.

He was, in other words, a tall, dark, very good looking, very *rich* Italian male with a sinful amount of sex appeal and all the conceit and arrogance that came with such an impressive pedigree.

It was no wonder he'd cut her out without giving her a chance to explain herself. A man like him was just too darn precious about his own status as the most eligible catch on the block to think of questioning if a woman might want to approach him for any reason other than to latch on to his great body and his lovely money.

Well, Mr Villani, Rachel told his elegant back. Self-obsessed millionaires are ten-a-penny these days. You only have to look around this room to see that.

But men of honour were a very rare breed indeed.

'I thought Elise said he was only into blondes,' she said to Mark. 'But you can't put a hair between him and that black-haired female, so what chance did I have of getting in there?'

'You idiot,' Mark said. 'Don't you know who the brunette is? That's his flighty stepsister, Daniella Leeson of Leeson Hotels fame. She's about to marry his best friend and that other hotel heavy, Gino Rossi—Don't you ever read any of the stuff I print?'

Rachel gave a slow shake of her head, still watching Raffaelle Villani as he paused in the foyer, framed like a masterpiece between the two open doors. He was helping his stepsister on with her coat now—all care and attention.

Gorgeous face in profile, honesty forced her to admit. With fantastic high cheekbones and black eyelashes so luxurious she could see even from this far away, how they hovered like sexy dark shadows just above those golden cheeks.

When he'd done with the coat he turned his stepsister round

and lifted her chin with a gentle finger, then smiled as he murmured something to make her smile back at him.

So he possessed killer charm too, when he wanted to unleash it, Rachel saw, and did not like the stinging flutter she felt suddenly attack the lining of her lower stomach.

Was this the side of him he'd used on Elise to make the silly fool risk her marriage for him? The way Elise told it, he had done all the chasing while she'd tried to keep him at arm's length.

No chance, Rachel denounced. There was no way any woman could hold this man at arm's length if he did not want to be held there. It was no wonder that poor Elise had dropped like a shot duck into his hands.

'I've ruined everything,' she murmured dully. 'Look, they're leaving.'

'The hell you have,' Mark said brusquely. 'We can't let Elise down after all of this planning. I can still rescue this.'

Grabbing one of her hands, he began pulling her towards the foyer.

'The trouble with you, Rachel, is you insisted on trying the wrong tack on him then blew it. This time you do it the way we planned it, okay? So listen,' instructed the man who got his highs hunting down and catching the rich and famous at their worst. 'I'm going to grab the lovely Daniella's attention. All you have to do is to move in on him the moment I move in on her. I can give you ten seconds at most, so don't hang around and, for God's sake, don't let yourself think! This will be our last chance.'

Their last chance…

They'd reached the foyer by now and Mark's instructions were playing across her tense chest muscles like sharp hammering throbs. Raffaelle Villani and his stepsister were already turning towards the main exit doors.

'Hey—Miss Leeson!' Mark called out. 'Where's your future husband tonight?'

Daniella Leeson paused, then turned on the delicate heels of her shoes, saw Mark with a camera already up at his face and switched on a false smile.

'He's…'

'Get going,' Mark muttered sideways at Rachel.

As if in a dream Rachel let Mark's urgency take her over. Her legs felt like jelly as she moved in. Raffaelle Villani was only just turning to watch his stepsister pose for the hated paparazzi so he didn't see Rachel coming at him from one side. Stepping right in front of him and without daring to think, she threw her arms up and clasped his face between her fingers, then stretched up on tiptoe and crushed her mouth against his.

She didn't know which of them was the more shocked as heat hit her body like mega-watt high voltage. His grunt of surprise vibrated against her lips. Lights flashed, her skin burned, her fingertips tingled where they pressed against his warm satin tight skin.

Seconds. It took too many seconds for his brain to relay to Raffaelle what was happening and by then her mouth was fusing hot against his. His hands leapt up—it was automatic to close them around a small waist with the intention of pushing her away.

A camera flashed.

He pulled his mouth free, found himself staring down at the same blonde who'd approached earlier. *'Madre de Dio.* What do you think you are doing?' he raked out.

The flash hit him again. She was staring up at him, all big blue apologetic eyes and smudged pink lipstick and her fingers had shifted from his face to the back of his neck.

'Sorry,' she whispered breathlessly. 'But you left me with no other choice.'

She began to pull away. The camera was still flashing. Instead of aiding her withdrawal, Raffaelle tightened his grip on her waist and made her stay exactly where she was.

He was blindingly, blisteringly furious. 'No choice about what?' he bit down at her.

She wriggled against him in an effort to free herself. What happened next made her breath catch and he knew why it did. She was plastered against him like a second layer of skin and the extra physical pressure had brought their lower bodies into contact.

'*Dio*,' he cursed again.

'Oh, God,' Rachel echoed. 'Y-you—you're…'

'I don't need you to tell me what I already know!' he raked out. 'I just need an explanation as to what the hell you think you are trying to pull off with this!'

'I…'

'Okay kiddo, let's go.'

Let's go…Raffaelle lifted his eyes to the photographer, wondered why he hadn't noticed the camera dangling round his neck before. Then answered his own question with a twist of his mouth. He had been too busy looking at her to notice him in any detail.

'Some set-up,' he gritted.

'Please let me go now.' She tugged at his iron grip on her waist.

'Not even if you decide to faint,' he incised, sparks flying from his eyes as he watched Daniella turn towards them and her eyes give a startled blink.

Indeed, he agreed with her surprised expression. The photographer was already shooting out of the door.

'You,' he raked at his attacker, 'are coming with me to explain yourself.'

Without giving her a chance to protest, he reached up to yank her claws out of his neck, then let go of one hand and used the other to begin hauling her towards the exit.

'Raffaelle—!' A bewildered Daniella called his name as she hurried after them.

Outside a cool breeze hit his angry face.

Just angry—? He was bloody blindingly livid. His instincts must be dulling for him to get caught out like this.

'Please…' the blonde pleaded.

'Be silent,' he snapped out and his hand tightened its grip on her wrist. He felt her wince; he didn't care. Dino, his chauffeur, drew his limo up at the kerb and climbed out of the car.

Raffaelle strode towards it with his captive almost tripping up behind him on her flimsy sparkling spindle-heeled shoes. 'Grab a cab and take Miss Leeson home,' he instructed his driver.

'But—Raffaelle—?' his stepsister wailed in protest.

He ignored her. He ignored everyone, including the blonde who was still desperately trying to get free. Opening the front passenger door to the limo, he tried to propel her inside.

She dug her heels in. 'I'm not—'

He picked her up and bodily put her into the car. When she tried to get out again, her mouth opening wide with the intention of screaming for help, he bent swiftly and smothered the sound with his mouth.

He didn't take pleasure from hard angry kisses, he told himself, particularly when he'd just been hit on by a woman who deserved a slap not a kiss. However the kiss gave him a hell of a lot more satisfaction, especially when her muffled scream rolled around his mouth and sent his tongue chasing it.

She quivered. She tasted of champagne and pink lipstick.

By the time he yanked his mouth away again she'd sunk into trembling shock.

'Now, listen to me,' he incised as he locked the seat belt around her. 'I don't know how much your partner in crime was paying you to pull off that stunt, but in case you did not notice, he was not the only sleaze-gathering scum working the room back there. The pack has scented a story and is about to descend on us.'

On that hard warning he straightened, slammed the car door shut, then strode round to the other side while Rachel twisted her head to stare dazedly at the press pack gathering at the main hotel doors. By the time she'd absorbed all of that, Raffaelle Villani had folded himself into the driver's seat next to her—a lean, dark, hard-muscled male with aggression bouncing off him.

His chauffeur had left the engine running. He snaked out a hand and threw the car into drive. They took off with a jerk just as the press pack tumbled over each other with their cameras flashing. Rachel watched as the whole debacle played out like a comic strip. Even his stepsister had her part to play. She was standing by the kerb staring after them while the chauffeur was politely trying to urge her into the back of a black cab.

Mark was nowhere.

Thanks, Mark, Rachel thought helplessly, visualising her darling half-brother rushing off to file his scoop without giving a second thought to what he had left her to face!

Rachel flicked a scared glance at the man sitting beside her, then shivered. If murder had a look to it then he was wearing it.

'Please stop the car so I can get out,' she begged and didn't even care that she was begging.

He didn't answer. Lips clamped together, he sent the car shooting out into the main stream of traffic. Several car horns blared in protest at his pushy arrogance. He ignored those too.

'Look, I know you're angry,' she allowed shakily. 'And I know that you have every right to be, but—'

'*Grazie*.'

'This is kidnap!'

'So sue me,' he gritted. 'That could be fun.'

Fun—? Rachel trembled and shivered as she sat tensely beside him. None of this had been *fun* from the moment she'd allowed Elise and Mark to talk her into it. One minute she'd been perfectly content, hiding away in Devon nursing her broken heart, the next minute she'd found herself staying up here in London with her half-sister and being embroiled in her complicated love-life!

'It w-wasn't what you think—'

'You don't know what I'm thinking.'

'I am *not* being paid to—'

'Hit on me?' he offered when those very same words dried in her throat. 'It is a relief to know I still have some natural pulling power then.'

He had loads of natural pulling power. That was his problem.

'Are you always this obnoxious when you've been caught off your guard?' she flared up on the back of pure agitation. 'So I hit on you—what's new there to a man like you? From what I hear, half the women in Europe have done it at some point in your blessed life—and not all of them because of your sex appeal!'

He sent her a glinting look. 'Did I hear a hint of scorn in your tone then?'

'Yes!' she flicked out. 'Men like you stroll through life as if you own it. You do what you want when you want to do it. You pick your women on looks alone and don't give a care whether they have feelings you could actually wound!'

Something sharp hit his voice. 'I wounded—you?'

'You mean you don't know?' The sarcasm was out before she could stop it.

They'd stopped at a set of traffic lights and he turned in his seat. Instantly the sheer size and power of the man flooded over Rachel like a simmering hot shower. She could feel his eyes skimming her face and her body as he checked her out while flipping through his huge data bank of women, trying to pinpoint who she was. Any second now and he was going to make a connection he could have made hours ago if he'd been more observant.

Rachel felt the stinging temptation to lie, if only to really confuse him, but— 'No,' she said finally.

Someone just like you did that to me, she added inside her head. Then she flicked him a hard resentful glance, heaved in a breath and saved him the bother of further taxing his no doubt phenomenal brain power.

'Elise Castle,' she breathed out.

CHAPTER TWO

THE name had its desired effect, Rachel noticed bitterly, as a long thick silence stretched between them and he didn't say or do a single thing.

She held her breath again while she waited for him to recover and begin spitting out a barrage of angry questions—but still nothing came.

In the end she took the initiative and broke the silence. 'The name means nothing to you?' she gibed.

Other vehicle headlights swished past the car windows, lighting their faces momentarily. Illuminated, she saw only the cold steel of his eyes as they fixed hers like lashing daggers and he kept his silence. In the darkness her gaze dropped for some reason to the single line straightness of his mouth.

A mouth that already felt disconcertingly familiar. She could still taste it. Her tongue even made a passing swipe at her lips in response to the thought.

Headlights lit up the car's interior again, dragging her attention back to his eyes. They'd narrowed and were watching her like a hawk waiting to pin its next victim. Rachel's breathing fell into small jerky fits. Her heart was pounding. He was frighteningly exciting to look at, all well cared for male with just the right balance between sensational good looks and raw masculinity.

Her mouth had to part to aid her quick breathing. He dropped his gaze and the result was a tingling quiver across her lips that sent the tip of her tongue nervously chasing it. Sexual awareness was suddenly alive and cluttering the atmosphere. Rachel felt her breasts grow heavy, their tips pushing out with a terrible knowing sting. He flicked those eyes back to hers again and he knew—he *knew*!

Then the traffic lights decided to change, demanding that he set them moving. She watched as if mesmerised as his dark head shifted back into profile, watched his long-fingered hands as he flipped the car into a slick right turn. More seconds ticked by and her chest felt as if it was burning beneath the pressure she was placing on it by barely breathing at all now.

'The name means plenty to me,' he finally answered. 'And you are not Elise.'

No, Rachel knew she wasn't Elise. She was her younger, less pretty, more sensible half-sister.

More sensible—when? She then scoffed at that. Sensible women did not get themselves into situations like this. Sensible women steered clear of the complicated love lives of others—and especially of frighteningly sexy men like him!

Sensible women did not fall in love with handsome Italians with a rich repertoire of words of love and a killer seduction technique—yet she had done it.

She had to close her eyes as an image of Alonso suddenly appeared in front of her. Tall, dark, beautiful Alonso, who had been so warm and attentive and flatteringly possessive when they had been out together, and so excitingly intense and passionate when naked with her in bed. They'd spent six glorious weeks living together in his apartment overlooking Naples. He'd vowed he loved her. 'I love you—*ti'amo mia bella cara*…' he'd murmured to her in his rich, dark, accented voice and she'd known without a doubt that she loved him.

Rachel shivered.

It was only when the time had come for her to return to England and he'd said, 'We had a wonderful time, hmm, *amore*? It is a shame it now has to end,' that she'd understood what a stupid, gullible, naïve fool she had been.

'I said you are not Elise,' this other Italian with the rich, dark accent prompted.

Rachel opened her eyes and let the real world back in. 'No,' she agreed. 'But very few people will be able to tell that from behind...'

A bell of understanding suddenly clanged loud in Raffaelle's head. Next to come was an action replay of the way this woman had thrown herself on him, followed by several camera flashes. Like a wild beast sniffing danger in the atmosphere, he picked up the scent of a deliberately constructed scandal involving him and the very married Elise.

But it was a scandal he believed he had already diverted. As far as he was aware, the lovely Elise had seen the error of her ways after his last spiked conversation with her on the telephone before he'd broken all contact with her and made his quick exit from London back to Milan. The grapevine, via Daniella, said she had not been seen on the social circuit since.

So what was *this* devious creature up to? Why had she gone to so much trouble to make out for the camera that she was Elise?

'Explain,' he commanded.

Not this side of midnight, Rachel thought tensely and clamped her lips together. Having come this far, she was not about to scupper everything by getting Mark's story pulled before going to print.

She'd already revealed more than she should have done.

'Look...' she heaved out instead. 'You're not an idiot, Mr Villani. You must know you're asking for trouble taking me against my will like this—so just stop the car and let me out now.'

'Not a chance in hell,' he refused.

And the way he turned his head to slide his eyes up her legs had Rachel tugging jerkily at the short skirt of her dress. She knew that look. It was as old as the human race. She'd let him see her attraction to him; now he was looking over the goods on offer.

'If you honestly think—!'

'Changing your mind about the hit, *cara*?' he taunted. 'Wondering if you might have bitten off more than you can chew with me? Well, let me confirm that you have done.' His voice hardened. 'You made the hit. I bought it. Now you are going to play it my way.'

'You're crazy,' she whispered.

Maybe he was, Raffaelle conceded. But no woman—*no woman*—played games with him and got away with it!

'I'm getting out of this car—' Rachel reached for the door handle. The automatic lock gave a clunk as it fell into place at the same time that he increased their speed.

True—true unfettered fear began to scream in her head as it finally began to sink in what a stupid, crazy, dangerous situation she had managed to get herself into here. What did she know about Raffaelle Villani, other than the details fed to her by Mark and Elise? How did she know he wasn't some kind of mega-rich sex maniac prowling Europe unhindered because his money could buy his victims' silence.

Just as he said, he had bought her...

Her skin began to creep, her fingers closing tightly around her small clutch bag so they felt the reassurance of her cellphone.

How much time did she need to call the police before he reacted?

She dared a quick glance at him, heart hammering, fingers tensely toying with the clasp on her bag. He didn't look like a lunatic, just a very angry man—which he had every right to be, she was forced to admit.

'Your partner in crime did not hang around to protect you,' he taunted grimly next.

He had to mean Mark. 'You don't—'

'Unless he is in one of the cars following behind us, that is…'

Cars—? Rachel twisted around to peer through the rear window.

'There are three back there I can pick out as belonging to the paparazzi,' she was told. 'And there are most likely more of them following not far behind them.'

Twisting forward again, she stared at him. 'But why should they want to follow us?'

'You are not that naïve,' he derided the question, flicking his eyes from the rear-view mirror and back to the road ahead. 'Or you would not have chosen Raffaelle Villani to pull your life-wrecking stunt.'

Life wrecking—? 'N-no.' Rachel gave an urgent shake of her head. 'You don't understand. This was not—'

'Not that it matters,' he interrupted. 'We are here now.'

As in *where*—? Even as Rachel thought the question, one of those shiny new apartment blocks that flanked the river loomed up close. With a spin of the wheel he sent the car sweeping on to its forecourt. He stopped it hard on its brakes and was already out of the car and striding around it to open her door.

Rachel didn't move. She was trembling like mad and her heart was thundering. She didn't look at him either, but just stared starkly ahead.

'Do you get out yourself or do I have to lift you?' he demanded.

Since she'd already learnt the hard way that he was perfectly willing to do the latter, swallowing tensely, Rachel took the more dignified choice, unfastened her seat belt and slid out of the car.

It was an odd sensation to find herself standing close to him. Nor did that sensation make any sense because she'd stood this close once already tonight and thrown herself right against him a second time, yet he hadn't felt this tall or as powerfully built or as dangerous as he did right now.

She shivered, panicked and was about to make a run for it when car doors started slamming. The paparazzi had arrived right behind them and were already piling out of their cars.

Raffaelle bit out a curse, then he was wrapping her beneath the hook of a powerful arm.

Cameras flashed. 'Look this way, Elise——!' one of them called out to her.

But she was already being ushered through a pair of doors.

'Keep them out,' Raffaelle instructed the security man manning the foyer.

Before Rachel knew what was happening, he'd marched her into a lift and the doors were closing the two of them inside.

It had happened so fast—all of it—everything! And she'd never felt so afraid in her entire life. Her head was whirling and her legs had gone hollow. The panic had not subsided and it sent the heels of her shoes screeching shrilly beneath her as she spun round, then she lifted an arm and hit out at him with her bag.

He fielded the blow like a man swatting a fly away. 'Calm down,' he gritted.

But Rachel didn't want to calm down. Hair flying about her slender neck as she struggled with him, 'Let me go—let me *go*!' she choked out.

Then she threw back her head and opened her mouth to scream.

Only it didn't arrive. Nothing happened. The scream remained just a thick lump pulsing in the base of her throat. And he didn't attempt to smother it like he had done outside the hotel but just stood there looking down at her while she stared up at him.

It was crazy—the whole evening had been crazy, but this

was *the* craziest part because it felt as if they'd both suddenly been frozen in time.

The panic receded. She forgot to breathe. As far as she could tell, he wasn't breathing either and he was frowning as if he too couldn't understand what was going on.

Gorgeous frown, she found herself thinking. Gorgeous black silk-hooded eyes. In fact he was, she saw as if for the first time, altogether totally breathtaking to look at. His facial bone structure was striking—the high forehead and good cheekbones, the long narrow nose and perfectly symmetrical chin.

And his eyes weren't really grey, but an unusual mixture of green flecked with silver. His skin was amazing, a tightly wrapped casing of honey-gold her fingers remembered with a tense little twitch. The satin-black eyebrows, those luxuriously long eyelashes that were hovering just above the cheekbones, and the mouth...

Don't look at his mouth, she told herself tautly, but she didn't just look, she stared at it. Slender, smooth, slightly parted. The tip of her tongue snaked out to wipe away the now familiar tingle she felt take over her own lips.

He breathed. The warmth of his breath brushed her face, scented with the heady fruits of a rich dark wine. She tried a tense swallow, looked back into his eyes and saw what was coming. He was going to kiss her. Not to stop her screaming or even in anger, but because—

Oh, God, she wanted him to!

He muttered something in Italian. She released the strangest-sounding groan. In the next second he'd captured her mouth and they were kissing—really kissing. Not stolen, fought-for, punishing or smothering kisses, but like two greedy, hungry lovers with a swift, hot, urgent necessity.

Their tongues flickered and slid in a wild, erotic dance of hungry heat. Without caring she was doing it, Rachel lifted her arms up over Raffaelle's shoulders and arched closer until she could feel every inch of him pressing against her, from his hard-packed chest to powerful thighs.

He was so pumped up and solid, his hands moving on a restless journey over the silk dress covering her slender body to the bare flesh of her shoulders, then back down to her small waist again. She became aware that she was purring like a well stroked kitten. He breathed something harsh, then picked her up with his hands and started walking without breaking the kiss.

Her hands were in his hair now, raking his scalp and scrunching its smooth style, the swollen globes of her breasts nudging at him high on his chest.

This should not be happening. This *should not be happening!* a shrill voice screamed inside her head.

The panic returned; Rachel yanked her head back at the same moment that he did the same thing.

Like two people who did not know what the hell was happening to them, they stared at each other again, her eyes wide dark pools of shocked horror and confusion, his blackened by stunned disbelief. Her mouth was burning, her lips still parted and pulsing and swollen as she panted for breath.

He put her down so abruptly she almost toppled off the thin heels of her shoes, her fingers trailing around his shirt collar then down the front of his jacket where they clung, because they had to, to his black satin lapels.

Anger burned now. A thick, dark, intense anger that pulsed from every hard inch of him as he used a key to open a door. Rachel had not noticed that they'd left the lift, never mind crossed another foyer to reach the door!

Manoeuvring them both inside, he kicked the door shut with a foot before peeling her off his front. She staggered dizzily. He walked away down a spacious hallway, then disappeared through another door.

She wanted to faint. She wished she *could* faint. She wished the floor would open up and swallow her whole. Every inch of her body was still alive and buzzing with excitement and a shrill ringing was filling her head.

The ringing stopped abruptly and she blinked. Then she heard his voice ripping out words in sharp Italian and realised the sound had been coming from a phone. She caught Elise's name and reality came tumbling over her like a giant snowball, dousing every bit of heat.

It took real willpower to make her trembling legs walk her down that hallway. But she needed to know what he was saying and to whom he was saying it.

The door was flung wide open on its hinges and she stilled in the opening, staring starkly across a spacious living room with wall-to-wall glass on one side and an expanse of warm wood covering the floor softened by a big creamy-coloured rug. Everything in here was clean-lined and modern. He was standing beside one of several black leather sofas that were carefully placed about the room.

His back was to her. He had a land line telephone clamped to his ear and his hair was still mussed. Her fingers tingled to remind her who had done the mussing. As she continued to stand there, he lifted up a set of long fingers and mussed it up some more.

'Daniella—' he snapped out, then stopped and sighed.

Whatever his stepsister said to him then made his voice alter, the snap going out of it and low, dark, soothing Italian arriving in its place, aimed to apologise and reassure.

Me too, please, Rachel wanted to beg. Reassure me too that this is all just a big nightmare.

But it wasn't and her heart was still beating too fast. The low dark flow of his voice seemed to resonate directly from deep inside his chest before reaching the rolling caress of his tongue.

Oh, God. She put a set of trembling fingers up to cover her

eyes. Did all Italian men have deep, sexy voices, or was it just that she had been unlucky enough to meet the only two that could do this to her?

Then an impatient 'Daniella,' arrived again. 'Take my advice and call Gino. Take your bad temper out on him, for I am in no mood to hear this.'

He had switched to English. Rachel dropped her hand in time to watch his shoulders give a tight shrug.

'If *Elise* upstaged you then count your blessings that she was more interesting to the cameras than you and your behaviour were five minutes before!'

Elise…Rachel tensed as a sudden thought hit her. If Raffaelle's stepsister had been fooled tonight into believing she was Elise, then maybe, between them, she and Mark had managed to pull this off!

Rafaelle's voice returned to smooth Italian. Rachel listened intently for the sound of Elise's name being spoken again but it did not happen. A few seconds later he was finishing the call.

Raffaelle put the phone down, then flexed his wide shoulders. He could feel her standing somewhere behind him but he did not want to turn around and find out where.

He did not want to look at her.

He did not know what the hell she was doing to him!

With an impatient yank he undid his bow tie, shifted his stance to angle his body towards the drinks cabinet, then plucked with hard fingers at the top button of his dress shirt as he strode across the room. His jacket came next. He lost it to the back of a sofa. The silence screamed across the gap separating them as he flipped open the cabinet doors and reached for the brandy bottle.

'Drink—?' he offered.

'No thank you,' she huskily declined.

Husky did it. He felt that low sensual voice reach right down inside him and give a hard tug on his loins.

'Keeping a clear head?' he mocked tightly.

'Yes,' she breathed.

Pouring a brandy for himself, he turned with the glass in his hand. She was standing in the doorway in her turquoise dress, with her arms held tensely to her sides. Her hands were gripping the black beaded bag she had tried to hit him with in the lift and her blue eyes were telling him that she was scared.

Some might say that she had asked for everything that was happening to her but Raffaelle was reluctantly prepared to admit that he had been behaving little better than a thug.

He took a sip of his drink, grimly aware that what had broken free in the lift was still busy inside him. He wanted her. He did not know why he wanted her. He'd been tempted by sirens far more adept at their craft than she was without feeling the slightest inclination to give in.

Yet he did—want to give in. In fact the want was now a low-down burning ache in his gut.

She wasn't even what he would call beautiful. Not in the classic Elise-sleek-catwalk-fashion-sense, that was. There again, neither had Elise been catwalk-sleek by the time he'd met her. And this woman's face did not possess the same striking bone structure that Elise had been endowed with. The eyes were the same blue but the nose was different—and the mouth.

The mouth…

Lifting the glass to his lips, Raffaelle half hid his eyes as he studied the mouth, wiped clear of pink lipstick now and still softly swollen from their kiss in the lift. Elise's mouth was a wide classic bow shape whereas this mouth was shaped more evocatively like a heart and was frankly lush. And Elise was taller, though he would hazard a guess the lost inches would not show on a photograph as this one had stretched up and plastered herself against his front.

The dress was expensive—you didn't live most of your life

around fashion conscious females without being able to pick out haute couture when you saw it. But it did not fit her. It was too tight in places, like across those two white breasts that were in danger of falling out of it, and it hugged the rounded shape of her slender hips like a second skin.

'Turn round,' he instructed.

She tensed in objection.

'I am looking for your likeness to Elise,' he informed her levelly. 'So humour me and turn around...'

She did. Raffaelle grimaced because he would have been prepared to swear that right now she would rather spit in his face than comply with anything he wanted her to do. The passionate kiss in the lift coming hard on the back of the way she'd looked at him in the car had made her so uptight and defensive he could almost taste her hostility towards him even as she stood there with her back to him.

And that was just another thing about her. Elise might have been a damn good liar but she had not possessed a single spark of passion or spirit. She'd been quiet and surprisingly shy for someone who had earned her living sashaying along catwalks and posing for glossy magazines.

But that was thinking with hindsight, because he had not known who Elise really was at the time. And he was looking in the wrong place if he expected to find the very married ex-model's nature in a woman who was definitely not her.

The back view did it, though. The back view with the straight hair and the narrow shoulders and tight backside told him exactly why this woman believed she could get away with pretending to be Elise from that angle.

'Had enough?' She spun back to face him so she could fix him with an icy stare.

It made him want to grimace, because if she was allowing herself to believe that such an expression was going to hold him back she was sadly mistaken. Despite the frost, she'd switched him on and now, he discovered, he was not feeling inclined to switch himself off again.

In fact he was beginning to enjoy the sexual sting that was passing between them.

The way he was standing there with his glass in his hand and his eyes half hidden, he reminded Rachel of a long, lean jungle cat lazily planning the moment when it would pounce.

Still dangerous, in other words.

The loss of his jacket wasn't helping. The bright white of his shirt only made his shoulders look wider and his torso longer and tougher, and the way his loosened bow tie lay in two strips of black either side of his open shirt collar kept on drawing her eyes to the triangle of golden skin at his throat.

Rachel's throat went dry. Oh, please, she begged, will someone get me out of here—?

Because looking at him was recharging the sexual buzz. She could feel it moving through her blood in a slow and sluggishly threatening burn, scary yet exciting—like a war she was having to fight on two fronts.

'Don't you think it is time that you told me your name?'

Rachel tensed, her eyes flicking into focus on his face. Then a strained little laugh broke in her throat because it hadn't occurred to her that he didn't know who she was.

'Rachel,' she pushed out. 'Rachel Carmichael.'

Something about him suddenly altered. For some unknown reason she felt as if the air circulating around him had gone as tense as a cracked whip. And the eyes—the eyes were not merely hooded now, they'd narrowed into sharp eyelash-framed slits.

'Well, hello, Rachel Carmichael,' he drawled in a very slow, lazy tone that made the hairs on the back of her neck stand on end. 'Now this has just become very interesting…'

'Why has it?' she asked warily.

'Why don't you come and sit down so we can talk about it?'

She had the impression that the jungle cat in him had just sharpened its teeth. Taut as a bow string and balanced right on the balls of her feet now, Rachel wondered if this would be a good time to try to make a run for it.

But the idea lasted for only a moment. He had not brought her up here to his apartment to let her get away before she had given him an explanation as to why she'd set him up tonight.

Making herself walk across the room took courage, especially when he watched her all the way as if she was performing some special provocative act designed purposely to keep his attention engaged.

Oh, God, did he have to look so sleekly at ease and so gorgeously interested?

Beginning to feel disturbingly hollow from the neck down, if she did not count the sparking sting making itself felt, Rachel picked one of the black sofas at random and sat down right on its edge.

The skirt to her dress immediately rode upwards to reveal more slender thigh than was decent with a peek of her stocking lace tops. Unclipping her fingers from the death grip they had on her bag she gave a tug at the dress's hem, only to notice to her horror that its bodice wasn't doing much to keep her modesty covered, either.

And still he stood there watching her every single move, deliberately, she suspected, building on the sexual tension that was fizzing in the air. Her heart was pounding. She refused to look up. She wanted to swallow but would not allow herself the luxury of trying to shift the anxious lump lodged in her throat.

Then he moved and she jerked up her head, unable to stop the wary response, only to feel almost dizzy with embarrassment when she saw how he was looking at her.

'I will have that drink now,' she burst out, desperate for him to turn away so she could pull up the bodice of her dress without him watching.

One of those sleek black eyebrows arched in quizzing mockery at her abrupt change of mind about the drink. He knew what she was trying to do. It was scored into his eyes and his body language.

'What would you like?' he asked politely.

'I don't know—anything,' she shook out.

He turned his back. Rachel feathered out a tense breath and hurriedly rearranged herself. In all her life she had never felt so out of sorts and out of place as she was feeling right now, sitting on this sofa, wearing this dress, with that man standing only a few feet away.

She was nobody's luxury appendage—never had been. She'd always left that kind of thing to the more beautiful and capable Elise. Playing the role given to her tonight had been tough on her pride, from the moment she'd donned the whole image. And the only man she'd ever thrown herself at in her whole life before tonight had been Alonso, and, she recalled with a grimace, he'd been more or less crawling all over her by then anyway.

And Alonso hadn't been rich. He'd just been a very junior car salesman with good lines in smart suits and a tiny apartment. He drove flashy cars but he didn't own them, and he'd earned less money than she had earned picking fruit on a farm just outside Naples.

A glass appeared in front of her. Glancing up, she unclipped one of her hands from her bag and took it with a mumbled, 'Thanks,' then sat staring at it wondering what the heck was in it?

'Splash of vodka topped up with tonic,' he provided the answer. 'And it is not spiked with something lethal, if that is what the frown is about.'

'I wasn't—'

'Then you should,' he intruded curtly. 'You don't know me, Rachel Carmichael. I might go in for drug-enhanced love-ins. How old are you, by the way?'

Rachel blinked. 'Twenty-three. Why, what has my age got to do with anything?'

'Just curious.' He sat down right next to her sending her spine arching into a defensive stretch.

Raffaelle saw it happen and smiled. The air circulating around them was alive with an ever increasing sting of awareness. He could feel it. He knew that she could feel it. What he could not figure out was *why* it was there and what he was going to do about it.

Liar, the dry part of his brain fed back.

'Okay…' Relaxing into the sofa, he stretched out his long legs. 'Now, start talking.'

Talking… Sending her tongue round her dry lips, Rachel looked down at the bag she was still clutching in one hand and made a small shift of her wrist so she could see the time on her watch.

It was just coming up to midnight. How long did Mark need to do his thing with his digital camera, write his accompanying piece, then file it with the newspaper via the Internet?

She looked at her bag with the comforting feel of her cellphone inside it, and wondered if she dared take it out and ring him to check?

Great idea, she then thought heavily. As if Raffaelle Villani was going to let her contact anyone until he had his explanation.

'Sit back and relax,' he invited.

What she did was stiffen up all the more. 'I'm perfectly relaxed as I am, thank you.'

'No, you are not. There is tension—here…' A finger arrived in the naked taut hollow between her shoulders, sending her spine into another muscle splitting arch as if she'd been stung by an electric shock.

The sensation flung her, gasping to her feet. 'That wasn't—necessary,' she protested.

'You think not?'

'No.' Taking a few shaky steps away from him, she put the glass to her mouth and sipped while he watched her through half hidden eyes and a knowing smile on his lips.

'We share chemistry, *cara*.'

Rachel laughed thickly. 'That of kidnapper and victim.'

'And who do you believe is the victim here—?'

Just like that, with one smooth question, he brought the whole madness which had made up this evening tumbling down to where it really belonged.

For which of them was the real victim? Certainly not her, she had to admit. He had every right to be angry. She had no right to be anything at all.

On the short sigh that quivered as it left her, Rachel finally took responsibility for her own misdemeanours. It was no use trying to pretend she was innocent when she wasn't. Or to wish Raffaelle Villani a million miles away because he'd ruined all their plans when he had stopped her from getting away back there at the hotel.

He was right about the chemistry too. Just turning to look at his long, lean, relaxed sprawl, giving off all kinds of innate sexual messages, sent her insides into an instant tight spiral spin.

Then—okay, she told herself grimly, let's keep this strictly to business, then maybe the—other—stuff will die a natural death.

On that stern piece of good common sense, she lifted her chin, pushed her eyes upwards to fix them on his face, then she steadied her breathing and plunged right in.

'As I just told you, my name is Rachel Carmichael,' she reminded him. 'Elise is my half-sister. W-we had different fathers, hence the different surnames…'

CHAPTER THREE

HE DID not move. He remained relaxed. His eyes told her absolutely nothing and his mouth held on to its smooth flat line.

So why did Rachel get the unnerving impression that he had already worked most of that out?

'Elise has been out of the modelling scene for over five years now since—since she married Leo Savakis—'

'And gave him a son.'

Rachel could only nod, pressing her lips together as she did so, because she knew without him adding that dry comment, how badly all of this reflected on Elise.

'Leo is an…awesome guy,' she continued. 'He is the very hands-on head of the Savakis shipping empire as well as being a respected international lawyer, expert in British, Greek and American corporate law—'

'Skip the CV. I know about Leo Savakis,' he coolly cut in.

Of course he would know about Leo. Most people who moved in high business circles would have heard about her brother-in-law's remarkable career.

'He's a very busy man.'

'Aren't we all?' drawled this high mover—in the business world at least.

'S-sometimes Elise feels—neglected.'

'Ah,' he sighed. 'So I am to get the sob story before you lurch into the ugly part.'

'Don't mock what you have never suffered, Mr Villani!' Rachel flared up in her sister's defence. 'When you've gone from being the face on every glossy magazine to a stay-at-home wife and mother with no identity to call your own, then you might begin to understand!'

He didn't even bother to respond to that heated outburst. 'So she feels—neglected...' he prompted instead.

'And lonely.' Once again Rachel steadied her breathing. 'When Leo works abroad he prefers Elise to stay put in London or on his island in Greece. He says it's all to do with security,' she explained. 'He's made enemies in his line of work and...'

'Naturally feels the need to protect his wife and his son.'

'Wouldn't you?' Rachel flashed.

He raised a black satin eyebrow. 'Are you working in defence of Mr Savakis here or his poor neglected wife?'

'Both,' Rachel declared loyally. 'I *like* Leo...'

But she wouldn't want him as a husband, she added silently. He was too overwhelmingly unreadable and dauntingly self-controlled. He adored Elise though, she was certain of it. It was just that...

'He's been virtually living in Chicago for the last twelve months, working on a high-profile case that only allows him back home for the occasional flying visit.'

'Hence poor Elise feeling lonely and neglected—'

'If you don't stop being nasty about her, I'm going to leave!'

He shifted his shoulders against the black leather, then moved his legs, bending them out of their lazy sprawl so he could rest one ankle on the other knee. Rachel's eyes were drawn to the lean bowl between his hipbones where the expensive black fabric of his trousers sat easily against—

Oh, please, someone help me! she thought despairingly and wanted to run away again.

He moved a hand next, lifting it up so he could stroke a long finger across the flat line of his lips. Above the stroking finger, his grey-green eyes feathered a ponderous look over her in a way that further fanned the sexual charge.

Did all Italian men have an ability to seduce just by using body language, or was it just her misfortune that they affected *her* like this?

Disturbed by the whole hectic physical war going on here, Rachel put some distance between them by walking across the room to stand staring out of one of the huge plate glass windows. London—the River Thames, Westminster and Tower Bridge—lay spanned out before her in a familiar night scene.

Behind her his silent study pin-pricked her spine.

He had not even bothered to challenge her threat to leave. It was as if he knew she was becoming more and more trapped here by the sexual pull and he was enjoying feeding it.

One of the friends she'd made during her stay in Naples had once claimed that Italian men could seduce you and make you feel wonderful about falling in love with them without so much as considering falling in love themselves. It was the Italian way. Apparently you were supposed to feel blessed that they'd bothered to notice you at all.

Because they were conceited and arrogant by nature, so confident in their prowess as mighty lovers, that the suggestion that they might not assuage your every sexual fantasy never entered their minds or their beds. Such an uncrushable self-belief was seductive in itself. Rachel had fallen for it with Alonso. Now here she was, feeling the pull again and with a much more dangerous beast than Alonso ever had been.

It was time to put it to death, she told herself.

Turning from the window, she looked back at him. 'Leo knows about your affair with Elise,' she announced.

And saw death happen to sexual promise as he flicked those eyes into sharp focus on her face.

'He was sent photographs of the two of you together in a restaurant here in London, then later being very intimate on a dance floor,' she pushed on.

His tight curse brought him to his feet.

'Elise got upset—'

'Naturally,' he gritted.

Rachel bit down hard on her lower lip. 'She denied everything, which was a bit stupid when Leo was standing there with the photographic evidence,' she allowed. 'F-fortunately the photos were dark and very grainy and she insisted that the blonde in them could be anyone.'

'She lied, in other words.'

'Wouldn't you have done in her place?'

His dark head went back. 'If I was so miserable in my marriage that I needed to look elsewhere for—company, I would be man enough to say so *before* the event!'

'Well, good for you, Mr Villani,' Rachel commended. 'It must be really great to be so sure of yourself that you *know* what you would do in any given situation! Well, Elise *lied*,' she stressed. 'And, right off the top of her head, she suggested that the woman in the photos could even be me. Leo wasn't impressed—I don't normally look or dress like this, you see—'

He flicked her a cynical look. 'Another liar in the family, then.'

'Yes,' Rachel sighed, seeing no use in denying it. 'I had been staying with Elise in London for a while to—to keep her company while Leo was away. She was so low and depressed I encouraged her to go out with an old f-friend from her modelling days and—and enjoy life a bit instead of moping around the house waiting for…' She stopped, shutting the rest of that away where it belonged.

By his expression she knew he knew what she meant.

'Anyway,' she went on after a moment. 'She took me up on the offer and really started to cheer up and be her old self! But I had no idea she was out there enjoying herself with another man…'

'Oh, call it as it is, *cara*, we had the hots for each other.'

'You don't need to be so crude about it!' she said heatedly.

'What happened next?' He was striding across the room towards the brandy bottle to replenish his empty glass and there was nothing languid in his movements now.

'Elise told Leo that *I* had been seeing someone while I was staying with her…'

'A someone who just happened to be me—?' Brandy splashed into the glass.

Rachel watched it and mentally crossed her fingers and hoped he had the steady head for it. 'She was fighting for her marriage.'

He swallowed the drink. 'So did Savakis call you up to demand confirmation and you lied to him for your sister's sake?'

'Leo didn't do anything.' Ignoring his sarcasm, she kept strictly to the point. 'Instead he chose to let the subject drop.'

'Generous man,' he drawled. 'Or a sadly besotted one.'

The idea of Leo being either generous or besotted was so alien to Rachel that she had to stop and think about it and still couldn't get either scenario to fit the Leo she knew.

'Things have been—strained between the two of them ever since, and now…' Rachel gathered herself in before she revealed the next bit. 'Elise has just found out that she's pregnant.'

Raffaelle responded to this with an abrupt stiffening of his long body. The glass clenched between his fingers, he turned a narrowed look on her face.

'Do go on,' he invited softly.

Rachel wished she didn't have to go on but she knew that she did. 'W-with the timing and—everything, there's a big chance that Leo might not believe the baby is his.'

'You mean he does not know about it yet?'

'Not yet,' Rachel murmured.

'And is it his baby?'

'Yes!' she cried out. 'Unless you are wondering if it might be your baby?' she then could not resist hitting back.

'I know it isn't.' His mouth was as hard now as his eyes were like ice.

Rachel shivered. 'It's Leo's baby,' she repeated firmly. 'Conceived during one of his flying visits home. He'd only been there one night when he was telling Elise over the breakfast table that he was flying back to Chicago the next day. S-so she rebelled at his arrogant assumption that he could just fly in and—' The rest was cut off and smothered. But once again she knew that he knew what she was getting at. 'So Elise decided to punish him by telling him she had started her period and so was off limits…'

Because, as Elise had said, if Leo thought he could fly in just to ease his libido, then he could go back to Chicago and to libido hell!

'*Dio*,' Raffaelle muttered. 'The sly machinations of a selfish woman never cease to impress me.'

'Nor am I impressed by the casual attitude of a man on the hunt for sex!'

'Was that remark aimed at me?' he demanded.

'Does it fit?' Rachel lanced back. 'Did you or did you not hit on my sister because you fancied your chances in her bed?'

Guilty as charged. His teeth came together. 'I did not know that she was married,' he declared stiffly.

'And that's your excuse?' Rachel denounced. 'Why didn't you know she was married?' she demanded. 'She was a famous ex-model, for goodness' sake! Her face used to be seen everywhere. Her marriage made the front pages of every glossy there is!'

'Does she look like the famous model any more?' he hit back. 'You know she does not! She carries more weight now and her face has altered. And she did not exactly go out of her way to tell me who she was!'

'What did she do then—pretend to be Catwoman, complete with rubber mask?'

Rachel saw him make a grab at his temper. 'She used a different name,' he said.

A different name—? That was one small detail Elise had left out of her account of her reckless rebellion against Leo.

'What name—?' She frowned at him.

He looked at her, then dared to laugh, though it wasn't a very pleasant-sounding laugh. 'Does—*Rachel Carmichael* mean much to you?'

Rachel suddenly needed to sit down again. Walking on trembling legs to the nearest sofa, she sank into its soft black leather and put the glass to her equally trembling mouth.

'I see you recognise the name,' he drawled hatefully.

'Shut up!' she whipped back; she was trying to think.

The devious witch, the calculating madam! She'd gone out there on the town stuffed full of rebellion, using *her* name as a cover-up, while insisting that Leo's precious security guards remained at the house to guard her son!

'No wonder Mark dragged me back here,' she mumbled.

'Who the hell is Mark?' Raffaelle Villani rapped out.

'My half-brother—the one with the camera,' she enlightened.

'You mean you are related to one of the paparazzi?'

Rachel shifted uncomfortably. 'Mark and Elise are twins.'

He didn't bother to say anything to that, but just stood there glaring into space. The atmosphere was pretty much too thick to breathe now and Rachel was wishing she was wearing armour plating because she had a horrible feeling she was going to need it soon.

'From where?' he demanded suddenly.

Looking up at him, she just blinked.

'You said that your brother dragged you back,' he enlightened her. 'From where—?'

'Oh—Devon,' Rachel responded. 'I work there on the family farm—organic,' she added for no reason she could think of.

His raking scan of her was downright incredulous. 'You…are a *farmer*?'

Her chin shot up. 'What's the matter with that, Mr Villani?' she challenged. 'Does it bruise your precious ego to know you're about to be intimately linked to a poor farming girl instead of some rich chick with a three-hundred-year-old pedigree—?'

Silence clattered—no, it thundered down as both of them realised at the same time what it was she had just said.

'"Intimately linked—?"' he fed into that rumbling thunder.

Rachel bit down hard on her bottom lip to stop it from quivering. The thickened air in the room began to curdle—or was it the vodka she wasn't used to drinking that was beginning to make her feel slightly sick?

'Explain that,' he raked out.

'I w-will in a minute,' she whispered. 'I just need to—get my head together to…' say what still had not been said.

Abandoning what was left of the glass of vodka and her bag to the floor at her feet, she made herself stand up again, preferring to meet what was about to come back at her from an upright position with her hands free rather than have him loom over her like a threatening thunderclap.

Why did he have to be so intimidatingly tall and big?

She found herself sending him a plea for understanding with her eyes as she lurched back into speech. 'Elise provided this d-dress and the invitation to the charity thing tonight,' she explained. 'Then she was packed off to Chicago with her son this afternoon f-for a surprise visit to Leo, while Mark and I…'

'Set up the sting on me?'

Pressing her lips together, she nodded, deciding not to object to the latest label he'd hung on them because it was the truth, and there was still more to come.

'Tomorrow morning you and I will appear together in a Sunday tabloid—'

'Saying what—?' he bit out.

Oh, God, she groaned silently. 'S-something like— Raffaelle Villani goes public with his latest w-woman…'

Having to really bite down hard on her bottom lip now, Rachel searched the hard angles of his face for a small sign that he wasn't into murder—but she didn't see it.

'It was important to convince Leo that the woman in the photographs he has in his possession and the one who will appear in tomorrow's paper are the same person and *cannot* be Elise if she is in Chicago with him!'

And that was the bottom line.

Suddenly he was a tall dark stranger standing there. A man so cold and so very still it was as if he had pulled on the same awesome cloak of implacability that Leo always wore.

The silence gnawed. So did the heightened tension which began sapping the defences that had kept Rachel going through all of this.

'It should have ended there,' she pushed into the taut atmosphere. 'If you had behaved as predicted and let me get away from you, I would have disappeared back to Devon and tomorrow's tabloid spread would have become Monday's bin liner—over and forgotten about—and my sister's marriage would have been safe!'

It was the way it worked, Mark had said. Raffaelle Villani

would have no case to deny. He might bluster and demand a retraction from the paper but that would be all he could do. Elise's name would not be mentioned by Mark and other than Leo receiving hard evidence that his wife was not the woman in the grainy photographs with Raffaelle Villani, everything else would just—go away.

But this man had not reacted as predicted. He'd grabbed and held on to her. And the pap-pack had caught their scent. Now she was stuck here in his apartment with the pack no doubt waiting outside ready to pounce on her the moment that she tried to leave.

And where was her darling quick thinking half-brother? Putting his twin's needs first, as he always did.

Now Rachel hadn't a clue as to where it was all going to go from here except—

It was time to beg, she recognised starkly. Time to appeal to one very cold and angry Raffaelle Villani for his under-standing and co-operation, when deep down she knew they deserved neither.

She moved towards him. 'Mr Villani,' she murmured huskily, 'please, just think about it. I was actually doing you a favour too tonight because if Leo—'

'What the hell is—*this*?'

Rachel hadn't realised she'd lifted a hand out towards him in appeal until his long fingers were suddenly clamped around her wrist.

'W-what—?' she said jerkily.

Grim mouth flattening, he lifted up her hand until her fingers dangled in front of her confused face. She had to blink twice to focus on the diamond-encrusted sapphire ring twink-ling back at her.

'Oh,' she said and swallowed. She'd forgotten all about the ring.

'You are betrothed—?' he enquired with blistering thinness.

'N-no.' Rachel shook her head. 'It—it's nothing; the ring is a f-fake, just w-window-dressing.'

'Window-dressing,' he repeated.

'Part of the look…' She was beginning to squirm inside again. 'Leo needed to see it if he was going to…'

'Believe you were not his wife?'

She nodded, then swallowed again. 'Elise's engagement ring is a big single yellow diamond. Th-this one is so glaringly different that it…'

Her voice trailed away, the hiss of his breath making it do so because she knew he had caught on.

'So, let me see if I have this clear,' he said grimly. 'You dressed yourself up to look like your half-sister—from behind, then you threw yourself at my neck, kissing me as if I am your…?'

He wanted her to say it. Her heart began thumping. He was going to make her confess the final full duplicity.

'L-lover,' she breathed.

'*Betrothed* lover?' His voice was getting softer by the second. Rachel licked her lips and nodded.

'And I was not supposed to issue an instant denial about this?'

'Th-there's a letter going to be h-hand-delivered here to you tomorrow along with the relevant newspaper,' she told him shakily. 'The letter will explain everything we have talked about and point out to you that to expose the photograph as a lie will leave you open to questions about wh-whose baby it is Elise is carrying.'

'*Madre de Dio*,' he breathed. 'You are truly devious.'

He was right and she was, but— 'This is serious, Mr Villani!' she cried out. 'You don't know Leo! He's one hell of a strict Greek! He's also an absolute killer expert on law! If he decides that his wife has been cheating on him with you and could be having *your* baby…for all your wealth and power, he will drag you to the courtroom and through the gutters along with Elise!'

He threw her hand away. 'I never touched her—!' he bit out angrily.

'Even this very trusting sister can't believe that!'

Her denunciation bounced off the walls and the sheets of plate glass while the air sizzled with his undiluted rage.

'One kiss, Mr Villani,' Rachel stressed urgently. 'One small kiss stolen from the wife of Leo Savakis and he will never forgive her, and you will find yourself stuck with the worst kind of enemy there is!'

He just turned and walked off, striding across the expanse of wood flooring and out through the door.

Rachel followed, quivering, shaken to the roots because it was only now, when faced with what this all meant to *him*, that she was beginning to realise how none of them had given much thought to how unfairly they were treating him in all of this.

She hurried after him. 'I'm so sorry…'

The husky quaver of her apology fell on stony ground. It had been such a useless thing to say anyway, so she didn't blame him for the filthy comment he threw back at her, as one of his arms flew out with an angry hand attached to it, which hit open another door to allow him to keep walking without altering his angry stride.

Rachel found herself coming to a trembling halt in yet another doorway. This one opened on to a shiny black and white kitchen and he was standing by a huge black mirror fronted fridge. One of the doors was swinging open, but by the way he was just staring Rachel received the pained impression that he didn't know what it was he was staring into.

'Please believe me when I say I did *try* to explain it all to you earlier—at the charity thing!' she tried again—frantically. 'I *insisted* to Mark that we should at least attempt to get your understanding and cooperation but…' she sucked in a breath

'…you wouldn't give me the chance to speak and then the whole thing j-just ran out of control!'

He slammed the fridge door shut and turned to face her. If her trembling legs would have let her, Rachel knew she would be running by now.

But—look at him, she told herself helplessly as he began striding towards her. He was so gloriously magnificent in his anger, his face muscles stretched tight across his amazing bone structure and his torso pumped up like a warrior about to begin a slaying-fest.

He reached for her.

She quivered. 'Y-you—'

He shut her up with his hard hot mouth to mouth that totally blacked out her brain. When he let her up for air again she was dizzy and disorientated, in no fit state to find herself being dragged by the hand down the hallway then out of the door to the lift.

His free hand stabbed the call button. Bright balls of panic spun in her head. He was going to throw her out. He was going to hand her to the wolves out there and—

'Please don't do this,' she begged him on the very—very edge of tears now.

He pulled her into the lift. They rode down with him standing there in front of her, with her wrist still his prisoner and the rest of her pinned against the lift wall by the steely glitter in his eyes.

'Think about it,' she begged unsteadily. 'You don't want to—'

He swooped and cut the words off the ruthless way, with another open mouthed onslaught that lost her the will to even stand.

But she had to stand. She had to follow where he pulled as they left the lift and crossed the foyer with a curious security guard looking on. Then a hard hand pushed open the main doors and Rachel lost the next few seconds beneath the glare of flashing flickering lights and the pandemonium of questions that burst out.

His arm was around her shoulders now, hugging her to him and keeping her upright.

'Smile,' he hissed and she smiled like an alien.

Then the words came, those low, smooth accented tones dryly confirming that no, as they could see, she was not Elise. She was in fact Elise's beautiful half-sister, Rachel Carmichael.

Then he let drop the big one, by calmly inviting their congratulations because they had just become engaged to be married.

The fake ring was displayed on her finger for the pack to snap to their greedy hearts' content.

How long had they known each other? Where had they met?

He answered all the questions with the relaxed humour of one who had all the answers, since he was merely duplicating facts from his short affair with Elise.

Breathing took on a shallow necessity aimed to maintain the fragile beat of her heart. The rest was a haze, a fog of nothing in which she must have performed well because no one suggested she was about to pass out or, worse, that she looked more like a horrified prisoner being hauled to the gallows than a happily betrothed future bride.

'Now you have what you came for would it be possible that you can do us a favour and leave us in peace?'

So lightly requested, so full of lazy charm. The pack laughed. He turned her within the iron grip of his arm. Silence hit with a deafening force as the doors closed with them back inside.

'Congratulations, Mr Villani, Miss Carmichael,' the eaves-dropping security guard said with a grin.

If the man holding her clamped to his side said anything in

response then Rachel didn't hear it. She was too busy trying to decide if she was dizzy with relief because he hadn't thrown her out there to face the paparazzi alone, or if she was dizzy with fear over what was still to come.

They travelled back up in the lift. She was in shock. She had been totally incapacitated by a man locked into his own agenda. An agenda that involved him seizing control of a situation they—*she* had taken away from him.

His apartment door closed behind them. Rachel shivered. And still the ordeal did not end there. The arm propelled her down the hall and in through another door. *It* closed with a quiet deathly click and only then did she manage to find the strength to break free.

She had moved three shaky steps before it hit her that this was a bedroom. A very male bedroom with very masculine items scattered around it and a very large bed standing out like a threat, with its very dark plum-coloured linen upon which it was too easy to imprint the solid frame of a dark-haired honey-skinned man.

She turned. He was still by the door and watching her. Not one small gram of anger had softened from his face. Her skin gave a fizz of alarm-cum-excitement because, even in anger, the way he was looking at her was stripping her bare to her quivering skin.

'Why—?' she breathed.

'You wanted my co-operation and you have had it,' he answered. 'Now I want what I want, and you, Miss Carmichael, are about to pay your dues.'

He started closing the gap between them.

'No.' Rachel shook her head and began backing away. 'I won't let you do this.'

'Oh come on, *mi amore*,' he taunted coldly. 'We are betrothed to be married. You wear my ring on your finger and my impeccably mannered family is going to try not to be shocked that my bride is wearing farmers' boots to her wedding and straw to decorate her hair.'

'Very funny,' she muttered, looking about her for an escape.

'They will tread daintily between organic lettuce and—'

'Will you just stop this!' His words might taunt but the rest was now getting scary. 'Look,' she said quickly. 'I know you are angry—and I know that you have every right to be.'

'*Grazie.*'

'Oh, God,' she choked as his hands closed around her waist and the shock of feeling them there again lit up her skin. 'I'm *sorry* about *everything,* okay?'

His dark head began to lower. Rachel tried to arch away.

'Your heart is racing.'

'Because you're *frightening* me!'

'Or exciting you.'

No, frightening—*frightening me!* Rachel repeated—though only inside her head where a strange tumbling darkness was gathering, closing around her like a cold mist that began to take her legs from beneath her and brought forth a string of soft tight curses as she began to go limp.

CHAPTER FOUR

SHE came around to find she was lying on the bed and her head was pounding. Someone moved close by and she flicked open her eyes as Raffaelle Villani came to lean over her.

With a startled jerk she tried to get up but he pushed her back down again.

'Be calm,' he said grimly. 'I do not ravish helpless females.'

Well, forgive me for not believing you, she wanted to say but, 'W-what happened to me?' she whispered instead.

'You—fainted.' His mouth tightened as he said that and his eyes were hooded; in fact his whole face was hidden behind a tightly controlled mask that did not make Rachel feel any safer. 'You are also very cold.'

It was only as a soft cashmere throw landed across her that she realised she was shivering.

'I should not have taken you outside to meet the press wearing only that dress.'

The press. It all came flooding back like a recurring nightmare and she closed her eyes again. 'I can't believe you actually did that,' she whispered unsteadily.

Straightening up, *'Mi dispiace,'* he offered stiffly. 'I have no excuse for frightening you as badly as I did.'

'I wasn't talking about you playing the sex maniac!' She

sat up and this time he did not stop her. 'I meant what you just did down there in front of all those reporters.' She grabbed her dizzy forehead and stared up at him. 'Have you *no* idea what it is you've done?'

'I did what I had to do,' he stated coldly.

'Great,' she choked. 'You did what you had to do and managed to escalate this whole thing right out of control!'

'It was out of control long before I became involved. You said as much yourself.'

So she had. 'Well, we are now stuck with a fake betrothal, complete with a fake ring and all the other fake stuff that is going to come with it.'

'But your sister's marriage will be safe, which, of course, makes the subterfuge, sacrifice and lies worth it?'

The sarcasm was still alive if the frightening anger had lessened, Rachel heard, and went to get up.

'Stay there,' he commanded, turning to stride towards the door. 'Give yourself chance to—warm up a little and—recover.'

Recover for what? Rachel wondered half hysterically. She was never going to recover from this awful night for as long as she lived!

Ignoring his command, she moved to sit on the edge of the bed, then sat trying to calm the sickly swimming sensation still taking place in her head.

'I have to find a way to get out of here undetected so I can go home,' she mumbled, more to herself than to him.

Still, he heard it and paused at the door. 'Where is home when you are in London?'

Usually with Elise but, 'With Mark, right now,' she replied, then squinted a look at her watch. 'He will be worrying where I am.'

'Not so I noticed, *cara*,' he drawled cynically. 'Not that it matters,' he then dismissed, 'because from now on you will be living right here with me.'

'I will not!' she gasped out.

He had the door open now. 'If my freedom to choose what I do with my life has been curtailed, then so has yours,' he declared. 'So, until we find a way out of this situation which does not involve *my* loss of face, you and I, Miss Carmichael, will in effect be stuck to each other with glue. So lie down again and get used to it.'

With that he walked out, leaving Rachel gaping at the empty space he'd last filled with his cold anger, which was just as bad as the hot anger from before!

'But that's just stupid—!' she fired after him. 'Betrothed people don't have to live together!'

If he heard her he did not come back to argue and, after a second, Rachel slumped her shoulders where she sat, wondering dully if he didn't have a point. Now the press wagon was rolling, nothing was going to stop it in the near future without someone—or all of them—losing face.

She closed her eyes, wishing her head would just stop spinning now so she could think.

She needed to ring Mark. The whole story had gone bottom upwards and she needed to warn him then get his take on what she should do next.

Ignoring the swimming room, she got up then just stood looking down at her feet. Her shoes had disappeared. Tugging the throw around her chilled shoulders, she began searching for them but they weren't anywhere to be found.

He must have taken them with him. To stop her from making a bid for freedom? He had to be crazy if he thought her mad enough to run out there where the paparazzi waited—with or without her shoes!

She did find a bathroom, though, which she was sincerely

glad about, since she had not been near one for hours and hours. It smelled of Raffaelle Villani: clean and tangy, with a hint of spice.

Nice, she thought as she washed her hands in the basin. The kind of expensive scents you expected to surround a super-elite male. Then she supposed she must also smell super-elite right now, bearing in mind that her body had been pampered by a whole range of expensive products Elise had provided along with the expensive hairstyle and dress.

She caught sight of herself in the bathroom mirror then and was actually taken aback because she hardly recognised herself—that sleek blonde thing with dead straight hair and heavy make-up.

Well, she thought grimly as she viewed the thick licks of mascara that lengthened her eyelashes and made her eyes look bluer than they really were, everyone just loved to tell her that she had the potential to look almost as good as Elise if she'd only take time with her appearance. Now it seemed they'd achieved their dearest wish, only—

She was not and had never wanted to be Elise, had she? And that person she could see in the mirror was just someone pretending to be something she was not.

The fraud, in other words—the fake.

The pink lipstick had all gone by now, she saw, but her lips still looked fuller than she was used to seeing them. Fuller and sexier because of too many hot kisses shared with a complete stranger.

A stranger who was in for a big shock when he eventually got to meet the real Rachel Carmichael.

Releasing a sigh, she turned away from the mirror and went back into the bedroom to search for that other item that had gone missing—her bag with her cellphone inside it.

It wasn't in the bedroom so she let herself into the

hallway, then walked down it and into the living room. The dress did not feel so indecently short now that her ankles were no longer elevated by four-inch heels, she noticed as she walked.

She heard the bag before she found it because her phone was already ringing. It had to be Mark—who else? she mocked grimly as she followed the sound and found the bag lying on the floor by the sofa she'd last sat down upon.

Her half-finished glass of vodka stood alongside it. As she bent to get her bag there was a moment when she considered picking up the glass first and downing what was left in true Dutch courage style before she told Mark what had happened.

In the end she didn't need to tell him. Pushing her hair behind her ear, she put the phone to it.

'Rachel, what the hell are you doing in Raffaelle Villani's apartment?' Mark's voice all but pounced.

'How did you find out where I am—?' she asked.

'Because it's all over the bloody Internet!'

A sound from behind her made her turn to find Raffaelle Villani propping up the living room doorway. His shirt sleeves were rolled up now, revealing tanned muscular forearms sprinkled with just enough dark hair to make her wonder where else on his body it might be.

Her stomach muscles quivered. Her mouth went dry. Fluttering down her eyelashes, 'It's nothing for you to panic about,' she said huskily into the phone. 'I—I've been explaining the—situation to R-Raffaelle.' The name fell uneasily from her lips and she caught the way one of his eyebrows arched in mocking note of that. 'He—he's being very understanding about it as—as I told you and Elise he would be once he'd heard all the facts.'

There was a short silence. 'I'm coming to get you.'

'No—!' Rachel pushed out. 'It—it's better that you stay away from here.'

'Because I'm the press? Because between the two of you—you've come up with this crazy engagement announcement that is flying round Europe as we speak?'

That far, that quickly—? Rachel swallowed.

'I'm your brother first, Rachel,' Mark was saying angrily. 'And if that bastard is—'

'Well, it's just a bit too late to remember that, Mark!' she cut in. 'After the way you left me standing tonight, I wish I didn't have a brother!'

'I thought you were right behind me until I reached my car.' He had the grace to sound uncomfortable. 'When I did think to look back, the rest of my cronies were piling out of the hotel and I couldn't see you anywhere, so I assumed you'd disappeared in the other direction.'

'And, happy with that very stupid idea, you just went home without me to post your scoop.' Wasn't that just typically Mark?

'I had a deadline,' he grunted.

I had a *life*, Rachel thought angrily. 'Well, it's too late to come at me with the brotherly concern now.'

'Yeah, you're right.' He sighed. 'Sorry, Rachel. So he's okay with all of this, then?'

Straight from apology back to business, Rachel noticed. 'Yes,' she said.

He sucked in a breath. 'So when are you coming back here?'

'Coming back?' She looked at Raffaelle Villani. He was standing there, waiting to hear her answer as much as Mark was.

And she knew suddenly that she was going nowhere. She owed it to this man to play the game the way he had decided it would be played.

'I'm not coming back,' she said to Mark, but it was this other man's wry tilt of his dark head that held her attention.

'We—we're still talking through our options,' she added. 'So I'm staying here f-for now.'

'Just talking?' Mark asked silkily.

She couldn't answer, not straight away anyway, because there was something about the way Raffaelle was looking at her now that—

'Yes,' she said.

But the gap had been too long for her streetwise, cynical half-brother. She heard him let out a long breath of air. 'I hope you know what you're doing,' he said grimly. 'He isn't the kind of man you want to become mixed up with.'

Great advice, she thought, after the event. 'I'll call you—tomorrow,' was all she said.

'I had better go and ring Elise to tell her she can stop worrying.'

And that was Mark, Rachel noted bleakly, back to prioritizing in his usual way—his twin always being a bigger priority for him than she ever could be.

'Okay,' she murmured. 'Tell her I—'

'Great,' he cut in. 'Got to go now, Rachel. I need to change my copy before it goes to print. Do you have any idea how much you've messed me about by making that announcement tonight?'

The phone went dead. Rachel stared at it. And, for the first time since this whole wretched evening began, she felt the thick push of weak tears hit her eyes and her throat.

Raffaelle watched as she continued to stand there with the cellphone in her hand. She'd gone pale again and if her body language was speaking to him then it was telling him that she had just been tossed aside like a used bloody pawn.

Anger pumped at his chest. He wanted to kick something—her twin siblings, for instance.

'What did you expect?' he demanded brusquely. 'A full rescue, complete with armour and swords? You are not the main player on this chessboard, *cara*—Elise is.'

'I know that,' she whispered and sank down on to the sofa.

He breathed out a sigh. 'At least her unborn child will get to know its rightful father.'

He'd meant that to sound comforting but it had come out sounding harsh. She winced, pressing her lips together and dipping her head. Her hair slid forward, revealing the vulnerable curve of her slender white nape.

Raffaelle brought his teeth together, his tongue sitting behind them and tingling with a mixed-up desire to taste what he could see and the knowledge that it was at real risk of being bitten off if he did not take more care about what he said.

With a reluctance to let his mood soften, he pushed himself away from the door and walked towards her. She heard him coming and stiffened her spine. When he leant down with the intention of picking up her glass to offer it to her, she actually shuddered.

'Please don't start dragging me around again,' she choked out.

Was that what he had been doing—?

Yes, that was what he had been doing, Raffaelle realised, and straightened up with a jerk. 'I'm—sorry,' he said.

'Everyone is sorry.' She laughed tensely. 'Doesn't help much though, does it?'

He couldn't argue with that so he threw himself down on the sofa beside her and released another sigh. 'Beginning to feel more like the real victim now, *cara*?' He could not seem to stop the taunts from coming. 'It is a strange feeling, don't you think—being kind of frustratingly helpless? If we then start to wonder how our present lovers are going to feel when the news hits the stands, the sense of frustration really begins to bite.'

'You have a lover?' Her chin shot up, her slender neck twisting to show him blue eyes stark with horror and the glittering evidence of held-in tears. His inner senses shifted, stirring awake from what had only been a very light slumber anyway.

'Do you?' he fed back.

'Of course not!' she snapped. 'Do you really think I would have got involved in any of this if I had a lover who could be embarrassed by it?'

'Whereas I was not allowed to make that choice,' he pointed out. 'So stop feeling sorry for yourself,' he finished coolly. 'You are still less the victim here than I am, so—'

'And you are just *so* loving being able to keep saying that to me!' Rachel got to her feet, restless, tense without knowing why.

Then she did know and she turned on him. 'So who is she—?' she speared at him as if she had the right to ask such a question.

Which she didn't, as the mocking glint in his eyes told her.

But it did not stop her stupid brain from conjuring up some other leggy blonde creature with a very expensive pedigree draping herself over him while he lounged in much the same way he was now—all long limbs and tight muscles and rampant sex appeal waiting to be adored because it was his due.

She took in a short breath, despising the heat of jealousy she could feel burning in her chest, as if a few angry kisses and a sham announcement had given her exclusive rights of possession over him!

It did not, but nor did it stop her crazy imagination from imprinting her own image of him. Her heart began pounding out a suffocating rhythm. This time she couldn't even look away! And to make it so much worse, having been crushed against him more times than was decent, she could even smell his sexy scent in her nostrils, feel the warmth of his mouth and the possessive touch of his hands on her—

'There is no one—fortunately…'

His deep voice slunk into her brain but she had to blink to make herself hear the words he'd spoken—then blink again to make herself understand what they meant.

He meant that there was no other lover in his life right now. Her mouth fell dry and her legs went hollow.

'I was just curious as to whether you had a man hanging about in the wings of this charade, ready to jump out and cause me more trouble.'

'Well, there isn't,' she confirmed and spun away, hating to hear him make that sardonic denunciation of her character because she knew he had every right to suspect her of every underhand trick there was going.

'Good,' he said. 'So I can sit here and enjoy looking at my newly betrothed's fabulous legs without worrying if I am encroaching on someone else's territory.'

The aforementioned legs tingled. She moved tensely. 'We are not betrothed—'

'And the way the neat shape of her *derrière* is teasing me as it moves inside that tight little dress...'

Rachel swung round. 'Is this your idea of having fun, just to get your own back on me?'

'With compliments?' he quizzed innocently.

'Those are not compliments!'

'You don't like me to tell you that I like what I see—?'

'No—!' she lashed out.

'But it's okay for you to look me over as if you cannot believe your good fortune, is it?'

Rachel froze as a guilty blush ran right up her body and into her face. 'I w-was not—'

'Are your breasts your own?' he cut in on her insolently.

Her mouth dropped open in complete disbelief that he had actually voiced that question. 'How dare you ask me that?' she seethed.

'Easily,' he replied cynically. 'They look real, but who can tell by just looking these days—'

'They are real!' she choked out. 'And I've had enough of this—'

'No, you haven't.'

With only that small hint that something was coming, he sat forward and snaked an arm around her waist, then tumbled her down on to his lap.

Her cry of alarm doubled as a shimmering gasp when she found herself contained inside all of that long-limbed, hard-muscled strength.

'W-what do you think you're doing?' Her clenched fists pushed at his shoulders.

The gleam in his eyes mocked her. 'The way you keep looking at me, count yourself lucky that I lasted as long as I did.'

Oh, God, she'd been that obvious? 'You said y-you wouldn't do this—!'

'You are no longer helpless.'

He caught hold of her chin and pushed it upwards, his eyes hiding beneath half-lowered eyelashes as he waited for her lips to part with her next cry of protest—then he pounced, dipping his dark head to match the full pink quivering shape of her mouth with his.

So they'd kissed in anger. They'd kissed in a terrifying state of untrammelled lust. They'd kissed to shock and to subdue. But this—this was different. This contained so much hungry, frustrated, heated desire that it stirred her up more turbulently than any kiss she'd experienced in her entire life.

He explored her mouth so deeply that the feeling of being taken over completely drained her of the will to fight. Her clenched fists stopped pushing and opened to begin stroking in tight, tense, restless movements that only stopped when she found the warmly scented skin at his nape.

One of his arms held her clamped against him, the other stroked the length of her silk-covered thigh. Her dress had rucked

up and the higher his hand glided the more she had to brace her
inner thighs to try to contain what was happening there. And her
breasts were tight, the nipples two stinging pinpricks pressing
against the solid wall of his chest through his shirt.

Her fingers became restless again, one set moving to his
satin cheekbone, then down in a delicate tremor to the corners
of their straining mouths. He muttered something as he caught
hold of her fingers and fed them down between them, until she
was covering the hard ridge of aroused flesh pushing at his
trousers. Frenzy arrived, a hot feverish frenzy of mutual desire
that had been bubbling beneath the surface ever since their first
kiss. Now it quickly spiralled out of control.

He caught hold of her hair and pulled her head back, his
mouth deserting hers to wreak a trail of hot kisses down the
arching stretch of her throat.

She was writhing with excitement, her skin alive to every
brush of his lips and flickering lick of his tongue. A simple tug
and the strap holding up her dress slipped off her shoulder. As
clear air hit the thrust of her breast his mouth was continuing
its delicious torment across its swollen quivering slope until
he claimed the nipple with a luxurious suck.

An explosion of pleasure swept down from her nipple to
low in her body, making her shudder, making her scythe out
hot breaths as she clung to him.

Then his mouth came back to hers again and his tongue
stung deep. Her deserted nipple was pulsating in protest at the
loss of his exquisite suckling. She groaned into his mouth. He
responded by lifting her up and bringing her back down strad-
dling him without breaking the deep hot-mouthed kiss. She felt
the thickness of his erection and couldn't stop herself from
pressing into it. He encouraged her by clasping the tight
mounds of her behind, now fully exposed because her dress
was bunched to her waist. Flaming heat ignited between her

thighs and she rocked her lower body, her fingers clutching at his silk-black hair.

When he stood up with her she didn't bother to protest. She knew what he was doing and where he was taking her. How he made it there without staggering she didn't know because his breathing was shot and his mouth had still not given up possession of hers.

The bed felt soft beneath her as he laid her down on it and she clung to his neck in case he decided to straighten and leave her, but he did no such thing.

Her dress was shimmied down her body. He stripped it from her legs with the deftness of a man who knew the easiest way to undress a woman without interrupting what was already happening with their mouths. There was no bra to remove—this dress was not the kind that permitted the wearing of one—and her stockings held themselves up, which left only her panties as a flimsy barrier to her complete nudity, but they stayed in place because he was now busy with his shirt.

She wanted to help; it was a feverish need that sent her fingers frantic as they tugged at shirt buttons, while his slipped lower to deal with his trouser-clasp and zip…

An impatient rustle of clothing, the fevered hiss of their breath, the heated scents from their bodies and the urgent touch of their fingers on newly exposed eager flesh…

And that deep drugging kiss just did not stop throughout all of it, not as she explored his muscle-packed contours or throughout each quivering gasp she made of pleasure when he explored her softer rounded flesh.

The impatient tug he gave at his shoes to remove them coincided with the reckless way that she dragged off his shirt.

Hot, taut satin skin adorned her hungry fingers once again, coated with a layer of male body hair. She scraped through it with her fingernails and felt him shudder with pleasure, her skin livening with excitement when she finally felt the full power of his naked length come to settle alongside her own. He was big and hot and amazingly, beautifully, magnificently built. Greedy for more, she rolled tight in against him and he accommodated her with a shift of his body that brought her into full contact with every part of his front.

The pouting buds of her breasts rubbed against the rough hair on his chest and she couldn't breathe for the tingling, stinging pleasure of it, yet she was panting, could barely cope with the thrills of excitement that went racing through her as he ran his hands down her spine and over her bottom and thighs to locate her stocking tops. He sent them sliding away with no effort at all. Her toes curled as the silk finally left them and he closed his fingers over her foot and used it to bend her leg over his hips.

Shock stung her into a quivering mass of pleasure when he captured one of her hands and fed it down to the velvet-smooth thickness of his penis, then urged her to stroke it between her legs.

He was big, a beautiful long-limbed muscular male with proportional length to his sex. She still had on her panties but she did not want them on; she wanted to feel him stroking like this against her with no barrier to dull the sensual ache.

Maybe he read her mind because he rolled on to his back, taking her with him, so she lay over him. Then he lifted her up and pushed her thighs together and ran his fingers into the scrappy fabric of her panties to stroke it away from the firm shape of her behind.

'Your skin is like silk,' he breathed against her urgent mouth.

When she caught the words with the flickering tip of her tongue he ran a forefinger into the tightly clenched crevice he'd uncovered and followed it all the way to the hot welcoming wetness between her legs.

He knew exactly what he was doing. Rachel just went wild as the dizzying tumult of thick, warm stimulation coiled around her senses. She moved with him in natural enticement and on a lusty growl he toppled her on to her back, then came to lie across her, their kiss completely broken for the first time.

His eyes were two intense black diamond orbs that he took from the burning desire suffusing her face to look down where his fingers now moved on her, following the path of pale dusky curls into soft female folds between her pearly-white thighs. The damp tip of his tongue appeared between his teeth as his dark head followed. For the next few minutes Rachel existed purely in the drugging eddy of his touch.

She was exquisite. The most receptive woman he had ever experienced. There was a brief moment when he let himself wonder what man had taught her to respond like this. Then, as something too close to jealousy ripped at him, he thrust the question away. His fingers made a slow sensual journey to search out her pleasure spots, allowing his thumb to replace his tongue in rolling possession of her taut little nub. He looked back at her face and watched her sink deeper into helpless response, urged on by his burning need to drive her out of her mind.

Her pale hair lay spread out across his pillow, her parted mouth warm and full and softly gasping, her lips dewy-red against the whiteness of her wonderful skin. Her eyes were closed, her slender arms thrown above her head in complete abandon and the two peaks of her breasts swayed and quivered as she moved her body in a natural sensual rhythm with his caress.

And his heart was thundering against his ribcage, the ache of his own steadily growing need pulsing its demand along his fully aroused length. She wanted to come. He could feel the anxious ripple of her inner muscles bringing her swiftly towards her peak. But thinking about another man making her feel this good made him determined to heighten her pleasure some more.

So he ruthlessly withdrew and, as she whimpered out a protest, he stripped her panties fully away. Without pausing, he then began a long slow, tormenting assault with his hands and his lips and his tongue over every inch of her smooth pale flesh. Dipping his fingers yet again into her hot sweet centre, he closed his mouth round one of her breasts. They were so perfect, two plump pearly-white mounds of womanly softness, with pink super-sensitive tips protruding from their rose-circled peaks. His fingers toyed with one while his tongue toyed with the other. She groaned and arched and gasped and quivered and tried to pay him back with the hungry nip of her teeth. Her hands were everywhere on him now, exploring and stroking, sometimes sending him into paroxysms of shudders when she decided to score her nails into his flesh.

By the time he covered her, she was nothing more than a shimmer of sensation and he took her face between his fingers, then urged, 'Look at me,' in a dark husky voice that made her tremble as she lifted her heavy eyelids and showed him dark blue passion-drugged eyes.

He was so very beautiful, she thought hazily. A dark passionate lover with the face of a fallen angel. Rachel held his gaze as he eased himself between her slender thighs and made that first slow silken thrust inside, surprise widening her eyes as she felt his girth and length. She was no virgin, but he was big so maybe experience had taught him caution with a new lover because she could see his fight not to give her all of him gripping the perfect mould of his face.

'Okay?' he asked huskily.

She nodded, her tongue making a circle of her lips as she willed her inner muscles to relax. With an erotic slowness that fanned the flames flickering between them, he followed her circling tongue with his own. Her fingers were clutching at the bunched muscles in his shoulders, her breathing reduced to short gasps of air as he pushed deeper still. She could feel the roughness of his thighs pressing along the length of her silkier thighs and the way his lean buttocks clenched as the first sense-shattering ripple of her muscles played along his length.

It was a slow, slow merging like she'd never experienced—a careful all-consuming invasion that sent her mind spinning off somewhere and her senses taking on a singing bright will of their own. She moved restlessly beneath him, wanting all of him—needing all of him—but where her hands clutched his shoulders she could feel their bulging taut muscles were trembling with stress as he held himself back. Impatiently she lifted her hips, closed her eyes, then let her muscles draw him in deep.

Nothing had ever felt like this, Raffaelle thought on a lusty groan as the full pressure of his hips sent her thighs spreading wider apart and she took him into that hot tight tunnel with a gripping greed which sent shots of sensation rippling down his full length.

He claimed her mouth with a devouring kiss and she kissed him back so desperately that he flung caution aside and allowed the powerful flow to take him over. Half expecting protest, he received eager encouragement instead as the tactile muscle play of her pleasure surrounded him in moist muscle-livened heat.

She was amazing, a pearly-white sylph with the moves of a siren. Her arms were wrapped around his shoulders, her fingernails scoring deep into his flesh. He moved with increasingly harder strokes and she moved with him, taking each driving plunge from his flanks with an exquisite contraction which rewarded each exquisite thrust.

Energizing heat poured into both of them, driving the whole thing right out there into a different world. The real excess began to build like an electrifying life-force that fine-tuned itself between agony and ecstasy, liquidising the senses and shutting down the brain. The white heat of her orgasm took her over, lifting her whole body from the bed in a quivering arch and holding it there while he thrust and shuddered and ground out hoarse words as she pulsed all around him and brought him to a shattering climax that carried them on and on.

CHAPTER FIVE

AFTERWARDS they lay in a tangle of slack limbs, racing hearts and heated flesh. His face was pressed into the pillow next to her head as he fought for breath and Rachel lay pale as death with her eyes closed, trying desperately to block out the wildly wanton way she had just behaved.

Hot sex with a stranger. Her insides turned over.

She had never done anything like this before in her life.

Which did not make her feel any better about any of it.

Nothing, she suspected, was ever going to make her feel good about it. This was Raffaelle Villani spread heavy on top of her. The man with a notorious reputation for getting off with long-legged blondes.

Now she knew what it felt like to be just one of a large crowd. Self-contempt engulfed her, followed quickly by hot suffocating shame.

Maybe she moved or maybe she even groaned. She didn't think she'd done anything but he suddenly shifted, levering up his torso so he could withdraw that all-powerful proof of his prowess from inside her, and the worst shame of all came when she was unable to still her damning quivering response.

At least the way he shuddered told her that he was experiencing the same thing.

Pushing up on to his forearms, he lifted his dark head off the pillow and looked at her. One of those thick silences seized the next few seconds while Rachel tried hard not to burst into tears. Her heart was still pounding, the desire to duck and hide away almost impossible to fight. It didn't help that his expression was so sensuously slumberous, like a man who was feeling very—very satisfied.

'I...'

It was the only word Rachel managed to drag free from the tension in her throat.

'You—what?' he prompted huskily, reaching up with a long, warm, gentle finger to run it along the trembling fullness of her pulsing lower lip.

'I th-think we got carried away...' She breathed the words out over his finger because he had not lifted it out of the way.

'Well, you carried me away,' he said with an odd half smile that did not seem to know whether to be cynical or just rueful about the whole thing. 'You were—special.'

'Th-thank you,' she mumbled unhappily.

'Quite an unexpected...gift to come out of this mess tonight, which makes me so glad I did not turn away from it when I had the chance...'

A gift—he saw her as a *gift*?

Cynical, Rachel named his half smile, and tensed as the warmth still sandwiched between their two bodies began to chill.

'Well, turn away now, Mr Villani,' she responded frozenly. 'Because it's the last *gift* you are going to get from me!'

She gave a push at his wide shoulders and obligingly he rolled away to lie on his side, watching as she scrambled off the bed, then began hunting the littered floor for something to wear to cover up her nakedness. Catching sight of her dress lying there on the floor in a brazen swirl, she shuddered, hating the sight of it, and made a wild grab for his shirt instead.

'You sound very certain about that.'

'I am.' Rachel had to fight with the shirt sleeves, which had become tangled inside out.

'We were really great together…'

'Well, you're such a great lover,' she flicked back. 'Better than most, if that gives your ego a boost.'

'*Grazie.*'

Get lost! she wanted to scream at him. A gift—a *gift*!

The shirt slithered over her now shivering body and she dragged the two sides together with fingers clutching at the fine cloth like tense claws.

Flushed, angry, and aware that any second now she was going to explode on a flood of wild, uncontrollable I-*hate*-myself! tears, 'Is there another bedroom I can use?' she asked, chin up, blue eyes refusing to do anything other than look directly at his smooth, sardonic, lazily curious face because she was determined to get away with at least some small part of pride intact.

'You don't need one. This bed is easily big enough for the two of us.' He was supremely content in his languid pose.

Refusing to get into an argument with him, Rachel turned to walk towards the bedroom door.

'I don't do one-night stands,' he fed gently after her.

She stopped, narrow shoulders tautening inside his oversized shirt. 'Neither do I…' she felt constrained to reply.

'Good. So we understand each other.'

'No.' Rachel swung round. '*I* don't understand!'

He was already off the bed and reaching for his trousers, so casual about his nakedness that she had to fight not to blush. He was incredible to look at: all golden and glossed by hard muscle tone, made all the more blatantly masculine by the triangle of black curls that swirled between his burgeoning pectorals and then drew a line down his torso to the other thick cluster curling around the potent force of his sex.

The stupid blush broke free when she recalled what that part of him had felt like erect and inside her. She tried to damp it all back down again but it was already too late because, as he was about to thrust a shockingly muscled brown leg into his trousers, he glanced at her and went as still as the dead.

Her breathing went haywire, her old friend panic rising up from places she did not know it could rise up from—her tender breasts, her taut nipples stinging against the cloth of his shirt and that terrible hot spot still pulsing between her legs, which made her draw in her muscles in an effort to switch it off.

He dropped the trousers. And she knew why he had. Seeing the way she was looking at him had turned him on like the floodgates opening on a mighty dam. What she'd thought potent before was suddenly downright unbelievable. He started walking towards her and she actually whimpered as she put out a trembling hand in the useless hope of holding him back, while her other hand maintained a death grip on the shirt to keep it shut across her front.

'No, please don't.' Her little plea came out all husky. Already her legs were threatening to collapse. 'We-we've made this situation messy enough as it is without adding intimacy to it—*please*!' she cried out when he just did not stop.

'I have just come inside you with the most amazing pleasure I have ever experienced,' his dark voice rasped over her. '*Intimacy* is here, *mia bella*. It is too late to switch it off.'

But it wasn't—*it wasn't*! 'I don't want—'

'Oh, you want,' he refuted. 'It has been vibrating out of you from the first moment we met. And I would be a liar if I did not admit to feeling the same way about you—so quit the denial.'

'Sex for the hell of it?' Rachel sliced back wildly.

'Why not?' Capturing her warding hand, he used it to draw her in close. 'We are stuck with each other for the next few months while this thing plays itself out, so why not enjoy what we do have going here which is not part of the lie?'

'If I walk out of here dressed like this and tell anyone waiting out there that I changed my mind because you just were not good enough—that should finish it,' she suggested wildly.

'Are you telling me that my finesse is in need of practice?' He threw back his head and laughed. 'Since we both know that you seem to be pretty much a natural sensualist, Miss Carmichael, I give you leave to teach me all you know.'

'What is that supposed to imply?' Rachel stared up at him.

He grimaced and she didn't like the cynical gleam that arrived back on his face. 'Either someone taught you how to give a man unbelievable pleasure or it just comes naturally to you,' he enlightened. 'I was attempting to give you the more honourable benefit of the doubt.'

He was daring to suggest that she'd been trained like a concubine to pleasure men—?

First a gift, now a trained whore. Rachel stiffened like a board. 'How dare you?' she breathed furiously.

'Very indignant,' he commended. 'But I have just had the life essence squeezed out of me by the kind of muscles I did not know a woman could possess and you kiss like a delightful, greedy, well-seasoned Circe, *amore*—dangerous, but I'm hooked.'

'I think this has gone far enough.' She went to twist away from him.

He spun her back, broke her grip on the shirt front and ran his two hands inside it in a sensual act of possession that claimed her slender waist. Two long thumbs stroked the flatness of her lower stomach and her flesh turned into a simmering sensory mass. When she released an agonised breath he watched the way her pale hips swayed towards him as if they could not stop from hunting out closer contact with the burgeoning jut of his sex.

'Look at you,' he murmured. 'You cannot help yourself. That deliciously damp cluster of curls I can see crowning your thighs is crying out to feel me there again.'

'No,' she denied, knowing it was horribly, shamefully true.

'If I do this…' he eased her in closer and gently speared a path between her thighs '…your slender thighs cling to me as if your life depends upon it…'

And she was clinging. Weak and helpless. He rocked his hips and her arms just lifted, then fell heavily around his neck as she gave herself up to the pure pleasure of it. Her head tilted back, her blue eyes dark and her soft mouth parting and begging for his kiss.

He did not hold it back. He ravished her mouth while other parts of him ravished the soft folds of warm damp flesh between her legs. It did not occur to her that he was as much a slave to what they were generating between them. To Rachel he was just displaying his contempt for her. Toying with her because the humiliation of being made such an easy victim of her half-sister's messy marriage still stung his ego and he wanted her to pay for making him feel like that.

This was payback—sexual payback. And he meant to make her keep on paying for as long as this thing took to pan out.

She was picked up and tumbled back on to the duvet. He came to lean over her, blocking out the light like a domineering shadow, everything about him so physically superior, strong, mesmerising—overwhelming yet so potently exciting at the same time.

His eyes glinted down at her, his face a map of hard angles built on arrogant sexual claim. She was about to be ravished a second time and the horror of it was that she knew she was not going to say no.

A telephone started ringing with the shrillness of a klaxon. Staring up into his face, tense and not breathing, Rachel thought for several seconds that he was going to ignore the call and continue with what he had started here.

Then his face altered, shutting down desire with the single blink of those long eyelashes, and he took hold of his shirt and grimly closed it across her breasts.

With that he levered himself off the bed, leaving Rachel to sit up and huddle inside the shirt while he went to recover his trousers and this time pulled them on.

He glanced back at her, nothing lover-like about him anywhere now. 'Get in the bed. Go to sleep,' he instructed.

Then he strode out of the bedroom, closing the door behind him, leaving Rachel coldly aware that she had just been put in her place.

As the *gift* in his bed, to use if or when he so desired it.

The telephone went silent. Unable to stop herself, Rachel got up and went to open the door as quietly as she could, meaning to creep down the hall and listen in on the conversation—just in case it had something to do with them.

She did not need to take another step from where she was. The door on the opposite side of the hall was open. He was standing in front of a desk with his back towards her and his trousers resting low on his hips.

'You think that ringing me at two in the morning will please me, Daniella—?' His tone did not sound pleased at all.

Rachel continued to hover, watching as his naked shoulders racked up tighter the more that his stepsister said.

'Daniella…' he sighed out eventually. 'Will you give me the opportunity to speak? I am sorry you have been hit by so many telephone calls,' he said wearily. 'No, the lady in question is not Elise,' he denied. 'She is who she has always been. It is everyone else who made the mistake. '

A lie. Another lie. Rachel felt the weight of every single one of them land upon her shoulders.

Raffaelle turned sharply, as if he could sense her standing here. She watched his eyes move in a possessive flow from her face to his shirt, then down her legs. The intimacy in the look conflicted with the coldness now in charge of his features. And she knew that not only had he brought himself under control, but she was now looking at the man she'd first met, undeniably attractive but cynical and hard.

On a wavering grimace Rachel dropped her eyes from him and stepped back into the bedroom. When Elise had picked him to have her rebellious affair with, she had chosen the wrong man, she thought heavily as she closed the door.

Pushing his free hand into his trouser pocket, Raffaelle suppressed the desire to either curse or sigh as he leant his lean hips against the edge of the desk while Daniella continued to yell in his ear.

He was angry with the interfering press, who were taking it in turns to call up Daniella in their quest for more information. He was also fed up because the whole thing was now driving itself like a train with no damn brakes.

And he was achingly bloody aroused and despising himself for feeling like that. Where did he get off, jumping all over a woman—a *stranger*—like some randy, feckless, uncontrolled youth—?

No wonder she'd looked at him just now as if he had crawled out from beneath a stone. No wonder she had gone back in the bedroom and shut herself away. She knew she was trapped; *he* knew he was trapped!

'No, Daniella,' he grimly cut in to her half-hysterical ranting. 'It is *you* who made the mistake two months ago. She was *never* Elise—have you got that?'

His cold tone alone had the desired effect.

'You mean you want me to *say* that I was mistaken?'

'No. I am telling you that you *are* mistaken.'

'So you *have* just got engaged to marry this Rachel Carmichael—the same woman who threw herself at you tonight?'

'*Si,*' he confirmed.

'Just like that—?' She was almost choking on her disbelief.

'No, not just like that,' he sighed out. 'I have been— courting Rachel over the last few months.'

'*Courting* her—?'

Bad choice of word. '*Seducing* her, then.'

Her struck silence made him grimace and he couldn't make up his mind if she was beginning to swallow the lies or simply being sensible for once and taking on board the grim warning in his voice.

'Is she pregnant—?'

'No!' he bit out, jerking upright from the desk and swinging round as a sting of stark alarm shot down his back.

Dio, he'd used nothing to stop it from happening, and he had not thought to ask her if she was protected!

What kind of crass bloody oversexed fool did that make him? Or her for not thinking about it—?

'And, since my personal life is no one's business but my own, *cara*, can I suggest a simple *no comment* from you would make me happy? Or, better still, Daniella—take the telephone off the hook!'

He cut the connection and tossed the handset back on its rest, then just stood there, not knowing what to do next.

Sex without protection with a woman he barely knew. Flexing muscles rippled all over him as he took on board the consequences which could result from such a stupidly irresponsible act.

With his luck tonight, she could already be in the process of conceiving his baby. Add all the other risks which came along with unprotected sex and he suddenly felt like a time bomb set to go off!

A growl left his throat as he turned back to the bedroom. Chin set like a vice, he pushed open the door. The room was in darkness. He switched on the overhead light and went to stand at the bottom of the bed.

She was nothing but a curled up mound beneath the duvet. 'I did not use protection,' he clipped out.

The mound jerked, then went still for a gut-clenching second. Then it moved again and she emerged, sliding up against the pillows, flush-cheeked—wary, defensive—sensationally delectable.

Dio, he thought.

'Say that again,' she shook out.

'I did not use protection,' he repeated tautly. 'I am not promiscuous and I have never taken such risks before in my life,' he added stiffly. 'I like to think that I can respect my…partner's history in the same way that she can respect mine.'

Rachel looked at the way he was standing there like some arrogant autocrat caught with his pants down by his bitch of a wife. Only his pants were up; it was his shirt that was missing and the bitch of a wife in this case was the *gift* he'd been handed and enjoyed thoroughly—before he'd thought to wonder where she had been before she'd landed in his bed!

As if it wasn't bad enough that she was sitting in the bed belonging to a man she had only met for the first time tonight, wearing his shirt and his scents and his touch on her skin—she now had to endure the kind of conversation that belonged in a brothel!

Next he would be asking how much he owed her for her services. Give him half a chance and she knew he would love to denounce her out loud as a whore.

Well, what did that make him? Rachel wanted to know.

'I am a clean-living, careful, healthy person,' she snapped out indignantly.

'I am relieved to hear it.'

He didn't look it. 'I don't sleep around! And if you hit me with one more rotten insult, Mr Villani,' she warned furiously. 'I think I am going to physically attack you!'

'My apologies if it sounded as if I was trying to insult you—'

'You did insult me.' She went to slide back down the bed.

'But we don't know each other.'

'You can say that again,' Rachel muttered.

'And it is an issue we need to address.'

'Well, you addressed it very eloquently,' she told him and tugged up the duvet with a *now go away* kind of shrug.

If he read it he ignored it. 'We have not finished with this.'

'Yes, we have.'

'No, Rachel, we have not…'

It was the alteration in his voice from stiff to weary that forced her to take notice. 'We still have the issue of another kind of protection to discuss.'

Another kind… Rachel froze for a second, then slid back up the pillows again, only this time more slowly as she finally began to catch on.

He put it in simple words for her. 'I did not protect us against—conception. I need to know if you did.'

It was like being hit with one hard knock too many; she felt all the colour drain from her face. 'I don't believe this is happening to me,' she whispered.

Taut muscles stretched as he pulled himself in like a man trying to field his own hard knock. 'I presume from your response that it is a problem.'

'I've told you once—I don't sleep around!' she cried out.

A nerve flicked at the corner of his hard mouth. 'You don't need to sleep around to take oral contraception.'

'Well, thank you for that reassuring piece of information,'

she said hotly. 'But, in my case, and because *I don't sleep around*, I—don't take oral contraception either…' The heat in her voice trailed into a stifled choke.

He cursed.

Rachel covered her face with her hands.

She had just indulged in uninhibited sex with a stranger without any protection; now his millions of sperm were chasing through her body in a race towards their ultimate goal!

Fertilisation. A baby—dear God…

Suddenly she was diving out of the bed and heading at a run for the bathroom. She thought she was going to be sick but then found that she couldn't. She wanted to wash herself clean inside and out!

Instead she just stood there with her arms wrapped around her middle and shook.

She heard him arrive in the door opening. 'I h-hate you,' she whispered. 'I wish I'd never heard your stupid name.'

Raffaelle shifted his tense stance, relaxing it wearily so he was leaning against the doorframe. He wanted to echo her sentiments but he did not think she was up to hearing him say it while she stood there resembling a skittish pale ghost.

'It happened, *cara*. Too late now to trade insults,' he murmured flatly instead.

She swung round to stare at him, blue eyes bright with anger and the close threat of tears. 'You think that kind of remark helps the situation?'

Pushing his hands into his trouser pockets, Raffaelle raised a black silk eyebrow. 'You think that your previous remark helped it?'

No, she supposed that it didn't.

Losing the will to stand upright any longer she sank down on to the closed toilet seat. 'I'm so horrified by what we've done.'

'I can see that.'

'I don't w-want a baby,' she whispered starkly.

'Any man's or just mine?'

Rachel looked at the way he was standing there in the doorway—*lounging* there half-undressed. A tall, lean, tightly muscled *supremo*, the image of everything you would want to grab from the human male gene pool.

Feeling something disturbingly elemental shift in her womb, she went on the attack. 'Being flippant about it doesn't help.'

'Neither does flaying yourself.'

She stared at him. 'Where the heck are you actually coming from?' she gasped out. 'You don't know me, yet you stand there looking as if you couldn't care less about what we've done!'

'I am a fatalist.'

'Lucky you,' Rachael muttered, pushing her hair back from her brow. 'Whereas I am wishing that yesterday never began.'

'Too late to wish on rainbows, *cara*.'

'Now you are just annoying.'

'I apologise,' he drawled. 'However, since we could well be in this for the long haul, I suggest you get used to my—annoying ways.'

'Long haul—?' Her chin shot up. What was he talking about now?

'Marriage comes before babies in my family,' he enlightened.

Marriage—? 'Oh, for goodness' sake.' It made her feel sick to her stomach to say it, but— 'I'll take one of those m-morning after pills that—'

'No, you will not,' he cut in.

She stood up. 'That is not your decision.'

His silver eyes speared her. 'So you are happy to see off a fragile life before it has been given the chance to exist?'

'God, no.' She even shuddered. 'But I think it would be—'

'Well, don't think,' he said coldly. 'We will not add to our sins if you please. This is our fault not the fault, of the innocent child which may result. Therefore we will deal with it the honourable way—if or when it comes to it.'

'With marriage,' she mocked.

'You must know I am considered to be quite a good catch, *cara*.'

Softly said, smooth as silk. A sharp silence followed while Rachel took on board what he was actually implying. Then she heaved in a taut breath. 'I suppose I should have expected that one,' she said as she breathed out again.

'I don't follow.' He frowned.

'The—you set me up for this accusation.' She spelled it out for him. 'The—you got me into bed deliberately so you could position yourself as the great millionaire catch!'

'I did not say that.' He sighed impatiently.

Oh, yes, he damn did! Inside she was quivering. Inside she was feeling as if she'd stepped into an ice cold alien place.

'I'll take the other option,' she retaliated and went to push past him. The hand snaking out of his pocket grabbed her by the arm as the other hand arrived, holding a mobile telephone.

'Let go of me.'

He ignored her and there was nothing relaxed about him now, Rachel saw as he hit quick-dial, then put the phone to his ear.

'Are we still under siege from the press?' he demanded.

He had to be talking to the security man in the foyer, Rachel realised. A new kind of tension sizzled all around them while he listened to the answer and she waited to find out where he was going with this.

The hard line of his mouth gave a twist as he cut the connection. Sliding the phone back into his pocket, he speared her with a hard look.

'The paparazzi is still out there,' he stated grimly. 'I do not expect them to leave us alone any time in the near future—understand?'

Rachel just stared at him, all eyes and weighty heart and pummelled feelings.

'Wherever you or I go from now on, I can almost guarantee that they mean to follow.' He made his point brutally clear. 'So think about it, *cara*,' he urged grimly. 'Do you want to take a walk out to the local all-night pharmacy and turn this thing into a tabloid sensation as the pack follow to witness you purchasing your morning-after medication—?'

Ice froze the silence between them as diamond eyes locked challengingly with frosted blue. Rachel thought about screaming. She felt like screaming! He really, truly and honestly believed that she was ruthless enough to calmly take something to rectify the wrong they had done, his wonderful *fatalist* attitude giving him the right to believe that his morals were superior to her own.

And why not? she asked herself starkly. What did he really know about her as a living, breathing person? Hadn't she flipped out the clever counter attack to his marriage deal? Wasn't she the cool liar and cheat around here, who could hit on a man and let him take her to his bed for no other reason than she'd fancied him?

Why not tag her as a woman who was also capable of seeing off a baby before she was even sure that there was one?

Hurt trammelled through her body, though, melting the ice and turning it into tears because she could not deny him the right to see her as a cold, ruthless schemer—she'd painted her own portrait for him to look at, after all.

He saw the tears and frowned. 'Rachel—' he murmured huskily.

She pushed his hand off her arm and walked away, only to pull to a hovering halt in the middle of the bedroom.

Nowhere to run. Nowhere to hide, she realised as her tears grew and grew. In the end she did the only thing she could see open to her right now and climbed back into the bed and disappeared beneath the duvet again.

Heart thumping, eyes burning, she pressed a clenched fist against her mouth to stop the choking sobs she could feel working their way up from her throat.

She heard him move. The lights went off. A door closed quietly. He had the grace to leave her alone with her misery and at last she let the first sob escape—only to jerk and twist her head on the pillow just in time to see him lift up the duvet and the warm dark shape of his now fully naked body slide into the bed.

Her quivering gasp was lost in the arm he used to draw her against him. Eyes like diamonds wrapped in rich black velvet searched her face, then a grimace touched his mouth.

'You're crying,' he said huskily.

'No, I'm not.' Squeezing a hand up between them, she went to brush a stray tear from the corner of her eye.

Or she would have done if one of his fingers had not got there before hers took the tear away; she could not hold back another small sniff.

'I would not have done it,' she mumbled.

'*Si*, I know that.' He sighed. 'We were fighting. You used your weapon well. I retaliated by cutting you to pieces. I apologise for doing it.'

'You're so ruthless it's scary.'

'*Si*.' On another sigh he sent one of his legs looping over her legs to draw her in a bit closer to him, then he caught her hand and pressed it to his chest.

She felt his warmth and his muscled firmness and the prickle of hair against her palm. It was all very intimate and very dangerous—especially so when she didn't try to pull away. The shirt formed a sort of barrier to stop the more frightening skin to skin contact, but—

She eased out a sigh of her own and tried to ignore what

was happening to her. 'I'm really sorry I got us both embroiled in this mess,' she whispered in genuine regret.

'But you did do it,' he pointed out with devastating simplicity. 'Now we have to deal with what we have.' He came to lean over her, suddenly deadly serious. 'And what we have is one story, one betrothal, one bed,' he listed. 'You will not, during the time we are together, give cause for anyone to question our honesty.'

'Our lies, you mean.'

He shook his dark head. 'Start believing in this, *cara*,' he advised. 'The fate of your sister's marriage rests on your ability to live, breathe and *sleep* the role you have chosen to play in my life.'

His life. Those two words said it all to Rachel. This was *his* life he was protecting. His reputation. His pride.

And why not—? she thought painfully. Her mouth quivered. The tip of his tongue arrived to taste her soft upper lip.

Rachel saw that grimness had been replaced with slumberous desire and knew what was going to happen next.

'No,' she jerked out.

But his tongue dipped deeper. 'Yes,' he contradicted in soft silken English.

'But I don't—'

'You do, *cara*,' and he showed her how much she did by trailing his fingers inside the shirt.

Her breast received his touch with livewire tingles. Don't respond! she told herself, but she did. Her mouth opened wider to turn the gentle contact into a proper kiss and the globe of her breast peaked pleasurably against his palm. It was terrible; she could not seem to control herself.

On a husky murmur he took the kiss back from her and from there it all began to build again.

It should have been a huge let-down after what they'd just

been fighting about—but it wasn't. What it was, was a slow, slow attack on every sensual front he could discover by using his lips and his tongue and the light-light tantalising brush of fingers. There was not a single millimetre of her flesh that was not gently coaxed into yielding its secrets—its every weakness exposed and explored until she felt like a slave to her own sensuality and an even bigger slave to his.

By the time he prepared to come into her, she was so lost in a hazy world made up entirely of him that she just lay there, watching while he produced the protection they'd both forgotten about the last time and expertly rolled it down his powerful length.

His eyes burned hers as he came over her. When he pushed inside, her groan brought his lips down to capture the sound. They moved together in a slow, deep, serious, dark journey, which left both of them totally wiped out by its end.

And, as sleep finally swept her into boneless oblivion, Rachel knew she had been totally taken over, ravished, possessed.

I wish, was the last conscious thought she remembered having and fell asleep wondering what it was she had been about to wish for.

She awoke cocooned in a nest of warm duvet and to the sound of a telephone ringing again. Only it did not sound loud, as if it was being muffled by the thickness of walls and doors. But the persistent sound pierced through her sleep like a sluggish pulse taking place inside her head.

She didn't open her eyes—didn't want to. Too many bad memories were already rushing back, the worst of them being the knowledge that she'd fallen into bed with a man she'd only met the night before, had hot, unprotected sex with him and now his physical imprint was so deeply stamped on her that she could still see him, hear him, feel him and smell him with every sensory cell she had.

The ringing stopped. Rachel let her eyes open. Daylight was shrouded by the drawn curtains but she could see just enough to know that the place beside her in the bed was empty and she breathed a sigh of relief.

At least she would have some time to get herself back together before she had to face him again.

Easing out of the bed, she rose to stand up with just about every muscle feeling the extra stretch as she looked around her for something to put on.

Her clothes had gone. So had the shirt she had been coveting last night like a last line of defence. What now? she asked herself. Were her missing clothes supposed to be sending her a message about where she fitted into his life?

Suddenly spying the cashmere throw he had used to cover her with the night before draped over a chair, she leapt on it and wrapped herself in it. The throw covered her from throat to ankle but she still felt like the wretched man's concubine, imprisoned for his exclusive use.

And he knew how to use her, she was forced to admit when her senses gave a tight little flutter in response to the thought.

Someone knocked on the door. She almost tripped over as she spun round to stare at it.

'Y-Yes?' she called out, puzzled as to why the heck he was bothering to knock when privacy had been something he had taken no heed of last night.

'Your things have arrived, Miss Carmichael,' a totally strange female voice announced. 'Shall I leave the suitcase here outside the door?'

'Oh—y-yes—thank you,' she answered, frowning because she didn't know what the woman was talking about.

She waited a few seconds before going to pull the door open a small crack to make sure the woman had gone before she looked down to discover the suitcase she'd hastily packed before leaving Devon was now standing on the floor. Clinging to the black throw with one hand and still frowning, she used her other hand to lift the case inside the bedroom and shut the door again.

Last time she'd seen this, it had been lying open and spilling its contents on to the spare bed in Mark's flat. So how had it ended up here instead?

Had Mark delivered it? Had he come here, then left again without bothering to see or speak to her to find out if she was okay?

Hurt thickened her throat as she heaved the case on to the rumpled bed and unzipped it. Inside it was everything she had brought up to London with her, plus all the extras that Elise had provided to help turn her into her look-alike.

There was also a piece of paper lying on the top of everything. Picking it up, she unfolded it to find it was a hastily scribbled note from Mark.

Did you have to send the chauffeur round to knock me up for your stuff at 6 o'clock in the morning? I'd only just crawled into bed!
Elise called you last night after I told her the good news, but your phone was dead. She and Leo wanted to congratulate you on your coming nuptials, if you get my drift. Call her later today so she can play the ecstatic sister for Leo's benefit.
I'm off to LA this afternoon for a few weeks. See you when I get back. Love M.

Mission accomplished, in other words, so it was back to normal life—for Mark anyway. No words of concern for how she was feeling. No sign of a rescue plan for her any time soon.

Rachel stared out at nothing for a moment or two. Then, as

a rueful grimace played its rather wobbly way across her mouth, she let the note fall on to the bed and turned her attention to selecting fresh clothes from the suitcase. At least she was now overloaded with expensive hair products and cosmetics, she consoled herself.

Dressed in a short bathrobe and fresh from his shower in one of the guest rooms, Raffaelle opened the bedroom door as the bathroom door shut with a quiet click.

He stood for a moment, viewing the evidence of her occupation, then walked over to the bed and picked up the note. His expression hardened as he read it. His eyes then drifted to the open suitcase, where it looked as if everything had been dumped in there at haste.

Did she feel deserted? She had to feel deserted because it was exactly what had happened to her.

Replacing the note where he'd found it, he turned then and strode across the bedroom to open the door which led into his dressing room. Ten minutes later he was dressed and letting himself out of the bedroom as quietly as he had come in while the running shower still sounded from the other side of the closed bathroom door.

CHAPTER SIX

IT TOOK nerve for Rachel to open the bedroom door and step into the hallway. She would rather be doing anything than facing Raffaelle Villani in the cold, harsh light of day.

Rubbing her hands up and down her arms in a nervous gesture as she walked, at least she looked more like herself, she tried to console herself. With Elise's image stripped away and her hair shampooed and quickly blow-dried, she'd seen the real Rachel staring back at her from the mirror—the one who wore jeans and a long-sleeved black knit top. Her make-up was minimal and her hair had reverted to its natural style.

All she needed to do now was to convince herself that she was the real Rachel, because she certainly did not feel like her inside.

She intended to go and hunt down her bag and her cellphone before she did anything else, but she never got that far. The door next to the kitchen stood open and, having glanced through it, she then pulled to a heart-sinking halt.

Raffaelle was there, standing by a long dining table. He was wearing a soft loose-fitting smoked-grey T-shirt and a pair of charcoal trousers that hung easily around his hips. And, if she had ever wanted to know the difference between expensive man dressed in a formal dinner suit and expensive man dressed casually, then she was looking at him.

The aroma of fresh coffee would have sailed right by her if he had not used that moment to lift a cup to his mouth. She was held transfixed by his height again, by his sensual dark good looks, by his mouth sipping coffee and his long golden fingers holding the cup.

Sensation quivered right down her front as each and every sense unfurled and responded to the sight of those hands, that mouth, the long legs and wide shoulders—to her exciting new lover. Her breasts grew tight and tender in her bra cups, her tongue grew moist in her mouth, her breathing stopped completely as a tight tingling erupted low down. It was like falling into a deep, dark pit of forbidden pleasures. She didn't want to feel like this but she could not break free from it.

Then he glanced up and caught her standing there staring at him. It was like being pinned to a wall by her guilty thoughts. Heat rushed up from her toes and through her body until it suffused her face to her hair roots while he just stood there with his cup suspended just below his sensual mouth.

The agony of mutual intimacy was nothing short of torture as she watched his eyes drop to the pair of simple flat black shoes adorning her feet, then begin a slow journey upwards, along well-faded denim that clung to her legs and her hips and the flatness of her stomach like a second skin.

His scrutiny paused right there and suddenly something else was adding to the turbulent mix. Rachel knew what he was thinking. She felt the muscles around her womb clench tightly as if it was acknowledging that it already belonged to him.

Maybe he saw the tightening because his eyes darkened. When he lifted them to clash with her eyes, the sheer power of what was passing between them put her into a prickling hot sweat.

He broke eye contact and she could feel her heart drumming against her ribs as he dropped his attention to her mouth, slightly parted and trembling, with its light coating of pink lipstick, then back to her eyes, looking out at him from a fixed hectic blue stare between quick flicks of mascara. Finally he let his eyes drift over her hair, where long and sleek straight had been replaced by a mop of silky loose curls that framed her still blushing face.

'Where did the curls come from?' he asked softly.

Forced into speech, Rachel had to moisten the inner surface of her lips. 'They were always there, just hiding,' she answered, lifting a self-conscious hand up to push the curls from her brow.

He continued to stare as the curls bounced back into place again. Shoulder-length straight now finished in a sexy blonde bubbly riot almost level with her pointed chin.

'They suit you,' he murmured.

'No, they don't,' she denied. 'But I was born with them, so…' She added a shrug, then stuck her hands into her jeans pockets and finally managed to drag her eyes away from him.

Raffaelle frowned as he watched the defensive body language.

'Is there any of that coffee going spare?' she asked.

'Sure,' he answered. 'In the kitchen. I will go and get it—'

'No.' She jerked into movement. 'Let me.'

She'd disappeared before he could stop her, fleeing like a scared fluffy blonde rabbit. It made him grimace—a lot of things made him grimace, like the tension she'd taken with her—the knowledge of what they'd done the night before. And the lack of awareness in her own natural beauty, for which he placed the blame firmly at her glamorous half-sister's feet.

Draining his coffee cup, he made the decision to follow her. Now the morning ice was almost broken he had no intention of letting it freeze over again.

She was standing by the coffee machine, watching it fill a cup.

'Here,' he said, striding over to offer his empty cup. 'I like it black.' He moved away from her before she had a chance to react to him. 'What do you like for breakfast—a fresh croissant? Cereal? Toast?' he listed lightly. 'There is some fresh orange juice in the fridge if you—'

'I don't want anything,' she cut in. 'Th-thank you,' she added. 'Just a caffeine shot then I will have to be going…'

'Going…' He turned slowly to look at her.

'Yes,' She was clearly refusing to look at him, staring down at her watch instead. 'I have a train to catch back to Devon and half the morning has gone already.'

'We've been over this,' Raffaelle reminded her. 'You are staying right here with me.'

'Yes, I know that.' She nodded, setting the blonde curls bouncing as she concentrated on the job of swapping her filled cup for his empty one beneath the stream of coffee from the machine. 'But I need to get some clothes if…'

'I will buy you any clothes you will need.'

Rachel stiffened. 'No, you will not! I have clothes back in Devon—and don't you *dare* make such a derisory offer like that again!'

'It was not derisory,' he denied. 'I was being practical.'

'Well, I'm trying to be practical too, and I can't just drop everything as if I don't have another life. I need a couple of days to—organise things with the farm.'

'You mean you actually run the farm yourself?'

More derision? Rachel stared at him but only saw honest disbelief in his face. 'Efficiently,' she stated coolly.

'So who is looking after it while you are here?'

'A—neighbour.' She frowned as she said that, wondering why she had put her relationship with Jack in such odd terms. 'But he has his own place to run, so I…'

Something altered in his demeanour, though Rachel wasn't sure exactly what it was.

'Use your phone to make your arrangements, as I have had to do,' he said coolly.

'God, you're so insufferable,' she gasped. 'It's all right for you. You're Mr High-flyer. You can order people about by phone, but I can't.'

Ignoring the high-flyer quip, Raffaelle walked towards her. 'You think?'

'I know.' Rachel nodded backing into the corner of the kitchen units as he approached, then feeling well and truly trapped by the time he towered over her. 'I've seen the way it works with Leo. W-when he needs something done he just throws his weight around by telephone.'

'But you need to be hands-on to water your organic lettuce,' he mocked.

'You don't need to be so derisive about it!' she flashed in her own defence. 'When this is all over with, Mr Villani, you might be unfortunate enough to have lost a deal or two because you weren't paying proper attention, but I risk losing my whole livelihood!'

'If you are carrying my child then this will never be over.'

Placed coolly into the argument, Rachel swallowed thickly. 'Don't start hitting me with the worst thing that could happen again,' she shook out huskily.

He went to say something, then sighed and changed his mind. Tension stung—antagonism that wasn't all to do with what they were arguing about.

'You said it was family-run thing,' he then prompted.

'It is,' she confirmed. Then she took a breath and altered that answer to, 'It *was* a family run thing until my parents were killed five years ago in—in a road accident. Now the farm is split three ways between me, Mark and Elise.'

'Which means that you do the work and they do nothing?'

'I like the work, they don't.'

'Loyal little thing, aren't you?' he mocked her. 'Has it not occurred to you yet that they are not very loyal to you—?'

Raffaelle wished the words back as soon as he'd said them. But it was too late. She'd already gone pale and she lost her cup so she could make a defensive fold of her arms across her front.

'My family loyalty is none of your business,' she muttered.

'You think—?' Anger with himself made his voice sound harsh. But since the anger was there now, he took a grip on her clenched left hand and prised it upwards. 'This ring on your finger demands that I should have your complete loyalty now.'

'It's fake.' She grabbed the hand back and thrust it beneath her arm again.

Things were starting to happen. Fights with women usually did end up as sexual battles and Raffaelle was beginning to feel the sexual pull. He reacted to it by snaking his hands around her slender nape and tilting her head back so he could claim her mouth.

She tasted of mint toothpaste and pink lipstick. He found he liked the combination. And she didn't try to fight him, which he liked even more. By the time he raised his head again, her arms were no longer defensively crossed but clinging to his shirt.

'This isn't fake,' he rumbled out deeply, still toying with the corner of her mouth. 'So let's forget about Devon and go back to bed. I don't know why we got out of it in the first place.'

'No.' She gave a push at him and when he released her she scuttled sideways. 'I've got things to do.'

'You mean you're running scared all of a sudden.' He grabbed her hand to pull her out of the kitchen and back into the dining room. 'If you are hoping to escape to a pharmacy in Devon,' he said brusquely, 'then first you should take a look at these…'

He brought her to a stop beside the dining table where a selection of the Sunday tabloids lay spread out.

Rachel froze, wondering how she had missed seeing them before. But she knew why she'd missed them; she'd been too busy drinking him in to notice anything else in the room.

In every photograph but one, she and he were standing outside the apartment block displaying the ring and looking convincingly loverlike and besotted. The only photograph that was different was in Mark's paper, which bore the clever caption, *'First public kiss for newly engaged lovers.'*

'My fifteen minutes of fame,' she jibed tensely, looking at the sleek stranger in the photographs, who happened to be her. Raffaelle looked no different than his tall, dark, handsome self and how he'd managed to pull off that smile without making it look cynical was worthy of a headline all by itself.

'This is set to last a lot longer than fifteen minutes, *cara*,' he responded dryly.

'Because you're newsworthy.'

'Which is the only reason why you hit on me in the first place,' he pointed out. 'This is what you wanted.' He waved a long finger at the photograph her half-brother had taken. 'I must admit you look very like your sister in that.'

The picture showed a clinch which looked like they'd been lovers for ever. That wave of tingling intimacy shot down Rachel's front again and she quickly shifted her eyes to the other more carefully staged photographs, all of which were accompanied by catchy tag lines aimed to turn them into tacky celebrity fodder.

'I did not want all the rest of this, though. That was your fault.'

'You cannot be so blind.'

It was the way he said it that made Rachel look sharply at him. It had been hard and sardonic—tones that repeated themselves in the expression on his face.

'Explain that,' she demanded.

'I meant nothing.' He went to turn away.

'Yes, you did!' She caught hold of his arm. 'And I want to know what you meant!'

He swung back to her, face hard, eyes angry. 'Did you never

think to question if your brother's cronies would know who his twin is? Of course they knew—' he answered his own question '—which is why they came after us and called out Elise's name. They saw you looking like her and him making his quick escape, then they saw a very contrived yet really juicy scandal brewing involving Elise, Leo Savakis and Raffaelle Villani in a gripping sex triangle. I can forgive you your naïvety, *cara*, if you are as shocked as you appear to be, but I will not forgive your stupid brother for not thinking this thing through and foreseeing the obvious outcome if I had not intervened!'

Rachel pulled out a chair and sat down on it. He was oh-so-sickeningly right. And the worst of it was that he seemed to have worked all of it out within seconds of her explaining it all last night.

'Now ask yourself how long you think it will take the press to sleuth out exactly who you are,' he persisted. 'And your fifteen minutes of fame becomes a roller coaster ride to hell and back while they dig into your past, with Leo Savakis waiting in the wings for you to fall off the rails and accidentally reveal it is all just a big ugly cover-up for his wife's transgressions.'

'You don't have to say any more,' Rachel whispered. 'I get the full picture.'

'Do you?' he rasped. 'Well, add this into the mix. Start running scared now and I will blow the whole lie sky high and damn your sister's marriage. I can take the heat of the repercussions if she cannot!'

He walked out of the room, leaving Rachel alone to stew on what he'd said. It didn't take long. He was right and she had been running scared when she'd made that bid to leave here and go back to Devon. But that had nothing to do with the lies, though they were bad enough. Her reasons did not even have anything to do with their stupid delving into unprotected sex! It was to do with him and what he did to her. What he made her feel. If he could affect her this badly in only one night, then she was going to be an emotional wreck by the time it came to the end.

If it came to an end, she then amended, recalling that marriage warning he'd made.

Raffaelle was pacing his study wondering what was the matter with him. Why had he bitten her head off like that?

Because she wanted to go home to collect some clothes and organise her life, or because she still persisted in defending her selfish family?

Or was it because she'd mentioned a man down there in Devon? A *neighbour* she had not bothered to mention before…?

He did not know. He did not think he *wanted* to know. Something was happening here that scared him witless each time he came close to looking at it.

He heard her moving about then and went to see what she was doing now. He found her in the living room with her bag in her hand.

'I—can't find my phone,' she said and she looked pale and defensive again.

'The battery was flat. I put it on the charger in my study. I'll go and get it…' Then he paused. 'Who do you want to call?'

Irritation ripped down his backbone because he knew it was none of his business who she wanted to call. By the expression on her face, she thought the same thing.

Still, she answered him. 'I will have to ring round a few people if I am not allowed to leave here—'

'No.' Raffaelle shook his head. 'We will do it your way, only we both go and we will use my car instead of the train.'

'But—'

'Ten minutes,' he said gruffly, turning away again. 'And don't keep me waiting. The sooner we leave, the sooner we can get back.'

He drove them in a silver Ferrari with the same reckless efficiency he'd driven the night before. But then, his driving had had to be nifty when they'd met with the paparazzi waiting outside for them to leave. They'd picked the car up from the basement car park but the moment they'd emerged on to the street they'd been spotted and all hell had broken loose as camera-toting reporters fell over themselves to get into their cars and give chase.

'I don't understand why they're still hanging around,' Rachel said after they'd lost their pursuers in a sequence of dizzying turns down narrow back streets. She hadn't dared speak before then in case she broke his concentration and they ended up hitting a wall. 'What do they think we are going to do? Get married on the apartment steps or something?'

'They don't know enough about you.' He sounded so grim that Rachel felt a cold little shiver chase down her spine.

'I hate this,' she whispered. 'I hated it when I used to get caught up in it with Elise. I don't know how you people live your lives like this.'

'We live in a celebrity-driven world,' he answered levelly. 'The masses are greedy for the intimate details of the rich and famous—or, for that matter, anyone who lives a high profile life. You have now joined the celebrity ranks, so get used to it, because this is only the beginning of it.'

The beginning of it...

After that Rachel did not speak another word. They reached the motorway and suddenly the powerful car came into its own, eating up the miles with the luxurious smoothness that promised to cut the journey time by half.

He stopped once at a motorway service station, led her into the café and bought sandwiches and coffee.

'Eat,' he instructed, when she stared at the unappetizing-looking sandwich he'd placed in front of her. 'You look like death and you have eaten nothing since you threw yourself at me last night.'

And I look like death because I hardly had any sleep last night, she threw back at him without saying the words out loud. Because out loud meant opening a Pandora's box full of what they'd been doing instead of sleeping.

The indifferent-tasting sandwich was washed down by indifferent-tasting coffee. Rachel was surprised he ate his sandwich or drank the coffee. They just didn't look like the kind of food this man would usually put anywhere near his mouth.

When they hit the road again he wanted to talk. 'Tell me how your family works,' he invited.

So she explained how her mother had lost her husband to a long-term illness while the twins had still been very young. 'A few years later she married my father and then had me.'

'So what is the age difference between you and the twins?'

'Six years,' she replied.

'And who did the farm originally belong to?'

'My father. But he—*we*—never differentiated between Mark and Elise and myself. And it isn't really a farm,' she then added because she thought she better had do before they arrived there and he saw it. 'It's what we call a smallholding, with three acres of land, a house, a couple of greenhouses and a couple of barns.'

'Another lie, *cara*?'

Rachel shrugged. 'It's run like a farm.'

'And the…neighbour that helps you out when you need it—what does he do?'

'Jack owns the land adjoining our land—and his *is* a farm,' she stressed. 'He's been good to us since our parents died.'

'Call it as it is,' Raffaelle said. 'He has been good to *you*.'

Rachel turned to look at him. 'Why that tone?' she demanded.

His grimace stopped her from becoming hooked on watching his face. 'I don't think I want to elaborate,' he confessed.

'Suits me,' she said and, turning the collar up on her coat, she leant further into the seat and closed her eyes.

His low laugh played along her nerve endings. 'You are prickly, Miss Carmichael.'

'And you are loathsome, *Signor*.'

'Because I don't mind saying that I dislike the way your siblings use you?'

'No. You are loathsome simply because you are.'

'In bed?'

Rachel didn't answer.

'You prefer, perhaps, this Jack in bed as your lover because he is so *good* to you.'

He was fishing. Rachel decided to let him. 'Maybe.' She smiled.

'But can he make you fall apart with pleasure there as I can, or does he bring the smell of farmer to your bed, which you must overcome before he can overcome you?'

'As I said. You're loathsome.'

'*Si,*' he agreed. 'However, when I said that I don't sleep around I meant it, whereas you seemingly did not.'

Rachel turned her head and flicked her eyes open to look at him. Once a liar always a liar, she thought heavily when she saw the grimness lashed to his lean profile.

And a tease could only be a tease when the recipient knew he was being teased. Sitting further up the seat with a sigh, she pushed a hand through her curls and opened her mouth to tell him exactly who and what Jack was—when her attention was caught by a giant blue motorway sign.

'Oh, heck,' she gasped. 'We need to take this next turn-off!'

With a startled flash of his eyes and a few muttered curses, he flipped the car across several motorway lanes with one eye on the rear-view mirror judging the pace of the traffic behind them and the other eye judging the spare stretch road in front of them. By the time they sailed safely down the slip road Jack's name had been washed right out of Rachel's head by an intoxicating mix of nerve-fraying terror for her life and the exhilarating thrill of the whole smooth, slick power-driven manoeuvre.

'Which way?' he demanded.

Rachel blinked and told him in a tense breath-stifled voice while her senses fizzed and popped in places they shouldn't. What was it about men and danger that struck directly at the female sexual psyche?

He glanced at her and saw her expression and sent her a wide slashing masculine grin that lit her up inside like a flaming torch.

'Scared, *cara*?' he quizzed.

'You—you—'

'Had it all under control,' he smoothly provided. 'Which, in Italian terms, makes the difference between a mere good lover and a fabulous lover.'

Rachel knew exactly what he meant, which was the hardest thing to take. If he stopped the car now she would be crawling all over him in a hot and seething sexually needy flood.

It was everything—the powerful car and the reckless man and the adrenalin rush still singing through her blood. She tried to breathe slowly and lost it completely when he reached across to her and gently stroked her cheek. Static fire whipped across her skin cells, she whispered something and turned her head. Their eyes clashed. For a short, short split second in time it was like falling into a vat of writhing, hissing, snapping snakes.

He looked away. The smile had gone but the atmosphere inside the car had heightened beyond anything real. Rachel sat on her hands to stop them reaching for him and tried to pretend it wasn't happening while he drove on with a sudden grim concentration that only made everything worse.

She gave directions in short, sharp, breathless little bursts of speech that only helped to increase the tension. He said nothing but just reacted with slick control of the car. They were both sitting forward in their seats. They were both staring fixedly directly ahead. She knew where this was going to end up just as he knew it. And the agony of knowing was as tough as the agony of having to sit here and wait.

At last—finally they turned into the private lane which led to the farm. Winter fields barely waking up to early spring spread out on either side of them, neatly ploughed and ready to sow. The old farmhouse stood in front of them, its rustic brick walls warmed by a weak sun. Flanking either side of it stood the adjoining barns and behind the house they could just see the greenhouse's glass glinting in the weak sunlight.

In front was the cobbled yard where Rachel's muddy old Jeep stood tucked in against a barn wall. On the other side stood another car, a Range Rover, making Rachel's heart sink, though whether that was due to disappointment, because she knew what was buzzing between the two of them was about to be indefinitely postponed, or relief for the same reason, she refused to examine.

Raffaelle brought the car to a stop in the dead centre of the courtyard, killed the engine, then climbed out without uttering a word. Rachel was slower in moving, unsure if her stinging legs would hold her up if she tried to stand on them.

He couldn't know what was coming and she didn't know how to tell him. One glance at his face across the top of the car and she was almost bowled over by the strict control he was holding over himself.

His eyes were not under control, though. They looked back at her with a possessive glitter that showered her with sexual promise.

She parted her paper-dry lips. 'Raffaelle—' she began anxiously.

'Let's go inside and find a bed,' he said huskily.

She quivered and swallowed, then heaved in a tense breath in preparation to speak again. The front door to the house suddenly swung inwards, snatching her attention away from him.

He looked where she was looking, shoes scraping on worn cobbles as he turned then went perfectly still.

A man stood in the open doorway—a tall, well-built, swarthy-looking man wearing brown cords and a fleece coat. He was also a man easily in his fifth decade, with eyes like ice that he pinned on Raffaelle.

'Jack,' Rachel murmured, feeling trouble brewing even before she saw Raffaelle tense up when she said Jack's name.

Damn, why hadn't she thought about this before she'd teased Raffaelle about her relationship to Jack?

And, oh dear, but Jack did not look pleased at all.

She hurried forward. Raffaelle stood frozen as he watched her walk straight into the other man's arms. He was trying to decide whether to go over there and punch the bastard for taking advantage of a vulnerable young woman left alone here to cope on her own. Or to reclaim what now belonged to him, then tell him to get the hell out.

In the end it was the other man who took the initiative.

'Jack…' Rachel burst into nervous speech as she reached him. 'This is…'

'I read the paper this morning, Rachel,' he cut in, looking across the cobbles with a set of grey eyes that were as cold as Raffaelle's own eyes.

He put her to one side so he could walk forwards. Rachel could feel the suspicion coming off him in waves. Jack knew her better than most people, so if anyone was going to smell a rat about her surprise engagement then it would be him.

'I n-need to explain.' She dashed after him.

'Mr Villani,' Jack greeted coolly.

Nerves jumping all over her now, Rachel rushed into speech yet again. 'Raffaelle, this is Jack Fellows.' Her anxious blue eyes pleaded with him to understand. 'He's my—'

'Guardian,' Jack himself put in. 'Until she is twenty-five, that is.'

'Well, that is a new name for it,' Raffaelle drawled.

'Jack is also my uncle,' she said heavily. 'M-my mother's brother…'

'And the one who looks out for her interests,' Jack coldly put in. 'So, if you are the same Italian who broke Rachel's heart last year, then you had better come up with a good reason for doing it or Rachel will not receive my blessing for this engagement.'

Oh, dear God. Rachel wished the ground would open up and swallow her. It just had not occurred to her that Jack would make such a mistake!

Now Raffaelle was looking at her as if she was one of the devil's children and she couldn't blame him. It had to feel as if each time he turned around he was being forced to answer new charges that someone in her family planted at his feet!

'Raffaelle is not Alonso,' she muttered to Jack in a driven undertone.

'Was that his name?' Her uncle looked at her in surprise. 'I don't recall you actually ever mentioning it.'

That was because she hadn't. She'd just come back here from her trip to Italy looking and behaving like a woman with a broken heart.

Her uncle turned back to Raffaelle. 'My sincere apologies for the mistake, Mr Villani,' he said and offered him his hand.

But it was too late for Rachel as far as Raffaelle was concerned. She sensed his anger hiding beneath the surface of his smile as he took Jack's proffered hand.

Then he switched the charm on. By the time he had finished explaining who he was and what he was, and trawled out the same story about how and where he'd met Rachel, he had her uncle eating out of his hand. It was like watching an action reply of the way he had handled the press the night before. And all Rachel could do was smile benignly once more and be impressed by his performance, while knowing retribution was close at hand.

He coolly assured Jack that he was no fortune hunter out to marry his niece for her share in the family pile. He assured him dryly that no, not all Italian men were so cavalier with the vulnerable female heart.

And of course he was madly in love with Rachel—what man would not be? His arm snaked out to hook her around her shoulders so he could draw her in close to his side.

I'm going to kill you the minute I get you alone, that heavy arm promised. And Rachel believed it—totally.

Then he apologised to Jack that the news of their betrothal had broken in the papers before he'd had a chance to come here and officially request Jack's blessing.

It was his finest moment, Rachel acknowledged from her subservient place at his side. Jack was old-fashioned, with traditional values. She could see from her uncle's expression that in Raffaelle he thought he was meeting a man after his own heart.

Jack had to rush off then but he offered them dinner to celebrate.

Smooth as silk, Raffaelle thanked him but regrettably had to decline. Apparently he had to be back in London this evening—to attend an irritating business dinner.

Whether there was a business dinner, Rachel did not know. But, of course, her uncle understood. Busy men and all that.

And Raffaelle's ultimate coup was to gain Jack's instant agreement that everything here would be taken care of while Rachel was away, because of course Raffaelle wanted her with him.

'Just be happy, darling,' Jack said to her, then he kissed her cheek, shook Raffaelle by the hand and left them, driving away while they stood and watched him—with Raffaelle's arm still exhibiting its possession across her shoulders in a grip like a vice.

Happy was the last thing she was feeling by the time her uncle's car disappeared out of sight. The moment he turned them to face the house Rachel tried to break free from him but his grip only tightened as he walked them across the cobbles.

The front door opened directly into the farmhouse-style kitchen, heated by the old Aga against the wall. Coming in here should have felt comfortingly familiar to Rachel but it didn't. The door closed. The arm dropped from her shoulders. Moving like a skittish kitten, she took a few steps away from him then spun around.

'I…'

'If you are about to utter yet another lie to me—' he cut right across her '—then let me advise you to keep silent!'

CHAPTER SEVEN

HER heart gave a thick little thump against her ribcage. It was like looking at a complete stranger again—a tall, dark, coldly angry stranger.

'I was actually about to apologise for the…misunderstanding with Jack out there.'

'You set me up.'

'It w-wasn't like that,' she denied. 'Y-you were fishing for information and I stupidly decided to tease you about my relationship with Jack.'

'I am not referring to your desire to pull my strings by intimating there was another man in your life,' he said. 'Though using your uncle like that is unforgivable enough.'

'Then what—?' she demanded.

'Alonso,' he supplied. 'The Italian heartbreaker I have been set up to play substitute for in your desire for payback!'

'That's not true!' Rachel protested.

His angry eyes crashed into her like a pair of ice picks. 'Not only is it true but you are the most devious witch it has ever been my misfortune to come into contact with!' he incised. 'This was never just about saving your half-sister's marriage! You always had this hidden agenda in which I paid for the sins you believe your other Italian lover committed!'

'No!' she cried. 'I'm *not* that petty! Elise's problems are serious enough without you adding such a crazy accusation into the mix! And anyway,' she said stiffly, 'you are nothing like Alonso. In fact I couldn't compare the two of you in any way if I tried!'

'In bed, perhaps?' he grimly suggested. 'Did you close your eyes and imagine it was him you were driving out of his head with your thrust-and-grind gyrations and those exquisite little muscle contractions?'

'No!' she said hotly. 'How dare you? That is such a rotten thing to say!'

'Then who did teach you to make love like that?' He took a step towards her. 'How many men, *amore,* does it take to produce such a well-practised sensualist?'

Blushing hotly, she cried, 'I'm not listening to this—'

She turned towards the door that led through to the rest of the house. The way he moved so fast to slam a hand against the door to keep it shut had her shivering out a shocked gasp.

'Answer the question.' He loomed over her.

Rachel folded her arms. 'You so love to throw your weight around, don't you?'

'Just answer.'

Anger flicked her eyes up to meet his. 'Why don't you tell me first—how many women have slipped in and out of your bed to make you such a *fabulous* lover?' she hit back. 'What was that,' she mocked when he clenched his expression. 'Do you want to tell me it's none of my business?'

'I am thirty-three years old, you are twenty-three.'

'Meaning the ten year difference justifies the numbers you clearly don't want to give?'

His shoulders shifted. 'I do not break hearts.'

Rachel released a thick laugh. 'You wouldn't know if you broke hearts! Men like you don't go into sexual relationships with the care of tender hearts in mind, *Signor*. They go into them for the sex!'

'In your experience.'

She tried to push past him, but the muscles in his arm bunched to form an iron bar she could not pass. 'Yes,' she hissed out.

'Gained mostly from this Alonso guy who took only what he wanted from you and trampled on the rest?'

'Yes!' she said again. 'Happy now?' she demanded. 'Have you got the required information nicely fixed in your head? I've had *two* lovers. Both Italian. *Both* with their brains lodged in their pants!'

For some reason she hit out at him, though she didn't understand why she had. The feeble blow barely glanced off his rock-solid bicep. And she was beginning to tremble now and didn't like it—beginning to bubble and fizz with anger and resentment and the most horrible feeling of all—humiliation at the way Alonso had treated her!

So maybe Raffaelle was right: when she'd agreed to hit on him to save Elise's marriage some subconscious part of her had wanted to pay back Alonso.

'So I am playing the fall guy.'

He was reading her thoughts. She swallowed tensely.

He turned to push his shoulders and head back against the door. '*Dio*, I cannot believe I fell into this trap.'

Rachel struggled to believe that she had fallen into it all too. 'I vowed I would never go near another Italian.'

'*Grazie*,' he clipped. 'I wish you had kept to your vow.'

Rachel turned away and walked over to the Aga and put the kettle on to boil. Why she did it she hadn't a single clue because she knew she could not swallow even a sip of anything right now.

But at least the move put distance between them. Silence

hummed behind her while she removed her coat and laid it over the back of a kitchen chair. Outside a weak sun was trying its best to filter into the room through the window on to scrubbed pine surfaces that had been here for as long as she could remember, yet she still felt as if she were standing in an alien place.

'Where did you meet him?'

The brusque question startled her into glancing at him. 'Who—?' she bit out.

His shoulders almost filled the doorway, his dark head almost level with the top of the frame. His face was still angry, the clenched jawline, the flat mouth, the glinting hard eyes, yet its harsher beauty still riveted her to the spot and claimed her breath and sent the hot stings of attraction streaking through her veins.

'My heartbreaking rival,' he provided and moved at last, shifting away from the door to pull out a chair at the table and sit down.

'In Italy.' Rachel moved to the sink and began toying with the mugs left there to drain. 'I was working on a farm just outside Naples—w-work experience,' she explained. 'He lived there. We met. Within a week I was moving into his apartment...' Wildly besotted with him and madly in love. 'He told me he loved me and, like a fool, I believed him. When it came time for me to come back to England, he said thanks for the great time and that was it.' She picked out two mugs at random. 'Do you want tea or coffee?'

'Coffee—when was this?'

'Last summer.' Shifting back to the Aga, she put the mugs down and picked up the coffee jar, then suddenly put it down again.

It had been only last summer when Alonso had taught her a lesson about Italian men she'd vowed never to forget. Yet here she was, involved with another and threatening to make the same mistakes all over again.

'I need to—do a few things before I can leave here. Can you make your own coffee—?'

She had disappeared through a door before Raffaelle could say anything—running scared again, he recognised as he sat there listening to her footsteps running up a set of stairs.

Then, on an angry growl, he got up and went to stand by the window. One part of him was telling him to go after her and insist she finish telling him the whole miserable story about her Italian lover—her *other* Italian lover, he grimly amended. Another part of him was wondering why he was not just climbing into his car, which he could see standing outside on the cobbles, and driving away from this…fiasco before the whole thing leapt up again and bit him even harder!

Because it *had* bitten him already, a voice in his head told him. She could already be carrying his child.

'*Dio*,' he breathed. He could not remember another time in his life when he had been so thoroughly stung by a woman.

And he did not need all of this hassle. He had many much more important things he could be doing with his time than standing here wondering what she was doing upstairs where he could hear her moving about just above his head.

Leo Savakis was not really his problem—none of this was his damn problem—except for the as-yet-unconfirmed child. He did not need to hang around until they discovered the result of their mindless love-in. A telephone call in a month would make more sense than hanging around her like this.

Yet some deep inner core at work inside him was stopping him from getting the hell out of here.

Lust, he wanted to call it. A hot sexual attraction for a devious female with cute curly blonde hair and the heart-shaped face of an innocent but who made love like the most seasoned siren alive.

He had taught her how to be that person—that other Italian lover had tutored her on how to give the best of pleasures to a man, had then dumped her as if that was all she had been good for—a student of his sexual expertise and a boost for his ego.

And then there was that thing with *real* teeth which was biting at him. He was used to being desired for himself. He was used to being the favoured one women revolved around, waiting with bated breath to find out which one of them he would choose.

Arrogant thinking? Conceited of him to know that he only had to crook a finger to have them crawling with gratitude around his shoes?

Yes. He freely admitted it. His clenched chin went up.

With Rachel Carmichael he was learning very quickly what it felt like to come in as second best in the heart and mind of a woman.

He did not like it. It gnawed at his pride and his sexual ego. And if he needed to find an excuse for why he was still standing here instead of driving away, then there it was.

There was no way that he was going to accept second best to any other man. By the time this thing between them was over, his Italian rival was destined to be nothing but a vague shadow in her distant memory.

She'd gone quiet.

Raffaelle looked up at the ceiling. What was she doing up there—lying on her bed pining for the heartbreaker?

Rachel was sitting on her bed with her cellphone lying in her palm displaying a text message from Elise.

Thank you for doing this for me. I will love you always. Leo is over the moon about the baby. He's taking us to Florida on a long overdue holiday. I could not be happier. He sends you his congratulations! Tell R thanks for his understanding. Have a great time playing the rich man's future bride!

What a wonderful game, Rachel thought bitterly. What a great way to waste several weeks of her life.

If she still had a rich future husband to play the game with, that was. He could have come to his senses and made his escape while she was up here moping—driven away in a cloud of dust and offended pride!

Getting up, she walked over to the window that overlooked the courtyard. The silver Ferrari still sat there glinting in the shallow sunlight. Relief was the first emotion she experienced—for Elise's sake, not her own, she quickly told herself.

Then the bedroom door suddenly opened and she turned to see him standing there, filling the gap like he had filled the other door downstairs and her senses responded, reaching down like taunting fingers to touch all too excitable pleasure points and she knew she was relieved he was still here for no one else's sake but her own.

'*Ciao*,' he murmured huskily.

'*Ciao*,' she responded warily, searching his face for a sign that another battle was about to begin and feeling the taunting brush of those fingers again when she saw that anger had been replaced by lazy sensual warmth.

'Need any help?' he asked lightly.

'Doing what?' Rachel frowned.

'Packing.' Walking forward, his gaze flicked curiously around a room made up of countrified furniture complete with chintzy soft furnishings. 'I see no sign of it happening yet,' he observed. 'But then—' his eyes came back to hers '—maybe you have other ideas for how we can spend the rest of the afternoon—?'

It was like being tossed back into the pit of writhing snakes again.

Switch off the anger and let desire rush back in, she reasoned. 'I d-don't think—'

'Good idea—let's both not think.' He moved in closer. 'That

small flowery bed looks the perfect place to spend a few hours thinking of nothing at all but this…'

But this—but this… His arms came around her and his mouth took over hers. No one needed to think about doing this, although—

'Why?' she whispered. 'Y-you should…'

'Be turned off you because you keep showing me different faces?'

His fingertips combed through the curls on her head as if to remind her of one of those changes she had made once already today and—damn her, but Rachel felt herself almost purring into his touch like a cat stroked by its beloved master.

He saw it and, on a soft laugh, caught her full, softly rounded, inviting mouth. It was one of those bewitching, tasty, compulsive kisses that clung, tongue tip to tongue tip. She swayed closer and his hands caught her waist to feel the slender arching of her spine for a few seconds before he gently but firmly drew her back.

'You get to me, Rachel, you really get to me. Though God knows why you do, because I certainly don't.'

'Not your usual type?' She could not resist the dig because while he frowned at her she was tingling in places that should not do that—the nerve-endings along the length of her inner thighs and between her legs.

He shook his head. 'Not my usual anything,' he muttered. 'You answer back, you disrespect, you lie and you cheat without batting an eye.'

'I don't cheat—!' she protested.

'Then what do you call the woman I first met last night with the long straight hair and the couture dress?'

A cheat. He was right.

'Well, this is the real me,' she said as she took a step back from him. 'The one with curls and jeans and—if you give me the chance—the one constantly fighting with dirt beneath her chipped fingernails…' She looked down at her nails, frowning now because they looked so different from what she was used to seeing: clean, well manicured and—pink. 'I am not made to be a *femme fatale*, Raffaelle. I wasn't even that good at it last night, only you didn't notice it because you were seeing what you'd been conditioned to expect to see at a function like that.'

'You were damn good at what came afterwards,' he said brusquely. 'I'll take a rain-check on the *femme fatale* bit if I can have more of that.'

Her chin went up, blue eyes coolly challenging. 'And the cheating face I'm supposed to show to the real world? Does it pop on and off according to what you require from me?'

To her surprise he let loose one of those lazy sexy smiles that melted the hardness out of his face. 'I think I like the idea of that. I will keep the sensual curly-haired Circe all to myself while the rest of the world gets the *femme fatale*.'

'Complete with fake ring to go with the fake relationship.' Rachel heaved out a sigh. 'We shouldn't be doing this at all.'

'Too late for regrets, *cara*. We have been over this already. We are both into this up to our necks.'

'Not the sex part.'

'Yes, the sex part!' he contended. 'It is here. We have it. And since it is the area where you really do get to me, we keep it.'

'If I say no?'

His laugh was derisive. 'You would have to want to say no and you don't.' He lowered his head to toy with her lips again. Electrifying, seducing. 'Do you—?' he challenged her for an honest answer.

Since her lips were clinging and her hands had already found their way beneath his T-shirt to the satin tight warmth of his skin she could not very well give any other answer than a weak shake of her head.

'Then say it so I can hear it.'

'I want you,' she whispered, swaying closer to him again, wanting, *needing*, body contact.

His hands on her waist held her back. 'Say my name,' he insisted.

Say his name… Alonso was suddenly looming up between them again. She tugged in a tense breath.

'I did not think of any other man but you last night, Raffaelle.' She felt she owed it to him to tell him that.

His murmur of satisfaction brought his mouth back to hers again with a full-on hot, deep, sensual attack. At last he was letting her have what she craved the most—skin-to-skin contact with him. Her fingernails curled into satin-tight flesh, then followed the muscular line of his ribcage across his chest, then around to his back so she could punish him at the same time as she arched even closer.

He shuddered, deserting her mouth. 'You ruthless witch,' he muttered as he took a moment to grip the edge of his T-shirt and rake it right off. Hers followed suit before he would allow her any more of his mouth.

Like that they strained against each other, exploring with their hands, tongues and lips. He was perfect. No man should possess a body like his. Rachel tasted his skin, her hands moving possessively over his hair roughened contours while he stood there and let her enjoy him, encouraging her with kisses and slow strokes of his hands.

Neither of them noticed that they were still standing in front of the window. Rachel with her back to it, Raffaelle with the sheen of the sinking sun painting his skin rich gold with a hot coral glow. He buried his fingers in her hair and pulled her head back to receive the full onslaught of his kiss.

Lights flashed, explosions took place. In the dizzying urgency of two lovers who needed to move this thing on to its next passionate stage, they missed that those explosive flashes came from outside the window.

The camera-toting paparazzo, who'd picked up their trail where others hadn't, slunk off down the driveway back to his car parked in the lane. He was smiling, pleased with himself, while the two captured lovers continued what they were doing, Rachel reaching up her arms to wind them round Raffaelle's neck as he lifted her up so her legs could cling to his hips. The bed was two steps away and he toppled her on to it, then bent to rid of her tight-fitting jeans.

He stood back. 'Tell me what you want,' he demanded as he began to strip.

'You,' she whispered.

'And who am I?'

'Raffaelle,' she sighed out—then sighed again as the full burgeoning thrust of him was arrogantly displayed.

He made her repeat his name throughout the long hours that followed. By the time they drove away from her home the intimacy between them had evolved into something beyond sex.

They arrived back at his apartment mid-evening. Raffaelle cooked them a meal while Rachel unpacked her clothes, grimacing at the array of sleek designer hand-me-downs Elise was forever giving to her, which most women would kill to own, but which she had rarely ever had an occasion to wear. Now they took up all of her hanging space in Raffaelle's dressing room as if they reflected the person she was now.

But she wasn't, was she?

They ate in the living room, lounging on a rug with their backs resting against one of the sofas and the television switched on. Rachel ate while she tried to concentrate on what was happening on the TV screen when really she was already hyped up about what was to follow.

Crazy, she told herself. You know none of this is real. You must be mad to let him get to you this badly.

Then he reached out to pick up her wineglass from the low table in front of them and handed it to her and their eyes clashed. What was good or bad for her became lost in what happened next. He moved in to kiss her; she fell into the kiss. The glass went back to the table and they made love on the rug between bowls of half-eaten pasta with the television talking away to a lost audience. Afterwards he carried her, satiated and too weak to argue, to bed.

'The pots and things…' she mumbled sleepily.

'Shh,' he said. 'I will see to them,' and he left her there.

By the time Raffaelle came back into the bedroom she was asleep. When he slipped beneath the duvet he did not disturb her—he did not think he had the energy to cope with what was bound to ensue if he did.

He closed his eyes, wanting sleep to shut out the next few hours before he had to make any decisions about how they were going to tackle the rest of this. The great sex was one thing, but the realities of life still waited out there for him to deal with.

Lies built on more lies. Smothering the urge to sigh, he shifted his shoulders against the pillows. She moved beside him, turning in her sleep to curl in close to him, her soft breath warm on his neck and a cool hand settling lightly on his chest.

He looked down at it resting there, with its pale slender fingers and pearly-pink varnished nails, and his skin burned in response to what he knew it could make him feel.

Lies or not, she was in his blood now. A fantasy siren most men would kill to possess. He closed his eyes again and tried to hunt down that illusive thing called sleep. His last conscious thought was the grimly satisfying knowledge that she was almost worth the temporary loss of his freedom and the trail of subterfuge he was about to embark upon.

Unless Mother Nature decided to get in on the act.

He fell asleep on that thought.

The next day brought fresh problems to deal with. He had been drinking coffee in the kitchen and trying to put his head in order while Rachel still lay lost in sleep in his bed, when his housekeeper arrived and laid a tabloid down in front of him.

'I thought you might want to see this,' she murmured embarrassedly.

But one glance at the photograph was enough to send him into the bedroom. 'Rachel, wake up.'

He shook her gently, then watched as she did her trick of emerging from the duvet in that way which grabbed at his senses.

'We need to talk,' he said grimly, then dropped the paper on to her lap.

Silence hung for the next thirty seconds while he stood there waiting and she looked down at the newspaper. There was something disturbingly erotic about the way the photograph had caught them and he knew by the way she suddenly dropped her face into her hands that this was one intrusion too far.

A nerve at the corner of his hard mouth gave a twitch. 'I suppose that being caught on camera like this will kill the suspicions of any mocking doubters and prove that we are indeed what we appear to be. But from now on both of us must be aware of what we do and what we say even when we believe we have complete privacy.'

'Life in the fast lane,' she named it bitterly.

'*Si*,' he agreed. 'I am used to it—though not to the degree that I feel the need to hide behind closed curtains,' he put in cynically. 'I would have expected that, having a half-sister like Elise and an insight into your half-brother's way of earning his living, you would know all the pitfalls of life in the fast lane.'

At last Rachel lifted her head to look at him. 'Are you implying that I set this up too?' she demanded.

'No,' he denied. 'I am simply advising you to draw on your knowledge gained from both of your siblings and think carefully before you move or speak.'

'It sounded more like a command to me.'

'Call it what you want,' he said. 'But accept that you will not go out without someone with you,' he instructed. 'I will assign one of my own security people to escort you.'

It was only as he said it that Rachel realised she was stuck here in London, in his apartment with nothing to do. Elise was away. Even Mark was away. She didn't know anyone else in the city! While it was very obvious by the way he was dressed that he was not going to hang around here if at all possible and keep her company.

'So I'm to be a prisoner now as well as your...' She severed the rest but they both knew what she had been about to say.

'It cuts both ways, *cara*,' Raffaelle said unsympathetically. 'I had a life and relative freedom with which to live it until you threw yourself at me. Now I have you, a bed and no life to call my own.'

'At least you get to go to work.'

'It is what I do during the day.'

'Well, lucky you.' Rachel handed him back the newspaper, then she curled on her side and tugged the duvet up to her ears. 'I might as well stay right here then, since it's the only place I am useful.'

He laughed. 'Hold that delightful thought until I return.'

Then he was gone. The door closed. He strode down the hallway and out of the apartment, then into the lift. It took him down to the basement where Dino and his limo awaited him. The moment he settled in the rear seat and opened his laptop his business cellphone began ringing and real life settled in. As he concluded his fourth complicated call of the journey, Dino was pulling the car to a stop outside the Villani building. He climbed out and strode in through the doors into familiar surroundings where that other excitement which came a very close second to sex waited to take him over.

Then it came.

'Congratulations, Mr Villani!'

'Congratulations, sir!'

Congratulations resounded from every corner. The curious smiles that accompanied them were due almost entirely to the photograph printed in this morning's paper, he judged.

His smile was mocking but fixed. And even that was wearing thin by the time he hit the top floor of the building.

'Congratulations, Raffaelle,' his secretary greeted him and dumped a whole load of telephone message slips down on his desk.

'What are those?' he asked dubiously.

'Congratulations and invitations, of course.' She grinned. 'I would hazard a guess that these are only the beginning. It looks as if you and Miss Carmichael will be dining out every night for months!'

He gave her them back. 'You deal with them.'

'Me?'

'Filter out the rubbish and sort the rest into some kind of order,' he instructed. 'Then I will look at them.'

'But wouldn't it be more appropriate if Miss Carmichael did it?'

Recalling the woman he had just walked away from brought a gleam to his eyes. 'No. She has better things to do,' he murmured dryly.

Like playing his personal little sex nymph.

CHAPTER EIGHT

THE SEX NYMPH WAS UP, showered and dressed in jeans and a T-shirt by the time Raffaelle entered his office building to a barrage of congratulations.

The sex nymph could not be more prim and polite when his housekeeper introduced herself as Rosa, the chauffeur's wife; apparently both of them travelled everywhere that Raffaelle went.

And the sex nymph had no intention of being anywhere near the bedroom by the time he got back home again.

She had come up with a much more practical way to spend her time.

Over a light breakfast prepared by Rosa, Rachel planned her day with the concentration of a tourist determined to miss nothing out. Only her tour would not consist of historical sites in the city; she was going to trawl the restaurants and food wholesalers specialising in organic produce.

Her nice new security guard arrived conveniently as she was about to leave. His name was Tony and he had the use of a car, which meant far less footwork.

Still, by the time she had been delivered safely back to the apartment long hours later, she was almost dead on her feet.

Raffaelle was crossing the hall towards his study from the living room as she stepped in through the door. Pinstriped jacket gone, shirt sleeves rolled up, tie knot hanging low at his throat and glass slotted between his fingers, he looked deliciously like the successful man just in from work and ready to wind down from his busy day.

Rachel paused, completely held by his sexual pull.

He paused too and looked at her, silky curls ruffled, face still chilled by the cold breeze blowing outside, woollen coat unbuttoned to reveal a white T-shirt with a neckline that scooped low at the front. He took his time taking in every detail with the slow—slow thoroughness of a seasoned connoisseur of beautiful women.

Knowing that she lacked the connoisseur's high standards right now sent Rachel's chin shooting up, blue eyes challenging him to say something derogatory.

'Did you enjoy your day, *mi amore*?' was the sarcastic comment that fell from his lips.

Defences heightened, she reluctantly supposed she should explain where she'd been. 'I went…'

'I know where you have been,' he cut in. 'Tony works for me, not for you.'

'Then, yes—' they could both play with polite sarcasm, she decided '—I had a very enjoyable day, thank you. And you?'

'I had an…interesting day,' he replied, watching her every step as she made herself walk forward. 'I spent it giving polite replies to polite invitations for us to dine with polite people who cannot wait to get a better look at my future wife.'

Recalling the revealing photograph in this morning's paper sent a rush of heat into her cool cheeks.

'Of course you did the wise thing and politely declined those polite invitations?'

'No, I accepted—most of them.'

Rachel pulled to a standstill. 'I hope you're just teasing.'

He took a sip of his drink, every inch of him vibrating with a kind of sardonic challenge that gave her his answer before he shook his dark head.

'The show must go on.'

'But I don't want to meet your friends!' she protested.

'Scared they might see through us?'

'Yes!' she said. 'Can't we just want to—be alone together—as real engaged couples prefer to be?'

'You're mistaking a new betrothal with a new marriage,' he countered. 'Honeymooners want to—be alone together. Newly betrothed couples want to get out there and—show off.'

'But I don't want to show off!'

A satin black eyebrow arched in enquiry. 'You don't think I am good enough to show off?'

'Don't talk rubbish,' she snapped. What woman in her right mind would say he wasn't fit to show off? 'I just don't think *we* are fit to be seen as an intimate couple within a group of your friends!' Stuffing her hands into her coat pockets and hunching her shoulders in self-defence, she went on, 'I presumed we would do—safer things like go out to quiet restaurants or something.'

'A restaurant it is.' He smiled. 'Eight o'clock. We will be meeting my stepsister and several other close friends of mine.'

Rachel's stomach started rolling sickly. 'Tonight?' she squeezed out painfully.

'*Si,*' he confirmed.

'W-why couldn't you be friendless?' she tossed out helplessly.

He just grinned. 'I'm sorry to disappoint you, *cara,* but I am certainly not friendless.'

'But your stepsister of all people. She *knows* we are fakes!'

His mood changed in a flicker. 'Stop playing the scared innocent, Rachel, when we both know you are far from it,' he clipped out. 'This is what you signed up for to save your sister's marriage. And lovers who fall on one other as often as we do are certainly not faking it!'

She pushed her hands through her hair. 'You know what I meant.'

'And you know what I mean when I say—get your act together,' he instructed, 'because we are going out in public tonight and I want the besotted *lover* by my side, not the farmer with a chip on her shoulder a mile wide!'

Rachel stared at him. 'What's that supposed to imply?'

He threw out an impatient hand. 'You compare yourself badly to your more glamorous sister,' he provided. 'You compare me with your ex-lover and hate the fact that I am Italian like him.'

'I do not!' she denied.

'Was he good-looking?' he demanded.

'What has that got to do with anything?' Her eyes went wide in bewilderment.

'Was he—?' he persisted.

'Yes!'

'How old?'

'My age—'

'And what kind of car did he drive?'

She sucked in an angry breath. 'A red Ferrari,' she answered. 'But that wasn't—'

'Great,' he gritted. 'Mine is silver. Is that a bad mark against me or one against him for being too flashy?'

'You're crazy,' she breathed.

Maybe he was. At this precise moment Raffaelle did not know why he was so fired up about a man he probably would not give a second thought to in other circumstances.

'Just go and get ready.' He turned his back on her and strode into his study, wanting to toss his drink to the back of his angry throat but refusing to allow himself the gut soothing pleasure while she was standing there staring at him. 'And I *don't* like flashy, so don't come out dressed in red!' he could not stop himself from adding.

Then he shut the door—*slammed* the damn door!

Rachel shook all the way into the bedroom. She shook as she removed her coat and laid it aside. She had absolutely no idea what all of that had been about and she didn't think that she wanted to know.

Did he hate her—was that it? she immediately questioned. Did he resent her being here so badly that he needed to take chunks out of her to get his own back on her for putting him in this situation in the first place?

Was he locked in his silly study *praying* that she wasn't pregnant with his child?

And he did not want to see the farmer dressed in flashy red when she came out. Her lips gave a quiver. He preferred to see the sleek Elise look-alike because at least he could relate to her and *pretend* she was his type!

Rachel stripped off her clothes and walked into the bathroom, not sure if she wanted to throw things or cry her eyes out.

The tears almost won the moment she stepped beneath the shower spray and she would have let them if he had not chosen that moment to push open the bathroom door and stride fully naked into the shower.

'No, don't stiffen up,' he said as she did exactly that. 'I am here to make you feel better, not worse.'

He drew her back against him, angling both of them so the shower sprayed down her front, then dropped his lips to her ear. 'I came to apologise for being bad-tempered out there.'

'You mean it's just hit you that you have to trail me in front of your friends having ripped my head off,' Rachel said.

'I had a bad day.'

He was tasting her earlobe now. Rachel jerked it away.

'Accepting invitations you had no desire to accept.'

'While thinking of you and that bed I had walked away from.' He chased the earlobe again. 'So I was bad tempered all day and came home more than ready to find you waiting for me. But you were not here; you were out enjoying yourself.'

'Playing the farmer to my heart's content.'

'I like the farmer,' he murmured lustily. 'She is toned and sleek and very sexy. I am also jealous of the ex-lover...'

That shocking confession finally stopped her from trying to pull away from him.

'Impressed by that?' he mocked.

'Yes,' she answered honestly.

'I thought you might be.' His mouth bit gently into the sensitive crook between her shoulder and neck.

Rachel's breathing feathered and she closed her eyes, giving herself up to this when she knew that she shouldn't. Wanting him to want her for herself and not just because she was here for the taking.

He found the soap and used it to paint every inch of her he could reach. Soon she was lost in a scented steam-filled world that shut out everything else.

Afterwards she felt lazy and languid and much too aware of him as her irresistible lover as the two of them moved around between the bathroom, bedroom and dressing room, preparing to go out.

Which had been the object of the exercise in the shower, she reminded herself. Several times he stopped her passing him by just fusing his mouth to hers in a slow clinging kiss and the lazily hooded way in which he watched her shyly lower her eyes and move away quickly only heightened an intimacy that was threatening to take her over completely if she didn't watch out.

She was relieved when he finally left her alone so she could finish getting ready without having him around as such a breathtaking distraction. By the time she joined him in the living room Rachel truly believed she had managed to get herself together—until he looked up from the broadsheet newspaper he was reading while lounging on a sofa and the whole whirlwind of awareness whipped into action again.

She'd chosen to wear a sleek short V-neck dress in dramatic matt black. Elise had donated the dress, claiming that it did not suit her because she didn't have the curves to fill it out.

Well, Rachel had the curves and, the way that Raffaelle was looking at her, he had not missed a single one. Her hair was loose, its curls carefully ironed out so the style was smooth and sleek. As he rose to his feet her blue eyes followed him, defiant yet anxious—just in case she did not look as good as she hoped she did.

But the look reassured her as he came towards her wearing the kind of black lounge suit that yelled couture *homme*. When an Italian male dressed he never ever dressed badly, was Rachel's single dry-mouthed heart pummelling observation.

'Beautiful,' he murmured as he reached her, sending pleasurable shivers chasing up her spine as he bent to brush a caress on her cheek. 'But I prefer the curls.'

'Different woman,' she answered with a small shrug.

His eyes narrowed, all the sensuality hardened out of his mouth. He said nothing for several long seconds and Rachel knew she had just managed to remind him of the real reason why they were together.

Maybe that was a good thing, she decided, as he helped her into the little black satin evening jacket she had brought into the room with her, still without saying anything else. They left the apartment and travelled in the lift down to where Dino waited by the car with the rear passenger door open. She slid in. The door clicked shut. Raffaelle rounded the bonnet and slid in from the other side. His long body folded with crease-free elegance into the seat beside her.

Lean, sleek, supremely sophisticated, she recognised. Crossing one silk-covered knee over the other, she fixed her attention on the partition which separated them from Dino.

Tension fizzed in the silence. Rachel found herself clinging to her little black beaded purse. The car swished along London's busy streets, recently drenched by a heavy downpour of rain. Everything outside the car seemed to glitter and sparkle in the darkness, everything inside the car was shadowed and oddly flat.

Raffaelle wished he knew what he was feeling right now, but he didn't. It was crazy to have been so taken aback by her reminder of what this was all about when they'd done little else but argue about it since they'd first met.

But he had been taken aback by it, stunned by the gut-twisting reminder that none of this was real—that *she* wasn't real.

Not tonight anyway.

She was the sleek look-alike sister of Elise Castle-Savakis, pretending to be a version of Rachel Carmichael that just did not exist. Even the dress was Elise's, classy and stylish and very sexy on Rachel, but he would be prepared to bet it was not of her own taste or choice.

He preferred the other Rachel with the curls and the spark of defiance in her blue eyes.

'Having second thoughts about risking me in there amongst your friends?' she asked suddenly.

Raffaelle blinked, realising that they'd come to a stop outside the restaurant. By the atmosphere inside the car, they'd been here like this for several seconds.

The restaurant was one of the best Italian restaurants in London. It was a place where the rich set ate. It was his kind of place and his kind of life, but neither were hers.

He turned his head to look at her. Barely an hour ago, she had been coming all around him in a breathtaking pulse of intimacy that still circulated in his blood. He looked at her silk-straight hair and her beautiful pearly-white complexion, the heavily accentuated black-lashed blue eyes and the sexy pink-coated mouth.

He could taste them. He could feel those soft pink-coated lips warm against his own whether she was this Rachel or the other Rachel. And if he was sitting here like this, wanting to know where the two Rachels became one, then he'd found it in that mouth and what happened to her when he claimed it.

'I won't embarrass you, if that's what's worrying you,' she stated, fizzing inside with resentment at the analytical way he was looking her over as if he was actually having to give some deep thought to the sarcastic question she had tossed out.

'You sound very sure about that, little farmer girl,' he said huskily.

'Well, I'm not,' she admitted honestly. 'I suppose I should have said I will *try* not to embarrass you.'

Easing his wide shoulders into the corner of the seat, his eyes glittered over her tense face. 'Do you really believe I will care if you do decide to embarrass me?' he asked curiously.

Rachel offered a shrug. 'I don't know you well enough to judge.'

'No, you don't…'

She didn't like the way he had said that, or the way he was looking at her now. Her tension was zinging along just about every nerve ending she had in her body and she wished he would just—

'Are we going to go in there or not?' she flicked out.

'In a minute,' he said smoothly, 'This conversation is just getting interesting…'

'No, it isn't.'

'Because it has nothing to do with whether you are going to embarrass me,' he said ignoring her interruption. 'It is to do with you being scared that I might embarrass you.'

Rachel stared at him. 'Why should you want to do that?'

'My thought exactly,' he said softly. 'Yet you *are* scared that I am going to take you in there, then just leave you to sink or swim.'

Her pink upper lip gave a vulnerable quiver. 'I was thinking more along the lines of being served up along with the main course,' she confessed.

He laughed. It was bad of him. But it was a very low, sexily-amused laugh and Rachel laughed too—one of those tense little sounds that jump up unexpectedly from the throat.

The atmosphere changed in that single moment, spinning the tension into a fine thread that eddied across the gap between them then morphed into something else. He moved so fast that she didn't see him coming, and then it was too late when he had taken arrogant possession of her mouth.

'You've stolen all my lipstick,' she protested when the kiss came to an end.

'I know.' He sat back a little, watching her as she fumbled in her bag for a tissue and her lipstick case. 'Keep on reapplying it, *cara*,' he advised as she reapplied a coating of pink with a decidedly unsteady hand. 'Because I find I like doing it. In fact I do believe I am becoming addicted to the taste.'

She handed him the tissue. 'It looks better on me than it does on you.'

And he grinned, wiping pink from his lips while his eyes tangled with hers. It was no use pretending that they weren't doing something else here, because they were.

Then suddenly he was being serious. 'Listen to me,' he urged. 'I don't want you to be anyone but yourself tonight, okay? I don't care if you want to spend the evening going on about the pros of organic produce. I don't care if you decide to ruffle your hair into curls or you march off to the kitchens to tout the chef for his business—'

'I'm not quite that uncouth!' she cried.

'You are missing the point,' he chided. 'The point being that I don't give a damn if you are just yourself and act like yourself. The only thing I do care about is that you stick to the main story as to how we met and keep in mind that, when we leave here, we go home to my apartment together as a couple, then to bed and to—this.'

Another kiss was on its way to her. 'Don't you dare,' Rachel drew her head back.

But he did dare—quickly, briefly, not enough to steal her lipstick a second time but more than enough to distract her from what he was about to do next.

She felt her left hand being taken. By the time she had the sense to glance down, the fake sapphire ring had been removed and he was already replacing it with one that looked exactly the same.

'W-what have you done that for?' she demanded.

'The fake might have been a good fake, *cara*, but it did not stand a chance of fooling the experts we are about to meet.'

'It fooled you when you saw it.' She was staring at the exact copy now adorning her finger.

'I was too angry to notice it then.'

'It's so—gaudy.' She sighed, staring at the ring as it shimmered and sparkled much more than its predecessor.

'Not to your taste?'

'Not to anyone's taste,' she said ruefully. 'It was only meant to grab Leo's attention... How did you get hold of this one so quickly?'

'I am the kind of man who gets what he wants when he wants it,' he answered with careless conceit.

He went to put the fake ring into his pocket.

'No—' As quick as a flash Rachel plucked it from his hand and pushed it into her beaded purse. 'I'll wear the real one when we are out together, but only then,' she informed him stubbornly. 'Otherwise I'll wear the fake one.'

'If you're afraid of losing it, it is insured—'

But Rachel gave a shake of her head. This had nothing to do with losing the real ring, but more to do with the fear that if she didn't hang on to the fake she would lose touch with reality.

'I will only wear it when we are out,' she repeated.

'And in our bed?' he demanded shortly.

Rachel thought about that for a second or two. 'I won't wear either ring,' she decided.

'Meaning our sexual relationship has nothing to do with the rest of this?'

Unless he was able to fake what was happening there as well. Then she nodded, because the sex was the only truly honest part of this.

He said nothing but just sighed and went to open the car door—then suddenly changed his mind. He turned on her, caught her chin in his fingers, then dipped his head for a third, definite, lipstick-stealing, full-blooded, possessive lover's kiss.

'The sexual part of this relationship does not stay behind in the bedroom, Rachel,' he stated harshly. 'Remember that, while you fix your lipstick again…'

He climbed out of the car then, leaving her sitting there trembling and shaken by the anger which had erupted from him.

What was the matter with him? Why should he care which ring she wore, so long as she didn't make *him* look the cheap fake?

Her lips felt tender and bruised this time as she reapplied the lipstick. He'd walked around the car and was now standing with her door open, waiting for her to join him on the pavement.

It was chilly outside and her satin jacket had not been made to keep the cold out. She shivered. He stepped closer, fitting her beneath his shoulder and curling his hand into her waist.

Gosh, don't we look the picture of romance? she thought dryly as he walked her towards the restaurant.

'Smile,' he instructed as he pushed the door open.

Rachel looked up to find that he was looking down at her. One of those frozen in time moments suddenly grabbed them, locking them inside their own private space.

'Heavens, Raffaelle,' another voice intruded. 'You were out there so long we were about to lay bets as to whether or not you were going to just take her back home again.'

'As you see, Daniella,' he came back smoothly, 'Rachel's manners are so much better than mine…'

He held Rachel's eyes as he said it. He watched her cheeks warm to a blush when she realised what Daniella had meant. Then he took hold of her hand and lifted it to his lips. The engagement ring sparkled as he kissed it. Her soft pink pulsing mouth gave a telling little quiver that shot an injection of heat down to his groin.

Someone else spoke—he did not know who. When he turned, he could barely make sense of the blur of faces all smiling at them.

What the hell was the matter with him? Was he sickening for something to have double-vision like this? It would be the first germ to catch him out since his childhood, he mused grimly, frowning as he looked back at Rachel.

Her face was in perfect focus. He did not like what that discovery was trying to say to him. With a taut shift of his shoulders, he pulled himself together and turned to face his dinner guests again, then switched on his lazy smile.

'*Buona sera*,' he greeted. 'My apologies for keeping you waiting when I know you are dying to meet my beautiful Rachel…'

CHAPTER NINE

MY BEAUTIFUL Rachel...

And so began the worst evening of his beautiful Rachel's life.

Raffaelle's stepsister did not believe a single word that either of them said to her. The others were more than happy to welcome her into their set, but they too were surprised and curious about this complete stranger who had arrived out of nowhere into Raffaelle's life.

Rachel supposed she should be relieved that Daniella seemed to have kept her suspicions to herself—or maybe she was too scared of Raffaelle to actually say what she thought outright. But she quizzed Rachel mercilessly about Elise.

'How is she?'

'Wonderful, taking a holiday in Florida with her husband and son.'

'You two met through Elise?'

'No, we met at a dinner party given by friends of Leo and Elise.'

Daniella had eyes like bitter chocolate which constantly flicked from Rachel to Raffaelle. 'Both of you were very secretive about this romance.'

'Rachel liked it that way,' her stepbrother answered. '*We* liked it that way. Look at what happened the moment we were seen in public. It turned into a witch-hunt.'

'When a woman throws herself at you in front of a reporter, it tends to have that effect. So does standing naked in a bedroom window.'

Rachel flushed but Raffaelle remained completely unruffled. 'Behaving like a spoiled child who does not like to know she has been left out of a secret is very unappealing,' he responded lightly.

Reducing her to the level of a spoiled child may have silenced Daniella but it did not kill her suspicions about Rachel not being who she claimed she was—as she made very clear the moment she got Rachel alone in the ladies' room.

'I *know* he was seeing Elise Castle because it was me who told him she was married with a small son! So don't try to pull the wool over my eyes, Miss Carmichael. That ring is a fake, just as everything else about you is fake.'

Rachel looked down at the sparkling diamond and sapphire cluster adorning her finger and grimaced. 'I don't want to fight with you, Daniella—'

'Well, I want to fight with you,' Daniella said fiercely. 'I *saw* you throw yourself at Raffaelle the other night. I *saw* his rage. I think you and Elise are trying to blackmail him!'

Apart from the fact that she was so close to the truth it was scary, Rachel had to feel for Daniella if only because she looked and sounded so worried and protective of Raffaelle.

'And you aren't drinking alcohol!' Daniella said suddenly. 'Are you pregnant, is that it? Did you have a fling with him, as well as your sister, and now you're demanding marriage?'

Rachel stared at the other girl as if she had just grown two heads. Was she psychic or what? 'I don't drink.' She iced out the lie with as much calmness as she could. 'And repeat your accusations to Raffaelle, if you dare,' she challenged.

Then she turned and walked out of the ladies' room. Raffaelle took one look at her flushed angry face and stood up before she could sit down.

His arms came around her. 'Problems?' he asked.

Rachel shook her head, aware of the others listening. 'Just a—headache,' she offered as a very weak excuse.

'Then we will leave.'

It was not a suggestion and Rachel did not argue with him. As they made their farewells Daniella came back to the table. One slicing glance at her stepbrother and her chin shot up in defiance.

To make everything feel even worse, a camera flashed as Raffaelle was helping Rachel on with her jacket. He'd lowered his head to kiss the side of her neck in one of those loving displays he'd been putting on all evening.

'What was it with Daniella?' he demanded the moment they were back in the car.

'She knows,' she responded.

'She knows what?'

'Everything,' she answered heavily. 'She thinks I'm blackmailing you over your affair with Elise.'

'You were blackmailing me,' he pointed out dryly.

'She also accused me of being pregnant because I wasn't drinking tonight, and of having a fling with you at the same time you were with Elise.' She grimaced. 'Great reputation you have there, *Signor*, when even your own family can believe you are capable of swinging it with two women at the same time.'

'She's fishing for information, that's all,' he answered coolly. 'And she—cares about me.'

'Lucky you,' Rachel mumbled.

'Do you say that because your family shows so little concern for you?'

That hit her right below the belt. 'My family care,' she insisted.

'Your uncle, maybe,' Raffaelle conceded. 'But even he made the quick getaway once he believed he had established that I was not your heartbreaker from Naples. I could have been lying to him. He did not hang around long enough to put me to the test.'

'He's a busy man.' She shifted tensely on the seat next to him.

'Like your half-sister and -brother are so busy they have not had time to check if I have chopped you into little pieces and dumped you in the Thames?'

'Sh-shut up,' she breathed.

They finished the rest of the journey in silence. As they travelled up in the lift to Rafaelle's apartment, Rachel stared fixedly down at her feet and he—well, she didn't know what he was looking at but she had an itchy feeling it could be her.

Once inside the apartment she headed for one of the spare bedrooms because there was just no way she was going to sleep with him tonight.

He didn't try to stop her, which only stressed her out more. She slept restlessly beneath a navy-blue duvet wearing only her bra and panties, woke up early the next morning and remade the bed, then crept back into the other bedroom to get some fresh clothes before Rosa arrived.

The plum-covered bed was empty and, by the look of it, Raffaelle had enjoyed a restless night too. She glanced at the closed bathroom door to listen if the shower was running, hoping to goodness that he'd already got up and dressed and taken himself off to work and out of the firing line.

'Discovered your sense of fair play, *amore*?' a smooth voice murmured.

She spun around to find him standing in the dressing room doorway wearing only a towel slung low around his hips. It was like being hit by that high wattage charge again.

'I—thought you would have left by now,' she said without thinking.

He just smiled then began walking forward. Rachel started to back away.

'Slept well?' he asked her.

'Yes, thank you.'

'Need any help tying that robe?'

She glanced down, then released a gasp when she saw the robe she had pinched from the other bathroom was hanging open revealingly. It was too big, a man's full-length heavy towelling bathrobe that trailed the floor at her feet and engulfed her hands. She'd thought she'd tied the belt, but the stupid thing had slid undone.

'Go away,' she shook out, trying to fight with the sleeves so she could grab the two ends of the belt.

But Raffaelle Villani wasn't going anywhere. He just kept coming until he was standing right in front of her. Then, while she mumbled out a protest, he pushed her fingers away and calmly cinched the belt around her waist. His fingers brushed the skin of her stomach as he did it. She breathed in sharply. He ignored the revealing breath, finished his task, then calmly turned away, dropping the towel from around his hips, and strode like the arrogant man he was back into the dressing room and closed the door.

It was the same as a slap in the face. She refused to sleep with him and he was showing her that it made little difference to him.

Rachel ran into the bathroom and wished she was dead, because her body was such a quivering mass of frustration that if he'd stripped the robe from her and thrown her to the bed, she would not have stopped him.

Her day was long and she was tired by the time she trailed into the apartment again. Rosa had gone home hours ago. Raffaelle was still out, which allowed her some time for herself to take a long bath behind a firmly locked bathroom door in an effort to relax some of the tension grinding at her every nerve and muscle.

She stayed in the bath longer than she'd meant to. By the time she let herself back into the bedroom she could sense more than hear that Raffaelle was home, though he was not in the bedroom, thank goodness, which gave her a chance to pull her jeans back on and a fresh T-shirt before she heaved in a breath and went looking for him.

He was in the kitchen making himself a sandwich, the jacket to his suit gone, white shirt-sleeves rolled up. He turned at the sound of her step. Her stomach dipped. She found herself running self conscious fingers through her curls.

'*Ciao*,' he said lightly. 'You look—pink.'

'I stayed in the bath too long,' she explained as naturally as she could.

He turned back to what he was doing. 'Want a sandwich?'

Her stomach gave a hungry growl. 'What's in it?'

'Take your pick,' he invited, pointing to the variety of salad things he had already sliced up. 'There's cheese in the fridge, some chicken and ham.'

Choosing the ham because she saw it first, she took over and handed it to him. Then surprised herself by staying there watching as he layered fresh bread with salad stuff.

'Not going to offer to do it for me?' He arched a look at her.

'Not me,' she said. 'I might grow the produce but I can't cook it,' she confessed. 'Ask me to make a sandwich like that and it will fall apart the moment you pick it up.'

'No culinary skills at all, then.'

'Not a single one.'

'Any good with a coffee machine?'

'Hit and miss.' She grimaced. 'I'm an instant coffee girl.'

'Tragic,' he murmured. 'Give it a try anyway.' He nodded to where the coffee machine stood. 'It's loaded and ready to hit the cup like the instant stuff does, only it tastes better.'

'That's an Italian opinion.' She moved across to the machine and fed it a cup as she'd done two days before.

Two days, she then thought suddenly—they felt like years. How had that happened?

'Tony tells me you have been treading the miles again,' he murmured.

She turned to look at him curiously. 'How often does he report in to you?'

The wide shoulders gave a shrug inside expensive white shirting that didn't quite stop the gold of his skin from showing through. 'Each time you stop somewhere.'

'Do you think it's necessary? I mean, I haven't seen a glimpse of a reporter in the two days I've been out and about.'

'Then you would make a lousy detective.' Turning he pointed to the newspaper lying on the table.

Going over to it, Rachel saw a photo of herself sitting at a table in a top Knightsbridge restaurant drinking morning coffee with its famous chef owner. A flush arrived on her cheeks because, not only was she aware that she had not seen the lurking reporter but she'd now realised that the only reason why she had been sitting there at all was because the chef had recognised her and his curiosity had been piqued.

'Where was Tony when this was taken?' she demanded. It was his job after all to stop this from happening.

'He did clear the reporter off, but not before he had managed to take this one photograph. Then the guy waited until you had left the restaurant and went back to quiz the chef.'

The chef had given an interview, getting a plug for his restaurant by happily telling the reporter what Rachel Carmichael did for a living. There was another photograph in a different paper showing Raffaelle kissing her cheek as he helped her on with her jacket.

'What it is to be famous,' she murmured cynically.

'Well, your secret other life is now out,' Raffaelle declared. 'Which means you can stop hiding behind the mask of Elise when we go out.'

'Daniella is going to love it.'

He turned with two loaded plates in his hands. 'I've spoken to Daniella.'

Rachel froze as he put the plates down on the table.

'She sends you her apologies and promises to behave the next time that you meet.'

'She had nothing to apologise to me for,' Rachel said flatly. 'Actually, I could like her despite…'

'Daniella not liking you?'

'Yes,' she said huskily.

He pulled out a chair and sat down on it. 'You can tell her you like her later when we meet up at the theatre—'

'*Theatre*—?' Rachel stared at him. 'I don't want to go to the theatre!'

'Sit down and eat,' he instructed. 'If you are eating for two you must have a good balanced diet.'

Rachel stared slack-jawed at him.

Steady-eyed, Raffaelle just shrugged. 'I'm the fatalist, remember? I work through problems sometimes before they are problems. It is what helps to keep me at the top.'

'You're not short on insufferable arrogance either. You and Daniella should share the same blood.'

He just grinned over the top of his sandwich. 'Tell me why you don't want to go to the theatre,' he instructed.

She pulled out a chair and sat down on it. 'I don't get the opportunity to go often enough to get to like it.'

'Well, that's about to change.'

'What kind of theatre?' she asked dubiously.

'Opera,' he provided. As her jaw dropped again, he said, 'Get used to it because it is the love of my life. Eat.'

Rachel picked up her sandwich. It arrived by instinct at her mouth because her eyes certainly didn't guide it there—they were still looking at him in horrified disbelief.

'I can't believe you want to put me through an *opera*,' she protested.

'We either go to the opera or we stay in and make love…'

And, just like that, their few minutes of near normality disappeared without a trace.

Rachel put down the sandwich. He chewed on his, his eyes gleaming with challenge.

'I'm will *not* be blackmailed into your bed—!' She flew to her feet.

'Then prepare for an evening of Tosca,' he countered coolly. 'Wear something long and—sexy. Oh, and take your sandwich with you, *mi amore*,' he drawled as she went to flounce out of the room. 'The opera starts early and supper will be late.'

She wore a long slender blue gown that faithfully followed her every curve. Raffaelle took one look at her and staked possessive claim with a hand to the indentation of her waist.

'*Mine*,' he declared huskily. 'Make sure you remember it while we are out.'

Sitting for hours beside a man who seemed to take pleasure in playing the deeply besotted lover throughout the interminable though admittedly moving music heightened her senses to such a degree that she had never felt more relieved to walk out into the ice-cold evening air so she could breathe.

They ate supper with a crowd of people including Daniella, who was quieter than the night before and was almost pleasant to Rachel, though Rachel could tell by the glint in the other woman's brown eyes that the pleasantness ran only skin-deep. Daniella was still suspicious and hostile and hungered for the real truth as to what was going on.

Rachel gave Daniella no chance of getting her on her own that evening, staying put in her seat and keeping her attention fixed on everyone else. At least they seemed to accept her at face value—it was difficult not to when the man sitting beside her rarely took his eyes from her face. Tension zinged between them like static. Rachel refused to so much as glance at him, smiling where she thought she should do and trying to ignore the ever increasing pulse of awareness he was making her suffer. She was quizzed about her occupation and it seemed a good time to launch into the benefits of organic farming with an enthusiastic vigour that set such an animated debate going she almost managed to forget Raffaelle was sitting there.

Then he reached out to gently take hold of her chin and turned it so she had no choice but to look at him. His expression was difficult to read, kind of mocking yet deadly serious at the same time.

'You are here with me,' he said huskily.

'I know who I'm with.' She frowned at him.

'Then don't ignore me.'

'I wasn't ignoring you. I was—'

'Smiling at every other man at this table but me.'

The idea that he might be feeling left out and jealous sent a different kind of sting singing through her blood. Her eyes must have showed it because his thumb arrived to rub across her lower lip in an intimate, very sexual proclamation that brought a telling flush to her cheeks.

But she could not pull back or break eye contact. It was too much like being plugged into an electric current again—lit up from the inside and sensually enlivened. He knew it, he built it until her breathing quickened and her eyes darkened. She could feel Daniella watching them. She heard someone else murmur dryly, 'Time to break up the party, I think.'

'Good idea,' he murmured and leant forward to replace the thumb with his mouth in a brief promise of a kiss that brought him smoothly to his feet.

They travelled back to his apartment in absolute silence. They rode the lift in exactly the same way. Rachel kept her eyes fixed on her feet again but refusing to look at him did not ease the sexual pull taking place. They walked along the hallway towards the bedrooms still accompanied by that highly strung clamour of perfect silence.

When they reached the door to his bedroom they paused. Still he said nothing and still she was fighting it until—

'Well—?' he asked softly.

Rachel drew in a tense, sizzling, battling breath, tried to let it out again but found that she couldn't. Her senses were singing out a chant of surrender and in the end she gave in to it, turning to reach for the door handle to his bedroom.

Without saying a single word he followed her inside and closed the door. Now she'd made the decision to come in here she did not go for modesty but just turned to face him and, with the light of a looming sexual battle lighting her blue eyes, she began to undress right there in front of him. His face was deadly serious as he watched her for a few seconds before he began to undress too.

Clothes landed on the floor all around them. Her dress pooled in a slither of blue silk at her feet. It was all part of the battle that they did not break eye contact.

Rachel walked towards the bed on legs that no longer wished to support her. Indeed they preferred to tingle and sting like the rest of her body, making sure they did not give her a moment to change her mind about this.

No chance—no *hope* of a last-minute reprieve. She wanted him so badly she couldn't think beyond the need.

He took up a position on the other side of the bed and the tip of her tongue crept out to curl across her upper lip as she let her eyes glide over him. Big, lean, hard and aroused. Her breasts grew heavy and her nipples peaked, the wall of muscle around her lower stomach contracting as she tried to contain the ache.

She lifted the duvet. He did the same. They slid into the bed together and arrived in the middle of the mattress in a limb-tangling clasp of body contact.

Then he kissed her. No, he punished her for putting them through twenty-four hours of denial.

That night Rachel learned what it was like to be totally taken over, excruciatingly sapped of her will by a man with a magician's touch. He wove sensual spells around every pleasure point. He drove her wild until she cried out. Then he possessed her, deep, tough and ruthlessly, staking claim in this final act of ownership that had her clinging and trembling and sobbing out his name as she tumbled into release.

And so began four hellish weeks trapped inside heaven.

When Raffaelle had said they were to be as if they were glued together, he'd meant it. Wherever his business took him, Rachel went with him, hopping from London to Milan, Paris, Monaco then back to London then Milan again. In one short month she learned what it was like to become a fully paid-up member of the jet set and how it felt to be recognised as the woman who'd managed to pin the very eligible Raffaelle Villani down.

Everywhere they went he took her out into public places—more restaurants, more theatres, nightclubs and private parties—all very select venues where they could be displayed as a couple.

It was almost all glitz and glamour. There were those in his close circle of friends who were the kind of people she could relate to mainly because they were easy to like. Then there were the other kind who hovered on the fringes of it all who would have sold their grandmothers to be included as a member of his inner set.

Then there was the seemingly endless stream of his ex-lovers from all over the world who had no problem with telling her what they used to be to him and thought it fine to discuss the ins and outs of having a lover like him.

'Have they never heard of the word discretion?' she tossed at him after one particularly vocal beauty had seen nothing wrong in singing his sexual praises to Rachel—in front of Raffaelle. 'Or does it stroke your ego to hear someone talk about you as if you were a stallion put out to stud and therefore free to be debated for your sexual prowess?'

'I don't like it,' he denied.

'Then don't smile that smug smile while they list your assets.'

'It is not a smug smile, it is a forbearing one. And you sound like a jealously disapproving wife.'

'No, just a lover who does not think you are so great in bed that you deserve so much attention,' she denounced.

'No—?'

She should have read the intimation in that *no* but she missed it.

'No,' she repeated.

'Maybe you found the Italian heartbreaker and sex tutor of innocents a better lover?'

She turned icy eyes on him. 'If you're fishing for information, then forget it. Unlike your ex-lovers, this one does not kiss and tell.'

He had been fishing for information, Raffaelle acknowledged. She might be the best lover he'd ever enjoyed but he had no clue as to where she placed him on her admittedly short list.

And he'd accused her of being jealous when he knew that was his issue. Jealous, curious, wary of the way she sometimes looked at him as if he was a being from outer space. Their age difference bothered him. Her youth and her beauty and that softer side she had to her that made some of his previous women appear sex-hardened and clinical. Did she see *him* like that: sex-hardened and clinical?

His male friends were drawn to her. He did not like to see

it because he knew exactly what it was about her that drew them. They wanted to experience what he was experiencing. They wanted to know what it felt like to simply touch a woman like Rachel and have her melt softly for them.

And she did melt. It was his only source of male satisfaction. In company, out of company, he touched her and she melted. He *looked* at her and she melted.

'Well, remember that I am the lover who takes you to heaven each night,' he said.

And, like Alonso, Rachel knew that he would break her heart one day.

He obsessed her mind and her body. She hated him sometimes, but her desire for him was stronger than hate. He knew it too and the inner battles she fought with herself turned him on. She watched it happen, watched right up until the moment they reached the lift which would take them into privacy and saw the social face he wore fall away to reveal the hard, dark, sexually intense man.

The lift became her torture chamber. The stinging strikes of his sexual promise flayed her skin. By the time they stepped through his front door she was a minefield of electric impulses, hardly breathing, hyped up and charged beyond anything sane.

Sometimes he would crash into that minefield right there in the hallway. Sometimes he would draw out the agony by making her wait before he unleashed the sensual storm. She learned to live on a high wire of expectation that allowed no respite and little sleep, with him even invading her dreams.

He knew every single sensitive inch of her. Sometimes he would coax her to stretch out on the bed with her arms raised above her and her legs pressed together, then he'd begin a long slow torture that she loved yet hated with equal passion because he would make her come—eventually—with only the lightest stroke of a finger or the gentlest flicker of his tongue.

It was an unashamed act of male domination which left her aching because he never gave in to his own need on these occasions or finished such torments off with an intimate, deep physical joining.

Why did he do that? Even after four weeks with him she still did not have an answer to that question.

And then there were those other times. The times when he allowed her to perform the same slow torment on him. He would lie there with his eyes closed and his long body taut with sexual tension while she indulged her every whim.

Being equals, he called it. She called it dangerous, because it had reached a stage where she could not look at him without seeing him lost in the throes of what he was feeling on those occasions. A big golden man, trembling and vulnerable, a slave to what she could make him feel.

The elixir which kept her rooted in their relationship, wanting—needing more.

And other things began to torment her which were far more disturbing than the constant overwhelming heat of desire. She knew she had fallen in love with him. She could feel it tugging constantly at the vulnerable muscles around her heart. If he touched her those muscles squeezed and quivered. If she let her eyes rest on him, those same muscles dipped into a sinking tingling dive.

But Raffaelle was not in this for love. He wanted her, yes. He still desired her so fiercely that she would have to be a complete idiot not to know that he was content to keep things the way they were right now.

If she had any sense she would be walking away from it. Elise and Leo were back in Chicago. Elise was happy, Leo was happy and keeping his pregnant wife and his son close to him; the crisis in their marriage was over.

All of this should be over now. And, if it wasn't for the

worrying prospect that her period was overdue, she would have no excuse left to call upon which could allow her to stay.

Then it all went so spectacularly pear-shaped that it threw everything they had together into a reeling spin.

They were in Milan when it happened. Raffaelle was tense, distant, preoccupied—busy with an important deal, he said. But Rachel wondered if the stress of waiting to discover if she was pregnant was getting to him too.

He didn't say so—never mentioned it at all and neither did she.

She knew that she needed to buy a pregnancy test. Putting it off any longer was silly when she was almost a whole week late. She was supposed to be going shopping with one of Raffaelle's many cousins but Carlotta had rung up to say she couldn't make it.

On impulse she snatched up her purse and headed out of the apartment. She should have called Tony to get him to drive her, but she didn't want anyone with her to witness what she was going to do.

She caught a cab into the city, then headed for a row of shops that included a pharmacy. Anxiety kept her locked inside her own thoughts as she walked, but the last thing she expected to happen was to be woken from them by a loud screech of brakes as a glossy red open top Ferrari swished to a sudden stop at her side.

The man driving that car did not bother to open the door to climb out but leapt with lithe limbed grace over the door. 'Rachel—*amore*!' he called out.

Shock held her completely frozen, her blue gaze fixed on his familiar handsome face.

'Alonso—?' she gasped in surprise.

'*Si*—!' He laughed, all flashing white teeth, black silk hair and honey-gold beauty. 'Is this not the greatest surprise of your life?'

CHAPTER TEN

HE BEGAN closing the gap between them, a lean muscled six-foot-two inch-Italian encased in the finest silver-grey suit. A man with so much natural charisma and self-belief that it just would not occur to him that he was anything but a welcome sight to her.

So Rachel found herself engulfed by the pair of arms he folded around her, then found herself being kissed on her cheeks and the tip of her nose, then her surprised, still parted mouth.

She tried to pull back but he was not letting her. 'I saw you get out of a cab and I could not believe my eyes!' he exclaimed. 'And look at you,' he murmured, running a teasing set of fingers through the bouncy curls on her head. 'Still my beautiful Rachel.' He kissed her mouth again. 'This has to be the best moment of my day!'

Well, not mine, thought Rachel, still rolling on the shock of seeing him. 'What are you doing here in Milan?'

'I could ask the same thing of you.' He grinned down at her. 'Though I would have to be blind not to know by now that you have captured the heart of Raffaelle Villani, eh? May good fortune always smile upon the bewitching,' he proposed expansively. 'He is totally besotted with you, as I was, of course…'

Across the street, on the shady side, sitting languidly at a lunch table with five business associates, Raffaelle happened to glance outside in time to see Rachel walking by on the sunny side of the street.

A smile warmed him from the inside. She looked beautiful in her simple white top and her short blue skirt which left a pleasurable amount of her long legs bare. And her silky blonde hair was shining in the sunlight, recently cut by an expert so the curls tumbled around her neck and her face like sensual kisses.

It was no wonder other men stopped to admire her as she walked past them, he observed, a smile catching the corners of his mouth as he saw one guy in particular actually spin around to take a second look.

Sorry, but she belongs exclusively to me, he heard himself stake the silent claim. Then he started to frown when another thought hit him. Where was Tony? Where was his cousin Carlotta? Why was Rachel out shopping alone when she knew the rules about going out without protection from the ever-watchful press?

The sound of screeching car brakes diverted his attention. A glossy red Ferrari with its top down had pulled to a sudden stop in the street. Its handsome young owner leapt out with lean grace and approached Rachel with his arms thrown open.

She had stopped to stare at him. What took place next lost Raffaelle the power to maintain a grip on his surroundings. The quiet hum of conversation taking place around the lunch table disappeared from his consciousness as he saw her soft pink mouth frame a name.

The man spoke, his gestures expressive, like the rakish smile he delivered as he gathered her into his arms, then kissed her cheeks, her nose and finally, lingeringly, her parted pink mouth.

A mouth that belonged to *him*. A mouth that did not attempt to draw back from the kiss.

So cold he felt frozen now, Raffaelle watched this other man run his fingers through her curls as he talked.

Small, familiar, intimate gestures. Soft parted pink lips that quivered when she spoke back to him.

They knew each other.

His heart hit his gut because it did not take much intelligence to follow the body language and know without a single hint of doubt who the man had to be.

Alonso. The heartbreaker. He was so sure of it he did not even think to question his certainty.

Had they arranged to meet—right here in broad daylight without a care as to who might see them like this?

How long had they been in touch with each other? Each time he had brought her with him here to Milan?

Was she still in love with him?

Dio. While she stood there in his arms, looking up at him like that, was her heart beating too fast and her throat drying up and her blue eyes helplessly drinking him in?

'Raffaelle…'

The sound of his name being spoken finally sank into his consciousness. Turning his head, he received the impression that it was not the first time one of his lunch companions had said his name.

'My apologies,' he said, managing to add a small grimace. 'My attention strayed for a few moments.'

'And why not, when the woman is as beautiful as the one seated in the window?' one of them said smiling.

Seated? Raffaelle turned again to focus on a table by the restaurant's window where indeed a very beautiful woman sat smiling ruefully back at him.

He had not noticed her before this moment.

He had not noticed any other women for a long time—not since Rachel came into his life.

His gaze flicked away from the smiling woman and across the street again.

He was in shock. He knew that. He knew that several important things were happening inside him even as he watched Rachel's other Italian lover fold an arm across her shoulders and guide her towards his car.

Car horns were blaring. The street was alive with impatient car drivers trapped behind Alonso's car.

'One quick coffee, then,' Rachel agreed as he swung open the door and helped her inside.

She should not be doing this. But they were drawing too much attention and getting into Alonso's car seemed the better of two evils if coffee somewhere was the only way she was going to get rid of him.

Alonso joined her in seconds, sliding into the seat beside her and sending her one of his reckless grins as he slipped the car into gear. He drove them away with a panache that completely disregarded the minor chaos he had been causing in the street.

'Like old times, eh?' he laughed at her.

And it was, just like old times, when he had used to sweep up in one fast car or another without a care while he waited for her to scramble in next to him. His handsome carelessness used to excite her then. Now it just scared her witless as she glanced quickly around them as they drove off, hoping she did not see a face she recognised in the street—or worse, a camera flashing.

'Somewhere quiet, Alonso,' she told him quickly. 'I can't afford to be seen with you.'

'Scared of what your rich new fiancé will say?'

You bet I am, Rachel thought. 'I call it respect for his feelings.'

'And a healthy respect for his bank balance too.'

Before she could challenge that last cynical remark, Alonso pulled into one of the less fashionable squares off the main street. Two minutes later they were sitting opposite each other at one of the pavement cafés that lined the square.

Rachel looked at Alonso and saw a man who worked very hard to look, dress, behave like the man he wished he could be but never would be.

And how did she know that? Because she had spent the last month with the genuine article, a man who didn't need to work hard at being exclusive and special, he just simply was. It was she who, like Alonso, had to work hard at playing the part of someone she was not.

The comparison hit her low in her stomach.

As if he could tell what she was thinking, 'You have done very well for yourself,' Alonso said.

Rachel didn't answer, giving her attention to the waiter who had come to their table. 'Espresso,' she told him. 'N-no, I don't want anything else.'

Alonso ordered the same, then casually dismissed the waiter with a flick of a hand. Had he always behaved with this much casual arrogance and she had been too besotted with him to notice?

'What *are* you doing here in Milan?' She repeated her question from earlier.

Sitting back in his seat and crossing a knee over the other, he said, 'I moved here six months ago—to a better position, of course.'

Of course, Rachel acknowledged. Alonso had always been ambitiously upwardly mobile. 'Still selling cars?'

'Super-cars, *cara*,' he corrected dryly. 'They are not merely cars but engineering works of art. But let us talk about you,' he said turning the subject. 'You must be happy with your new lover. What woman would not be?' His mouth turned cynical as his eyes drifted over her. 'No longer the rosy-cheeked innocent up from the country, eh?'

Recalling that innocent young girl Alsono had known last year, with—if not quite straw in her hair as Raffaelle described her—then pretty close to it, made her smile.

'No,' she agreed.

Their coffees arrived then, putting a halt on the conversation while the waiter did his thing. Eventually, Alonso sat forward to catch the hand she'd used to reach for her cup.

'We had a good time, didn't we?' he said softly. 'I missed you when you left me to go home.'

'Did you?' Not so Rachel had noticed.

'Ah, *si*,' he sighed. 'I almost came after you but—life, you know, got in my way…'

Another new conquest had got in his way, he meant.

'And maybe I did you a very great favour,' he added. 'For look where you are today—betrothed to man with more connections in this city than any other that I know of. A man in possession of his own bank! I salute you, *cara*.'

Leaning towards him, Rachel let him lift her fingers to his lips. She let him try to seduce her with the rueful tease glinting in his sensual dark eyes. She even added a smile.

'You know what, Alonso,' she then said softly. 'You were a beautiful charmer last year when I met you, and you are still a beautiful charmer now.' He smiled and kissed her fingertips. 'But why don't you just tell me what it is that you want from me, because I am going to get up and leave here any minute…'

There was a moment of sharpened stillness, then he sat back in his seat and laughed. 'How did you guess?'

Living the part of a rich man's woman had taught her how useful other people believed she could be to them. 'Raffaelle does not need another new car,' she told him. 'He has too many of them already.'

'An introduction to him and his friends could bode well for me in the future, though.'

'Or ruin your career,' Rachel pointed out. 'Raffaelle knows about you and me, *caro*.'

He caught on, which Rachel had known he would do. The smile died from his features, taking with it all the charm and leaving behind only a rueful kind of petulance.

Then it changed. A sudden well-remembered gleam hit his eyes. 'I don't suppose you would enjoy a little light diversion this afternoon with your old lover—for old time's sake before we part again?'

The business side done with, he was back to playing the sexy charmer. Rachel couldn't help it, she laughed. 'No, I would not!' she refused, still bubbling with amusement at his downright audacity.

His lazy smile reappeared and he reached across the table to gently brush her smiling mouth with his thumb. 'Shame,' he murmured. 'We were so good together once, hmm, *carisima…*'

Across the square on the shady side, a camera caught them for posterity as Rachel reached up to close her hand around his so that she could remove his touch from her mouth.

'One day,' she warned him seriously, 'some beautiful creature is going to come into your life and knock down your outrageous conceit.'

'But she will not be you?'

'No.' She'd tried to do that once and had failed, had survived the experience and had now moved on—though to what, she was not certain about.

Still, it was a good feeling to realise that she was completely free of Alonso. So maybe meeting up with him had not been a bad thing to happen in her life right now.

Getting to her feet, '*Ciao*, Alonso,' she murmured softly, then simply turned and walked away from him.

He did not try to stop her. Maybe he'd read the look in her eyes and knew he had lost the power to make her feel anything for him.

Or, more likely, he simply did not care enough to want to stop her. Who knew? It was just a good feeling to know that she no longer cared.

The camera toting paparazzo had already gone, missing the moment that she'd walked away from her old love with no regrets. And, by the time she reached the main street again, Alonso had been pushed right out of her thoughts by more important things.

Buying a pregnancy testing kit took courage, she discovered. She was constantly glancing around her to check if anyone was watching her and she found herself wandering aimlessly around the shops, putting off the evil moment for as long as she could.

Which in the end turned out to be a foolish exercise because, having found the courage to buy the darn thing, she had been back at the apartment for barely two minutes when Raffaelle arrived home unexpectedly, forcing her to shove her purchase into a bedside drawer.

He was in a strange mood, cold and distant and sarcastic as hell when she tried to speak to him. She needed to tell him about her meeting with Alonso, but he just cut her off with a curt, 'Later,' then locked himself away in his study and did not come out again until it was almost time for them to leave for the restaurant where they were meeting his friends for dinner that evening.

His mood had not improved by the time he'd taken a shower and changed his business suit for a more casual version made of fine charcoal-coloured linen. Her simple black halter dress drew no comment—but then why should it when he'd seen her wearing it several times before?

But she was hurt by the sudden loss of his usual attention. Confessions about surprise meetings with old lovers just did not suit the kind of mood he surrounded them with as they left.

He did not look at her. He did not touch her. When she dared to open her mouth and ask what was wrong with him, he ignored the question by turning to say something to Dino who was driving them tonight.

What with his bad mood, the stress of knowing that the pregnancy test was still burning a hole in the bedside drawer, plus the memory of her meeting with Alonso sitting heavy on her conscience, the last person she needed to see as they walked into the restaurant foyer was his stepsister Daniella, who was standing beside a tall, dark, handsome man. The elusive Gino Rossi, Rachel assumed, by the way Daniella was tucked so intimately into his side.

Raffaelle made the introductions with brusque, cool formality that made both her and Gino Rossi's responses wary and brief. After a moment Raffaelle then turned away and centred his attention on the rest of his friends, determined to get through this damn evening before he decided what he was going to do about what he had witnessed today.

In the inside pocket of his jacket, a photograph of Rachel with her lover being cosy across a café table was trying its best to burn a hole into his chest. The fact that she had been too engrossed to notice the paparazzo who took it only fed his simmering rage. It was perhaps fortunate for him that he was close friends with the newspaper owner to whom the freelance reporter had offered to sell the photograph.

He was now assured that the picture of his betrothed being intimate with another man would not appear in the tabloids, but at a cost to his dignity as well as his wallet, plus an invitation to this evening's dinner party, along with a promised exclusive interview about his wonderful life to date.

A life that included details about the lying, cheating, two-timing blonde wearing his ring right now.

He allowed himself a glance at her, standing there looking

paler than usual with an oddly fragile look to her slender stance. A frown cut a dark crease across his brow. Why fragile? Was her conscience pricking her? Did she possess one? Had she spent the afternoon comparing her old lover with her new lover?

Which of them had won the contest?

A curse rattled its way around his throat and he looked away again, wondering when the hell she had got to him so badly that he even considered that damn question?

Dio. Rachel was bad for him. She had been bad for him from the moment he'd set eyes on her. Her type, her *kind,* were poison to a guy like him and maybe it was time that he got himself the cure.

The owner of the newspaper arrived then, like the perfect answer to his thoughts. Tall, blonde, and beautiful, and dressed in rich, dark purple that moulded her long, slender curves, Francesca de Baggio was the kind of woman who answered most men's desires.

Raffaelle went to meet her. They embraced with murmured greetings to each other that showed the intimacy of lovers from eons ago. As his lips brushed her cheeks he smelled her sensuous perfume, felt the smoothness of her skin at her shoulders beneath his palms. As her red lips lingered at the corner of his mouth he waited for the expected tingle to light him up from the inside.

It did not happen.

'*Ciao, mi amore,*' she moved those red lips to whisper softly in his ear. 'The betrothed does not look happy. Have you beaten her soundly?'

Almond-shaped eyes that matched the colour of her dress gleamed up at him with a conspiratorial smile. Anger erupted inside him, fresh anger—*new* anger—leaping on a desire to jump to Rachel's defence.

'You know better than I do how a photograph can misrepresent the truth.'

The almond eyes widened and filled with amusement. How was it he had forgotten that Francesca was in the tabloid business because she loved the trouble it allowed her to cause?

'His name is Alonso Leopardi,' she informed him softly. 'He sells cars for a living and loves them as much as he loves women. He also rents an apartment above the café they were sitting at being so…cosy. Convenient, hmm?'

Raffaelle was hooked like a fish and he knew it. It was perhaps fortunate that Gino and Daniella came up to greet Francesca then, because it saved him from making a bloody fool of himself by letting Francesca see that she'd reeled him in.

Looking round for Rachel, he could see her nowhere. For a tight, thick, blood-curdling second he thought she must have walked out. For a blinding, sickening, sense-drowning moment he actually saw her in his head, making a run for it, grabbing a cab and heading for her heartbreaker in a white-faced urgent adrenalin rush of need.

A clammy sweat broke out all over him. He took a step away from the group of his friends now gathering around Francesca to welcome her into their fold.

Common sense was telling him not to be so stupid. Rachel would not just walk out on him—even if the way he had been behaving tonight was enough in itself to justify her walking out.

He saw her then, right over on the other side of the busy restaurant. She was just stepping into the ladies' room with her blonde head bowed slightly and a slender white hand pushed up against her mouth.

She'd looked pale all evening, he remembered. His mind flipped from hating her to worrying about her. How could he have forgotten the baby they could have made, which might be making its presence felt as she made a quick dash into the Ladies'?

Concern wanted to send his feet in her direction. Only common sense warned him not to make a scene here. Turning back to Francesca, he saw her watching him with an eyebrow arched curiously. Dragging on his social cloak, he forced himself to smile as he walked back to her.

Rachel was fighting the need to be sick in the toilet. The clammy sweat of nausea had flooded over her the moment she'd seen the way Raffaelle had walked into the arms of the beautiful blonde.

'Ex-lovers,' Daniella had whispered to her. 'Don't they look amazing together? He adored her once but she left him for her now ex-husband. We thought he would never get over it— maybe he didn't. He spent the afternoon with her,' she confided with relish. 'I know because Gino told me Raffaelle cancelled a meeting with him to go to her. Now she's here. An interesting development, don't you think?'

Was it? Rachel discovered that she no longer knew anything. Her head was thumping too thickly to think. A month—a month in which she had lived and slept with him, had trailed around Europe with him as his pretend future bride. But what did she really know about Raffaelle, other than he was a fantastic lover and was willing to go to any lengths to protect himself from getting a negative press?

By the time she felt able to rejoin the party, everyone was gathered around a long wooden table. Still fighting down nausea, Rachel found herself having to take the only seat left available between Daniella and another male friend of Raffaelle's, whose name she couldn't recall right now.

Raffaelle was sitting at the other end of the table. The beautiful Francesca was next to him. She had arrived here on her own and Rachel supposed that, given the odd number of men to women, the dinner placements had become muddled.

But it was the first time that Raffaelle was not occupying the seat beside her like a statement of possession.

Had he even noticed that she was not sitting on his other side?

Not that Rachel could tell. His attention was too firmly fixed on his new dining partner. And she was not the only one to notice the change in place settings, or the difference in him. Others kept sending her brief telling glances, then looking down the table at him.

Raffaelle did not notice. He was too busy plying his beautiful companion with wine and food, while Rachel could barely bring herself to swallow a thing. And, to top this whole disaster of an evening, having her handsome fiancé sitting beside her was enough protection to give Daniella's tongue back its sharpened edge.

'How is Elise?' she began innocently enough.

'Fine,' Rachel responded. 'She's still in Chicago with her husband and son.'

'And your…half-brother? The one with the camera? Is he still enjoying playing tricks on the rich and famous?'

How Daniella had managed to discover that Mark was her half-brother Rachel just did not feel like finding out right now. 'Mark is fine,' she answered in the same level tone and tried to change the subject. 'How are your wedding plans coming along?'

'Wonderful.' Daniella smiled happily. 'I'm here in Milan for my dress-fitting. Isn't that dress you're wearing—?' She named a top designer. 'Did Raffaelle buy it for you? How much do you think you have stung him for by now?'

'My dress is not by that particular designer,' Rachel answered quietly, 'and I pay for my own clothes.'

'Well, don't bother buying anything expensive for my wedding, darling, because by the look of it you will not be coming.' Daniella flicked her eyes down the table. 'Knowing Raffaelle as well as I do, I think I can positively predict that you are on your way out and Francesca is definitely on her way back in.'

One short glance down the table was enough for Rachel to

confirm why Daniella felt so very sure about that. If it wasn't enough that he had ignored her all evening, the way he was smiling that oh-so-familiar lazily sensual smile at the beautiful Francesca was the final straw for her.

'You know what, Daniella?' She turned back to her tormentor. 'Watching you marry that poor fool sitting next to you is the last thing on earth that I want to do.' The poor fool heard what she said and turned sharply to look at her. She ignored him. 'So dance on my grave, if that's what turns you on, *darling*,' she invited. 'And, while you're doing it, tell your stepbrother from me that he can have his Francesca with my absolute blessing!'

Then she stood up. The nausea instantly hit her again. She pushed her chair back and walked away. Silence had fallen around the table. How many of them had heard her exit line she did not know and she did not care.

Raffaelle tuned in too late to catch anything but the sight of Rachel's taut back retreating and the uncomfortable silence that followed. Gino was frowning angrily at Daniella. His stepsister had gone very pale. Someone else muttered a soft, '*Dio*.'

And the whole table watched as he came to his feet. Someone touched his hand. It might have been Francesca. He neither knew nor cared.

He strode after Rachel. 'Where the hell do you think you are going?' he raked out, catching hold of her wrist to bring her to a standstill between two tables.

It came out of nowhere, the rise in anger, the sudden swing round. Next thing she knew, she had slapped him full in the face.

A camera flashed.

His eyes lit up bright silver. 'That's tomorrow's trash out of the way,' he gritted, then hauled her up against him and kissed her hard.

The flashes kept on coming. The whole restaurant had

fallen into complete silence to witness Raffaelle Villani fight with his future bride. By the time he set her mouth free her lips were burning and her heart was thumping and tears were hot in her eyes.

'I wish I'd never met you,' she hissed up at him, then wrenched free of him and walked away.

Outside the air was cool and she shivered. Dino stood leaning against the car in the car park but he straightened the moment he saw Raffaelle appear.

'Rachel—'

'Stay away from me.' She started walking away from both the driver and Raffaelle, her spindly heels clicking on the hard pathway's surface. Inside she was a mass of muddled feelings, nausea and the pumping, pounding need to just get right away from everything.

She managed about ten metres before the car drew up beside her, at the same time as a figure leapt out of it and a hard hand arrived around her waist.

She tried to pull free; the hand tightened. 'You know how this works,' Raffaelle said grimly. 'You decide which way we do it.'

A camera flashed. They both blinked as it happened. Raffaelle muttered something nasty as his free hand pulled open the car door. Shivering, Rachel stiffened away from him and entered the car under her own steam.

The door closed her in. He walked round the car to get in beside her. With no glass partition in here to give them privacy, they were forced to hold their tongues, so the silence pulsed like a third heartbeat between them.

Anger, hostility, a tight sizzling *hatred* that ran dangerously close to its unrequited flipside flicked at the muscles in Raffaelle's face and held Rachel's frozen in her own private hell.

If he had not drunk so much wine, keeping up with Francesca in his attempt to divert her curious attention away from Rachel, Raffaelle knew he would have kicked Dino out of the car and taken his place, just to give himself something to do and stop himself from wanting to reach out and kill her for making him feel like this.

And—yes, he freely admitted it—he had been happy to give this woman sitting beside him something useful to think about! Did she think she was the only one of them who could play this game of falseness?

Game, falseness; the two words ricocheted around his head as a brutal reminder as to what this relationship was really about.

Rachel sat beside him with her face averted, fingering the ring on her finger and only realising as she felt its duller contours that she was still wearing the daytime fake.

Looking down, she could see that she had forgotten to swap the ring for the real one. So what was that little error trying to tell her?

You can't live a lie and expect it to spin itself into the truth?

They arrived at his apartment still steeped in thick silence. The journey up in the lift was just as cold and reined in. They entered the apartment. Rachel tossed aside her purse and just kept walking. He followed her into the bedroom and shut the door.

She could feel his anger beating into her. She refused to turn and look at him. 'If you want a row, then you're going to have to save it until tomorrow,' she tossed out coldly. 'I'm not—feeling too well, so I'm going to take a shower, then I'm going to bed and I would prefer it if you found somewhere else to sleep.'

Kicking off her shoes, she headed for the bathroom.

'Pleading a headache, *cara*?'

The drawling tone made her wince. 'Yes, actually,' she answered.

'Perhaps even pining for your Italian heartbreaker—?'

What had made him bring up Alonso now of all times? Rachel stopped walking to turn and look at him. He was standing in front of the closed bedroom door, tall, lean, spectacularly arrogant, with that coldly cynical expression lashed to his handsome features that just said it all.

CHAPTER ELEVEN

AN ICY chill chased down Rachel's spine. 'You know I bumped into Alonso today,' she murmured.

The tense shape of his top lip twisted. 'Is this *bumped into* an English euphemism for recklessly planned to meet with him in broad daylight on a busy street?'

Refusing to take him up on his cold sarcasm, she replied, 'No, it means bumped into by *accident*.'

'And, having spent the afternoon in his company,' Rafaelle said coldly, 'how would you prefer to describe that to me?'

Rachel frowned. 'But I didn't spend the afternoon with him.'

Shifting out of his taut stance, he walked forward, a long-fingered hand sliding into his inner jacket pocket, then smoothly out again. He halted by the bed, placed a photograph down on it.

Rachel glanced at it briefly. So someone *had* seen them together. She looked back at him. 'If you want to say something, Raffaelle,' she challenged. 'Then just come out and say it.'

'You drank coffee with him.'

'Yes.' She nodded.

'You then moved on to his apartment situated above the café.'

'You have photographic evidence of that too?'

He sliced the air with a hand. 'It stands to reason.'

'Does it?'

'*Si*—!' he bit out.

Suddenly all the rage he had been holding in all evening burst to the fore. He took a step towards her. Rachel took a step back. The raking flick of contempt in his eyes as she did so tensed up her trembling spine.

'You can give me a better explanation as to where you did spend the rest of the afternoon before you returned here?' he demanded.

Refusing to let his anger intimidate her, 'Can you explain where you spent *your* afternoon?' she hit back.

'*Scuzi*—?' He had the gall to look shocked!

'And then you could go on to explain how you had the rank bad taste to bring your *afternoon friend* into my company at dinner tonight!'

'Francesca is—'

'An ex-lover of yours, I know.' She said it for him. 'With darling Daniella around, I do tend to find these things out.'

His angry face hardened. 'We were discussing what you did with your afternoon, not what I did with mine.'

'Well, let's just say, for argument's sake, that we both did the same thing!' she threw back. 'As least you were saved the embarrassment of watching me fawn all over Alonso at dinner, whereas I did not warrant that much respect!'

His wide shoulders clenched inside expensive suiting. 'I did nothing with Francesca this afternoon but spend the time negotiating the price for that photograph! She owns the damn newspaper that bought it!'

'So she deals with the dreaded paparazzi?' Rachel's blue eyes lit up with bitter scorn. 'What lovely loyal people you and I surround ourselves with. Maybe we should introduce her to my brother and between them they could happily make a mockery out of both of us in two countries at the same time!'

'None of which explains what you did with your ex-lover,' he grated.

Her stomach was still churning and her heart was beating much too fast. 'I drank coffee with him, then I walked away. End of subject,' she said and turned back to the bathroom.

'It is the end of nothing.' His roughened voice raked over her as he grabbed her shoulder to spin her back round again, his face hard like granite. 'I want to know the truth!' he bit out.

Dizzy and nauseous, maybe she was not going to need to do any test, Rachel thought shakily. 'I've just given you the truth.'

'And your coffee took four hours to consume?'

Rachel made herself look up at him. 'Your negotiations for the photograph took just as long?' she challenged him right back. 'Or was your time spent on a certain *kind* of negotiation?'

He went white, stiffened and let go of her. 'You will not sink me down to your level, Rachel.'

'My *level*?' She stared at him.

'Your propensity to lie, then, without blinking an eye.'

Well, her eyes certainly blinked now and she took an unsteady step backwards. 'I have never lied to you, Raffaelle,' she breathed out unevenly. 'No—think about that,' she insisted when he parted his hard lips to speak. 'We have a relationship built on lies, yes,' she acknowledged. 'But I have never lied to *you*!'

The way his top lip curled really shook her. This, the whole thing they had going between them, suddenly showed itself up for what it really was—a relationship built on sex and disrespect, which had never stood a chance of being anything more than the tacky way it felt to her right now.

'Scoff at me all you want,' she invited. 'But while you're doing it remember that three months ago you wanted my sister. This month you decided that you might as well have me. Next month you will probably put Francesca back into your bed.

The way you are going through them, Raffaelle, there won't be a woman left in Europe you will be able to look at without experiencing *déjà-vu*!'

Rachel spun away then, needing to head fast for the bathroom. But she didn't make it that far. The room began to swim and she pushed a hand up to her head, swaying like a drunk on her spindly heels.

'What—?' she heard him rasp in a mad mix of concern and anger.

'I don't—f-feel well,' she whispered, before everything started to blacken around the edges and his thick curses accompanied his strong arms which caught her as she started to sink to the ground.

Her own piece of *déjà-vu* followed, as she opened her eyes to find herself lying on the bed with him looming over her. The same look was there, the same closed expression.

A flickering clash of their eyes and she knew what he was thinking.

'It might not be,' she whispered across the hand she pressed against her lips.

He opened his mouth to say something, then closed it again—tight. Then he straightened up and she knew he was drawing himself in ready to deal with the worst.

'I will call a doctor—'

The fatalist at work again, she recognised. 'No,' she shook out and, when he paused as he was turning away from her, Rachel heaved out a sigh and slowly sat up. 'Y-you don't need to call a doctor,' she explained. 'I h-have something…' She waved a hand towards the bedside drawer.

Without saying a word, he walked over to the drawer and opened it. Long fingers withdrew the paper bag containing the only purchase she had made that afternoon.

Such a small purchase for something so important, Rachel

thought bleakly as he withdrew what was inside the bag, then just stood looking down at it.

The mood was different now, still tense but thick and heavy. She looked at his profile and saw that the drawbridge had been brought down on his anger and what he was thinking.

'When did you buy this?'

'Today,' she answered. 'Th-this afternoon.'

'I thought we agreed that you would not risk making intimate purchases like this,' he said with super-controlled cool.

A strained little laugh left her throat. 'There was no one I could trust enough to get them to do it for me and I…needed to know.'

'Did you?'

The odd way he said that brought her head up. 'Of course— don't you want to know?'

He did not answer. There was something very peculiar about the way he was standing there, tense and grim.

'If you're concerned that I've given the paparazzi something else about us to feed on, then I was careful,' she assured him. 'In fact,' she said, sliding her feet to the floor, 'you wanted to know what I did with my afternoon. Well, wandering round the shops trying to fool any followers into leaving me alone before I dared to buy the test was it.'

He said nothing. Rachel wished she knew what was going on in his head. Hurt was beginning to prick at her nerve endings. Didn't he think this situation was difficult enough without him standing there resembling a block of stone? Was he scared in case they discovered she was pregnant and that sense of honour he liked to believe he possessed would require him to marry her when he didn't want to?

Standing up, she went to take the package from him. 'I'll go and find out if it's—'

His fingers closed around it. 'No,' he said gruffly.

Rachel just stared at his hard profile.

'We—need to talk first,' he added.

'Talk about what?' she said curtly. 'If I am pregnant we will deal with it like grown-ups. If I'm not pregnant, then I go home.'

'What do you mean, we deal with it like grown-ups?' At last he swung round to look at her. His face was pale and taut.

Rachel sighed. 'If I am pregnant I'm not marrying you, Raffaelle,' she informed him wearily.

'Why not—?'

Why not—? If she dared to do it without risking setting her queasy stomach off again—Rachel would have laughed. 'Because you don't want to marry me?' she threw at him. 'Because I can take care of myself *and* a child! And because I refuse to tie myself to a man who just *loves* to believe the worst of me!' She heaved in a breath. 'Do you want more—?'

'Yes,' he gritted.

She blinked, not expecting that response.

'Okay.' She folded her arms across her shaking body and looked at him coldly. 'You don't trust me. You think I am a liar and a cheat. I give you perhaps a couple of months held in marital captivity before you start questioning if the baby could be some other man's.'

'I am not that twisted!' he defended that last accusation.

She put in a shrug. 'Trapped by a child on purpose, then.'

'We've been through that. I *don't* think that!'

'You've got your old lover already lined up ready to take my place.'

'Francesca was not lined up for anything other than to get that photograph,' he sighed out.

'Well, guess what?' Rachel said. 'I don't believe *you*.'

Now that was a twist in the proceedings, she saw, as he stared at her down the length of his arrogant nose. She made a grab at the package.

This time he let go of it.

On a shivering breath she turned and walked into the bathroom, then closed and locked the door.

By the time she came out again, she was stunned, shaken, totally hollowed out from the inside.

Raffaelle was standing by the window, his body tense inside his well-cut jacket. When he heard the door open he spun round, then went perfectly still.

'Well—?' he said harshly.

Rachel pressed her pale lips together and gave a shake of her head.

Tension sizzled. 'Is that a *no*, as in you are *not* pregnant?' he demanded.

Hands ice-cold and trembling where she clutched them together in front of her, Rachel nodded.

He moved—one of those short, sharp jerks of the body. 'You have to be pregnant,' she thought she heard him mutter beneath his breath. 'Why did you feel sick—why the fainting?' he asked hoarsely.

'W-women's stuff,' she mumbled dully. 'It—it's like that sometimes.' She added a shrug. 'The real thing should h-happen any day now…'

Silence fell, one of those horrible awkward, don't-know-what-to-say-next kind of silences that grabbed at the air and choked it to death.

Rachel couldn't stand it. She was in shock. She wasn't really functioning properly on any level. She'd been so sure that the answer to the test would come out positive, and if she did not find herself something practical to do she knew she was going to embarrass both of them by bursting out crying with sheer disappointment!

With no control at all over her trembling legs, she walked like a drunk towards the dressing room. 'I'll pack,' she whispered.

'What the hell for—?' he raked out.

'Time to call it quits, I think.' She even added a flicker of a wobbly smile.

'No,' he ground out roughly. 'I—don't want you to go.'

White as a sheet, Rachel shook her head. 'It might as well be now than next week—next month—'

'No,' he repeated.

'But there's no reason left for me to stay now!'

His wide shoulders squared. 'Am I not a good enough reason?' he demanded harshly. 'Have our weeks together meant so little to you that you could just decide to leave me like this—?'

Stunned by the harsh husky agony in his tone, Rachel was further shocked to see how pale he looked.

Tears burst to life. 'Raffaelle…' she murmured pleadingly. 'You know we only—'

'No,' he cut in on her yet again. 'Don't say my name like that—don't *look* at me like that.'

'But there is no baby!' She had to say it—*had to!*

'To hell with babies,' he bit out fiercely. 'We can make babies any time! This is about you and me and what *we* want. And *I* want you to stay!'

Was he saying what she thought he was saying? She just stared at him, not daring to trust what her ears were telling her. 'Francesca—'

'Forget about Francesca,' he said impatiently. 'I am blind to Francesca. I am *blind* to any woman who is not you.'

She took a wary step towards him. 'Are you saying that you want me to stay even without a baby—?'

He threw out an angry hand. 'Why do you need me to keep on saying it?' he thrust out. 'I want you to stay…because I want *you* to stay!'

'H-how long?'

'*Dio*, woman,' he breathed savagely. 'What are you trying

to do to me?' His silver-green eyes gave an aggressive flash. 'For ever, okay? I want it all: the love, the ring, the marriage—the whole damn crazy package!'

'Then why are you so angry about it?' she cried out.

He squared his wide shoulders. Pale and tense, 'It would not hurt you, Rachel, to give me some small encouragement to feel happy about loving you,' he pushed out.

Then he turned his back to her and grabbed his nape with long angry fingers. Rachel hovered, wanting to go to him but still too scared to move.

Then, why are *you* scared? she asked herself. He had just said he loved her and she was standing here giving him every impression that she—

She closed the gap between them, running her arms around his waist and pressing herself in close to his rigid back. 'I'm sorry,' she whispered. 'But I've loved you so much and for so long when I *knew* I didn't have the right to feel like this!'

A sound ripped from his throat and he spun in her arms. His eyes were like twin black diamonds, still angry, possessive—real.

'No—w-wait, I need to say this—' she shivered out when she saw what was coming. 'I knew that I had no right to fall in love with you after the way I had hit on you without giving a thought to the trouble I was going to cause! Then w-we thought we had made a baby so I used it as an excuse to stay and—'

'We used it.'

'But it just wasn't fair of me to load you down with my foolish feelings when—No!' she protested. 'I've not—'

Finished...

What a waste of breath, Rachel thought as she fell into the kind of kiss that made words redundant.

By the time he lifted his head again, streaks of desire were burning into his cheekbones. 'Any reason why we cannot continue this...discussion in bed?' he said huskily.

What discussion? Rachel thought dryly as she wound her arms around his neck. 'You want to…talk?' she asked innocently.

His mouth twitched. 'No.'

'You perhaps want to say something about the way you unleashed your charms on another woman tonight?'

He tensed. 'You want me to apologise—'

'I want you to *pay*,' Rachel told him. 'At least you were saved from watching me act like that with Alonso.'

'But I did see.' He grimaced. 'I watched the handsome bastard leap out of his car and take you in his arms. I watched him kiss you as if he had every right to do it, and I saw the adoring expression on your face as you looked up at him!'

'It wasn't adoring, it was shock!' Rachel protested.

'You *let* him kiss you.'

'Italians are always kissing each other.' She dismissed that accusation.

'You let him drive you away in his flashy red car.'

'It was either that or get caught in the street by a snooping reporter.' Then she frowned. 'Where were you when this was happening?'

His sigh was rueful. 'Making a fool of myself over lunch with five important business associates, by just getting up and walking away,' he confessed. 'Then I got the call from Francesca and my day just continued downhill from there.' He ran his fingers through her hair, his eyes hooded. 'When you walked out of the restaurant I thought you were going to go to him.'

Rachel stared at him in blank disbelief. 'Since when have you been so short on ego to *think* such a thing?'

'Since I met you,' he said. 'You have a unique way of eating away at my ego.'

'That's such a lie,' she denounced. 'You've done nothing but bully me and want sex from me since we met!'

'You hit on me, but not because you wanted me. And you taunted me with other lovers.' He shrugged.

'I've had *one* lover before you,' she reminded him. 'My *one* lined up against your many who have trailed themselves past me seems a pretty pathetic comparison to me.'

He touched his tongue to the corner of her sulky mouth. 'I love you,' he murmured. 'Can we forget the others?'

Rachel sighed out a groan because he was right and harking on about old lovers had nothing to do with what they had here. 'Just take me to bed and love me, Raffaelle,' she begged.

He did not need asking twice. Their clothes fell away like rags for jumble. He pulled her against him, lips almost bruising in their intensity, his hands sliding possessively along her slender curves until he found the indentation of her waist, where he gripped and lifted her off the ground.

For a few clamouring seconds when her legs wrapped round him she thought he was going to do it standing right there with no preliminaries. Their mouths were straining and he was on fire, pumped up and ready for her. And she was pretty well much the same.

Then he turned and toppled them on to the duvet. What followed was the kind of fierce, fevered loving that staked absolute possession and claim. He gave her all of him and she took it greedily and gave back the same.

Afterwards they lay spread across the mattress, Rachel nothing more than a slender, soft, boneless creature lying beneath him, still lost in a wonderful, sensual world.

'In all my life,' Rafaelle murmured as he gently kissed her back down to earth again, 'I have never known the power of what you can do to me.'

So, gravely serious, opening her eyes, Rachel smiled at him. 'Hit on, trapped, taken over,' she said approvingly.

His eyes began to glint. 'Now you are asking for trouble,' he warned and climbed over her to land lightly on his feet by the bed.

'I didn't mean it—!' she cried out, sitting up jerkily.

He'd moved to the dressing table; now he was back by the bed. Stretching out beside her, he took hold of her left hand.

'Oh, I forgot,' she said, staring as the fake ring was removed from her finger.

The real one glittered and flashed as he slid it on to her finger. They lay there beside each other while he held up her hand. 'Hit on, trapped and marked as mine for ever,' he said turning her own words back on her with some very satisfied-sounding additions.

Then the fake ring spun in the air as he tossed it carelessly away.

'Did I tell you I love you?' Rachel said softly.

He rose above her, eyes dark and slumberous in his golden face. 'Tell me again,' he commanded.

'Love you,' she obliged and sealed it this time with a warm clinging kiss.

'And you will be my wife?'

Warm, dark, golden, gorgeous—she placed a finger on the thoroughly kissed fullness of his lower lip, loving the very possessive sound of *my wife*.

'Tomorrow.' She nodded gravely.

'Even though you get Daniella as a stepsister-in-law?'

'You get worse from me,' Rachel said. 'You get a fully paid-up member of the paparazzi as your brother-in-law.'

'Stung again—' he sighed '—you are going to have to work very hard to make it worth my while.'

The kiss she laid on his mouth worked very hard to make it worth his while.

'By the way,' she murmured a long time later, flickering innocent blue eyes up to look at him, 'you forgot to use any protection…'

The Italian's Chosen Wife

KATE HEWITT

To Cliff,
For believing in me and showing
it in so many ways.
—K

Kate Hewitt discovered her first Mills & Boon® romance on a trip to England when she was thirteen, and she's continued to read them ever since.

She wrote her first story at the age of five, simply because her older brother had written one and she thought she could do it too. That story was one sentence long—fortunately, they've become a bit more detailed as she's grown older.

She has written plays, short stories, and magazine serials for many years, but writing romance remains her first love. Besides writing, she enjoys reading, travelling, and learning to knit.

After marrying the man of her dreams—her older brother's childhood friend—she lived in England for six years and now resides in Connecticut with her husband, her three young children, and the possibility of one day getting a dog.

Kate loves to hear from readers—you can contact her through her website, www.kate-hewitt.com.

**Don't miss Kate's exciting new novel,
Mr and Mischief, out in June 2011 from
Mills & Boon® Modern™.**

PROLOGUE

'I WISH *that* was on the menu.'

Alessandro di Agnio's lips thinned in distaste at his companion's expression. He leaned back in his chair, his cool gaze flicking over the waitress chatting in Italian at the nearby table. Her hand rested on her hip, and he could hear the warm gurgle of her laughter from where he sat. There was, he noticed, a tomato sauce stain on her blouse. Her hair was falling from its pins, and she ran a careless hand through it.

His eyes narrowed. 'I believe we're here for the food.'

Next to him, his potential client Richard Harrison chuckled. 'Relax, di Agnio. It's just an expression.'

Alessandro smiled, his expression now calm, urbane, in place. He took a sip of iced water. 'She's quite pretty, in her own way. Now, to the business at hand…?' He raised his eyebrows, still smiling, although his eyes were cold and the expression on his face was at best remote.

Richard leaned back in his chair, his own expression that of a mouse intent on teasing a cat. His lower lip stuck out in a boyish pout. 'You know, I didn't come all the way to Spoleto just to talk to you. I thought we were going to have some fun.'

'Of course. You know what they say about all work and no play.' Alessandro shrugged lightly, although his eyes were still hard.

'Then how about a little play?' Richard asked, his tone turning petulant. 'I've heard so much about your playboy reputation. A few years ago there wasn't a tabloid in this country without your picture splashed across its pages! Coming here, I was expecting a little something more than lunch at a second-rate trattoria.'

Alessandro smiled again, this time a mere stretching of his lips. He didn't need to be reminded of tabloids. Yet he also knew how much Di Agnio Enterprises would benefit from Richard Harrison's business.

'I didn't realise my reputation stretched so far,' he said after a pause, his voice flat. 'Of course you need only choose your pleasure. Dinner? Dancing?'

'Her.' Richard pointed to the waitress—still chatting, Alessandro noticed, and obviously not an industrious worker. He heard another peal of laughter, warm and inviting. She leaned forward, hair tumbling into her face, one hand swiping it away as she murmured provocatively. Everything about her told him she was relaxed, carefree, available. Easy.

He'd known women like that. Knew what they wanted, what they expected. Of him.

The customer she was talking to had to be seventy years old at least. And he was eating it up. Probably wanted to eat *her* up, as well.

'Her?' Alessandro repeated. Icy disbelief laced his words. 'I don't pick women like sweets in a shop.' Not any more. He injected a faint, dry note of humour into his voice as he added, 'I didn't think my reputation was quite that notorious.'

'I don't mean like *that*,' Richard said impatiently. He was gazing at the waitress with the longing of a child for a toy—or, as Alessandro had said, a sweet. A forbidden one, sticky and delectable. 'She's a waitress. Why don't you hire her to wait on us tonight? A quiet dinner for two, at your villa.' Richard's eyes lit up lasciviously.

Alessandro eyed his companion with cold dislike. 'To wait on us?' he repeated. 'And nothing else?'

Richard grinned. 'We could see what happens.'

Alessandro didn't bother to hide his disgust. His guest was actually suggesting they hire the waitress as a virtual prostitute. 'I think not.'

'Why such a prude, di Agnio?' Richard taunted. 'From what

I hear, you've done that and worse.' He paused meaningfully. 'A lot worse.'

Alessandro did not dignify his companion's remark with a response. He knew his own past. He knew what people believed. He chose to ignore it, as he had ignored every telling, incredulous remark since he'd taken the reins of Di Agnio Enterprises two years ago.

'If it's pleasure you're seeking,' he said, with quiet, menacing derision, 'you'll find a wider range of amusements in town, not with some two-bit part-time whore.'

'You don't need to be crude.' Richard sipped his wine, his expression thoughtful as he gazed at the waitress. She'd finally cleared the table, dirty plates stacked on one tanned arm.

Still chatting, Alessandro noticed with scathing disdain. He watched her lips curl into a smile that promised all too much.

'She reminds me of home. I bet she's American.'

'Why don't you go talk to her, then?' Alessandro questioned silkily. 'I'm sure you don't need my intervention.'

'But I want it.' Richard's eyes met Alessandro's, watery blue clashing with midnight steel. 'And you need my business, di Agnio, so why don't you just humour me?'

A muscle ticked in Alessandro's jaw. He rested his hand flat on the table, resisting the desire to curl it into a fist. He would not be threatened—not by the potential of Harrison's business, not by the ghosts of his own past.

He was free. He was free of all that.

He smiled. 'You'll find I don't need your business quite as much as you think,' he said lightly. 'And perhaps you need mine a bit more than you'd like me to believe.'

Richard's expression hardened. Fear flickered in his eyes, and one limp, well-manicured hand bunched the tablecloth. 'Where did you hear that?'

'I like to stay informed.' Alessandro's smile widened, predatory, in control. Richard saw, and seemed to shrink a little. 'There's a dinner and dancing club on the Via Filetteria that will do very well for tonight.' Alessandro spoke firmly, as a parent to a child, and saw with satisfaction that Richard Harrison's momentary flare of rebellious authority had died out.

'I just liked her, that's all.'

Alessandro glanced again at the waitress. He could understand her appeal, on a basic level. She was pretty enough, and there was an aura about her that exuded—what? Warmth? Sexuality? Availability, perhaps?

A woman to be pleasured—used—once, and discarded.

If he did that. Which he did not.

Not any more.

Then she turned and caught his gaze. Her hair was piled untidily on top of her head, strands of indeterminate brown falling to frame her face. Nothing special, Alessandro decided dismissively, despite her youth and obvious sex appeal. She knew how to work a room, a man.

Then her eyes widened, her gaze fastened on his.

Her eyes were the golden-green of sunlight on an olive grove, iridescent, filled with promise. With hope. Her lips parted into a smile, tender in its uncertainty.

Alessandro felt his insides tighten. Something flared to life within him—something he'd suppressed, had thought banished for ever.

Need.

He turned back to Richard, who was oblivious to the silent yearning exchange. 'On second thoughts, I've changed my mind,' he said, in a voice that brooked no argument, no opposition. His fingers toyed with then tightened on the stem of his water glass. 'A quiet dinner at home will suit my needs.'

CHAPTER ONE

'MEGHAN, there's someone here to see you.'

Meghan Selby struggled against the knot in her apron strings and sighed tiredly.

'Please tell me it's not Paulo,' she said, as the other waitress, Carla, placed a stack of dirty plates on the counter.

'Who?'

'My landlord.'

Carla wrinkled her nose. 'What does he look like?'

'Short, fat, greasy-haired.' She suppressed a shudder.

'Why would he come here?' Carla asked, curiosity evident in her eyes, and Meghan shrugged evasively.

'Who knows? But I don't know many other people in this town.'

'Well, it's certainly not him.' Carla's efficient fingers went to work on the knot. 'This man is tall, built, wavy-haired and asking to see you.' She released the untangled strings and grinned. 'He's gorgeous, actually. Is there something—or someone—you're not telling me about?'

'I wish.' Meghan slipped off her apron with a quick, grateful smile. 'It's probably just someone who's lost his wallet.'

Carla raised her eyebrows. 'Why wouldn't he ask Angelo, then?'

She shrugged. The truth was, she'd no idea why a strange man would ask for her, and she didn't really want to know. She didn't want to attract attention from any men, strange or familiar. The sooner she dealt with the one waiting outside the better.

She'd been waitressing in Spoleto for six weeks, and she knew instinctively it was time to move on. She enjoyed Carla's friendship, and Angelo, who owned the trattoria, was like a doting uncle. She'd made a few friends in town, but she felt the inexorable need to shake the dust from her feet before the money ran out, before anyone got too close. Before her past caught up with her.

'I'll see you tomorrow?' Carla queried, and Meghan pretended not to hear. Best not to make any promises.

'I'd better go and see about my mystery man,' she joked, and Carla laughed.

'I can't wait to hear all about it.'

A quick glance in the bar's mirror revealed a stain on her shirt, and her hair, which had been in an almost sleek chignon this morning, was now a flyaway tangle.

'You look gorgeous, *cara*.' Angelo, sixty-three years old and full of spicy humour, grinned at her. 'Got a date?'

'Nope,' Meghan replied, trying for a breezy smile. She didn't plan on having any dates for a long time. She tucked a strand of hair behind her ear—not that it did much to help.

'See you tomorrow.'

She nodded, still making no promises, and went outside.

The man waiting under the red and white striped awning of Trattoria di Angelo was striking even from a distance. He wore a charcoal-grey suit, excellently cut, his hands thrust into the pockets of his trousers, stretching the cloth of his jacket against an impressive pair of shoulders.

He looked up as she approached, navy eyes clashing with hers. The sheer force of those eyes—the power, the *knowledge* in their midnight depths—made her take an involuntary step backwards even as her heart stumbled in beat.

She recognised him, of course, as the man who'd dined in the trattoria earlier. Someone important in business, or so Angelo's significant look had implied when he'd asked her to wait on them.

She remembered the way the man had looked at her earlier that afternoon, his eyes blazing into hers. Searing, branding.

Knowing.

As if he knew who she was. *What* she was.

That wasn't possible, Meghan reassured herself, and yet one look from beneath those dark, frowning brows told her this man had summed her up—and dismissed her—in a matter of seconds.

Opinions, impressions already formed, and they hadn't exchanged a word.

She straightened her shoulders, her expression hardening as a matter of instinct and self-preservation. She stopped a few feet from where he paced restlessly on the cobbled pavement.

'You wanted to see me?'

'Alessandro di Agnio,' he introduced himself brusquely, and thrust one hand out for her to shake.

Meghan inclined her head in introduction, resisting the impulse—the desire—to take his hand. Long, tapered fingers, strong, square nails. No, she didn't want to touch him. Didn't want to invite that particular temptation into her life.

'I don't think I know you,' she said, for he was still staring at her, eyes narrowed, mouth thinned in…what? Disapproval? Dislike? Disdain? Whatever it was, Meghan didn't like it.

He dropped his hand, smiling slightly in rueful acknowledgement of her rebuff.

'No, you don't. Not yet. But I hope you will very shortly.' His mouth curved in a small wry smile that flickered along her nerve-endings, skittered across her pulse. 'I wanted to hire your services for the evening.'

Meghan recoiled in spite of her best intentions to stay aloof. His words echoed in her brain. *Hire your services.* His meaning, the desire darkening his eyes, the faintly sneering curl of his lip, were plain enough.

She lifted her chin, summoned her strength. 'Services? I think you're talking to the wrong woman, *signore.*'

There was a moment of charged silence as he regarded her in obvious distaste. 'Perhaps I am. I need to hire a waitress for a private dinner party at my villa.' He raised an eyebrow, humour and contempt mingling in those dark, knowing eyes. 'Or were you thinking of some other kind of services?'

Humiliation burned colour in her cheeks. Her stomach felt as if it were coated in ice…or acid. Still Meghan glanced at him coolly, refusing to be unnerved. Condemned. 'A strange man asks to see me in the middle of the street—wants to hire my *services*—what am I supposed to think?'

'I can hardly put myself in your place, but I would imagine most women wouldn't immediately think they'd been mistaken for a whore.'

'Most women wouldn't appreciate being looked over like a piece of meat,' Meghan replied shortly. The word echoed in her numb brain. *Whore*.

A faint blush stained Alessandro di Agnio's sharp cheek-bones, and he gave a slight nod of acknowledgement. Meghan knew his type well enough to know there would be no apology forthcoming.

'I'm sorry,' he said, surprising her. 'You're a beautiful woman, and Italian men admire that. Some are more obvious than others. I promise you, I want to hire you as a waitress only, at my villa. It's a private dinner party for two.'

No doubt the business colleague from lunch, Meghan surmised. She'd seen the way his watery eyes had roved over her, the way his little mouth had pursed in greedy desire.

Yet she wasn't afraid of that man.

She was afraid of this one.

Afraid of his power, his effortless control, the way his eyes swept her from head to foot…the way her body reacted, tensing, tingling.

He had the face of an angel, Meghan thought, with those liquid eyes and sculpted lips. Not the innocent round-faced cherubs she'd seen in frescoes, but something elemental, beautiful in its power. His jaw was square, cheek-bones chiselled. A dangerous angel.

She shook her head. 'Why me?'

'I want a pretty girl as a waitress.' He shrugged, unapologetic. Unashamed. 'Someone to lighten the atmosphere, add a bit of flair. It's not an uncommon desire.'

Meghan cringed just a little bit at his words. A pretty girl. That was all she was, all she'd ever be. So little, so damning.

'Lighten the atmosphere?' she repeated, with a scornful note of incredulity. 'I'm not an entertainer.'

'Aren't you?' His eyes burned her from head to toe, and a slow smile stole over his features.

Meghan flushed angrily. He might not have said it in so many words, but she knew what he thought. Perhaps even what he expected. 'You don't know me, *signore*,' she said in a voice of restrained fury. '*You don't know me.*'

'No, I don't.' His eyes flicked coolly back up to her face. 'Not yet. So what will it be? I'll pay you double what you make at Angelo's.' There was an impatient edge to his voice. 'Triple. I'm sure you could use the money.' His dispassionate glance raked her again, taking in her worn white tee shirt with its tomato sauce stain, the black skirt that was cheap and shiny from wear.

Meghan refused to be embarrassed. She was a waitress; of course she was poor. Of course she could use the money.

And yet she didn't like the way Alessandro looked at her. As if he were buying goods, services, and cheap ones at that.

'Well?'

Meghan knew she should say no. Whatever Alessandro di Agnio said about hiring her as a waitress, she knew there were other expectations involved. A man didn't look at her like that if he just wanted her to serve food.

And yet Alessandro di Agnio hardly seemed like the kind of man who needed to purchase his pleasure.

Her stomach roiled with nerves; doubt wound tendrils around her heart. She didn't know what kind of man he was. She wasn't sure she wanted to find out.

She certainly didn't want to go to his villa alone, unprotected. Vulnerable.

Unless she could be stronger than that. Unless she could make it work to her advantage. Get through dinner, leave with euros in her pocket and a smile on her face.

Nothing changes the past.

No matter how far you run.

'One night,' Meghan clarified.

His lip curled. 'You want more?'

'Certainly not,' she snapped. 'I'm leaving Spoleto anyway.'

'Things not to your liking?'

Meghan's mouth hardened into an unforgiving line, a deter-mination darkening her eyes. 'It's time to move on.'

'Then earn triple the last night you're here,' Alessandro sug-gested smoothly.

Meghan lifted her chin. Her pulse raced, blood rushed in her ears. 'Maybe I will.'

His eyes fastened on hers, and Meghan saw the hunger in them turning them opaque. She saw expectation, anticipation. Satisfaction. The deep, primal look of a conqueror regarding his spoils.

And she knew that, no matter what Alessandro said, he thought he was getting something more than a waitress for the night.

And was he?

No. For once she would prove who she was. What she was. And what she wasn't.

'Yes, I'll do it,' she said, her voice coming out strident. 'What time do you want me to come? And where?'

'Villa Tre Querce. It's five kilometres outside of town. I'll send a car.'

'No.' She didn't want his car showing up at the grotty hostel she currently called home, and she didn't want to take anything else from Alessandro di Agnio. 'I'll take the bus.'

'The buses don't go to Tre Querce,' Alessandro informed her shortly. 'I have a car and a driver. Give me your address, and I'll send him to fetch you at seven o'clock. We'll dine at eight.'

'That doesn't give me much time,' Meghan protested. 'It must be six o'clock now.' Already there was a slight chill in the spring air, descending damply from the mountains, rolling in on a fine mist.

'All the more reason for me to send the car,' Alessandro coun-tered, and his tone brooked no opposition. 'Tell me your address.'

Meghan shrugged. Let him see where she lived. It was dire, she knew that, but who cared?

She didn't. He certainly didn't.

'It's the Arbus Hostel on the west side of town,' she informed him coolly. 'On the Via Campelo.'

His mouth tightened in disapproval. 'I don't know it.'

'You wouldn't.'

'My driver will be there at seven.' He paused, his gaze flicking the length of her, taking in, no doubt, her mussed hair and stained shirt.

'You have something to wear?'

Her eyebrows lifted in challenge. 'I'm waitressing, remember? I think I have something suitable.'

'This isn't the trattoria,' Alessandro warned her. 'I expect you to dress…and behave…appropriately.'

The warning stung. 'It's a little late now for second thoughts, isn't it?' Meghan said, her smile cautious. 'You've already hired me.' Her voice turned ragged as she added, 'I'm not going to show up in nothing but high heels and a frilly apron, even if that's what you actually want—'

'Stop it.' Alessandro's voice cut across her. 'I've told you what this position entails—waitressing and nothing more. Do you not trust me?'

Meghan dared herself to meet his eyes, to feel the force of their magnetic onslaught. Trust? What a joke. She barely knew him, and even if she did, the only trust she had was in herself, in her ability to protect herself. 'Is there any reason,' she asked quietly, 'why I *should* trust you?'

Alessandro gazed at her in silent consideration. He shrugged and looked away. 'No,' he said after a moment, his voice flat and expressionless, 'there isn't.'

Meghan sagged slightly. Of course there wasn't. She was walking into the lion's den, and she wasn't even armed. All she had was her dignity and her determination to prove herself, and right now they didn't count for much.

'I'll see you, then,' she said after a moment, thankful her voice was steady. She began to turn away, only to have Alessandro reach out. He put his hand on her arm, his fingers wrapping around her wrist, pulling her towards him.

Meghan stiffened with shock and a little fear. Shock at his touching her, the simple, possessive way he drew her to him. Thoughtlessly, and yet with care. As if already he expected something from her, deserved something from her.

The fear was at her own reaction. She didn't resist. She let him pull her, her legs moved woodenly, helplessly, closer. Her pulse kicked into high gear with the simple touch of those fingers on her wrist, holding her. Gently.

He kept holding onto her, a slight smile playing about his mouth, his eyes raking in her appearance, their gaze a caress…and an assessment.

'I don't even know your name.'

Her lips opened soundlessly as her mind spun. 'Meghan.'

He nodded. He let go of her wrist, smiling as she pulled her arm protectively inwards. 'I'll see you at seven.'

Meghan's legs trembled as she watched him walk away. She shook her head, resisting the urge to wrap her arms more tightly around herself. Had she really agreed to waitress? *Why*? It should have been so easy to walk away.

Yet it wasn't, and she hadn't.

She couldn't escape her past, she reflected bleakly. The exchange with Alessandro di Agnio reminded her of that. If anything happened tonight it would be nothing more than she deserved.

CHAPTER TWO

MEGHAN hurried through the darkening streets of Spoleto towards the Via Campelo and the hostel she'd been calling home.

Not a very pleasant home at that, with its tiny dark bedrooms, dripping ceilings and grimy sheets. She'd seen worse on her travels, but Paulo, the proprietor, was a particularly unpleasant landlord.

Meghan had seen him for what he was right away. First it had just been leering grins and wandering eyes, soon followed by coarser remarks and wandering hands.

She'd bought a padlock for her door, and more than once she'd woken up to hear the stealthy, futile turning of the door handle, weak with relief that she was at least that safe.

Now she tried to avoid him altogether. Still, it was another reason to leave Spoleto. With the money earned from waitressing for di Agnio she could buy a train ticket to her next destination...wherever that was.

'*Ciao, bellissima.*' Paulo leaned over the front desk as Meghan slipped in the door. His white undershirt sported large patches of dried sweat, and his mouth curled in a knowing grin, revealing tobacco-stained teeth.

Meghan didn't bother to answer. She slipped by before he could reach one hand out to squeeze or pat, and hurried to her room, fastening the padlock.

There was no time for a shower, so she just splashed water on her face and arms from the tiny cracked sink in the corner of the room.

She threw her dirty clothes in the corner and pulled on a fresh white shirt and simple black skirt—her waitressing uniform. She hadn't brought much with her when she'd left home. It had all been so quick in the end.

Dressed and ready, she sank onto the bed, the broken springs creaking in protest. Her momentary burst of energy spent, she felt weak. Limp. Unreal.

The conversation with Alessandro di Agnio played in her mind, forever on pause and rewind.

Why had she agreed? she asked herself again, and couldn't come up with a satisfactory answer. At least not one she was willing to face.

In the last six months of travelling through Europe, she'd become a professional at deflecting comments, invitations, innuendoes. A woman on her own was considered fair game, easy prey by many, and Meghan already knew of her own damning allure.

So why hadn't she just said no to Alessandro di Agnio? It would have been easy. It would have been safer to have just walked away.

Because he's different.

The thought was ludicrous, laughable. Stupid.

He'd summed her up quickly enough—easy American, slutty waitress. He wasn't going to change his mind.

She was the one who would prove she was different. *This time.*

'I won't see him again after tonight,' Meghan muttered, and it was both thanksgiving and supplication.

He certainly wasn't expecting to see *her* again, she reflected with a wry bitterness. One night only, limited engagement.

She pulled her hair back into a sleek ponytail, her only concession to vanity a bit of face powder and lipgloss. The last thing she wanted was for di Agnio to think she was tarting herself up.

She locked her room and went in search of Paulo.

'I'll have my deposit back, please. I'm leaving tomorrow.'

Paulo looked at her with calculating lasciviousness. 'I don't remember you putting down a deposit. I said you didn't have to, because you were so pretty.'

Meghan gritted her teeth. 'Nice try, Paulo. I have the receipt.

Two weeks' stay in this hovel. That will cover last week's rent, and the rest I want back. Now.'

His expression hardened. 'Don't talk mean to me, *principessa*. I know what you are.'

'I'm a waitress,' Meghan snapped, her already frayed temper now reaching breaking point. She might have been unnerved by Alessandro di Agnio, but she certainly wouldn't be so shaken by this piece of wheedling slime.

'You need the money?' His eyebrows rose. 'You're in trouble, perhaps?'

'No, and no,' Meghan retorted. 'But that doesn't stop me from wanting what's mine.'

'Maybe *I* want what's mine.' There was a thread of dangerous need in Paulo's voice, and Meghan's scalp prickled in alarm. She took a step away, but not fast enough.

Paulo grabbed her arm and pulled her to him. Meghan slammed against his soft belly with a suppressed grunt, his hands tight on her wrists, pinning her against him.

'One kiss.'

She could smell his stale smoky breath, his old sweat. She could smell his lust, and everything in her recoiled.

'Get off me—' Meghan tried to push herself away, but Paulo only held her tighter.

'One kiss, *bella*, that's all. And then you can have your money.'

'Go to hell!' Meghan spat raggedly. 'I won't give you anything—'

'You've been wanting it.' Paulo's face had turned angry even as his eyes were bright with desire. Meghan wanted to retch. 'I've seen you—the looks you give me—'

She closed her eyes, swallowed bile. 'You're fooling yourself, Paulo, and I can call the police—'

'But you haven't, have you?' he said with soft menace. His lips, moist and slimy, were inches from hers. 'I've wondered about you, *bella*. What are you trying to hide? Why don't you leave? You could, you know. There are other hostels in Spoleto.' He shook his head slowly. 'But you never did leave…so that must mean you want it.'

'You're wrong.' Meghan's voice shook. Her body shook. She felt weak and helpless, and the realisation angered her. She would not be a victim again. She would not allow someone as pathetic and disgusting as Paulo to control her.

Except she couldn't prevent him.

He was too strong, and every time she struggled the hands grasping both her wrists, forcing her to press up against him, tightened.

'Let me go,' she cried desperately, and Paulo's eyes glittered.

'I want to hear you beg.'

'You will be the one begging. To the police.' The voice from the doorway was like the crack of a pistol. Paulo's grip slackened, and Meghan stumbled away, a trembling sob escaping from her before she could prevent it.

Alessandro stood in the doorway, his face white with rage. His whole body was tensed, coiled, ready to spring. He stared at Paulo with glittering eyes.

'I'm calling the police.'

'You can't prove anything,' Paulo said sullenly, but he looked nervous.

'You'll find,' Alessandro said, in a voice that was deadly in its quiet calm, 'that I can prove whatever I want. When the *carabiniere* arrive they will only need my word to see you rot in jail.'

'She wanted it—' Paulo began, but Alessandro cut him off with one sharply raised hand. Every movement was efficient, precise. Taut with suppressed emotion.

'Do not tell me what any woman wants. You should not presume to know.' He dropped his hand. 'Do you know who I am?'

Paulo's eyes shifted nervously, speculatively, to Meghan. 'No…'

'I am Alessandro di Agnio. This hostel will be shut down by morning.'

Paulo's face paled and his mouth dropped open. 'Di Agnio…but you can't do that! There are people staying here—I own it—'

Alessandro's face was implacable. 'It will be shut.' He snapped open his mobile phone. 'Now I am calling the police.'

'Signor di Agnio—' Meghan's voice came out in a choked whisper. She was still reeling from shock, her senses struggling to catch up. She dragged a breath into her lungs, ran a hand through her mussed hair. 'Please don't involve the police.'

Alessandro turned to look at her sharply. 'What? Are you in trouble with the police?'

Meghan almost laughed at his assumption. 'No, I'm not. I just don't want them involved—the time and hassle it will cause. There will be a report to give, no matter what your word means in Spoleto.'

He searched her face, as if looking for an answer to an unspoken question. Meghan said nothing.

'Please, let's just go.'

The silence was taut as Alessandro gazed at her. Paulo watched them from behind his desk, his expression one of a trapped mouse, scenting both freedom and danger.

Alessandro snapped his mobile shut. He didn't even glance at Paulo as he said, 'The hostel will close tonight. For good. I do not want to see you in Spoleto again.'

He walked out, and Meghan had no choice but to follow.

Outside his car idled at the kerb. It was not, as Meghan had half-expected, a sleek sports car, the embodiment of most Italian males' fantasies. It was instead a luxury executive model. Alessandro opened the door and stood aside for her to get into the front passenger seat. Every movement spoke of barely curbed impatience.

Meghan stared at him with wide eyes, suddenly realising the enormity of his presence. 'I thought you were going to send a driver.'

'I decided to come myself instead.'

Somehow this didn't surprise her. Alessandro di Agnio was a man who was in control. Always. Wordlessly she slipped inside.

The car was cool and the leather seat soft and inviting. Meghan leaned her head against the seat and closed her eyes. She didn't want to talk, and to her surprise and relief Alessandro remained silent as he got in and pulled away from the kerb, navigating Spoleto's evening traffic with superb confidence.

Meghan opened her eyes and stared blindly at the traffic—cars and mopeds weaving around each other on the narrow cobbled streets. As they broke free from the city and its traffic the Umbrian hills, cloaked in purple twilight, spread out before them, and the sounds of urban life were replaced by the quietness of meadow and field.

She snuck a peek at Alessandro's profile. The sharp, clean line of his tensed jaw, his powerful shoulders still encased in the charcoal-grey suit, his hands easily gripping the steering wheel—all radiated power. Confidence. Control.

Over her.

No. She couldn't let that happen.

Yet she felt as if the whole situation had started slipping away from her from the moment Alessandro had walked into the hostel.

No, she realised with a sigh, from the moment he'd asked her to waitress.

If she'd ever thought she was in control of this situation, of *him*, she'd been massively deluded.

She wasn't in control of anything—least of all her own spinning emotions.

Alessandro slotted her a sideways look out of steel-blue eyes, his lips tightening as his gaze swept over her.

'Are you all right?' he asked, and Meghan jerked back in surprise. 'What?'

Alessandro gestured to her wrist. A purple bruise was already starting to blossom on the tender skin. Meghan glanced at it and shrugged.

'I'm fine. I should have known Paulo would try something. I suppose I thought he was too much of a coward to live up to his filthy talk—'

'Why do you stay there?' Alessandro asked abruptly. 'There are plenty of hostels in Spoleto. Inexpensive hotels. You don't need to endure his filth.'

Meghan shrugged again. 'It was cheap and convenient,' she said, staring out of the window.

'Cheap I can believe. I'm surprised the building wasn't condemned. Convenient? No. What is convenient about being molested? Raped?'

'I wasn't raped.'

'You could've been.'

'Oh, am I supposed to thank you now?' Meghan asked, her voice sharp with sarcasm. 'I'm sorry, but I don't do the whole damsel in distress routine.'

'I've realised that.' The wry humour edging his voice took the wind straight out of her sails. Meghan sagged back against the seat.

'I'm sorry.'

'I'm not. I'm glad I was there in time.'

Meghan touched a finger to the bruise on her wrist. 'So am I,' she admitted quietly.

Alessandro watched her, his expression forbiddingly grim. 'At least no other women will suffer Paulo in this city,' he murmured, almost to himself, and Meghan lurched upright.

'Do you mean you were serious when you said you were shutting down the hostel?'

Alessandro looked affronted. 'Of course I was. Did you think I was bluffing?'

Definitely not, she conceded silently. 'But you can't just do that, can you? He said he owned the building.'

'He was lying. It's owned by a local businessman. I checked on it before I arrived.'

Of course, Meghan thought. In control. Again. 'If you don't own it, how can you make him close it down?' she pressed and Alessandro shrugged impatiently.

'Since you're American, you don't realise what the di Agnio name means in Italy— especially in Umbria.'

'You're powerful,' Meghan surmised, and he chuckled dryly.

'Most women find that attractive.'

'I don't.' She looked away. 'At least not when I'm on the wrong side of it.'

He glanced at her, curious. 'Do you think you are now?'

Was she? It was a question Meghan didn't want to ask herself. Certainly didn't want to answer. 'The thing about power,' she said after a moment, her voice brittle, 'is that it can easily be abused.'

'Agreed.' Alessandro's voice was terse. 'As in the case with

Paulo, don't you think?' he continued after a moment. 'At least you don't have to endure his attentions any more.'

'Then where am I supposed to sleep?'

'I can find you another hotel. Or you could sleep at my villa.'

Meghan reared back at his blatant offer. 'Thanks for the offer, but no thanks,' she replied sharply. 'I'd rather stay with Paulo.'

'Don't be absurd!'

'Don't think you can control me,' she fired back, fury starting to boil. Anger felt good. Clean.

'Control? Is that what you think this is about? I was protecting you back there!'

'I don't need protecting.'

He raised one eyebrow in scathing contempt. 'Really? It didn't look like it from where I was standing.'

Meghan gritted her teeth. 'I can handle Paulo.'

'You were obviously handling him when I came in,' Alessandro slung back at her. He shook his head in incredulous derision. 'Do you honestly think you could have controlled him?'

'I…' Meghan trailed off. *More than I can control you.*

The frightening thing was, she realised, she couldn't have controlled Paulo. She could have been—perhaps *would* have been—raped.

She bent over, suddenly feeling nauseous, the events of the evening catching up to her consciousness with sickening speed. 'I think I'm going to throw up.'

In one fluid movement Alessandro pulled the car over onto a stretch of grass and flung open his door. He went around to Meghan's door and yanked it open, ushering her out with one arm around her shoulders.

Meghan pushed away from him and stumbled into the grass where she retched helplessly. She'd never felt so low, so utterly humiliated, and that was saying something.

That was saying quite a lot.

She stood up, wiping her mouth, her hair falling about her face, while Alessandro watched impassively. He handed her a starched white linen handkerchief, and Meghan dabbed at her lips uselessly. She didn't want to sully it.

'It's to be used,' he said, his voice tart, and Meghan managed a weak smile.

'Sorry.'

'I'm the one who should be sorry. I should have remembered how shock can be delayed. Here.' He handed her a bottle of water and Meghan opened it, drinking gratefully.

'Thank you.'

'Are you ready?' he asked after a moment, and Meghan was suddenly aware of how dark it was. A car hadn't passed them since he'd pulled over, and nothing but meadows and clusters of elm trees surrounded them, the hills no more than shadowed mounds in the distance.

She could hear the whisper of the wind through the grass and the bare branches of the trees. She could hear her own breathing. They were very much alone.

'Yes, I'm ready.'

Alessandro opened the door for her, and Meghan slipped inside.

'I'm sorry about that,' she said again, once they were on the road, and Alessandro shrugged.

'Don't apologise.'

The car climbed higher into the Umbrian hills, and they spent the rest of the short drive in silence. Soon a high stone wall appeared, running parallel to the road.

Alessandro swung the car through an opened pair of ornate iron gates, and then up a long, twisting drive, the hills steep on either side.

Automated outdoor lights flashed on as the car approached the portico, and Meghan glimpsed a long, rambling villa of mellow stone and terracotta roof tiles. Several large pots lined the entrance, spilling a riot of begonias onto the tiled steps.

Alessandro stopped the engine and went around to open Meghan's door. She stepped out with murmured thanks. She smelled the fresh tang of pine, and the air was sharper, colder. She wrapped her arms around herself.

The front door opened, and a stout woman with a shiny black bun of hair, a spotless apron and a forbidding expression stood there. Meghan quailed under her heavy-browed, frowning gaze.

'Meghan, this is Ana,' Alessandro said, 'the housekeeper and guardian of Tre Querce.'

He spoke rapid Italian to Ana, too fast for Meghan's basic grasp of the language, and the woman gave an obviously disgruntled response.

'Ana will show you to a room,' he continued in English. 'You can freshen up and meet me in the lounge for dinner.'

Meghan turned to look at him in surprise. It almost sounded as if she were a guest rather than a waitress. 'Shouldn't I be in the kitchen?' she suggested hesitantly, and Alessandro gave her a knowing look.

'You are not the cook.'

'I'm a waitress,' she threw back at him, and his smile was far too understanding.

'Yes. I know. So you've told me.'

With jerky, unnatural steps Meghan followed Ana through a cool tiled hallway and up a wide staircase, her hand clutching the smooth wrought-iron banister.

Silently Ana led her down the upstairs hall, passing a row of closed doors, before ushering her into a bedroom spare and clean in its elemental luxury.

A large double bed dominated the room, the duvet and pillows encased in pure white linen. An oak dresser with iron fixtures stood against the wall, a strip of mirror above.

Disapproval radiated from every stiff line of the older woman, from her thinly pressed lips to the tightly clasped hands at her ample waist. Meghan couldn't blame her. What did she think she was? How had Alessandro explained her presence?

Why was she here?

Ana left without a word, and Meghan sank down on the bed, enjoying the softness, relieved to be alone even though her nerves felt as if they were jangling and jumping throughout her taut body.

Why was she here?

She looked in the mirror. Her hair had come undone, her face was pale and tense, her eyes as wide and frightened as a doe's.

Why was she here?

It wasn't for the money. She could have left Spoleto without it, Meghan acknowledged. Admittedly, it would come in handy, but still…

She didn't need it. Didn't even want it, perhaps.

She owed nothing to Alessandro di Agnio, nothing to anyone. Yet she'd agreed. Willingly.

What did that make her? Meghan wondered. To agree to come to a strange man's house, despite the desire in his eyes, the assessment of his gaze, the innuendo in his tone.

He knew what she was.

Everyone knows what you are.

The voices from her past clamoured inside her head—a knowing hiss, a contemptuous snarl.

Had she come here to prove Alessandro di Agnio wrong… or right?

Or to prove something to herself? And to Stephen.

She stood up, filled with a sudden restless energy, and moved to the French doors that looked out on the villa's gardens. She saw a swimming pool set in resplendent grounds, closed now, and beyond that terraced gardens, shadowed and bare.

Meghan shivered. The night air in the mountains was cool, and her simple white shirt didn't give her much warmth or protection. She took in a shaky breath and set about repairing herself.

A few minutes later, her hair neat and her face clean, she stepped outside. The villa was quiet. She couldn't hear the murmur of voices or the clank of pans from the kitchen. Nothing.

Carefully she walked down the front stairs. A single light flickered in the foyer, and a pair of double doors had been left slightly open, leading to what looked like the lounge.

Meghan's heart thudded in fresh anxiety and she wiped her palms along the sides of the skirt.

She supposed she should go in there, search out Alessandro and his weasely friend. Do what she was being paid to do. Pass out *hors d'oeuvres*. Make conversation, smile. Flirt.

Except, quite suddenly, she couldn't. The thought made her ill; she was sickened by the very fact that Alessandro had asked and she'd agreed.

She couldn't do this.

She *was* doing this.

She shook her head, biting her lips, and half slunk down the hallway in search of the kitchen.

Ana looked up in frowning surprise as Meghan entered the spacious room. Gleaming chrome appliances and granite worktops gave way to a breakfast nook and more French doors that led out to the terrace and swimming pool. Although it was in darkness, Meghan could imagine the stunning view of hills Tre Querce possessed.

'I'm here to help,' she began awkwardly in Italian. 'I mean…to serve. You know?'

Ana stared at her. A pot bubbled on the stove, emitting a wonderful spicy scent. A green salad was in the process of being made on the worktop, next to fat red tomatoes and yellow peppers in a basket.

'Signor di Agnio doesn't want you here,' Ana said after a moment, choosing her words with care. 'He wants you in the lounge. Now.'

Meghan shook her head. Her nerves were taut as wire, threatening to snap. She couldn't face it…them.

'Perhaps,' she finally said, speaking slowly as she searched for the right words. 'But I came here to serve the food, and this is where the food is.'

'No.' Ana shook her head.

Meghan clenched her fists at her sides but kept her smile in place. 'Why don't I just put an apron on?' she suggested, and, spying one hanging on a hook by the door, slipped it on before Ana could protest.

The housekeeper shrugged, and turned away with a grunt.

Meghan scanned the worktop, wishing she could make herself useful. She wondered about the men waiting for her. What did they really expect? Would Alessandro come and find her?

She shivered. It was stupid to have come here, to have thought she could exorcise her personal demons by seeing this little arrangement through. She didn't have the strength, the power.

The control.

All she wanted to do now was run away. Hide. But where?

She suddenly appreciated how isolated Villa Tre Querce was, how isolated *she* was.

How alone.

Vulnerable.

'I thought you'd be hiding in here.'

She turned to see Alessandro standing in the kitchen doorway, one shoulder leaning against the frame. He'd changed out of his suit and now wore a casual white button-down shirt, open at the neck to expose the tanned column of his throat. He wore faded jeans with a leather belt, casual yet expensive, and fitting him far too wonderfully.

It was not, Meghan thought, an outfit a man wore to a business dinner. He looked too relaxed, too comfortable in his own skin for her liking. He looked ready to be entertained, amused, enjoyed.

She wanted business suits, papers and briefcases, laptops and mobiles. A business dinner, with both men too involved in their work to spare her a glance.

Except that was not how it was going to be…how Alessandro would let it be. She could tell that right now, in the way his lips curled upwards in a predatory smile, his eyes taking in her appearance, resting on her face with a flare of hunger, desire.

She was not making that up, she knew, nor the answering flicker in her own core.

She swallowed. 'Where else would I be? And I'm not hiding.'

'Of course not.' Humour lurked in those steely eyes, in the twitching of his moulded lips. He took a step into the kitchen. 'I thought I told you to meet me in the lounge.'

'Is your dinner companion in there?' She hated the fact that her voice wavered. 'Has he arrived already?'

'You'll see.' He twitched the apron from around her neck, balling it in his fist before tossing it aside. 'You don't need that.'

One more piece of her armour taken away. One more layer stripped bare.

'I didn't want to get my uniform dirty.'

He raised one eyebrow. 'Uniform?' he asked with obvious scepticism, before turning to leave the kitchen, clearly expecting her to follow. And, wordlessly, she did.

She followed him to the lounge, its double doors opening to a room scattered with comfortable sofas upholstered in varying shades of cream. The few pieces of artwork on the walls were vivid splashes of colour, still-lifes of flowers, scenes of Umbria in bold strokes, that made Meghan pause to admire their sheer vivacity.

Then she looked around. The room was empty.

'Where is your guest…?' she began, but something in Alessandro's satisfied look as he stood in the doorway made the question die on her lips. She had a bad feeling about this.

'*You* are my guest, Meghan,' he said softly. 'There is no one else.'

CHAPTER THREE

'No.' MEGHAN said the first word that came to mind, desperately wanting it to be true. 'No, no, no.'

'Yes.' Alessandro smiled. He seemed pleased. Far too pleased. As if he'd given her a gift, a pleasant surprise. A *treat*.

'You hired me to be a waitress,' Meghan pointed out in what she hoped was a reasonable tone. 'For a dinner party. That's why I'm here.'

'I hired you,' he agreed, 'but, as you remember, it was for a quiet dinner for two. There are two of us in this room right now.'

His words drenched her in icy shock. Meghan stared incredulously. 'You never even intended for someone else to come? What about the man you ate lunch with?'

Alessandro's expression hardened. 'He has other plans for the evening. He is a business acquaintance, nothing more.'

'And what am I?' Her voice rose shrilly, and she pressed a fist to her lips. She moved around the room restlessly, seeking escape, but there was none. She didn't have a car. She didn't even know where the villa was. She had no place to go in Spoleto. And Alessandro was blocking the door.

She'd walked straight into a trap. She'd agreed to it willingly. Who wouldn't think she deserved this, that she wanted this? Disgust roiled through her, washed over in sickening waves. Terror followed on its heels. She closed her eyes, struggling for composure. Control.

She opened them, saw Alessandro regarding her with a

mixture of curiosity and compassion. She took a deep, shuddering breath. There was always Ana in the kitchen. She could handle this. She had to handle this.

'Whatever you thought about me, it's wrong. I don't want to be here. I don't want to have dinner with you. Take me back to Spoleto now or I'll press charges.'

Alessandro raised his eyebrows, taking in her words with a thoughtful nod. 'You're scared,' he said after a moment.

Meghan laughed shrilly. 'Of course I'm scared! A strange man—a powerful man—has trapped me in his house, alone! Under false pretences! Now, let me go.'

He continued watching her, his expression assessing but not without compassion. Meghan didn't care. Couldn't think. She paced the room, caged and desperate.

'Why weren't you frightened,' he asked after a moment, 'when you believed I'd hired you to serve my lunch guest and me? Then there would have been two men here with you. Shouldn't that have been twice as alarming?'

Meghan whirled around and glared at him, fear replaced momentarily by anger. 'It was a *business* arrangement.'

He shrugged. 'Then consider this such an arrangement as well. I'll pay you the same rates. I just want to have dinner with you.'

'I don't want to be paid!' she snapped. 'I'm not a whore!'

Alessandro stilled, his expression chilling. 'I don't remember calling you that.'

She closed her eyes, pressed a hand to her chest as if she could still the frantic racing of her heart. 'If you wanted to have dinner with me,' she said after a few seconds of silence, her breathing ragged, uneven, 'then there are more normal ways to have gone about it. You could have asked me straight out. It's called a date.'

'Admittedly I've used unconventional means.' He shrugged, unperturbed. 'I had to.'

'Oh? And why is that?'

'I'm a powerful man, Meghan. You remember that power can be abused? It works both ways.' He smiled softly. 'Picture this. A man is charmed by a pretty young waitress when he sees her in a restaurant. He likes her smile, and the way her eyes remind him of sunlight. He wants to get to know her better, but he also understands that his position and wealth either frighten women off or attract the wrong kind. So he makes up a little pretence to bring this woman he desires to his house. Nothing far-fetched, nothing sordid. And when she arrives, he intends to surprise her with a quiet, romantic dinner. A chance to know her, and for her to know him. And then he drives her home.'

Meghan stared at him, arrested. Her lips parted, but no words came out. Her mind whirled, thoughts twisting away before she could snatch them, drag them to clarity. 'It wasn't like that.'

'Wasn't it?' Alessandro's quiet, sad little smile made her heart ache with regret and wonder.

It wasn't like that.

She shook her head. She couldn't believe. Couldn't let herself. 'You can romance it up all you want now, because you think I want to hear those silly pretty words. But you as good as admitted what you really want…what you really think of me. We both know that.'

'What I want to know,' Alessandro said softly, 'is why you think so little of yourself.'

'I don't,' Meghan snapped—a matter of instinct, yet her words sounded hollow. She turned away. 'Why can't you just take me home?'

'Because I don't want to.' Alessandro sat in an armchair, ivory silk striped with gold, his legs elegantly crossed, his body relaxed. 'Where do you come from?' he asked pleasantly. 'Why have you been travelling around Europe? Waitressing to pay your way, I presume?'

'Stop it.' She shook her head. 'This is a farce. I'm not sitting here talking with you, discussing my life with you.'

'It would perhaps make things more pleasant.'

'I don't *want* things to be pleasant,' she snapped. 'I want to leave here. Now.'

'Then answer my questions. Ask some of your own. It's called making conversation, you know.'

'All right.' She dropped her hands, took a deep breath. 'Here's a question…Alessandro. If I have dinner with you, will you drive me back to Spoleto afterwards?'

'If that's what you want.' The implication was obvious. Dinner would be enough to make her change her mind. He smiled; it felt like a caress. 'I like the way you say my name.'

Meghan stared at him, watched as the heat in his eyes flared, turning them from steely-blue to indigo, and she wondered helplessly, hopelessly, if dinner would indeed be enough.

'You do not need to be frightened,' Alessandro said quietly. 'That was never my intention. You can trust me.'

'You told me not to,' Meghan snapped, and Alessandro's expression hardened for a moment.

'I told you there was no reason to. Now there is.'

'Oh, and what is that?'

He smiled, although his eyes remained flinty. 'Because I said so.'

She opened her mouth to utter some scathing reply, the words not yet formed in her head, but then something left her. Her energy, perhaps, or at least her self-righteousness. Her ability to continue a verbal battle with this impossible iron-willed man. And her fear.

She sank onto a cream leather sofa and leaned her head against its soft back. 'You speak English very well,' she said after a moment.

'Thank you. I should. I spent most of my boyhood in England.'

'Why?'

'I went to boarding school at seven, in Winchester,' he explained. 'All of my siblings did.'

'You have brothers and sisters?'

'One sister.' He opened his mouth to speak, and then shut it abruptly. Meghan almost asked what he'd been going to say, but the shuttered look in his eyes made her realise that topic was now off limits. All of his siblings had gone to boarding school, yet he only had one sister? Something didn't make sense.

'Who are the di Agnios, anyway?' she asked. 'Something big, obviously, but what do you do?' She sat up straight, the thought of the Mafia suddenly shooting through her. Surely not…

'We're entrepreneurs.' The rich laughter lacing his words showed he knew exactly where her train of thought had led her.

'Primarily jewellery, but we've branched into property, finance—
a bit of everything really.'

'Di Agnio…' With a jolt Meghan remembered passing boutiques of that name, shops with locked doors and luxurious velvet
cases in their display windows. As far as jewellery went, it was
strictly top-shelf. 'It's a family business?'

'Yes. I am the CEO.'

Well. She sat back again, realising sickly the kind of life he
must lead—so different from hers. It would be nice, to have that
kind of wealth, power, control. Safety.

She took a deep breath, let it out. 'All right, then. Let's have
dinner.'

Alessandro grinned, and the effect was quite devastating.
Meghan drew in a shaky uneven breath at the sight of him, the
harsh lines of his face relaxed into laughter, the whiteness of his
smile contrasting with his tanned skin and navy eyes, now
glinting with humour.

When Alessandro di Agnio frowned he was forbidding. In
repose he was handsome, even beautiful. But when he smiled
Meghan wanted to walk straight into his arms.

And that was a place she could not go.

'Then you take me home,' she added, and he nodded.

'Of course. If you wish.'

'I will wish it,' Meghan snapped, and he merely chuckled.

Damn him. Damn his arrogance, and damn him for being
right. Already she felt herself wondering, weakening.

Wanting.

A smile played about his mouth as he held out his hand.
'Shall we?'

She still had things to prove. She would still walk away with
her dignity, her pride, her heart.

Her heart? The last thought, slipping treacherously through
her numb brain, made Meghan almost gasp in surprise.

There was no way her heart was involved with this man.

'All right,' she agreed tonelessly.

She walked past him, towards the kitchen, but Alessandro
pulled her back gently, his hand warm and firm on her elbow.

'Wrong way, *gattina*.'

Meghan jerked. 'What did you just call me?'

His lips quirked in a smile. '*Gattina*. It means kitten.'

'I don't like nicknames.'

'It was meant to be an endearment.'

'As in sex kitten?' she said contemptuously, and Alessandro shook his head.

'I was thinking more of an actual kitten, baring her tiny, tender claws.' He trailed his fingers from her elbow to her hand, stroking the tender palm, electrifying her skin with the lightest of touches. He raised her palm to his lips, gave it the barest brush of a kiss. A promise. Mesmerised, Meghan could only watch. And feel.

This was a bad, bad idea.

'This way,' Alessandro said, sounding faintly amused, and gestured to the other set of double doors leading into the foyer.

Numbly she followed Alessandro through the foyer and into a mahogany panelled dining room. Candles were lit, casting flickering shadows on the dark walls and tiled floor.

The green salad she'd seen earlier in the kitchen was now placed on an imposing table, one corner set intimately for two.

Meghan swallowed, and the gulping noise was loud in the room, where the only sound was the guttering of flame.

Alessandro laughed softly. 'Come here. I don't bite.'

Reluctantly Meghan moved towards him on wooden legs. 'Are you trying to seduce me?' she whispered. *Because it just might be working.*

'No. When I seduce you, you'll know.'

The languorous promise in these words sent both panic and anticipation fizzing through her in dangerous bubbles. 'I don't want to be seduced,' Meghan said, and knew how feeble her voice sounded.

'You don't want to be hurt,' Alessandro corrected. 'There's a difference.'

She lifted her chin. 'Is there?'

'I believe with me there is.' His voice, though gentle, allowed no argument. 'Now enough about seduction. Let us turn our attention to eating, which in Italy is just as sensual an art.'

Meghan sat at the table, watched as Alessandro poured wine from the bottle chilling in a bucket and served her a generous portion of salad bursting with tomatoes, basil and mozzarella.

'This looks delicious—thank you,' she murmured, and Alessandro smiled, a wicked, teasing glint in his eye.

'Is there anything else I may get for you? Ana will bring the antipasti later.'

With a start, Meghan realised Alessandro was the one serving her. Everything was mixed up tonight. She moved as if to get up, although she wasn't sure what she intended to do. Pour the water? Run to the kitchen? Curtsey?

He shook his head. 'The only thing I want you to do now, Meghan, is to enjoy.'

She opened her mouth to issue a sharp retort, the stinging reply that had become her habit, her defence. Alessandro watched her with an expectant little half-smile on his face, and Meghan hesitated.

She'd spent the last six months holding herself apart—apart from men, from pleasure, from life. Sometimes it felt as if it was the only way to get through each day—and, more importantly, to get back the dignity and self-respect she'd lost in Stanton Springs, Iowa.

Yet now, for one evening, even just one moment, she wanted to let go. Not completely, not out of control, because she knew she wasn't ready for that.

She just wanted to enjoy…something.

Food.

She sat back in her chair, managing a rather stiff-lipped smile. 'All right.' She took a bite of salad, felt the burst of tomato on her tongue. It felt different. Sweeter. The room seemed different. More vivid. And she felt different. More alive.

Alessandro watched her with an indulgent, affectionate smile, and Meghan took a sip of wine, the taste sharp and tangy.

Her senses were heightened to the feel of the cool, smooth wine glass in her fingers, the cotton shirt against her arms, her breasts. She saw Alessandro's languorous gaze, the way he watched her move, sleepily, yet with a flared awareness in his eyes that thrilled her.

This was so dangerous.

She knew Alessandro would not abuse her. He wouldn't spread malicious lies or treat her with cruel contempt.

But he would hurt her. Meghan put her wine glass down with an unsteady clatter. Yes, he would hurt her if she let him…if she gave him her heart.

Alessandro watched Meghan eat with a pleasure he normally reserved for more physical activities. He enjoyed seeing the way her eyes widened, the slow smile that spread over her features at the simplest of pleasures.

He'd no doubt that she was unaware of how sensual, how desirable she looked simply eating a tomato. She was, he was beginning to realise, quite unaware of her effect on him.

If only he was as unaware. The desire—the need—for her pulsed through him, an ache, a hunger that made him want. Yearn. He didn't like it. He didn't *want* to want anything—certainly not a woman from nowhere who looked at him with her heart in her eyes, shadowed by both fear and desire.

She was the last thing he needed.

Yet he wanted her.

And she wanted him. She was denying it with nearly every fibre of her being, but he saw the way she looked at him, the way her eyes flared and her lips parted.

She was afraid. The realisation humbled him. He would have to tread carefully.

Still, it was only a matter of time.

The thought pleased him, yet as he cradled his wine glass between his palms he felt a ripple of unease. Guilt.

He wasn't in the habit of buying women. And certainly not of lying to them. Since taking over Di Agnio Enterprises two years ago Alessandro had become known for his no-nonsense demeanour, as well as the brutal honesty he favoured with clients and friends alike.

Two years ago, on a chilly spring evening much like this one, he'd put away the trappings of a different life, the sweet-talking lies that had smoothed the already slippery path to pleasure.

He'd put them away for ever, even if some still wondered. Doubted.

Even if he did.

He lived for his work now, for seeing Di Agnio Enterprises rise in stature and earnings, for seeing his family name respected once more.

He did not live for pleasure.

He no longer cared about desire.

So why had he lured—and he knew that truly was the word for it—Meghan to his villa?

For seduction?

The thought made him frown, and he saw Meghan's gaze flicker uneasily over his countenance. She was as attuned to the variations of his mood as he was to hers.

He smiled. 'Have some pasta.' Ana had brought in the pasta dish a few moments earlier, her lips pressed in a thin line of disapproval, although she'd restrained herself from saying anything.

Alessandro had watched Meghan flush and look down at her plate, clearly embarrassed.

It was his fault she felt humiliated. He'd never meant her to feel so shamed, yet he knew he'd assumed things of her…things that he still wasn't sure were true or not.

Had he brought her here simply for pleasure?

For sex?

Was that what he wanted? Was that the kind of man he was…still?

He didn't know. Didn't know what to think of her, of himself. He took a sip of wine. When he'd seen her at Angelo's she'd seemed like any other of the many women he knew. Women who were free and easy with their favours, their bodies. There was no shame in that these days, although Alessandro recognised in himself a deep-seated disapproval of the freedom in women which he himself had enjoyed.

You didn't marry women like that.

He wouldn't marry a woman like that.

But was Meghan that kind of woman? He'd assumed it, and strangely *she* seemed to have assumed it.

But was it true?

And why had he brought her here?

Frowning again, Alessandro realised he couldn't answer those questions. Not yet. Which meant Meghan had to stay a bit longer. Until he discovered why he'd brought her here.

Until he discovered why he needed her.

CHAPTER FOUR

MEGHAN felt as if she were in a daze. Dazed by food, by wine, by pleasure. Drugged by her own senses and the novelty of letting herself feel…everything.

After their initial charged confrontation, Meghan found herself relaxing and enjoying the simple pleasure of conversation. She told Alessandro how she'd learnt Italian, and about some of her travels; he shared his experiences in the same places.

Meghan had to smile at the differences. She'd been slumming it with hostels and third-class train fares, while Alessandro travelled around Europe in a company jet, staying in five-star accommodation with a fresh magnum of champagne in every room.

And yet…they'd both found Notre Dame ostentatious, and fallen in love with the history of Père Lachaise, the famous Parisian cemetery. They'd both bypassed Brussels for Bruges, loving the historic city, with its church spires and cobbled streets.

Some things, Meghan thought, rose above money and status.

She found herself sneaking looks at him while he ate, watching the long, clean column of his throat as he sipped his wine, noticing the way his faded jeans moulded to his body as he sat, relaxed and half sprawled, in his chair. Watching his moods chase the colours in his eyes from navy to steel to indigo, a rainbow of blues.

Every movement, every look, every softly spoken word or dry chuckle, created a yearning in her soul—almost made her lean towards him, craving contact. Touch.

She wanted him.

Despite what he'd thought, despite what he still expected. Despite the danger.

The realisation of her own need stunned her. She'd never expected to feel the flooding, weakening sensation of desire again. Never expected to want a man, to want to take pleasure as well as to give it.

Her mind spun as she considered this, the novelty of reawakening sensation, need. It was intoxicating. It was scary.

It was desire.

The shame that followed on its heels like a mocking shadow, the fear she tasted in her mouth, were more familiar.

Meghan took a sip of wine, but it could have been water. A pulse beat in her throat, and despite the liquid her mouth was dry. She put the glass down carefully. 'I think I've had enough.'

Alessandro raised his eyebrows, waiting, sensing the *double entendre*.

'It's late,' she continued stiltedly. 'I should go.'

'Go where?'

'You could drive me back to Spoleto.' Even as she said it, Meghan knew it wasn't going to happen. Didn't want it to happen.

Alessandro smiled. 'I could.'

They were both silent. Meghan stared at her plate, at the remains of one of the most delicious meals she'd ever had. Silence thrummed between them—heavy, oppressive, expectant.

She looked up, her eyes wide, luminous. 'What happens now?' she asked, her voice little more than a whisper.

Alessandro regarded her steadily. 'What do you want to happen now?'

'I…' She licked her dry lips, resisting the urge to gulp down the rest of her wine. 'I…I don't know.' The enormity of this admission caused a humiliating flush to steal across her cheeks. She was as good as saying she wanted him.

And she *did* want him. Perhaps she even wanted him to know. She stared at him now, openly, hungrily, wondering how hard and broad his chest would feel against her own womanly softness, how his mouth would feel on hers, covering it, possessing it, how his hands would stroke and touch her body.

Wondering how sensual, how tender he would be.

Wondering how she would respond.

She wanted to know, and she was terrified.

Alessandro reached across the table to cover her hand with his own. 'Meghan, you may sleep in the spare bedroom. There need be nothing between us tonight.'

She was far too conscious of the heavy warmth of his hand on hers, the way it made tiny shocks ripple all the way up her arm. The strength of it, the security, the desire.

Tonight, she thought. The meaning was obvious. There would be another night, and perhaps another, and, if she were lucky, a few more.

And what then?

Could she really sell herself so cheaply simply for desire's sake? Shame scorched her face, her soul.

'Tomorrow I leave,' she reminded him, although her words sounded hollow. 'Unless you plan to keep me here until… until…' She trailed off, courage deserting her.

Humour glinted in Alessandro's eyes. 'Maybe I do.'

'What if I say no?' Meghan demanded shakily. 'Are you going to force me?'

Alessandro swore softly. 'Do you think that is the kind of man I am? To force a woman? What has happened to you to think such things?' His eyes narrowed, though his voice was soft. 'Who was the man who hurt you, Meghan?'

The question echoed numbly through her, through the empty, scarred places inside. *The man who hurt you.* She stared down at her plate, the colours blurring into a sorrowful rainbow, her thoughts hopelessly scattered.

'You don't have to tell me if you don't want to,' Alessandro said quietly. 'But I think that it would help me to understand.'

Meghan forced herself to look up, blinking through a haze of devastated emotion and memory. 'What is there to understand?'

'Why you're so suspicious. Afraid. Ashamed.'

'I'm not!'

Alessandro simply inclined his head.

'Let's just say I'm coming out of a bad relationship,' she

finally managed. Meghan bit her lip, took in a shuddering breath. She felt cold, empty, even though the waves of emotion Alessandro had caused to crash through her still lapped at her nerves, her senses. 'Look, I'm suspicious, and I don't know what kind of man you are. You tricked me into coming here, after all.'

Alessandro's face was harsh in its sincerity. 'I promise you, I won't hurt you.'

'You might not mean to,' Meghan muttered.

His face blanked for a second, and he inclined his head in silent, brutal acknowledgement. Meghan looked down.

Alessandro leaned forward, rested a hand on her arm. His fingers were gentle, caressing, yet they burned. Made her ache, made her want to know how they would feel on her skin. All over her skin.

Meghan stared at his hand, the clean strength of it on her own pale fingers, as he murmured, 'Stay, Meghan. Spend the night— alone—and we can have the day tomorrow. To enjoy. Be tourists, if you like.'

'And see what happens?'

'Why must you think of the future? Let us just enjoy each other's company. It brings me pleasure to be with you, to look at you. Do you not feel the same?'

His voice was a caress, and Meghan found herself nodding, helpless. 'Yes…'

'Then let us enjoy it,' Alessandro said simply. 'Enjoy each other. And leave it at that.' He removed his hand, and Meghan felt bereft. Stupid to want his touch. Foolish to crave it when she knew it could only lead to hurt. Pain and shame.

'And then I leave,' she stipulated.

Alessandro shrugged. 'If that is your desire.'

'It is.'

'Very well.' He gazed at her, one hand curled around the stem of his wine glass, his eyes glittering.

'I'll sleep in the spare bedroom,' she said after a moment. He smiled and nodded.

'You know where it is? I can show you, if you like.'

'N-no,' she stammered. 'That's not necessary.'

He chuckled, enjoying her discomfiture. 'As you wish.'

Meghan lifted her chin. 'And I'll lock the door,' she added with her last mustered spirit, and for a moment Alessandro looked almost hurt.

'I'll take your word for it,' he said quietly.

The lights had been dimmed in her bedroom, the covers turned back. Meghan saw that a hot water bottle had been thoughtfully placed between the smooth cotton sheets and a nightgown—also cotton, and surprisingly modest—had been laid out on a chair.

She felt like a treasured guest. A captive guest. Yet she had chosen these bonds. She couldn't blame Alessandro any more.

This was her choice.

This was her desire.

Her hand hovered over the lock. She knew Alessandro would not try to come in; even to suggest it had been an insult. *She* was in control now.

Yet the fear she'd lived with for six long months was too deeply ingrained into her soul, her spirit. Biting her lip, Meghan turned the key, heard the audible click, and somehow knew Alessandro had heard it as well.

Too tired to think any more, to wonder what Alessandro intended to do or how she might respond, she changed and slipped into bed. Sleep blessedly came within a few minutes.

When she woke, sunlight was filtering through the linen curtains and casting shifting patterns on the floor.

Her eyes reminded him of sunlight.

Gilded words, or the truth? Meghan sighed and leaned back against the pillows. Her experience with Stephen had caused her to question everything that came out of a man's mouth, to think the worst of every admiring look he might give.

To doubt and to fear.

When would it stop? Meghan wondered. When would *she* stop? Yesterday morning she couldn't have imagined ever wanting a man again. She certainly couldn't have imagined the desire she would feel, as potent as a drug, as heady as new wine.

Desire.

Meghan closed her eyes. That was all it was. Desire. Sex. Not love.

Never love.

She could not, absolutely could not, fall in love with Alessandro di Agnio.

Love was dangerous. Love made you a fool and a victim.

Meghan was never going to fall in love again.

So, she thought with a rueful smile, all she needed to do was enjoy this day and make sure not to fall in love with Alessandro. Tonight she would leave Spoleto, and his life, for ever.

The thought made her wince. She wasn't ready to leave. How ridiculous, when only twelve hours ago she'd shrilly demanded her release.

Impatient with the thoughts chasing circles in her head, she threw off the covers. She would enjoy the day. Then she would say goodbye.

That was simply how it had to be.

A light knock sounded at the door, and Meghan whirled in surprise. 'Who is it?' she asked carefully, in Italian.

'Ana, *signorina*. I've brought you some clothes.'

'Just a moment…' Meghan hurried to the door and turned the key. 'Come in.'

The housekeeper bustled in, her expression ominously neutral as she placed a bundle of clothes on top of the bureau. 'Signor di Agnio thought you might wish for a change of clothes.'

'That was thoughtful of him.'

Ana inclined her head in what could have been a nod or a shrug. Her expression remained bland as she waited for Meghan's dismissal.

'Where did they come from?' Meghan asked, her curiosity piqued.

'The clothes?' Ana's mouth thinned in disapproval. 'They belong to Signor di Agnio's wife.'

'*What*?' Meghan stared at the housekeeper, her eyes wide with shock. Alessandro was *married*? 'His wife?' she repeated.

Ana inclined her head. 'Paula di Agnio. She lives in Rome.'

Married. Somehow Alessandro had forgotten to mention that little detail. Did he think it wasn't important? That she wouldn't care?

Meghan closed her eyes. *Liar*. She'd begun to believe Alessandro was different, that even if he only wanted sex at least he was honest about it.

He was a liar, like all the rest.

Like Stephen.

And she'd fallen for it, begun to believe his tender little act, because her heart and body still cried out for understanding, compassion.

Love.

No. Not that. Not that any more. Ever.

'Is there anything else you need, *signorina*?' Ana asked diffidently. 'There are toiletries in the bathroom. A toothbrush, deodorant—whatever you require.'

Meghan opened her eyes, blinking the room back into focus from behind the thick haze of tears that had come unbidden. 'Thank you.' Her voice came out rusty, and she cleared her throat. 'I'll be down shortly. Thank you for everything.'

Ana nodded, her expression still diffident, and left the room.

Meghan stared at the bundle of clothes. His wife's clothes. Did he actually think she would wear them? Could he judge her any lower?

Her mind still reeling from the housekeeper's unexpected news, Meghan dressed in her outfit from the previous night with numb, blunt fingers.

In the luxuriously appointed bathroom she found all the necessary toiletries, and was glad to wash her face and brush her teeth. As she stepped into the hallway she felt protected again, hardened enough to do battle.

To find out just what Alessandro had been keeping from her.

Her resolve wavered slightly when she stepped into the lounge and saw him waiting there. He turned when he saw her, and the spontaneous smile of affection and admiration made Meghan's heart stumble. Then his expression darkened.

'Why are you wearing your clothes from last night? Your…uniform?'

'Ana told me where the other clothes came from,' Meghan replied, her voice choked.

'Oh?' Alessandro's expression became guarded, a shutter closing over his eyes, turning them almost black, and Meghan's heart sank.

'Why didn't you tell me you were married?'

'*What*?' He stared at her incredulously, before suddenly laughing aloud, the sound pure and clean, filling the room. 'She told you that?'

'She said the clothes belonged to Signor di Agnio's wife.'

'Ah.' He nodded slowly, the laughter gone, not even an echo. 'Well, they do—but to a different Signor di Agnio's wife.'

Meghan stared at him in confusion. 'Who? Your father's?'

'My father is dead.' He bit out the words. 'The Signor di Agnio Ana was referring to is my brother. He was married to my sister-in-law, Paula.'

'Was?' she repeated uncertainly. 'Are they divorced?'

'No, my brother is also dead.' He paused, his eyes like iron as Meghan stared at him, unsure how to respond. 'This was his villa,' Alessandro continued. 'I use it for business purposes now.'

'Oh.' Meghan felt a blush crawl up her throat. 'I thought…'

'I know what you thought, *gattina*.' Amusement glittered in his cool eyes. 'You can sheath your little claws, because now you know Ana was just making trouble.'

'Why would she—?'

He cut her off swiftly, with a chuckle and a shake of his head. '*Da tutti i san*—you insist on thinking the worst of me at every turn! Married! What next?'

'I couldn't help it,' Meghan mumbled. 'Maybe I misunderstood the Italian…'

'Oh, really?' The look he gave her was far too perceptive. 'Tell me, this relationship you were in? Was the man married?'

Meghan's mouth was dry, her lips numb. 'I don't want to talk about it,' she finally managed.

He shrugged. 'Whoever he was, he has a lot to answer for. Now, I'm starving, and there is a full day before us. One without arguments, I hope. Why don't you get changed into the clothes that do not belong to my wife—a woman who does not yet exist—and meet me in the kitchen?'

The humour lighting his eyes made Meghan smile ruefully. Somehow Alessandro had dispelled the tension that had thrummed between them. She felt light, almost happy.

'All right,' she agreed, and hurried upstairs.

Back in the bedroom, Meghan tugged on a pair of designer jeans, a bit loose in the waist, but otherwise fitting her well, and a black cashmere turtleneck sweater. A leather belt fitted snugly around her hips, and she pulled her hair back with a clip.

She glanced in the mirror and was surprised to see her cheeks flushed, her eyes sparkling.

She looked like a woman on the brink of adventure. A woman desired.

Instead of the usual plunging fear in her belly at this thought, Meghan felt a warm tingling. A glow.

Smiling to herself, she headed down to the kitchen.

Thankfully Ana had disappeared, leaving them alone at the round pine table set in a comfortable nook overlooking the pool, still covered, and the terrace set with loungers and pots of flowers.

'It must be beautiful here in the summer,' Meghan said a bit wistfully, and Alessandro slotted her a thoughtful glance.

'It is. Now, eat.'

The food set before them was a feast. Meghan hadn't been overly fond of the Italian breakfasts she'd encountered so far, but set before her now was an array of mouthwatering dishes.

One eyebrow raised, Alessandro handed her a steaming bowl of eggs scrambled with mozzarella and basil. 'I prefer the full English breakfasts I had at school—done the Italian way, of course.'

'Of course.' Meghan helped herself to eggs, fresh orange juice, and toast with apricot preserve. 'Ana is a good cook,' she said, after the first few delicious mouthfuls.

'Who said Ana made it?' Alessandro challenged, and Meghan stared in surprise.

'You didn't…?'

'No, unfortunately you're right. I can't cook—more's the pity.' The smile tugging at Alessandro's mouth turned into a fully-fledged grin that made Meghan's answering smile die on her lips. Her throat was dry, her heart hammering.

She could not resist this man. Not when he smiled like that, his eyes warm, full of laughter, yet with heat just below the surface, simmering. Ready to blaze.

Meghan swallowed a mouthful of eggs and took a sip of orange juice, grateful to avoid Alessandro's gaze. He continued eating, and the rest of their breakfast passed with blessed uneventfulness.

'So,' Alessandro said a short while later, as he poured her a second cup of coffee, 'today I want to show you Umbria.'

'Which part?' Meghan asked, picking up the thick ceramic mug. The coffee was strong and smelled like heaven. She took a sip. 'I've seen Spoleto, of course, and Assisi.'

'We can take a driving tour. There are many beautiful sights in Umbria. Villages, mountains. Spoleto is lovely, but there are other hidden treasures. Treasures I want to show you.'

Meghan's hands tightened around her cup. She couldn't resist imagining a day out with him, basking in the spring sunshine, revelling in the mountain breeze. Holding hands, laughing over silly jokes. A proper date. Something normal people did. People who liked each other, who fell in love.

'It sounds lovely.' She hesitated, the escape clause she'd provided herself with still looming, a hopeless distraction. 'I still need to get my things.' Just thinking of Paulo, the hostel, even her haversack, seemed unreal. A different lifetime.

'I've sent for your things,' Alessandro replied with a dismissive shrug. 'They'll be in your room by this afternoon.'

Meghan put down her coffee cup with a clatter. 'You had no right—'

'Why must it be about rights? I did what was most convenient.'

'Convenient for *you*!'

Alessandro's eyes glittered. 'Are you going to fight me on every point? Or shall we enjoy the day together?'

Meghan sagged. He was right. She couldn't seem to get out of the battle stance—ready to doubt, to question, to attack. 'I'm sorry. That was…thoughtful of you.'

'Wasn't it?' He beamed at her. 'You're learning.'

Meghan gritted her teeth. 'Don't push it.'

Alessandro chuckled. 'I won't. I know well enough I need to take my time with you.'

It was a beautiful morning—perfect for driving through sun-touched hills—the sky a deep, pure blue, studded with fleecy clouds. The wind was chilly but the sun was warm, and Alessandro rolled down the windows so the breeze ruffled their hair as he drove down the steep, winding road away from Villa Tre Querce.

'I thought you'd be the kind of man to have a convertible,' Meghan admitted as they drove.

He glanced at her, his expression unreadable. 'I'm not quite sure what that says about your opinion of me. But I did have a convertible once.'

'What happened?' Meghan teased. 'You crashed it?'

'As a matter of fact, I did,' he replied flatly, staring straight ahead. Meghan opened her mouth to mumble some kind of apology, but the set of Alessandro's jaw made her close it again.

The day was too beautiful to dwell on anything unpleasant, and Meghan revelled in the sensual pleasure of wind and sun.

They drove for nearly an hour on twisting, narrow roads, up hills and through valleys, villages huddled on the distant mountains, the spire of a church's tower silhouetted against an azure sky.

At the base of a particularly steep hill Alessandro pulled the car over and killed the engine.

'Now we walk.'

'Walk?' Meghan held one hand over her eyes to shade them from the sun as she squinted up at road ahead of them, twisting steeply upwards into nowhere. 'What's up there?'

'You'll see.'

She took his hand, warm, dry, strong, liking the way his hand encased hers.

'Close your eyes.'

'What?' She jerked in surprise, withdrawing her hand by instinct, but Alessandro held onto it. His thumb caressed her palm, and Meghan suppressed a shiver, affected by the simple touch. 'Why should I close my eyes?' she asked.

'Just do it.' Alessandro paused, his eyes dark, intent. 'Please. Trust me.'

Trust him? Every instinct in her rebelled. She didn't *do* trust. Except something deep within her heart, her soul, wanted her to trust this man.

And that was the most frightening thing of all.

Meghan glanced up at the road, at Alessandro's steady gaze, then finally shrugged and laughed.

'Why not?' she said lightly, and, closing her eyes, let him lead her as if she were a child.

The road was steep, and with her eyes closed Meghan felt as if she could tumble backwards into an abyss at any moment. Alessandro tugged gently on her hand, leading her onwards, upwards.

'Keep them closed,' he ordered sternly, and a bubble of laughter escaped her.

'I'm trying.' She stopped for a moment, chest heaving. 'I'm also out of breath. I'm not used to this kind of hiking.'

'I thought you'd been travelling around Europe.'

'My general mode of transportation has been train or bus,' Meghan returned tartly, 'and I stick to the cities. I haven't been wandering out in the hills like some Umbrian nomad!'

He chuckled softly. 'Now's your chance.'

With her eyes closed she was all the more conscious of the sun warm on her face, the dry scent of pine and cypress mixed with the heady fragrance of wild lavender and rosemary.

She was also exquisitely, achingly conscious of Alessandro's hand encasing hers, the way his fingers held hers lightly yet with such certainty, such possession. The way the simple touch seemed to reach inside and touch her where she was most vulnerable, most needy.

Her heart. Her mind. Her soul.

'Are we almost there yet?' she asked, her voice coming out in a rusty croak. She tried instinctively to pull her hand away, but Alessandro's grip only tightened.

'Don't be frightened.'

'Who said I was scared?'

'I can tell. We're almost there.'

Wherever 'there' was. Since they'd been walking she hadn't

heard another person or even a car in the distance. The only sound was the wind in the trees and the faint tinkling of a far-off goat's bell.

'Can you hear it?' Alessandro asked softly.

Meghan strained to listen, and realised she could now hear in the distance what sounded like rushing wind. The light breeze caressing her face could hardly cause such a sound, and she shook her head in confusion. 'Yes, but what is it?' She started to open her eyes again, only to have Alessandro cover them with his hand.

'Don't spoil it,' he murmured. 'A little bit longer.'

The feel of his hand on her face, his thumb reaching down to caress her cheek, her lips, made Meghan stumble. Gently Alessandro tugged on her hand until she came forward, and he wrapped his arm around her waist, pulling her against him, her back against his chest, his other hand still covering her eyes.

'Let me go,' Meghan said breathlessly, even as desire—forbidden, treacherous, molten—coursed through her veins.

'I don't want to.'

'What about what I want?'

'But I don't think you want me to, either.' She could sense rather than see his smile. His hand still covered her eyes, his fingers brushing over her cheeks, her chin, her lips, as if he were memorising the touch of her. The feel of her.

She sagged against him. She couldn't help it. His chest was hard, unyielding, and yet she still seemed to mould herself to his contours. She felt the betraying hardness of his own desire against her back, and it only made her want to press closer.

Her insides were turning to liquid; a pulse deep inside was thrumming to life. Her breath hitched and his thumb traced her half-open lips, ran along her teeth.

His own breath feathered her hair, and he tilted her head upwards, still covering her eyes, and brushed her lips in the soft kiss of an angel.

Meghan's lips parted soundlessly, helplessly, and he deepened the kiss, turned it into something achingly sweet, wonderfully gentle.

Desire was flickering, licking through her, weakening both

her limbs and her resolve. She reached up with her fingers, tugged at the hand that covered her eyes.

She wanted to look at him, and yet the feel of his lips plundering hers was so exquisite she didn't want it to stop.

'Alessandro…' It came out as a whisper, a plea.

He chuckled.

She jerked back slightly, still caught in his embrace, his hand still covering her eyes. 'You think this is funny?'

'A bit,' Alessandro replied, unperturbed. 'But enough. I want you to see me when I make love to you. I want you to look into my eyes and see how I want you.'

He paused, his thumb outlining the fullness of her mouth again. Meghan's lips parted in silent invitation. She couldn't help it.

'And I want to see in your eyes how you want me.'

He removed his hand from her waist and led her onwards once more. 'Keep them closed,' he warned, and dropped his hand from her face.

Meghan longed to open her eyes—if just to see the expression on Alessandro's face. Smug because he'd made her want him so easily? Would there be the residual flicker of desire in own brilliant eyes?

Somehow she kept them closed. It had become a matter of pride. Of trust.

He tugged her along the stony path and she followed, her limbs still weak, flooded with sensation. With need.

Alessandro had recovered from their kiss more quickly than she had, she thought ruefully.

He held her hand gently, helping her over rocks and twisted roots. Meghan clung to him, moving carefully over the unfamiliar ground.

The rushing sound had become increasingly louder with every step, and when Alessandro finally brought her to a stop it was a roaring in her ears. She could feel the spray of water on her face.

'Now open them.'

Meghan obeyed, and found herself staring at a magnificent waterfall, a pure cascade of rushing whiteness that dropped over a hundred metres into a restless surging river below.

She clapped her hands in delighted surprise. 'A waterfall! I'd no idea!'

'Cascata delle Marmore. It's beautiful, isn't it?' Alessandro leaned against the balustrade of the viewing balcony he'd brought her to. The waterfall was like a huge sheet of streaming glass, surrounded by dense green foliage and trees. Meghan felt as if she were on a tropical island, despite the cool breeze teasing her hair into her eyes.

She stared at the water, rushing blue-green turning to pure white foam. It was both beautiful and frightening in its sheer power. 'I didn't realise there were natural waterfalls in this part of Italy,' she marvelled.

'It's not actually natural,' Alessandro told her. 'The Romans built it nearly two thousand years ago. They created viaducts to drain off the swampy land around the River Velino and pour the excess water off the Marmore Cliff into the Nera. Now it's only turned on for a few hours a day. The rest of the time it's little more than a trickle.'

'You mean it's not real?' She felt a twinge of disappointment that this powerful beauty hadn't been here since time began. Wasn't even *meant* to be here.

Alessandro turned to her, one eyebrow raised. 'What's real?' He gestured to the falls, raising his voice over the sound of rushing water to be heard. 'That looks rather real to me.'

'I suppose you're right,' Meghan said slowly. 'I certainly wouldn't want to go over it in a barrel!' she joked, then shook her head. 'I don't know—somehow it would be more impressive if it hadn't been manufactured by man.'

'Isn't that what makes it so amazing?' Alessandro countered. 'It was a swamp, a stagnant river—useless, dangerous, even— and they made it into something beautiful.'

'And still dangerous,' Meghan couldn't resist saying.

'Yes. Still dangerous.'

What were they really talking about? The falls, or something deeper? An even stronger current that threatened to pull her under, drowning her self-respect, her independence, and leaving only need.

A current that, like the falls, had been manufactured, created by an impossible and unreal situation.

Currents like that couldn't last. What was once a torrent would become a trickle, turned off at the source, by the source.

Alessandro. This was his game, she knew, and he was calling all the shots. He was in control.

Just one day, she reminded herself. One day couldn't be dangerous.

Except perhaps it could, with Alessandro.

'Come on.' Alessandro put an arm around her shoulders easily, as naturally as if he'd done it many times before. 'We can have lunch in Montefranco.'

Back in the car, he gave her a knowing glance. 'Still disappointed the falls aren't real?'

She shrugged. 'I can't deny they were beautiful.'

'Do you know the story behind them? Nera was a wood nymph who fell in love with a shepherd boy. The goddess Juno was jealous, so she turned Nera into a river.'

'The River Nera,' Meghan surmised. 'Bad luck for her, falling in love with the wrong man.'

'Perhaps,' Alessandro conceded with a wry smile. 'But do you know what her shepherd Velino did?'

'Found a shepherdess?'

He chuckled softly. 'No, he was so anguished at the loss of his love, he threw himself off the Marmore Cliff. His tears became the waterfall, and so they are joined for ever, the Rivers Velino and Nera. Their love lasting into eternity.'

Meghan smiled tightly. 'A sweet story.'

'You don't believe in lasting love?' There was a cynical edge to his voice that was impossible to miss.

'No, I don't,' Meghan said baldly. 'Do you?'

Something flickered in his eyes—disappointment? Relief? Who knew? Meghan looked out of the window, refusing to be drawn in. It didn't matter what Alessandro thought about everlasting love, because there was nothing *lasting* about their situation.

'No,' he said after a moment. 'No, Meghan. In that respect I'm like you.'

And, strangely, Meghan suddenly felt sad for them both.

Two people together, bound by desire and disillusion.

Montefranco was one of Umbria's classic hillside towns, its houses and churches perched on the green slopes as if they'd sprung up from the soil. Alessandro led her to a little trattoria tucked away on a narrow cobbled street, and the proprietor, a jolly man in an apron-covered suit, greeted him like a friend. After speaking briefly in his usual rapid-fire Italian, Alessandro slowed down to introduce Meghan.

'Antonio—my friend from America—Meghan Selby.'

He made her sound like a pen-pal. Smiling, Meghan shook the older man's hand. Yet how else could he possibly explain her presence?

It didn't make sense. This entire day didn't make sense. It was something out of a story, a fantasy, and it would end tonight.

Meghan's mouth turned dry. Tonight…when she walked away with a wave and a smile. If she could.

And if she couldn't…?

'You know what they say,' Antonio said, 'a friend of Alessandro di Agnio's is a friend of mine.' He turned to Alessandro, still speaking slowly for Meghan's benefit. 'So good to see you! It's been too long.'

'I've been busy, Antonio,' Alessandro said as he clapped the older man on the shoulder.

'I know! I know! All this work in the city—no time for rest, for play. I never thought I would say that to you, of course…' His chuckle faltered at Alessandro's wintry look.

'You along with many others.' He smiled, but it was as if a light had gone out in his eyes, turning them from blue to lifeless black.

'The poached cod is delicious,' Alessandro told her after they'd both silently perused the menus. 'If you care for fish.'

Meghan grimaced. 'Sorry, I'm a smalltown girl from the Midwest. I'm not much of a one for seafood.'

He chuckled. 'How about the *strascinati* with black truffle sauce? The truffles are famed in this region. It's a long-guarded secret where you can find them.'

'Do you know?' she asked, and Alessandro gave an eloquent, arrogant shrug that forced an unwilling laugh from her lips.

'Of course. You must try the *vino santigrano* as well. It's made locally, from some of the best vineyards in all of Italy.'

'Sounds like you know the menu,' Meghan commented. 'Do you come here often?'

'Do you mean, do I bring all my women here?' Alessandro said, his eyes alight with rueful humour.

'Something like that.' She smiled in admission, a tell-tale blush stealing across her cheeks.

'I told you—I like food.'

It was, she realised, not an answer to her question. How many women had he had? He was a man who knew women, who understood them, who was made for lovers...if not for love.

Alessandro steered the conversation into calmer waters, regaling her with tales and antics of the Umbrian locals, peppered with the mythology of the region.

Antonio himself brought the food and poured the wine, and Meghan could feel herself relaxing, enjoying. Laughing. Flirting.

'Try this.' Antonio had laid a sumptuous-looking rolled pastry on the table between them, and now Alessandro lifted a forkful to Meghan's lips.

Closing her eyes, she opened her mouth, and Alessandro slid a forkful of heaven inside.

The taste of chocolate, raisins and walnut melted onto Meghan's tongue. It was delicious. It felt like a sin. 'Mmm...what *is* this?'

'*Attorta*...a speciality of Umbria.'

Meghan opened her eyes to find Alessandro smiling at her, his gaze heavy-lidded, languorous. Sensual.

The pastry turned tasteless in her mouth, her throat so dry she could barely swallow.

Desire pulsated between them, coiled around Meghan's heart, her lungs, until she found she couldn't breathe. When she finally managed to drag air in, her breath came out in a shudder.

Alessandro smiled. 'Have another bite.'

Obediently, Meghan opened her mouth, and Alessandro slid

in another forkful. She could feel a drip of chocolate on the corner of her mouth and, mesmerised, watched as Alessandro wiped it before licking it off his own finger.

'Mmm.'

She closed her eyes briefly. 'What's going on here?' she whispered.

'We're eating dessert.'

'Alessandro, you know what I mean.'

He shrugged, though his eyes blazed into hers. 'I want you. You want me.'

'It's not that simple.'

'Isn't it?'

Meghan shook her head. 'I wish it were.' She gazed down at the crumbled remnants of their shared feast, delicious while it lasted but gone so quickly. She'd travelled that route before.

She would not do it again.

She looked up, her eyes wide and bleak. 'I won't sleep with you.'

'So you've said.' Alessandro took a sip of wine, looking amused.

Meghan sighed wearily. 'I know you think you'll wear me down eventually, and in truth you might get close. You might even win.'

'Is this a battle?' he murmured.

'You know it is. If I sleep with you I'll lose my self-respect, my dignity. I'll have given into desire, and I'll hate myself for it.'

'Why couch it in those terms? Why can't we love each other as two responsible, mature adults?'

Meghan laughed without humour. 'Because it's not about *love*.'

'You said you didn't believe in love.'

There was no mistaking the look of surprise on Alessandro's face, the heavy-lidded languor replaced with a wary tension.

'I don't. That doesn't mean I'm going to give myself to every—any—man I'm attracted to. I don't operate that way. Sorry.'

'So. You don't believe in love, but you won't make love with someone out of simple desire. What are you going to do? Become a nun?'

Meghan gave a shaky laugh. 'At times that prospect is appealing.' She twirled her fork between her fingers. 'I don't know what is going to happen in the future.' Her tone and face were bleak as she considered the prospect. The future was something she avoided thinking about. Sometimes it didn't seem as if she had one at all. 'I just can't ever see myself falling in love again. If that means being alone, then I guess I'll just have to get used to that.'

'It's not easy, being alone,' Alessandro said after a moment.

Meghan glanced at him, surprised by the guarded note in his voice, the vulnerability in his eyes. 'Sometimes it's safer.'

He nodded thoughtfully. 'Safety is important to you?'

'Yes.'

'This man you were with—you loved him? And he made you feel unsafe?'

'Of course he did,' Meghan replied shortly. 'Stephen was married. I didn't know it—'

'Stephen?' Alessandro's eyes darkened. He reached across the table to pluck the fork from her hand. He took her fingers in his, stroking her wrist with soft, tender movements. 'This Stephen— he was an ass. Even I can see that. But you can't let one man— one experience—spoil the rest of us for ever.'

'I'm sure,' Meghan said with a little smile, struggling to hold onto her composure as the fluttery little movements on her wrist went straight to her heart, 'you'd like to be the man to break the pattern.'

'One man, one relationship, is not a pattern.'

'Well, no.' Meghan glanced down, her eyes suddenly blurred with tears as memories rushed to the surface—memories she had firmly stamped down when she'd fled Stephen's apartment, fled the memories and the tears and kept running.

She still hadn't stopped.

'Meghan? *Gattina*?' Alessandro lifted her chin with his fingertips. 'What is wrong? What did I say?'

'Nothing.' Meghan blinked back the tears and smiled. 'I'm sorry.'

'No, I am sorry. We've wasted enough time indoors. We can walk through the town, up to the old fortress. There is a beautiful view from its walls.'

And as easily as that, he dispelled the tension, the sorrow.

Meghan let herself be led, her hand in his, out into the Umbrian sunshine.

The last thing she wanted to think about was Stephen, or the night she'd finally had the courage to walk away.

That was a memory she had locked deep into her soul. Something she never, never wanted to talk about. Certainly not to Alessandro. Not to anyone. Ever.

The fortress was built into the hill, overlooking the tumbled buildings of the town, and Meghan could imagine how it had once been formidable, impenetrable.

Now its walls were crumbling, mellow in the sunshine, and children played in the street below. Meghan let Alessandro lead her up the steps onto the top of the crenellated wall, the Umbrian countryside spread out before them in a peaceful patchwork of earthen colours.

A teasing wind blew her hair around her face and she breathed in the clean, pine-scented air, as pure and satisfying as a drink of water.

Alessandro and Meghan silently surveyed the panorama of tumbled hills and olives groves, taking in the majesty of an unchanged landscape.

'Did you grow up here?' Meghan asked after a long moment.

'Yes and no. As I told you, I went to school in England. My parents' main house of residence is in Milan. And yet…' He smiled with wry honesty. 'This was home.'

'Your brother's villa?'

'Yes. It was my father's before that.'

But not yours, Meghan realised silently, wondering what lay behind his careful choice of words.

'Well, it's beautiful,' she said with a smile. 'I happened on Spoleto by chance, but I'm glad I came.'

'So am I,' Alessandro murmured, and sudden expectant tension thrummed between them, heavy with meaning, with possibility.

Meghan stared out at the countryside, blind now to its charms.

'I should take you back to Spoleto tonight,' Alessandro said suddenly. His face looked hard.

Meghan's stomach plunged icily. She realised she was disappointed. She had expected to stay. She'd expected Alessandro to want her to stay.

'If that's what you want,' she said, only just managing to keep her voice steady.

Alessandro raked a hand through his hair. 'You know it is not!' He dropped his hand, tracing her cheek with his fingers. 'But you are haunted, Meghan, by the past. This man—he is like a shadow. I can almost see him at your shoulder.'

Meghan touched his fingers briefly with her own, her fingers winding around his, clinging. Pleading. 'I don't want him there.'

Alessandro smiled sadly. 'Neither do I.'

He cupped her cheek and she closed her eyes, revelling in the touch, the tenderness. She couldn't go yet. She couldn't leave this man—this hold he had on her senses, her soul. Perhaps even her heart. It wasn't love. She knew that. It was desire; it was need.

'Don't take me back yet,' she whispered.

His hand stilled. 'Are you sure?'

Meghan opened her eyes, swallowed audibly. Panic was fast setting in. 'I don't mean… I'm not…'

Alessandro smiled. His thumb caressed her lips. 'I know.'

He drew her naturally to him, in an embrace that was gentle rather than passionate. 'Stay,' he murmured against her hair. 'God knows, I don't want you to go.'

Meghan knew their time had been extended by only a day, perhaps two. Soon she would have to move on, and so would Alessandro. Their lives had never been meant to intertwine.

This was going to end. It was just a matter of when…and what happened beforehand.

The drive back to Tre Querce was quiet, both of them lost in their own thoughts. Meghan gazed out of the window at the fallow fields and bare vineyards, the sky above streaking lavender and gold.

She'd never reacted to any man the way she reacted to Alessandro—even Stephen hadn't affected her so profoundly, so deeply…as if he were stroking not just her hand or her body, but her soul.

Her whole body—her whole self—yearned towards his touch, his understanding. The two, she realised, were intimately connected.

He didn't love her.

He made no promises.

And yet…she wanted him.

She *wanted* him.

More than she'd ever wanted anything in her whole life.

More than your self-respect?

Meghan closed her eyes against the setting sun now blazing over the hills and fields.

I don't know.

As Alessandro turned the car up the twisting drive, Meghan wondered what the night would hold. She turned to look at him, and he sensed her gaze and smiled, reaching over to twine her fingers with his.

'Don't be afraid, Meghan. There don't have to be any shadows.'

Shadows. Meghan thought of Stephen. She could still see his face, hear his words.

I thought this was what you wanted.

How could he have thought that? How could he have twisted everything so horribly, so shamefully?

Alessandro was nothing like him, Meghan told herself. She knew that. He'd proved it to her again and again over this day. No matter how they'd started—what she'd thought—what *he'd* thought—it was different now.

Everything was different.

Could be different…if she let it.

If she let the shadows fade away.

Alessandro's hand tightened briefly on her own. 'Ana has the night off.'

So they would be alone. Meghan swallowed. 'Alessandro, I want—'

Meghan broke off, her heart still hammering, as Alessandro braked sharply in front of Tre Querce and cursed in Italian under his breath.

There was another car parked in front of the villa, a racy red convertible, and the man leaning against its hood was one Meghan recognised.

It was Alessandro's companion from lunch at Angelo's. As the man's eyes flashed to Meghan her own stomach lurched. There was no mistaking his knowing, lascivious grin or what it meant.

CHAPTER FIVE

'WELL, well, well.' Richard Harrison pushed himself away from the convertible and strolled towards Alessandro's car. 'You sly dog. Keeping her all to yourself.'

Alessandro flicked a cool, contemptuous gaze towards Richard. 'I don't recall inviting you here,' he replied, in a voice of dangerous silkiness.

'I was bored, and I do believe it's your job to entertain me.'

'You're not a child, Richard, as much as you behave like one.'

Richard's watery blue eyes blazed for a second. His mouth turned down sulkily. 'You need my business, di Agnio.'

Alessandro chuckled dryly, although his expression remained diamond-hard. 'You should realise by now, Richard, that there are very few things I need. You and your string of second-rate department stores is not one of them.'

Richard's face suffused with colour, turning puce. He clenched his fists, half raised one. 'You'll regret that.'

'I don't think so.'

Meghan's hand was slippery on the door handle as she grasped it. She heard the men trading insults, but it sounded like no more than dogs snarling at one another. She couldn't take it in. The one salient detail that had made its way into her numb mind was Richard's careless sentence.

Keeping her all to yourself.

They'd discussed her. Talked about her.

Richard's gaze roved over Meghan with crude, insulting

boldness, his eyes lingering on her breasts and thighs, sweeping over her as if he owned her, as if she could be bought. His thin lips turned up in a revolting smirk, and his watery eyes gleamed with lust. 'She's just as pretty as I said.'

'I think you should leave, Richard.' Alessandro's voice was calm and dispassionate, but a muscle ticked in his jaw and his eyes were like black ice.

Richard raised his eyebrows. 'What was it you said? There are better amusements in Spoleto than a two-bit part-time whore? It seems there aren't, my friend, and I think it's time you started to share.' He moved towards her, pale eyes glittering, and Meghan couldn't move. Couldn't think except to hear the sickening echo of his words.

Alessandro's words.

Two-bit part-time whore.

Just as she'd suspected and Alessandro had denied.

Just as she'd *known*.

She watched, transfixed, trapped, as Richard reached for her, his wet lips parted, his eyes glittering with lecherous intent.

He never managed to touch her. Alessandro moved with swift, calm certainty.

She heard rather than saw the crunch of Alessandro's fist into Richard's jaw. He staggered and fell onto the pavement by her feet.

She stared down silently. She still hadn't moved.

'I could sue you!' Richard choked. He clutched at his bleeding mouth, his face contorted with humiliated fury.

Alessandro massaged his knuckles. There was a fierce, primal light of satisfaction burning in his eyes as he gazed down at Richard. 'I don't think so,' he said calmly. 'Now, you'd better get off my premises before I do something worse to that pathetic baby face of yours.'

Richard glared. 'You've just lost a hell of a lot of business, di Agnio. I know what this deal meant to Di Agnio Enterprises!'

Alessandro's smile was sardonic. 'I'll live.' He turned his back on Richard in dismissal, and put his arm around Meghan's shoulders. 'Are you all right?'

'I'm fine.' Her voice came out as brittle and sharp as shattered glass. She *felt* as if she were nothing more than a handful of shattered glass, a fistful of jagged splinters. Shaking off Alessandro's arm, she moved towards the villa. 'I'll just get my things.'

She walked on numb legs to her room, the villa streaming by her blind eyes in a blur of colour.

Almost dispassionately she saw that her haversack had been placed at the foot of her bed. Who had fetched it? she wondered. How many minions worked for Alessandro, in a life she didn't even understand, with a power she could not begin to fathom? A power abused.

She stuffed her crumpled white shirt and black skirt into the bag. She could return the clothes she was wearing to Alessandro later. There was no time to change.

She was zipping up her bag when Alessandro strode into the room.

'What the hell are you doing?'

In the distance she heard the roar of the convertible heading down the drive. She spoke through stiff lips. 'Leaving.'

'Just like that?'

'Just like that.' Meghan tugged at the zipper of her bag, refusing to meet Alessandro's eyes. She couldn't do that and get out of here. She knew she couldn't.

'You can't.'

'Yes, I can.' *Barely.* The zipper had finally closed, and she swung the haversack onto her shoulder. She still hadn't looked at him.

It was the only way she could keep the desperate shards of self-respect and sanity together.

For surely if she stayed one moment longer than necessary—if she let Alessandro talk to her, touch her—they would be scattered.

Stolen.

'If you won't drive me, I'll walk.'

'It's over five kilometres to Spoleto,' Alessandro warned. His mouth was a thin line of anger, his eyes black, his body tense and ready to spring, although there was a loose-limbed grace to his movements even in his fury.

Meghan shook her head wearily. 'You can't keep me prisoner here, Alessandro.'

'Were you prisoner at the falls? At lunch? With me all day? When you begged me to let you stay? Don't throw that one at me this time, Meghan. It won't work.'

'I enjoyed today,' Meghan said, with a dispassionate calm she was far from feeling. 'But I didn't *beg*.' She felt sick, and she prayed she wouldn't throw up. Prayed she wouldn't cry. 'Now I want to leave.'

'No.'

'I'll walk—'

'No.' He took her gently by the shoulders, his touch like a promise. Meghan closed her eyes. She didn't need this. Couldn't need it.

When he spoke his voice was a caress. 'Look at me, Meghan.'

Damn him. Unwillingly, despite every good intention she'd ever had, she met his eyes.

'Why are you doing this? Is it because of Richard? He's a pig—*porca*—'

'Two-bit, part-time whore.' The words came out in a sorry little whisper.

Alessandro stared at her, his eyes blazing, filled with an urgency that almost undid her.

'You believe what he said?' he finally demanded hoarsely.

Meghan spoke through numb lips, her voice a rusty whisper. 'Tell me it isn't true. Tell me you didn't say it.'

Alessandro was silent, his gaze hard and unyielding. Then he released her, running a hand through his hair, and Meghan sagged against the bed. Her haversack fell to the floor.

'I did say it.'

Tears pricked her lids. She'd begun to think perhaps it wasn't true. Only now did she realise how much that brief flicker of hope had cost her. Damn him. Damn him for making her feel.

Feel so very much.

'But I didn't know you then,' Alessandro continued in a voice of determined calm.

Meghan tossed her head, blinking back tears. 'It was *yesterday*, Alessandro.'

'A day is a long time.'

'Not long enough.' And yet far too long.

One day wasn't supposed to be dangerous.

And yet it was. It *was*.

Wearily, every limb leaden, she stooped to pick up her haversack.

'What do you want from me?' Alessandro demanded. 'Complete trust—faith in you before I even know you?'

She shook her head. 'Don't you see? You judged me then, in the restaurant.'

'Fine. I admit it. So?' He stared at her, head tilted with casual instinctive arrogance, eyes blazing blue fire. 'Harrison liked the look of you. He wanted to invite you here to serve us and see what happened.'

Meghan swallowed painfully. 'And that's just what you did.'

'It is not! I rejected his offer—coldly, in disgust. Yes, I called you a two-bit part-time whore. I admit it, and I will not apologise. I didn't know you then—hadn't spoken to you, hadn't looked into your eyes.' His own eyes burned now into hers. 'And when I did I wanted you. I wanted you for myself. Not as a waitress. Not as a whore. As a woman.'

'Yet when you first invited me here you *did* think that of me…didn't you? It wasn't until later—'

'What does it matter when it was?' Alessandro exclaimed. 'We are arguing about details!'

'No,' Meghan said, her voice stronger now. 'We're not. All that lovely nonsense about a pretty girl and wanting to get to know her, needing a pretence because of your prestige and wealth—it was just that. Nonsense. Lies. You didn't mean any of it.'

'I did.'

'Don't lie to me!' Meghan's voice rose in frustrated anger. She wanted truth—at least now. She deserved that much. 'I thought you were honest. I was beginning to believe— But you're as low and slimy as every other man I've known, thinking I'm a slut without even knowing my name! Lying to me to get what you want!'

'Don't compare me to that filth who used you,' Alessandro warned in a dangerous voice. 'I've been very patient with you, Meghan.'

She laughed incredulously, and the sound turned into a sneer. 'Patient? Waiting twenty-four hours before you demand to be serviced? *I don't think so.*'

Alessandro's face was white with anger. 'Have I demanded *anything* from you?' he asked, in a low voice that still managed to thrum with power.

'Should I be thankful?' Meghan snarled back, too hurt to care how she sounded, how her words might hurt. She wanted them to hurt. She wanted, savagely, to bring Alessandro as low as he'd brought her, though she doubted it was possible. He didn't care what she thought. He didn't care what she felt. 'I won't be your night-time entertainment,' she declared.

'As I recall, you haven't been providing any such entertainment,' Alessandro retorted, his voice a predatory hiss. 'Perhaps that's the problem.' He moved towards her with slow, purposeful strides, and the sudden intent look in his eyes, the harsh lines of his face softening with deliberate languor, made Meghan step backwards and stumble against the bed.

'Don't touch me!'

Alessandro prowled closer, an elegant stalking beast. Meghan pressed further against the bedframe, her heart thudding so hard she could feel the blood rushing in her ears.

She fell backwards onto the mattress, throwing one hand out to keep herself from becoming entirely helpless before him.

'I'm not going to touch you,' Alessandro informed her silkily. He stood above her, hands on hips, his whole body radiating lithe power, raw hunger.

His eyes glittered with intent and Meghan lay there, helpless, trapped by her own damning need.

'I'm not that kind of man. But I am going to tell you how I *would* touch you if you let me. If you wanted me to.'

Meghan opened her mouth soundlessly, her eyes wide.

'Do you know how I would touch you, Meghan? No, of course you don't. I don't think you've ever been touched that way. I imagine the man who took your innocence—because he did, didn't he?—I imagine he used you for his own pleasure. He didn't think about your needs—your desires—at all. Am I right?'

She wanted to speak. She *would* speak. She would tell him to go to hell, and then she would get up and walk away.

Except she didn't.

'When I touch you, Meghan,' Alessandro continued, his voice a caressing whisper, 'you'll want me to. You'll want me to because you'll know that I want you, and you can want me, and that it can be *good*. Nothing shameful, nothing sordid.'

'No…' It came out as a plea, although whether to stop or continue Meghan didn't even know. She was mesmerised by his words, by the unabashed hunger in his eyes, the desire he was not afraid to show.

The desire he was not afraid to feel.

'First I'll touch your lips. I've touched them already…just a taste. I want more now. I want more of you.' He paused thoughtfully, his eyes glittering. 'I think I'll love touching your lips. They're soft, and they'll taste of walnut and raisins. Like the *attorta* we shared. Do you remember? Nutty and moist and so very, very sweet.' His eyes moved from her mouth to her throat, and Meghan felt the damning blush staining her skin. Giving him evidence.

'I'll touch your throat there, where I can see your pulse. It's beating quite wildly now.' He smiled, and Meghan saw the desire in his eyes—pure, blazing. Elemental. 'Then I'll move lower. I'll touch your breasts. I wonder what they look like? As golden as the rest of you? I want to feel them in my hands.' He raised his hands, palms upwards, cupped, and Meghan moved slightly, leaning towards him, craving the thought of his touch.

'I'll touch you everywhere,' Alessandro continued, his voice ragged now. 'Stroking and kissing and bringing you to heights you've never climbed, places you've never been. Shattering you into a thousand pieces and then putting you back together again. And then you'll touch me.'

Meghan shuddered. She couldn't help it.

'You'll touch me, and I'll want you to touch me. It will be like a gift.' He closed his eyes briefly, his expression straining, pained. 'I want that very much, Meghan. I want you to touch me.'

He stood very still, his head thrown back, the column of his throat brown and exposed and clean. Then he lowered his head and opened his eyes. Meghan saw the naked vulnerability there. He'd bared himself to her, she realized.

No other man had given her so much while seeming to promise so little.

He'd given her control. It felt precious.

Slowly, her legs trembling, she stood up. She was so close to him she could feel his breath on her cheek. Still he did not move.

Her hand shook as she lifted it, placed it deliberately on his chest. She could feel his heartbeat race under her palm, the muscles jerk in response, and a little smile stole over her features.

'You see what you do to me?' Alessandro's voice was choked.

Meghan looked up. There was so much in his eyes—so much need, so much pain, so much desire. It stunned her, left her breathless.

And yet he didn't move. His whole body was taut, straining, still.

She slid her hand up, across the solid width of his chest, along his neck, letting her fingers coil in the crisp curls of hair at his nape.

He remained motionless, though his breathing was uneven, ragged.

She stood on her tiptoes, using her hands to pull his face down to hers. She brushed her lips against his, surprised at their softness, daring him, willing him to respond.

He moved.

His arms came around her, drawing her to his hard length with a gentleness that still gave witness to his urgency. His mouth turned the barest brush of a kiss into something far deeper and more demanding.

Meghan surrendered.

She didn't know how they got to the bed, how they ended up lying in a tangle of limbs until she wasn't sure where she ended and Alessandro began. His hands were on her, hot, sure, seeking. She felt him smile against her throat as he reached to cup the fullness of one breast.

'You're so beautiful.'

Meghan let her own hands roam along the smooth expanse of

his back. When had he taken off his shirt? She didn't know if she'd taken it off; everything was a softened haze of desire, of need.

Nothing mattered but this moment, this time of touch and taste and feel.

Oh, how she felt.

She felt his hands as they slid across her stomach, temptingly lower. She felt his lips as they traced a fiery path of ardent need, tender desire, down her throat, pausing where her pulse leapt and jerked. She felt him smile against her skin.

Then he moved to her breast, taking his time, teasing her with his tongue, laughing softly at her arching gasp when he took her nipple into his mouth, and the shock of feeling was without fear, desire without shame.

The need he was creating within her was a thrumming pulse in her core, a glorious ache begging to be satisfied. And she knew he felt the same. Felt the pressure of his desire against her middle, heard his ragged gasp as he moved lower with his hands and his mouth.

'Alessandro…' It came out as a supplication as she lay there, subject, slave, to his devotions.

She tried to take control. She let her own hands drift lower, reaching for the pulsing heat of him. She saw his eyes darken with desire, heard his breathing hitch.

'*Mia gattina*…those claws are sharp!' He chuckled softly, capturing her hand with a groan. 'We have time…we have time…'

Meghan shook her head in protest. She didn't want to slow down. She didn't want to wait. She knew if she waited, if she let time and memory catch up to sensation, she would hesitate. She would start to doubt, to question, to fear.

To feel shame.

Now she just wanted to feel, feel *this*—his hands, his mouth, his body—with her senses and not her heart, to lose herself in the beauty and passion of being touched, caressed.

She wanted to feel…and to forget.

She knew that, and she pulled him to her to kiss him, hard, to banish the memories. The ghosts.

And then it stopped.

Alessandro pushed himself away from her, back onto his

knees. His face was flushed, his breathing ragged. He pulled a hand through his hair and exhaled slowly.

'We need to stop.'

Meghan stilled, stiffened in shock. Humiliation came—a fast, hot rush of feeling. She was suddenly conscious of how she must look, her hair in a tangle around her face, her lips swollen, cheeks flushed. Her shirt was hitched up around her neck, her bra clasp undone.

And Alessandro was looking at her with a quiet sorrow that made everything they'd just done seem dirty.

'Why?' She pulled her top down, and Alessandro stilled her hand.

'Don't. You're lovely.'

'You're not looking at me as if you're thinking that right now,' Meghan said, her voice coming out far more tremulous than she'd meant it to. 'What's wrong?'

'Nothing's wrong.' Alessandro stretched out beside her, tracing one finger along the tender skin of her navel. Meghan shuddered lightly.

'I'm rushing things,' he said after a moment. 'When we make love, it won't be like this.'

'Like what?'

'Rushed. Frenzied. Because we are angry.'

It took a great deal of her pride and courage to say, 'If I was angry, it was at myself. For wanting you.'

He paused, sitting up on one elbow to regard her thoughtfully. His fingers drifted up to touch her chin, tilting her face so their eyes met. He traced the outline of her lips with a fingertip.

'He hurt you very much, didn't he?'

Meghan opened her mouth soundlessly. She hadn't expected *that*. Hadn't expected tenderness on the heels of such passion, understanding coupled with desire. She nodded, helpless to deny what he already knew. 'Yes, he did.'

Undone by compassion where she'd expected condemnation, she felt tears sting her eyes. She forced them back. Lying next to him, her sorrow plain to see, Meghan felt far more exposed than when her clothes had been rucked up.

She tried to shrug away, but he stilled her with one gentle hand on her shoulder.

'Don't hide from me.'

'What do you want from me?' Meghan whispered. He wanted her body; she knew that. Understood it, even. Yet now he seemed to be asking for more. Her emotions, her desire, her soul.

Her heart.

Except he didn't want that, did he? He couldn't possibly want that.

Alessandro's eyes darkened even as he continued to stroke her face with tender, absent movements, a gesture of unthinking intimacy. 'I want you to want me,' he said at last. There was a hidden vulnerability in his voice that made Meghan ache.

Want him? Of course she wanted him. He had to know it. It was in her every look, her every word.

Her every thought.

'I do want you,' she admitted with a little laugh. 'I think that's obvious.'

'But you're ashamed,' Alessandro said quietly. 'Ashamed to be with me.' There was an ache in his voice, of need and pain, that Meghan couldn't begin to understand. It almost sounded as if he thought she were ashamed of *him*...rather than herself.

'I can't help that. I...I have a lot to get over, I suppose. When you touch me I want to forget. I want to feel and not to think.'

'That's only half of the experience.' He smiled down at her, his expression softened with tenderness, yet a shadow lingering in his eyes. 'You can make love with your body *and* your mind.'

'I suppose you're the expert?' Meghan said, and it came out halfway between a joke and a jibe.

'Perhaps with the body.' Alessandro's mouth tightened briefly before he smiled and brushed the hair back from her forehead, tangling his fingers in the silken strands. 'Like you, I'm waiting for my mind to catch up.'

Meghan's mouth opened soundlessly at this admission. *We're so alike*. Yet they were impossibly different. 'Where do we go from here?' she forced herself to ask, though at the moment she didn't want to know. She didn't want to leave. She didn't want Alessandro to leave.

She didn't know what she wanted.

'We wait.'

'For what?'

'For you to come to me of your own free will, with no shame, no fear, no frenzy. For both of us to give…completely.'

Meghan struggled to sit up, pushing her hair away from her face. Alessandro dropped his hand, still smiling.

'That's asking quite a lot.'

'I don't mind.'

'Maybe I do.'

He raised one eyebrow. 'Do you want to leave me?'

Meghan let out a shaky breath. 'No. But I should.'

'Why? What is this *should*?'

'Alessandro…' She closed her eyes, felt his fingers drift along her face. 'There's no future for us, is there? I'm not…'

'You're not what?'

She bit her lip. How could she explain her doubts, her fears, without opening the Pandora's box of her past? 'You thought I was a whore.' She hadn't meant to say it, didn't want to remind him, knew from the chilling silence that she shouldn't have. Her old wounds were too fresh, the scars raw and red.

Alessandro stiffened, his hand dropping from her face. Meghan opened her eyes.

He rolled off the bed, standing there, his chest brown and bare and glorious, his expression like iron.

'You still think I invited you here presuming you were a whore, that I hired you for a whore's work.' He shook his head, the movement sharp and contemptuous. 'This is old ground, Meghan. And I'm getting bored with it.'

'As you're bored with me?'

His voice was level, almost a drawl. 'Just about.'

Meghan swallowed painfully. He had the ability to hurt her so easily. 'But you judged me,' she whispered.

'Yes, I did. But you're the one judging *me* now.' There was a moment of taut silence, then Alessandro's hand slashed through the air. 'I won't have it, Meghan. I won't be judged—condemned on old evidence. I've had enough of that!' His voice was savage, yet as he turned away his head was bowed, as though under a burden too great to bear. 'I won't have you throwing one thing I said into my face time and time again,' he continued in a low voice. 'I *can't* have it. Nothing I ever say or do will prove what I am. You damn me on one piece of flimsy evidence. I will not be damned. Not by you.' His voice shook slightly. 'Not by you.'

Meghan stared, stunned by the force of his emotion. Her mind spun.

He turned back to her, his voice now cool. Cold. 'You must take responsibility for your own actions. Stop blaming me, or that other man, for your own desires. You may have been a victim before, but you are not one now. And I won't let you act like one.' He shook his head, his expression suddenly weary. 'There are too many shadows, Meghan. Perhaps for both of us. I'll drive you back to Spoleto, or wherever you want to go, tonight. It is better that way. It has to be.' With that, he gazed at her one last time, smiling sadly, then turned on his heel and left.

CHAPTER SIX

MEGHAN sat back on the bed, her mind still numb, yet whirling. Spinning horribly with implications she had pushed away, refused to consider.

You may have been a victim before, but you are not one now.

She lay back against the rumpled sheets and mussed pillows, an ache of regret throbbing through her, threatening to rise up into an overwhelming howl of misery.

She'd wanted control. She'd entered Alessandro's villa—his life—so she could prove something to herself. To him.

She'd wanted to prove that she was in control, that she wasn't a victim. She'd been determined to show how she could be in control of her own life, her own body.

She'd failed spectacularly.

She was such a fool.

She took a deep, shuddering breath. If she wanted control this was the time to take it with both hands, and show Alessandro she understood.

Meghan pushed the tangled mass of hair back from her flushed face. A glance in the mirror confirmed her suspicions; she was a mess. She splashed cold water on her face, yanked a brush through her hair until it lay in waves against her shoulders, and changed into a fresh pair of jeans from her haversack. She picked one of her favourite blouses, a silky, cream wraparound that emphasised the clean lines of her throat and collar-bone and left all the rest to the imagination, barely hinting at the soft curves it hid.

It was wrinkled and cheap, but it was clean, and it was hers. She didn't want to wear borrowed clothes for this.

Taking another breath, in a vain attempt to calm her wildly beating heart, she walked downstairs.

The villa was quiet, cloaked in darkness, but Meghan saw a lamp burning in the lounge. The double doors were closed, although one had escaped its latch.

It was enough of an invitation. It would have to be.

Meghan pushed the door open with her fingertips. Alessandro stood in the centre of the room, his back half turned, staring at one of the vivid oil paintings on the wall with a preoccupied scowl. When she saw the ferocity of his expression Meghan almost turned back.

Then he saw her. He stilled, then turned slightly towards her, one eyebrow raised, his face now frighteningly impassive, as if a mask had dropped into place. He didn't speak.

'I wanted to tell you I'm sorry,' Meghan began, her voice thready. 'You were right.'

'Oh?' He gave her nothing—no quarter, no mercy.

'I *was* acting like a victim,' Meghan continued painfully, her face flushing with humiliated acknowledgement, 'and it wasn't fair to you. Despite our…beginnings, you've given me nothing but honesty and understanding since then. I realise that now.' She swallowed, bowed her head in submission, and waited for his judgement.

Alessandro was silent. Meghan could hear her heart pounding.

'How convenient for you,' he said after a long moment, his voice dry, and yet with a chill.

'Alessandro, please.' Meghan looked up, took a step forward, reached a hand out in helpless appeal before dropping it. The man she'd thought she was beginning to know was warm, vibrant, alive.

The man in front of her now was a shadow of that man, no more than a reflection in ice.

He did not have compassion in his eyes. Tenderness did not soften his face. His eyes were black and cold, the beauty of his face made up only of harsh planes and angles.

'You really do want me to leave,' she said unsteadily.

He shrugged, an elegant twisting of his broad shoulders. 'Maybe you were right. Maybe I'm bored with you, as you suggested.'

Meghan felt sick. Alessandro was a man who didn't bluff. She should have known she'd wasted all her chances. She took a step backwards. 'I'll go and get my things.'

'Are you quite certain you want to return to Spoleto?' His expression was sardonic. 'You did say you were finished there.' He raised his eyebrows, coldly amused. 'So where are you going now, Meghan? Where are you running to? Have you decided that yet?'

'I'm not running,' Meghan retorted automatically, and Alessandro gave a sharp bark of laughter.

'Oh, no? But you give such a good impression of it.' He shook his head in disbelief. 'You're not a woman. You're a child. So young and naïve. You look to others to condemn or absolve you. You blame them for your mistakes—your choices—and you run away when it gets too hard. You have to take responsibility for your actions, Meghan. Lord knows I did—much as it hurt.'

Meghan jerked back from the verbal assault. He'd assessed and discarded her whole character in a matter of seconds. He'd given her reasons, motivations, faults, without understanding the truth.

Without knowing it.

'Don't,' she whispered. 'You don't know what you're talking about.'

'No? Then tell me.' Alessandro's face darkened even as he shoved his hands in his pockets, his body chillingly relaxed. 'Tell me about Stephen. He was married, you said? And you didn't know?'

Meghan's eyes widened in shock. 'No, I didn't! I told you that! He never told me…I never…'

'Yes, you've told me many things.' He made it sound as if she'd offered him a tissue of lies. 'This place you lived—Stanton Springs, was it? A small town? You told me you were—what was the phrase?—a smalltown girl.'

'Yes,' Meghan whispered wretchedly. 'It was a small place.' She knew where this was going, knew where he was leading her without mercy, without understanding. Without forgiveness. And she could do nothing but follow—follow down this damnable path to its terrible destination.

'I've heard about these towns in America. Friendly places, yes? Everyone knows everyone else. You all say hello in the street. Like one of those American television shows.' His eyes glinted with both knowledge and power.

'Yes,' Meghan agreed softly. 'It's just like that.'

He lifted his chin, prepared for the final thrust. 'So tell me now, how is it that you didn't know he was married? Because you *did* know, didn't you, Meghan?' His eyes were like blue flames, burning into hers, into her consciousness, her soul. Searing her. 'You must have known who he was. You must have said hello to his wife. You must have lived a lie. Isn't that right? That's what is eating you alive—why you have these shadows. Why you can't move on. You knew, and you pretended you didn't. Even to yourself. You knew, Meghan.'

It was too much—too close to the truth, and yet so horribly far from it. 'I didn't know!' Meghan shouted. Tears spurted from her eyes and her voice choked. 'I didn't know, it wasn't that small a town. He told me he was single! Damn you—damn you to hell, Alessandro di Agnio! I don't care what you say—what he said— I didn't know!'

He stilled, tensed. 'What did *he* say?'

'He said I should have known…that no one would believe I didn't know,' she choked out. The words, the confessions, tumbled from her lips. They'd been stamped down for so long, and now they couldn't come fast enough. 'He said everyone would assume I'd known—he was a model citizen, so was his wife. How could I not have known?'

'Indeed,' Alessandro said in a soft voice.

'But I didn't.' She was begging now, pleading for him to understand, to believe—as foolish a gesture as she knew that had to be. Who begged their accuser to understand? 'I didn't. I realise now how naïve I was. He was so charming, so…taken with me. I never stopped to question, to wonder why we always met in hotel rooms, seedy restaurants. I assumed he just wanted to keep a low profile because of his job. I thought it all so thrilling, but it's obvious now. Back then…then I was so starstruck, thinking myself so lucky, so in *love*, that I had no idea…no idea…' Her voice trailed off brokenly.

'No idea?' Alessandro prompted coolly.

'No idea of what I was getting into,' Meghan finished in a whisper. 'No idea what would happen. No idea that someone could think…'

'Think what?'

This was dangerous. Memories were dangerous. Her vision blurred and she clutched blindly at the chair. 'He thought I was nothing more than a whore,' she said, her voice so low that Alessandro leaned forward to hear. 'A whore,' she repeated disbelievingly. 'If you wonder why I thought that was what you meant by services, if you can't understand why it hurts so much that you thought that of me—even for a moment—then now you know.'

Alessandro regarded her quietly for a moment. 'Why would he think that?' he asked. 'Is there something you're not telling me?'

'He just did.' Meghan cut off a half-sob, took a shuddering breath. Her nerves were shattered, her emotions splintered. She felt as if Alessandro could sweep the broken pieces of her into his hand and blow them away. 'He just did, anyway.' Her voice came out dull, flat. She pressed her fist to her mouth, bit down on her knuckles. Hard. She couldn't say more. She couldn't tell him any more.

'And you started to believe it?' he surmised thoughtfully.

Meghan swung round to face him, horrified. 'No, of course I didn't! I would never—!'

'Yes, you did,' Alessandro countered softly. 'You've believed it all this time, haven't you? You think it was your fault. And you've never forgiven yourself.'

'*What*?' She jerked back as if she'd been slapped. 'Forgive myself? You think I need that?' She shook her head so hard her hair tangled against her face, and she brushed it away in one angry, impatient gesture. 'I forgave myself a long time ago—if there was anything to forgive. *Which there wasn't*.' Her breathing hitched and she forced herself to sound calm.

There was no truth in what Alessandro was saying. There

was no *sense*. Could he actually think she was to blame for what had happened? For what she hadn't *known*? For what had happened next…?

'Perhaps there wasn't anything to forgive,' Alessandro agreed evenly. 'But you blamed yourself all the same, didn't you? You tell me now you didn't know. But maybe there was a little whisper in your heart. Deep down you thought, you must have known. You must have at least suspected.'

Meghan stared at him transfixed. Horrified. She felt stripped bare…again. This time more vulnerable than ever before, and it hurt. It hurt so much. More than physical blows. Still, she could not look away from Alessandro's gaze, his eyes blazing with knowledge. Knowledge of her heart, her mind.

'Maybe I did,' she whispered, the words torn from her.

'That's why you thought I was propositioning you outside the restaurant.'

'You were—'

'No. I told you. Richard Harrison—the man here earlier—wanted to proposition you.' Alessandro's lips curled in distaste. 'I wanted no part in that plan.'

'You still thought—'

'Yes.' He held up a hand, cutting her off. 'Until you told me I was talking to the wrong kind of woman.' He smiled sadly, spreading his hands wide. 'It stunned me at first. But what kind of woman assumes she's being propositioned that way? Not a true whore—because that kind of woman would take it in her stride, sidle up to me and make an offer. Another woman—most women—would ask me what I meant, perhaps, or assume that since I'd called you out of the restaurant I naturally wanted your services as a waitress. But you didn't. And it made me wonder.'

Meghan swallowed. Her throat was dry, as if it were coated in sandpaper. 'What did it make you wonder?' she whispered huskily.

'It made me wonder why you thought you were a whore when you so obviously weren't. That's why you flirted that way, isn't it? Why you stayed at that hostel—why you never reported Paulo. Why you keep thinking I'm treating you like one, thinking of you as one. Because you think you deserve it.'

Meghan shook her head. 'I don't deserve it.' Her voice broke, and she couldn't keep the tears from clogging her throat, her eyes. She blinked them back; they fell anyway, tracing silver tracks down her face. 'I *don't*.'

Wordlessly Alessandro put his arms around her, drawing her to him. Meghan let herself be pulled against him, let him tuck her chin against his chest.

He couldn't see her face, yet his thumb still traced her cheek, wiping away the tear that slipped softly, silently down—as if he'd followed its track with his heart. He was holding her as close as a lover, as gently as a child.

'*Mia gattina*, of course you don't. Of course. I know that. Perhaps you know it in your mind, but not in your heart. Where it matters.'

She closed her eyes. For a long moment there was nothing but the sound of their own ragged breathing. Alessandro stroked her hair softly.

'What…what happens now?' Meghan asked in little more than a whisper.

Alessandro tensed, then sighed, a shuddering breath that made Meghan realise he was not as much in control as she'd thought. She'd been laid bare, but somehow, in some way, so had he.

He understood.

Why? How?

'What happens now?' Alessandro repeated almost musingly. She felt rather than saw his smile. 'Now you marry me.'

The silence in the room was deafening, a roaring in her ears. Meghan froze, then forced herself to move away. She stared at him, looking for humour, for mockery. For something to tell her he was not, could not possibly be, serious. There was nothing in his face to indicate he was joking. He looked bland, impassive, yet Meghan suspected that blank look was his brand of armour. What did that mask hide? What emotions? What hopes?

Marriage?

Meghan shook her head.

'You're joking.'

'Do you really think I would joke about marriage?'

She shook her head slowly, hating the sudden flare of hope and need that he had ignited within her. 'Why would you want to marry me?'

'Just because you think so little of yourself doesn't mean I do.'

'You just acted like you thought very little of me indeed,' Meghan said through stiff, numb lips. 'You called me a child, you blamed me for what happened—'

'I drove you to confession,' Alessandro corrected quietly. 'Absolution.'

'Oh, is that what that was?' Meghan slapped her forehead in a parody of understanding. 'Sorry. Silly me. Because it sure didn't feel that way. It felt like you were condemning me for every single thing I thought you didn't believe!'

'I don't,' Alessandro said calmly. 'Not now. But I knew you did, and I had to show you that. Only then would you be able to move on. Stop blaming, stop being the victim.'

'Thanks for the psychotherapy.' Meghan turned away in disgust—disgust at herself for falling into his trap, and for the damn thing *working*.

He knew her better than she knew herself, and it didn't make sense. It wasn't fair. She didn't like feeling so vulnerable, so exposed, so *raw*.

And yet, she realised with sudden, sweet surprise, it was a relief.

It was a relief to be known and not judged. To be accepted, not condemned. To not carry the burden of her secrets, her shame, alone.

'Marry me, Meghan.'

It was tempting. Far, far too tempting. To marry a man she barely knew, a man she shouldn't trust.

Except she did trust him. More, she knew, than she'd ever trusted anyone else.

'Alessandro, it's crazy.' She tried to laugh; it came out as a wobble. 'We barely know each other.'

'Actually, I think I know you rather well.'

That much was true. How had he slipped beneath her defences, her *skin*? When had it happened? How had she not seen, felt, realised until now, when she was exposed and empty and he was tempting her with promises, with hope?

With a second chance.

'I don't know you,' Meghan pointed out. That was true, too. She didn't understand him at all—couldn't fathom how such tenderness could be coupled with a refusal to love, how his smiles hid a seething darkness, a vulnerable need so at odds with the strength and control he radiated.

'You know you can trust me, at least. Don't you?'

'Yes…' She just didn't know where that trust would lead her.

'So why not?'

'*Why*? Why not an affair? A few days at your villa and then a sweet parting? Isn't that what you had in mind all along?' Her chin lifted in challenge even as the words rent her soul.

Alessandro raised his eyebrows. 'Is that all you think you're worth? An affair? Not marriage?'

'I thought *you* thought that was all I was worth,' Meghan responded quietly.

He inclined his head in cool acknowledgement. 'Now you know that's not true.'

Meghan tried to laugh, to pierce the unreality of the situation. 'You haven't fallen in love with me, have you?' She'd meant it as a joke, but it fell horribly flat. It came out as a plea, a prayer.

'No,' he said slowly. 'But then you haven't fallen in love with me either. We don't believe in love, remember? Or was that a lie?' His expression turned hard for a moment.

She looked away, out of the window. Twilight was descending on the hills with a purple softness, a peace was cloaking the world that felt so removed from the shattered atmosphere of this room.

'No, it wasn't a lie.' She'd loved Stephen, and he'd used it to his advantage, to control her, time and time again. She'd accepted the snubs, the sneaking around, the hasty moments and couplings, because she'd thought that was what you did when you loved someone. You accepted whatever they gave. You gave whatever they were willing to take.

No matter how much it hurt. No matter how much it cost.

'Good.'

She looked at him curiously. How could such a gentle and tender man be so hard, so unforgiving? 'Have you ever been in love?'

'No.'

'Never? And you never want to be?'

'No. Love is a cheap emotion, used to manipulate and blame. I'm not interested in love.'

'You've loved *someone*, surely?'

Alessandro's mouth twisted in a bitter smile. 'My heart's not broken, if that's what you mean.'

Meghan shook her head. 'There must be some reason why you don't want to love…be loved. It's a natural human desire. You know my reason. What's yours?'

His eyes narrowed, blackened. 'Don't analyse me, Meghan. Don't try. Just understand this. I won't love you. Ever. And I won't be loved.' His voice tightened ominously. 'And, Meghan, if you think you can make me change my mind, you can't. I don't love. Anybody. Not even my mother, my father. Not you. You should know that from the start. I thought, in fact, that such a…condition might appeal to you. No danger—isn't that right?' He smiled mockingly. 'Our hearts don't need to be involved. *Won't* be involved.'

She would have had to have been deaf not to hear the warning. 'But why should I marry you?' she protested, hating how weak her voice sounded.

His smile was lethal, predatory, possessing. 'You desire me. It is a good basis for marriage.'

'Physical desire?' Meghan didn't bother keeping the disbelief from her voice. 'Sex?'

He shrugged, unperturbed. 'Why not? If we were married there would be no shame in that.' His gaze roamed over her again.

Meghan felt a blush stain the tender skin between her breasts, crawl up her throat. She watched Alessandro watch that humiliating, revealing stain, a smile playing about his lips. He stared at her, his expression smouldering, daring her to respond, to deny what pulsated between them.

'A high price for you to pay to sleep with me,' Meghan couldn't help but jibe, and Alessandro slashed his hand through the air.

'Do not debase yourself to me. Ever.' He paused, his words

becoming a caress, a temptation. 'You would have security, Meghan. No more waitressing, no more grotty hostels. No more running.'

'I don't need you for that,' she whispered.

'No, but it would help, wouldn't it? What about when you go back home?'

'I'm not going back home!'

'Not now,' Alessandro agreed, his tone far too placid, too convincing. 'But never? Can you honestly say you will never see your family again?'

Meghan swallowed. 'I don't know.'

'If you are married to me you can go home with your head held high, a husband at your side. A rather powerful husband. I could buy out all the poky little shops in that town if you wanted me to.'

Meghan managed a shaky laugh. 'I'm not interested in revenge.'

'I'm not talking about revenge. I'm talking about power. Power that won't be abused. Power that you will have at your disposal. The power not to be ashamed. Afraid.'

Colour scorched her cheeks once more. Alessandro caught her hand in his, stroked the tender skin of her palm.

'Can you tell me you don't want that?' he asked softly. 'Can you tell me that isn't tempting to you?'

Meghan looked down. His finger stroked her palm, her wrist, her heart. How did he know? How could he possibly guess the thoughts racing through her mind so easily?

Power. The thought called to her with a siren song, lured her forward to a treacherous future. She could be secure. She could live without fear. Safe from the past, the knowing looks, the scorching shame.

She couldn't wander her way through Europe for ever; it was a half-life at best. She'd put off thinking of the future because she was afraid to face it.

She knew she could start over in another town, begin another life, but the prospect held no appeal. The shame would still be there—the fear that someone would believe what Stephen had, would act as Stephen had.

With Alessandro as her husband she would never need to be

afraid again. She would be in control…with him. She could hold her head high.

She could finally have power, and it would not be abused.

She shook her head. It was crazy, but it was tempting.

'And what do you get out of this bargain?' she asked after a moment, uneasy suspicion rippling through her.

'I get a wife who won't expect me to love her. A wife I desire. Most women want to marry for love. I'm not interested in deceiving or disappointing them. The women who don't want to marry for love are usually after money. Mine. I'm not interested in them either.'

It sounded chilling, as soulless as a business transaction at a bank. 'If you're so against love,' Meghan asked quietly, 'why marry at all?'

He hunched one shoulder in a half-shrug. 'I told you before. It's not easy being alone.'

'Get a dog,' she snapped, and he smiled faintly.

'I don't want a dog.'

'What *do* you want, Alessandro?' Meghan asked, and she held her breath for the answer.

His expression stilled, blanked. Although his face was a mask, she sensed the urgency underneath. 'I want you.'

Meghan's heart lurched. Yearned. This was what she wanted to hear. Yet she was still afraid. She couldn't trust it. Not this time. Not again. 'Why me?'

'I don't know,' he admitted, with an honesty that stung just a little. 'But I want you, Meghan. I want a life…a life that's different. A life together.'

'But without love?' Meghan clarified, after her heart had stopped stumbling. 'It sounds kind of cold.'

'It doesn't have to be.'

'Tell me how.'

'Companionship, desire, affection.' He ticked them off on his fingers. 'Don't those mean something to you?'

All too much. 'What's the difference?' Meghan challenged. 'Wouldn't you call those things love?'

He levelled her with one knowing look. 'Would you?'

No. Love was needing someone like air or water. Needing

despite the desire or affection. Needing even though it hurt, even though pain sliced through you, even though it killed you.

She glanced away. 'What about children?' There was an ache of longing like a physical pain, deep in her belly.

'Do I want them? Yes. I need an heir. Someone to run Di Agnio Enterprises when I am gone. Someone to pass it on to.'

'And would you love your children?' Meghan asked, her throat raw and aching.

Alessandro paused. 'I would certainly give them every affection, every opportunity.'

Meghan shook her head. Was it possible to have affection and desire—to enjoy them—without love? She didn't know. Didn't know if she could take the risk to find out.

His hand circled her wrist and he pulled her towards him, caressing her with his words. 'You can stop running, Meghan. You can stop hiding who you are, what happened to you. I already know, and I accept you. I believe you. Does it really matter if I don't love you?'

She was so near she could feel his breath feathering her face. She lifted her head, saw the truth, the heat blazing in his eyes.

She was tired of running. Of being alone, afraid, ashamed.

'I wasn't looking to be rescued,' she said in a low voice.

He smiled, skimming his fingers along her cheek. 'We never are.'

'And you? Will I be enough for you?' Meghan asked, a thread of uncertainty, of fear, in her voice. 'What if you get tired of being married? Being married to me? What then?'

Alessandro looked down at her, blinked slowly as he took in her words. When he spoke his voice was quiet, yet as strong and taut as a wire. 'I honour my promises,' he said. 'I honour my word. No matter what you…or anyone…thinks. That is the man I am. The man I mean to be.' He spoke with a fierce determination that roughened his tone and burned in his eyes.

She wanted to believe. She wanted to so much.

'It can happen,' he promised softly. 'It can happen for both of us. We can forget the past, what people thought, what they believed. We can be something new—something wonderful and true—to each other.'

It sounded wonderful. But was it real? And could it happen without love? And what was *he* running from?

'I…I need to think about it,' she said, her voice a raw whisper. 'It's too big a decision to make so quickly.'

'I can give you tonight,' Alessandro said. 'Tomorrow I have to return to Milan, to deal with business. Insulting Richard Harrison—as satisfying as it was—is sure to have repercussions.'

'And if I say no in the morning?' Meghan asked, transfixed by the unreality of the situation.

'I'll take you to the station in Spoleto. Or the airport—wherever you'd like to go.'

A ticket to her next destination. The thought had no appeal. Her travelling, once exciting and vibrant, was now just another excuse to run away.

Yet the realisation that he would dismiss her so easily—so coldly—chilled her to the marrow.

'And if I say yes?' she whispered.

'You come with me to Milan, meet my family, and we get married.'

Alessandro spread his hands, smiling, although there was a coolness, a remoteness in his eyes that stung Meghan's soul. Who was this man? Would she ever understand him?

'As soon as possible.'

'That easy?' she asked, in both disbelief and hope.

'That easy.'

The sky was inky black, studded with stars, as Alessandro prowled along the terrace outside. He'd already knocked back a glass of whisky, the fiery liquid burning all the way to his gut, and it hadn't helped.

What had he done?

He'd asked Meghan Selby—a virtual stranger—to marry him. A pretty young woman he'd mistaken for a whore—who'd mistaken *herself* for a whore.

He laughed aloud—a rasping sound that echoed in the still night and held no humour.

He didn't think Meghan was a whore. She was, he thought

with something close to regret, far too innocent. Too naïve… about him.

He recalled the aching vulnerability in her eyes, the shadows of both remembered and anticipated pain, and cursed himself— not for a fool, but for a madman.

A devil.

What kind of a man but a devil offered marriage to a woman who had been so badly hurt—who surely deserved only love and tenderness when he could offer her neither?

He could pretend to be tender. He could say the right words, do the right things. Because he knew what the response would be, the response he wanted.

He knew how to play her.

He was good at that. He'd always been good at that.

Alessandro raked a hand through his hair and cursed softly. He'd finished with hurting people, with acting selfishly and leaving ruin and grief in his wake.

That was his old life. He'd put it aside two years ago, along with the memory of a smoking ruin and the still, lifeless form of his older brother.

And yet now he was risking not only his own soul—which he'd long since condemned—but someone else's.

Meghan's.

A woman who deserved so, so much more than he could give.

A woman who deserved so much more than him.

He stared out at the midnight sky, at the sliver of moon, pale and luminous, suspended above a still world, silent save for the rustling of leaves in the olive trees.

Eyes like sunlight on an olive grove.

Why had he asked her to marry him?

She would have agreed to an affair. He could have worked her out of his system, left her at the train station with a diamond bracelet and no backward glances.

He'd done it before. Many times.

So why marriage? Why now? Why her?

Because I'm not that man any more. I don't want to be that man any more.

His lips twisted into a smile—a smile of self-loathing and also of self-acknowledgement.

He *was* that man. That wouldn't change. He could pose, he could pretend, but underneath ultimately he knew who he was. Everyone knew who he was.

Everyone but Meghan.

He wasn't like her—judged, condemned falsely by one twisted man. He'd been condemned by the truth.

The truth of who he was.

And yet…he wanted her. Wanted her with a desire that shook him, paralysed him with its blinding need, its power. Even made him a little bit afraid.

He wanted a saviour.

The realisation made him hurl his whisky tumbler onto the paving stones, where it shattered. Some things couldn't be fixed.

Not the tumbler. Not him.

He was past redemption, past saving. He knew that; he'd been told it many times. He saw it in his own soul and he accepted the truth, as everyone who knew him had accepted it.

No matter how hard he tried, how far he ran, it wouldn't change.

He couldn't change.

She could change me.

It was a joke; it wasn't fair. He couldn't expect Meghan to save him, love him. Didn't want it.

Didn't want to need it.

He didn't want—*shouldn't* want—some pathetic, needy smalltown girl trying to fix him. Trying to love him. No matter what she said, he knew she would start to love him. He saw it in her eyes—the hope and the fear.

I won't love…or be loved.

Except she had eyes like sunlight, and when she smiled he felt…hope.

But there was no hope, could be no hope. Not for him.

He was damned.

If he married Meghan he would be dragging her down with him. Taking her with him to hell.

But he still wanted her. And he would have her. No matter what it took. No matter what it cost.

Because, Alessandro acknowledged with a bitter, mocking toast to himself, that was the kind of man he was. He was a selfish bastard who took his pleasures where he could, how he could, no matter who he hurt.

And he would hurt Meghan. He might try not to for a while, but the truth would out.

His own nature would out.

No matter what he'd tried to prove in the last two years, the reality was his own blackened soul…and what it would do to Meghan.

Hating himself, Alessandro turned back inside.

CHAPTER SEVEN

MEGHAN awoke to sunlight washing the room in shades of yellow and cream, a slight breeze from the open window ruffling the curtains.

She leaned her head against the pillow, willing herself to enjoy the simple sensual pleasure of the moment before the thoughts, the memories, the doubts came rushing back in.

And so they came, hurtling through her mind with stunning force, leaving her breathless when she hadn't even moved.

She'd almost made love with Alessandro.

He'd stripped her bare, taken away her pretences, her pride.

He'd asked her to marry him.

Meghan pressed her fists to her eyes, wanting to cry, needing the release, but she'd already shed all her tears.

Her eyes were dry and gritty. It had been a long, sleepless night. Yet now, despite the agony of remembering, of allowing herself to process all that had happened, she realised she felt calm.

She felt strong.

She sat up in bed, pushing her hair away from her face. Today was a new day. Today was the beginning of a new life.

Last night, somewhere between midnight and dawn, she'd decided to marry Alessandro.

It had been a long night of doubt, of uncertainty, and yet also of hope. Her mind told her to run far, far away from Villa Tre Querce, from the hold Alessandro had on her.

And yet she also knew she would never be able to run far

enough. In the space of a few days he'd already marked her heart, her mind, her soul.

Even her body.

Just the thought of his hands on her, his fingers lightly skimming her skin, made her shiver in remembered pleasure.

I want you to touch me.

She drew her knees up, resting her chin on top. The breeze blowing from the window was warm, a sign of oncoming summer.

A new life.

What would life be like with Alessandro? The question sent a delicious shiver of anticipation through her, yet chasing it was the sharp bite of fear.

It could all go so horribly, horribly wrong.

Meghan closed her eyes as doubt assailed her once more.

Why was she doing this? It would be easier, safer to run away. Find a new place since she couldn't return home.

Home. Just the word—the concept—brought pain slicing through her as a grim smile twisted her features.

You knew. You wanted it. You deserved it.

The voices of the past, still haunting her. The shadows, she realised, still there.

Would they ever go away?

You haven't told him the truth.

The treacherous whisper of her conscience made her shudder. She could not tell Alessandro the truth. She could not share with him the extent of her shame. Admittedly it was hard for him to believe that she would think so little of herself simply because she hadn't known Stephen was married.

If he knew how low she'd been brought...how ashamed she'd been...

The shadows flickered about the room, the echoes of Stephen's taunts and leers like whispers in the corners.

And now? Wasn't she just opening herself to the possibility of even more pain, more humiliation than ever before?

Yes, Meghan thought. She was.

Except now the power would be on her side. She would never

be helpless again, never a pawn in someone else's filthy desire, disgusting needs. She would never again be a victim.

Unless she was Alessandro's.

The thought chilled her. If she fell in love with him, if she let him inside her heart even just a tiny bit, it could hurt.

It could hurt so much.

But that was a risk she was going to have to take.

When she'd run out of Stanton Springs she'd also run out of choices. She couldn't go home. She couldn't keep running. Not for ever.

Alessandro had been right when he'd asked, 'Does it really matter if I don't love you?'

Even though the question had caused her pain, she recognised the truth. It didn't matter. It couldn't.

She didn't want to love him; he wouldn't love her.

They could still be happy. And she would have power. Control. At last.

Why wouldn't he love anyone? What was his secret? The truth behind the need?

That is the man I am. The man I mean to be.

If it were within her power she would help him become that man. She would make it happen.

Maybe one day he would tell her. And maybe, Meghan thought grimly, she would tell him. The truth. The whole truth.

Maybe.

Her stomach churning with nerves, but also with a new, fiery determination, she sprang out of bed. She dressed in her own clothes—faded jeans and a butter-yellow jumper. She pinned her hair back carelessly on top of her head and scanned her reflection in the mirror. She was pale, too pale, and her eyes looked huge, but there were freckles on her nose from the sun yesterday, and she couldn't quite contain the smile lurking underneath her fear.

Dragging a shaky breath into her lungs, she headed downstairs. The house was silent, waiting, as Meghan descended the sweeping staircase, one hand on the wrought-iron railing.

Was Ana back? How would the taciturn housekeeper respond

to the news that her employer was marrying? That he was marrying Meghan?

Meghan took another breath. She needed air.

She found Alessandro in the kitchen, drinking coffee and reading the newspaper as if he hadn't a care in the world. His head was bent and his hair fell boyishly over his forehead. He raked it back with one careless hand, absorbed in the paper.

Meghan's heart felt as if it had been squeezed, as if Alessandro had reached right inside and tugged even when he'd barely moved. Even when he hadn't seen her.

Ana stood at the stove, preparing breakfast. She flashed Meghan a quick, malevolent glance before her face went blank and she turned back to the eggs on her stove.

Meghan shifted uneasily. She had an enemy there, and she didn't even know why.

'Alessandro?'

He turned quickly, smiling easily, although Meghan could see the shadows in his eyes. Something was troubling him, and she wasn't sure if it was her.

'*Buongiorno*. Did you sleep well?'

Meghan laughed dryly. 'Not really.'

'No?' Alessandro shrugged, spreading his hands. 'You had a lot to think about, I suppose.'

'Maybe I'd already made my decision,' Meghan retorted, nettled a bit by his arrogance.

'Maybe you had.'

He looked so calm, so urbane, dressed in pale cream trousers with a leather belt, a light green button-down shirt open at the throat, scuffed yet exquisitely made leather loafers on his feet. His hair was still damp and curly from the shower.

'What do you think it was?' Meghan couldn't resist asking. She folded her arms, staring him down.

Alessandro chuckled. 'Meghan, I don't *think* what it was. I know.'

'Oh?' She was half inclined to tell him she wouldn't marry him now. He didn't have to look so certain!

'You'd made up your mind before I had even left the room,'

Alessandro continued. The smugness was gone, replaced by simple soft honesty. 'And if you hadn't, it didn't matter. Because I'd made up mine.'

'You can't force me to marry you!'

'Who said anything about force?' His eyes had darkened dangerously, and Meghan felt her pulse thrum in response. It didn't take much to have her swaying into him, longing for his look, his touch.

She was conscious of Ana behind them, pots and pans clanking ominously as she moved around the kitchen.

He reached for her hand, pulling her to him slowly, even though she made a pretence of resisting. When she stood only inches away, their bodies still not touching, he brushed his lips against her palm.

'You look beautiful like that—so natural, so unaffected.'

Meghan looked up, startled. 'Sloppy, more like.'

'No.' Alessandro touched her cheek, trailing his fingers down to gently grasp her chin. 'I meant what I said. You're beautiful.'

'Thank you,' Meghan whispered. 'You're beautiful too.'

Alessandro smiled, and she saw it reached his eyes.

'And you'll marry me.'

She wanted to argue, to deny it simply to resist his autocratic dictates, but she couldn't. It was true, and she wanted it to be true.

I can make you happy, she thought.

'Yes.'

Alessandro's smile deepened, and she saw a new satisfaction there, deeper than any she'd seen before. A hunger satisfied.

'Thank you,' he said simply, humbly, accepting her acceptance as a gift, a treasure. Meghan's heart ached.

I can make you happy. Give me a chance. Even if there's no love. The words buzzed in her mind. She almost said them, gulping them back, choking on air.

Alessandro smiled. 'Let's eat.'

Over breakfast, with Ana serving in courteous if rather stony silence, Alessandro informed Meghan of their plans.

'We must leave for Milan after breakfast. I have business to attend to, and I want to introduce you to my family. The sooner they know you, the sooner we can get married.' His expression darkened briefly before he turned brisk and businesslike again.

'Why does it have to be so quick?' Meghan asked. Her mind was spinning and she took a steadying sip of coffee. 'We could take time to get to know each other. Be sure we're not making a mistake.'

'I'm not making a mistake,' Alessandro replied with easy confidence. 'And I want to marry quickly because I want you in my bed every night.'

Meghan flushed. 'And we need to be married for that?'

He paused, his lips twitching. 'You do. I won't have you feeling guilty or ashamed about what happens between us. Ever.'

Meghan was conscious of Ana clearing their dishes. She didn't think the housekeeper understood much English, yet surely Alessandro's intimate caressing tone came across in any language?

'Thank you for that respect,' she managed stiffly.

Ana loaded the dishwasher while they finished their coffee, and then retreated to another part of the house. Meghan watched her broad back disappear with a twitch of unease.

'She doesn't like me,' she said suddenly.

Alessandro glanced up from the newspaper headlines he'd been scanning once more. 'Who? Ana?'

'Yes, she disapproves of me. I can tell. She glared at me when I came into the kitchen.' Meghan toyed with the handle of her coffee mug. 'Is it always going to be like that?'

'Not when we are married,' Alessandro replied in a flat, final tone. 'And you'll discover that Ana doesn't disapprove of you. She disapproves of me.'

Meghan looked up in surprise, but Alessandro had moved on. He swept the newspaper aside with unconcern and smiled.

'There are other matters to attend to in Milan. You will need clothes—that haversack cannot hold much. I have a flat in Milan, but perhaps you would like to live somewhere new? I leave such decisions to you.'

'I'm sure the flat you have now is fine,' Meghan said faintly. She was reeling from the barrage of information. What was she actually going to *do* in Milan, in her new life?

'You know, I was a teacher in Stanton Springs,' she said hesitantly. 'Languages. I quit my job when…'

'A teacher?' Alessandro glanced at her swiftly, assessingly.

'Well, of course if you want to teach again in Milan I have no problem with it. Perhaps at one of the English or American schools? Something part-time, so you can travel with me if needed?' His voice lowered, filled with promise. 'I don't want to leave you alone...or to be alone myself.'

She nodded. 'Yes...part-time. I'll look into it.'

'*Buon*. But first my family, and the wedding.'

The thought of meeting other di Agnios sent a stab of fear through her. Taking another sip of coffee to quell the nerves rising queasily upwards, Meghan asked, 'What exactly is your business? You mentioned the jewellery boutiques, the property and the finance, but are there other things as well?'

'My grandfather started with the jewels. My father chose to branch out into property, electronics, shipping.' He shrugged. 'A piece of every pie. The jewellery, of course, is our flagship enterprise—what we are truly known for.' He drummed his fingers on the table. 'The man you met yesterday, as unpleasant as he was, owns one of the largest chains of department stores in the United States. We were negotiating a contract to feature Di Agnio jewels in select stores—our own boutique within the department store, as it were.' He shrugged. 'It's no matter.'

'It sounds like quite a big business deal,' Meghan said after a moment.

'There are other deals,' Alessandro replied in dismissal. 'And no deal, business or otherwise, is worth making if you lose your self-respect.'

'Is that what we're making?' Meghan asked suddenly. Her hands tightened on her coffee mug. 'A business deal?'

Alessandro frowned. 'Marriage is a contract, certainly,' he replied. 'But I do not consider it business.' His eyes narrowed. 'Having second thoughts, *cara*?'

'What if I was?'

'I would tell you it is too late. We drive to Milan within the hour.'

'Too late?' Meghan echoed incredulously. 'Are you always going to be this bossy, Alessandro? Because I won't have you ordering me around—'

In response, Alessandro plucked the coffee cup from her

fingers and set it on the table. 'Go and get ready. I've just decided I want to leave as soon as possible.'

'You mean,' Meghan retorted, 'you want to stop this conversation.'

'As a matter of fact, yes. Why don't you pack your things? It won't take long.'

Wordlessly Meghan rose from the table. She wasn't going to waste her energy or emotions on arguing over such petty things. She knew she'd need to save them for later—for the bigger, more important battles that were sure to come.

She went upstairs. Stuffed her few paltry possessions into the worn haversack.

'What am I doing?' she muttered, a bubble of hysteria rising inside her, threatening to escape in a wild peal of laughter. 'What am I *doing*?'

She was leaving for Milan to meet the di Agnio family…to be introduced as Alessandro's fiancée. Bride.

It was so crazy. It was so real. She didn't know what to do but continue to move forward, one inch at a time. If she looked further than the next day, the next moment, she would fall into an abyss of fear and doubt.

'I washed your things.' Ana stood in the doorway, her expression close to a glare. Meghan's waitressing uniform was folded neatly in her hands.

'Thank you, Ana,' she replied in Italian.

Meghan took the clothes hesitantly. Disapproval and dislike rolled from the woman in waves, and she felt compelled to say something.

'You know I am marrying Signor di Agnio?' she said, and Ana nodded stiffly.

'You will—' she began, struggling to find the words. 'You will make him happy?' It was as much an order as a request.

Meghan blinked in surprise. 'He told me you didn't like him,' she blurted out.

'I don't like the man he has become. The boy he was…here…I loved.' Ana blinked and shrugged, impatient. 'Goodbye, *signorina*.'

She left the room, and Meghan stuffed the clothes into her haversack, her mind whirling.

The man he has become.

The man I mean to be.

What was the difference?

'Ready?' Alessandro asked from the doorway. He'd shrugged on a beautifully tailored jacket, worn with unselfconscious ease and grace. 'It takes about two hours to drive to Milan. We'll go straight to my mother's house, if you don't mind.'

With the sunshine turning the distant green fields to gold, Meghan watched the Villa Tre Querce disappear as they drove down the steep, winding hill and through the wrought-iron gates.

'When will we be back?' she asked after a moment.

Alessandro glanced at her. 'To the villa? Who knows? We can plan a honeymoon, of course. Somewhere different...somewhere neither of us have ever been.'

Meghan regarded him thoughtfully. It almost sounded as if she were not the only one who was used to running away.

What are your secrets? she wanted to ask. *What are you hiding from me?* She could hardly ask for the truth now, when she was hiding so much herself. There was time. There had to be time.

Neither of them spoke as Alessandro drove past Spoleto into Tuscany. The fields on either side of the motorway were a blur of browns and greens, and Meghan leaned back in her seat and closed her eyes.

She was, she realised, completely exhausted. She must have dozed, for she woke up as the car began to climb the foothills into Lombardy. Alessandro smiled at her as she sat up, shrugging strands of hair from her eyes.

'We're about an hour away. I've telephoned my mother. She expects us for lunch.'

'Great.' Meghan swallowed nervously. 'Maybe you could tell me about your family?'

He shrugged. 'There is not much to know. My mother, Gabriella, lives in the house I was born in—in Milan. My father died four years ago of a heart attack. My sister, Chiara, lives in London. She works for Di Agnio Enterprises there.'

'And your brother?'

He pressed his lips together, shook his head. 'I told you before. He is dead.'

'Right. I'm sorry.' Meghan felt as if every word she spoke was prodding a nest of vipers, full of poisonous secrets. 'When did he die?'

'Two years ago.'

'Was it from a disease?'

'Car accident.' He spoke so tightly that Meghan almost didn't hear the bitten-out words.

'And what about his wife...?'

'She lives in Rome. You'll find Paula will have nothing to do with me. With us. We needn't consider her at all.' Alessandro spoke so dispassionately, so coldly, that Meghan knew it was a subject she must drop.

For now.

'So I'm just meeting your mother today?' That was easier than a houseful of faceless disapproving di Agnios. One woman she hoped she could handle.

'Yes. Chiara, I hope, will fly to Milan for the wedding.' He glanced at her enquiringly. 'That is, if you agree to a wedding in Milan? Naturally I assumed you did not wish to return to Stanton Springs.'

'Naturally.' Meghan felt the beginnings of a headache. She massaged her temples. 'A wedding in Milan is fine. Something small.'

'Of course. Small, but tasteful.' His mouth quirked in a smile. 'Elegant. Do you wish to notify your family? Perhaps there is someone—a friend—you would like to attend?'

Meghan thought of her family—her two older sisters, safely married and quick to judge, the disapproval and disappointment of her parents who hadn't been able to understand how it had come to this. As for friends—Stephen had pushed them all away, and now she was too embarrassed to tell them the truth.

No one wanted to hear a truth like this. Not in a small town.

'No,' she said after a moment, her voice a thread of sound. 'There's no one.'

Alessandro's mouth tightened, but he did not insult her with pity. 'Just as well. Everything will be easier to arrange.'

The fields and foothills gave way to houses as they entered Milan. On the horizon Meghan saw a cluster of skyscrapers bearing silent witness to the fact that Milan was one of the most glamorous and cosmopolitan cities in Europe.

'Will…will your mother like me, do you think?' Meghan asked, trying to keep her voice diffident.

Alessandro laughed once—a sharp, bitter sound. 'Don't waste your time trying to make people like you, Meghan.'

She blinked. 'But, Alessandro, this is your mother. Of course I want her to like me.'

'Why? She doesn't like *me*.' He stared straight ahead, his expression grim.

'Is that why you don't love her?' Meghan asked after a moment.

'No. I don't love her because I don't love anyone.' Alessandro flexed his hands on the steering wheel as he navigated the increasing city traffic. 'You're not thinking you can change me, Meghan, are you?' he said, his voice pleasant but with the hint of a warning. 'Because I told you once before—you can't. Don't make the mistake of entering this marriage thinking you can change me, save me.'

Save me. The words echoed through Meghan's mind. Did she think she could save Alessandro? Make him believe in love?

No, surely not. Surely she wasn't that desperately naïve. Besides, Meghan thought, you couldn't save anyone. You could only believe they were worth saving.

Did Alessandro think he needed saving? Didn't he think he was worth it? The questions buzzed round in her brain with no answers.

Meghan stared straight ahead. The gothic spires of Il Duomo rose in the distance, as elegant and ostentatious as the decorations on a wedding cake.

'No,' she said flatly. 'I'm not that foolish.'

'Good.'

She glanced at him curiously. 'If you don't care what your mother thinks, why introduce me to her at all?'

His mouth tightened, his fingers flexing once more on the

steering wheel. 'She's family,' he said shortly, and Meghan knew it was time to drop the subject.

A few minutes later they entered a residential section of Milan, where the elegantly fronted town houses were as grand as small *palazzos*. On a large, sweeping square with a fenced green in the middle, Alessandro pulled his car to a stop.

'Here we are.' A dark-suited man had exited the house and approached the car before Alessandro had even killed the engine.

He opened Meghan's door and she clambered out, standing on the kerb while a brisk wind blew her hair into tangles.

The man opened Alessandro's door, and Alessandro tossed him the keys.

They exchanged some rapid Italian, and Meghan caught enough to understand that the man was taking the car round to the back.

'*Grazie*, Manuelo,' Alessandro said, and Manuelo gave a short bow. He asked something else in Italian, but the wind carried the words away. After hesitating for the briefest of seconds, Alessandro answered. Meghan heard her name being mentioned, and cast him a curious glance after Manuelo had left.

'What did you say about me?'

'You're staying here,' Alessandro explained briefly. 'I'll reside at my flat until our wedding.'

Alarm prickled along her spine. 'Why can't we stay together?'

Alessandro barely spared her a glance. 'It's not appropriate.'

Appropriate? Surely staying in separate rooms, chaperoned by Alessandro's own mother, was appropriate enough? Meghan wondered uneasily how Alessandro's attitude towards her might change now that she was becoming his wife and not just his lover.

And yet she knew he was doing it to protect her. To make her feel safe, secure, unashamed. Just as he'd promised. She smiled at him.

'Thank you.'

He shrugged in response. 'It is my duty.'

They entered the town house through a pair of impressive double doors covered with an intricate iron trellis.

The foyer was decorated in cool marble, with a crystal

chandelier suspended above a polished mahogany table with a large bowl of chrysanthemums on it.

Gabriella di Agnio entered from a short flight of steps that led to the rest of the house. She was a small, slender woman in her mid-sixties, dressed in a designer suit in cerise, her silver hair elegantly coiffed.

Meghan immediately felt gauche and underdressed, standing there, dazzled by wealth and glamour, dressed only in a jumper and jeans.

Gabriella's pale blue gaze swept over the pair of them before she inclined her head.

'Alessandro.'

Alessandro inclined his head back. 'Mamma.'

It was hardly a warm greeting, Meghan thought. Tension crackled in the air.

'I'm so glad you came. And your companion—Signorina Selby.' She smiled graciously at Meghan, and Meghan ducked her head back.

'Thank you.'

'Luncheon has been served in the dining room. Will you come?'

'Of course.' Alessandro put his hand on Meghan's back, propelling her forward with gentle pressure.

Gabriella watched this careless movement with narrowed eyes before smiling and leading the way upstairs.

Meghan imagined she could almost see the thread of hostility pulsating, taut and thin as a wire, between Alessandro and his mother. Why didn't they like each other? What had happened?

The dining room was a long, narrow room, with frescoes painted on the walls and ceiling. Meghan drew her breath at the beautiful and obviously old paintings. She'd seen similar work on the walls and ceilings of churches in Umbria and Florence.

The Di Agnios, she realised afresh, were rich. Powerful.

It was unfamiliar, and yet soon it would be hers. Hers.

The wealth…the safety.

The table was set with a fragrant dish of beef risotto. There was an opened bottle of red wine on the sideboard.

Alessandro and his mother sat at opposite ends of the long

polished table, and Meghan was forced to sit in the middle. She felt as if she were watching a tennis match.

'I didn't realise you were in Umbria,' Gabriella began, as she beckoned a servant forward to serve the risotto.

'Business,' Alessandro replied briefly.

'Are you back in Milan for long?'

Alessandro's mouth tightened imperceptibly. 'A few weeks. Maybe more.'

'Business is well?' Gabriella persisted, her voice eerily neutral.

'You should know—you check our stock prices every day.' Alessandro's mouth curled upwards in a mocking smile.

'I like to know what's going on. Now,' Gabriella replied with dignity.

'I know how much it pains you to see me at the helm,' he countered silkily, although his eyes glittered with—what? Meghan couldn't be sure. Rage?

Hurt?

'You almost wish I would make a mess of things, don't you, Mamma?' The word sounded crass. 'It would be easier for you, then, wouldn't it? You'd finally be justified.'

Gabriella dabbed at her lips with a linen napkin. When she raised her head to look at her son, her expression was stony.

'No, Alessandro. I don't want that.' She paused, a new bleakness in her eyes. 'I have never wanted to be justified.'

He shrugged—restless, unconvinced. 'I said almost.'

Meghan gazed down at the risotto on her plate, steaming and richly scented with saffron. Her mouth was so dry she didn't think she could manage a bite, delicious as it looked. She didn't want to look at either Alessandro or Gabriella, or to feel the bitter antagonism that vibrated between them.

She was relieved when the wine was poured, and she took a grateful sip of the rich, ruby liquid. It slid like velvet down her throat.

'What about you, Signorina Selby?' Gabriella turned her rather brittle smile on Meghan. 'Are you staying in Milan for long?'

'I…' Meghan looked helplessly at Alessandro. Obviously his mother was missing some salient details about their relationship.

'As a matter of fact, Mamma, Meghan will be staying as long as I am.' Alessandro smiled, but his eyes were cold and hard. 'We're getting married.'

The silence in the room was a physical thing, a separate presence, stifling, choking. Alessandro kept eating, and Meghan listened to the clink of his silverware while his mother simply stared, her face quite blank.

She recovered herself admirably, giving Meghan a forced but gracious smile. 'Then of course I must offer my felicitations. When is this wedding to be?'

'Next week.' Alessandro barely looked at her as he kept eating. Meghan stared down at her food. Colour scorched her face. She ate a forkful of risotto, and it turned to ash in her mouth.

'So very soon?'

He glanced up darkly. 'For the simple reason that I want to begin my new life with my bride, Mamma. No matter what conclusions you have jumped to about her or me.'

Good heavens, did Gabriella think she was pregnant? Meghan's cheeks burned hotter.

'I am very happy for both of you, then,' Gabriella said after a tiny pause.

There could be no mistaking that she was not pleased with this news. And what mother would be? Her son had brought home a stranger—one from another country, another *world*—and announced he was marrying her within a week.

Was this what Alessandro called appropriate?

'I'd appreciate it,' he said now, 'if you could take Meghan out to buy some suitable clothes. She has very little with her, and of course there is no one with better taste than you, Mamma.' Somehow he turned it into an insult. 'I will be quite busy for the next few days, managing some business from America.'

'I would be delighted.' Gabriella turned to Meghan with a smile that bordered on genuine. 'It will give me a chance to know my future daughter-in-law a bit better.'

Better than what? Meghan thought. A complete stranger? She pressed her napkin to her lips, suppressing the bubble of hysterical laughter that threatened to escape.

This was so, so crazy.

So wrong.

Yet when she'd been with Alessandro it had felt so *right*.

The man he'd been with her, alone in Umbria, was so different from this angry, haunted stranger.

Who was he?

Had she made the most enormous mistake of her life in agreeing to this?

And could she get out of it?

Somehow she thought that would prove difficult to do.

She glanced up, saw Alessandro take a sip of wine. He was gazing at his mother with a disappointed, almost sad look on his face, before the mask of masculine authority slipped back into place.

I'm not making a mistake.

Meghan clung to that hope, thin as it was.

Right now it felt as if it was all she had.

After lunch Alessandro excused himself to go to the office, announcing that he would be back for dinner. Gabriella showed Meghan to her room, tactfully suggesting she might appreciate a rest.

Meghan was grateful. Not only was she exhausted, but she couldn't endure an afternoon of strained conversation with Gabriella—and she had a feeling the older woman felt the same.

She drew the heavy brocade drapes, kicked off her shoes, and crawled under the soft duvet, closing her eyes against the oppressive environment of the house around her, the tensions unspoken, unrecognised, and yet so very evident.

Sleep came with blessed speed.

When she awoke the room was in shadow, late afternoon sunlight filtering through the crack in the curtains. She stretched, luxuriating in the warm, comfortable bed, knowing the memories and fears would rush back soon enough.

Then she realised someone was sitting on the edge of the bed, watching her.

It was Alessandro.

She gave a soft little gasp of surprise and tried to sit up. He stayed her with one hand on her leg, his touch burning even through the heavy material of the duvet.

'Don't. You looked so relaxed, so at peace. I've never seen you sleep before.'

His voice was soft, his face cloaked in shadow. Gently he stroked the length of her leg, and Meghan felt the stirrings of the desire that he so easily evoked in her.

'I was tired.'

'I know.' There was a smile in his voice, she knew, even though she couldn't see it. She heard it—heard the tenderness. 'It hasn't been easy for you. I'm sorry. My mother...'

'Why doesn't she like you?' Meghan asked, glad for the darkness that cloaked her question. 'And why don't you like her? You could have given me a little warning, Alessandro.' She didn't mean to sound reproachful, and she tensed for the anger, the withdrawal she was sure would come.

Instead he sighed with an aching weariness. 'You agreed to marry me, didn't you? Just me. Not my mother. Not anyone else.'

'Yes, but other people affect us. They matter.'

His hand moved up her leg to the joining of her thighs, fingers deftly, knowingly moving, stirring delicious feelings inside her. She found herself parting her legs, gasping as he teased her through the covers.

'Alessandro...'

'No one needs to matter,' he murmured, his voice a caress, a promise. 'No one needs to matter but us.'

He moved his hand treacherously upwards, creating flames of need everywhere he brushed his fingers. Across her navel, over her breasts, and then her face. He cupped her cheek, leaning forward so he was almost on top of her. She arched upwards, wanting the contact, the closeness. The touch.

'I look forward to mattering to you very much.'

He stretched out on top of her, and everywhere his body touched hers it burned. Ached.

Meghan moved as a matter of instinct, pressing against him, desiring more, wanting more.

Wanton.

'I think,' Alessandro whispered, 'it will take a long time. A lot of…experience.'

His hand left her face, slid under the duvet with practised ease to caress her breast, teasing her nipple to an aching peak through the soft fabric of her jumper.

Meghan moaned slightly, pushing herself against his hand. She saw Alessandro watching her, his eyes dark, intense, taking pleasure in her pleasure, in the response he so easily evoked in her. His own breathing was ragged, and she could feel the evidence of his desire.

'Alessandro…'

'I want you.' He moved his hands to cup her face once more. 'I want you so much.'

She reached up with her arms, running her fingers through the crisp softness of his hair, pulling his face down to hers.

'Meghan…' he groaned, then captured her mouth with his own. The kiss was deep, demanding, endless.

Needy.

Meghan revelled in the feel of him, the taste of him, in the knowledge that he wanted her as much as she wanted him.

He ended it first, pulling away with a ragged gasp.

'*Gattina*, I can't stand much more of this.'

There was a deep, restless ache of longing within her. A hunger demanding to be satisfied, a thirst to be quenched. Meghan closed her eyes, her own breathing uneven.

'Neither can I.'

'We will be married as soon as it can be arranged.'

Meghan pulled at him, wanting him closer. *Wanting* him. The pulsing ache in her needed to be eased. 'Alessandro…'

He covered her seeking lips with his fingers. 'We will wait till we are wed. Difficult as it is…and, *da tutti i san*, it is difficult for me.'

She gave a little groan. 'Who made that rule?'

Alessandro chuckled. 'I suppose that is up for debate. But I'm making it now. When we make love there will be no shame. No shadows.'

Meghan wanted to argue. The need, the desire was so strong.

She wanted to tell him there were no shadows. But she knew she would be lying.

She needed to tell him something else first.

'All right,' she said as she pushed up to a sitting position. 'I can wait. I have as much self-control as you do.'

'I look forward to shattering it one day soon,' Alessandro said softly.

He was so patient with her, Meghan realised. So tender. Even though he didn't love her. Perhaps it could be enough for them to build a life, a marriage upon. The thought gave her hope; it made her happy. 'You're a good man, Alessandro.'

He stilled, tensed, swinging around to look at her with a gaze that was dark and unyielding. Cold. 'Why do you say that?'

Meghan shrugged, discomfited by his sudden change of mood, his quiet, lethal tone. 'Because you are.'

He shook his head; Meghan thought she heard him laugh softly. She didn't like the sound.

'Dinner is in half an hour. My mother keeps a formal table. Will you be ready?'

A formal table? With a rush of nerves, Meghan realised she didn't have anything appropriate to wear. 'I'm afraid my haversack doesn't hold evening gowns,' she joked, but Alessandro just shrugged.

'There are some clothes in the cupboard in this room. I imagine something suitable can be found there. And tomorrow you will go with my mother to buy a new wardrobe, as I said.'

Meghan gave him a teasing little smile. 'And who do *these* clothes belong to?'

Alessandro watched her for a moment, his face expressionless, his tone bland. When he spoke, it was with cold decision. 'I imagine,' he replied, 'they belong to one of my mistresses. I will see you at dinner.'

He slipped from the bed and the room, leaving Meghan alone in the darkness with the shock and pain caused by a comment so cruelly, so casually delivered.

CHAPTER EIGHT

'I THINK we will find all that you need on the Via Montenapoleone,' Gabriella told Meghan the next day, as they took the di Agnio limousine into Milan's shopping district. 'The best shops are there—including the flagship Di Agnio boutique.'

Meghan nodded, barely taking in her future mother-in-law's words. She was hopelessly distracted by the remorseless echo of Alessandro's voice.

One of my mistresses.

After he'd left the room Meghan had opened the cupboard and found a range of clothes, from casual dresses and jeans to screamingly expensive evening gowns.

His mistresses' clothes.

Why had he said that?

Meghan had sighed as she'd taken in one designer gown after another, her hands roaming mindlessly over silk, satin and crêpe. Of course she'd known he'd had lovers. Mistresses. He was a virile, beautiful man. Of course he had. He'd hinted at it before.

But why mention it then, in the twilit intimacy of the darkened bedroom, her lips still burning from his kisses, her senses still scattered by his touch? The remark had been delivered with the cruel, cold accuracy of an arrow to the heart…and it had met its target.

He had, Meghan knew, been warning her.

Don't fall in love with me. The voice in her head was as loud as if he'd actually said it.

And hadn't he? He'd warned her before. She should have realised a single moment of tenderness, companionship, desire was simply that.

A moment in an otherwise barren marriage.

A marriage of convenience…for both of them. No matter how it felt, no matter how it seemed.

He wanted someone to give him an heir. A willing woman in his bed who wouldn't demand love. Someone to keep him from being alone. Lonely.

A woman who wouldn't *bother* him too much.

And she wanted power. Safety. Security. Release from the fear and shame.

That was why she'd agreed. *That* was the promise she would build her life upon.

Not flimsy dreams of love, of affection, but the man Alessandro had said he meant to be.

She'd finally picked one of the gowns—a simple design of black silk that had swirled about her calves and was the least revealing—and had gone downstairs.

Dinner had been stilted, strained. Gabriella had tried to make conversation, Meghan had helped her woodenly, and Alessandro had sat in flinty silence, preoccupied, refusing even to meet Meghan's gaze, indifferent to his mother's.

After dinner he'd excused himself, and when Meghan had woken in the morning he'd already gone to work. She wondered if she'd actually see him again before the wedding.

The wedding. She could leave, she reminded herself. Slip out while he was at the office and never come back.

Keep running.

The trouble was, she didn't want to.

She was damned by her own need.

Her own desire.

'Here we are.' Gabriella's voice was bright, her manner only a little stiff, as the car slowed to a stop on a long, glittering street lined with the most famous and expensive designer names in the world. Boutiques with a single garment hanging in the window and a lock on the door.

The next few hours were a blur of clothes and fitting rooms. Gabriella spoke rapid Italian with sleek saleswomen who examined Meghan's body and thrust clothes at her as if she were no more than a problem, a rather difficult problem, to be fixed.

Three hours and a dozen designer bags later, Gabriella glanced consideringly at Meghan and said, 'I know Alessandro has not mentioned it, but since you are to be married, perhaps we could do your hair? Your make-up? There is a salon on the next street that can take you now.'

Meghan nodded dumbly. She hadn't had a haircut in over six months.

'*Buon.*' Gabriella smiled. 'As sudden as this arrangement may be, every bride wants to look beautiful on her wedding day, yes? And what of your dress?'

'Dress?' Meghan repeated uncertainly. She was humbled by Gabriella's acceptance, by the woman's friendliness.

'Wedding dress,' Gabriella explained. 'There are few shops that can fit and alter a dress in so short a time.'

'It's going to be a very small wedding,' Meghan said hurriedly. 'I can wear something simple. One of the dresses you bought for me.'

'No, that will not do. You need a proper dress—a bride's dress.' Gabriella paused. 'You can wear mine.'

'What?' Meghan was stunned.

Gabriella laughed lightly. 'I know, it is old—but they call it vintage these days, yes? And it is a timeless classic, I assure you. I have a seamstress who can alter it in a matter of hours.'

'I can't—' Meghan began, and Gabriella fixed her with a pale, penetrating stare so similar to her son's.

'But why not? You are marrying my son, are you not? You are going to be my daughter-in-law. You need a dress. Of course, if you don't like it you must not wear it. We can find something else.'

'It's not that.' Meghan stared down at her hands. 'It's just…' She looked up, open, honest. She had to know. She would not start this life, begin in this family, with mistrust. 'Why don't you hate me?'

Gabriella looked taken aback. 'But why should I hate you?'

'I've known Alessandro for a very short while. I'm not from your…class.' She stumbled over the words, the explanation. 'I'm not even Italian. Perhaps you had someone in mind for him already…'

Gabriella shook her head. 'No, my dear. The only thing I have in mind for Alessandro now is his own happiness.'

'Yet…' Meghan swallowed. 'There's so much tension between you.'

Gabriella smiled, the movement strained. 'Alessandro is very angry with me.' She paused, weighing her words. 'I have not considered his happiness in the past as much as I should have. In all honesty, I have not considered…him. It was easier to forget. And then there was the—'

'Forget your own son?' The words came out before Meghan could stop herself, and she winced as pain shadowed Gabriella's features.

'Alessandro was not an easy child—nor, for that matter, is he an easy man. I realise now my own blame in who he became. It is why he is so angry.' She shrugged sadly. 'If you make him happy, then how can I complain?'

'I hope I will,' Meghan whispered.

'You will.' Gabriella shrugged off the serious talk. 'With your new hair and make-up, in my wedding dress… *Da tutti i san!* Who could resist you?'

Meghan found herself smiling back. '*Da tutti i san,*' she repeated. 'Alessandro says that. What does it mean?'

'By all the saints. His grandmother used to say it a lot. He was…very close to her.'

Meghan was intrigued by this glimpse into an Alessandro she didn't know, couldn't fathom. 'Did she die?'

'When he was nine. She lived in Umbria, at the villa.' Gabriella shot her a quick, speculative look. 'You know it?'

'Yes.' Meghan couldn't keep a tell-tale flush from warming her face. 'I thought it had belonged to Alessandro's father.'

'Yes, it was my husband's family home.'

'And then Alessandro's brother's?' Meghan pressed, seeking more information.

Gabriella's lips pressed together. 'Yes, it belonged to Roberto. Now it is Alessandro's, as perhaps it should have been all along. Enough talk. We must eat. Shopping is hard work. And tonight you can show Alessandro your purchases. He will be pleased, I hope.'

Meghan nodded. Her stomach had turned queasy, roiling with nerves and doubts. The last time she'd seen Alessandro he hadn't looked pleased at all, about anything.

About her.

Had he changed his mind?

With lurching fear, she realised she didn't want him to. How had she started to believe in this, in *them*, so quickly? So *much*?

Especially when she didn't even know what *them* meant— what they would be to each other. How a marriage would *work*.

That evening Meghan gazed at her reflection in amazement.

The clothes had been put away, she'd had a nap, and she'd awoken refreshed, ready.

And beautiful.

She touched her hair, now highlighted and styled in gentle waves to her shoulders. The hairdresser hadn't changed her look; he'd just made her better. More herself.

It had taken, Meghan acknowledged wryly, a lot of money to accomplish that.

The make-up she'd painstakingly applied emphasised her golden-green eyes, making her lashes thick and long, sweeping down to delicately tinted cheeks. Her lips were full and sensual without being pouty. She smiled, intrigued by her new self.

She glanced down at herself, dressed in one of the gowns purchased that morning. It was a pale amber, the colour of morning sunlight.

'It complements your eyes,' Gabriella had said in approval. 'Very nice.'

Looking at herself, Meghan had to agree. The dress was simple, pouring over her body like liquid sunshine without being too revealing, too obvious.

Hinting, not screaming.

Promising.

Taking a deep breath, Meghan turned away from her reflection, the image in the mirror having bolstered her confidence enough. It was time to go downstairs and meet Alessandro.

The central staircase of the town house twisted in a spiral down to the foyer, and as Meghan descended the marble steps she saw Alessandro at the bottom, dressed in a navy blue suit, his back to her. One hand was shoved in his trouser pocket, the other raked through his ebony hair.

Meghan paused on the step, silent and watching. Watching him. Was she imagining the vulnerability in his stance? She must be, for every lithe movement radiated power, strength, authority. Control.

Need.

The word came from nowhere; the thought was stunning in its force.

Surely Alessandro could never need anything?

Surely he could never need her?

Need was more than desire.

Need was love.

He turned, and his eyes blazed for a moment, sweeping over her, drinking her in.

Meghan felt heat everywhere his eyes roamed. Treacherous, wonderful heat. It weakened her, made her sway, and Alessandro saw and smiled.

He reached for the banister, gripped it hard, and Meghan realised with a ripple of shock that he was just as affected as she was.

She walked on trembling legs down the last few steps into the foyer.

'Hello, Alessandro.'

He reached for her fingers, gently pulling him to her. His lips brushed hers, and when he spoke it was a whisper against her mouth.

'Why don't you hate me?'

Meghan tensed, startled. 'Why would I hate you?'

He kissed her again, moved his lips to her temple. 'I didn't mean to hurt you, *gattina*.'

Yes, you did. Meghan smiled through the sudden sting of tears. 'It's all right.'

'No.' His voice was low and almost savage. He kissed her again, hard on the mouth, his fingers digging into her shoulders before he relaxed, his hands softening into a caress. 'No,' he said against her lips. 'But it will be.'

He stepped back, scorching her with one primal, possessive look. 'You look ravishing.'

He took her hand, linking their fingers as he led her into the dining room.

'So,' Gabriella began when they were seated, the food served and wine poured, 'you say this wedding is next week? Have you made preparations? Secured a church?'

Meghan glanced enquiringly at Alessandro, as curious to know the details as her future mother-in-law.

'We will be married on Friday, at the San Pietro church,' Alessandro informed them both. 'There will be a reception afterwards at the Principe di Savoia.' He glanced at Meghan. 'I would have left the arrangements to you, but you are a stranger to this city. I thought it would be easier to arrange it all myself. I hope that is agreeable to you?'

'Of course,' she murmured.

'The Principe di Savoia is Milan's most luxurious hotel,' Gabriella informed her. 'You will be well served there.' She turned to Alessandro, her thin eyebrows raised. 'And how many guests are you inviting to this celebration, may I ask? Have you taken care of the invitations as well?'

'It will be a small affair, as Meghan and I both want. Family only. A few friends.' He smiled, his voice becoming a drawl. 'You must invite who you like though, Mamma. I imagine you have plenty of friends who are eager to witness the spectacle…your prodigal son getting married.'

'Thank you.' Gabriella clearly chose to ignore the jibe. 'Chiara is coming?'

'I spoke to her on the telephone,' Alessandro confirmed. 'She can only come for the day. You know how busy she is.'

'How busy she chooses to be,' Gabriella agreed. 'And what of your family, Meghan?'

'I don't have anyone coming.' It came out as a wretched confession. Meghan lifted her chin. 'I've been travelling for a while now, and I've…lost touch with people from home.'

Gabriella maintained an eloquent silence at this news, and Meghan knew how odd it must sound. No friends, no family?

No one.

She took a bite of the antipasti—rigatoni in a delicate cream sauce. When would she tell her family? she wondered. When would she go back?

The thought was too depressing, and so she pushed it away. There was enough to deal with here. She had her own shadows, but so did Alessandro.

She wondered if she would ever find out what they were.

After dinner Gabriella excused herself, and Alessandro and Meghan were left alone in the elegant drawing room that faced the front of the house.

A tension thrummed between them, taut and expectant. Meghan realised they hadn't had much experience in being alone, living as a couple, doing normal, boring things.

The intensity remained. It wouldn't go away.

How long could they keep this up?

She moved around the room, seeking bland conversation, something innocuous, safe.

Like the villa, the drawing room was decorated in shades of cream and ivory, the muted colours punctuated by the vivid oil paintings on the wall.

Meghan inspected one while Alessandro poured them drinks.

'Is this by the same artist as the ones in the villa?' she asked. 'I don't know much about art, but it looks similar.'

'So it is,' Alessandro agreed, his voice neutral. She knew he was at his most dangerous when his face turned blank, his voice toneless, the mask dropping into place.

She needed to be careful. She needed to know.

He knocked back half of his *negroni* before handing Meghan her own glass.

'Who is the artist?' she asked, and Alessandro took another sip of his drink.

'My brother. You can see my parents were very fond of his work. They have his paintings in nearly every room of this house.'

Meghan studied him, his careless pose, and yet there was restless energy radiating from every taut line of his beautiful body. The mood had suddenly turned sour, savage, and she wasn't sure why. 'Are you jealous of him?' she asked uncertainly, and he raked her with a cool, contemptuous gaze.

'Jealous? He's dead. What is there to be jealous of?'

'I meant before that.' Meghan spoke cautiously, feeling each word as though in a darkened maze of memories, every turn leading to an unforeseen trap. A danger.

'Was I jealous of my brother?' Alessandro spoke musingly, his expression distant. 'Perhaps I was, a little. You've given me an amusing bit of therapy there.' His tone turned sardonic. 'I'd never considered that before.'

'Don't.' Meghan put her glass of *negroni* down, untasted. 'You sound like a little boy—mad at his mother, jealous of his brother.'

His eyes turned so dark she couldn't see his pupils. It was as if his muscles, his mood, were carved from ice. 'You know nothing about it.'

'No, I don't. So why don't you tell me?'

'I've told you all you need to know.'

'I want to know more,' she persisted, her voice breaking a little. 'Alessandro, I want to understand you.'

He laughed, a harsh sound, raking a hand through his hair before setting his glass down so hard it rattled. 'Trust me, Meghan,' he said savagely, 'you do *not* want to understand me.'

Meghan trembled inwardly at his words, but she stood her ground. 'Tell me why not, then.'

He glanced at her, eyes blazing, punishing. His smile was a cruel slash of colour on his face. She took an unsteady step backwards.

'Why do you think I chose you?' he asked, his voice a deadly purr. 'And not some Italian girl, like you said? Someone from my own class, culture? Because face it, Meghan…' he glanced at her with a searing contempt that made her feel tarted-up and dirty '…you're not.'

'I know I'm not,' she whispered, hurt despite her intention not to be, despite her realisation that he was trying to hurt her and she was letting him. This was perhaps hurting him as much as it was her.

Why did he do this to her? To himself?

Why?

'I chose you because you don't know my family, you don't know me, and it can stay that way. I don't *want* you to know me. I don't *want* you to understand me. I don't love you, and you don't love me, remember? So let's enjoy each other's company—and bodies—without any unnecessary complications. Is that understood?' His mouth turned upwards in a mocking smile.

Meghan stumbled back a step, sickened. 'What about the promises you made to me, Alessandro? What about *the man you mean to be*? Is this it? Because if so, I don't want any part of you.' The words rang out, echoing, condemning.

The smile died on his face, leaving it blank and empty. He stared at her for a moment, and Meghan opened her mouth to deny what she said, to apologise. She wanted him. She wanted *all* of him. She wanted to understand, to explain, to…

Help. Help him.

'It's too late for regrets,' he said tonelessly. 'For either of us. You will marry me, Meghan. You don't have any choice. And neither do I.'

'We both have choices,' Meghan protested, though her voice sounded feeble. 'This may have been a deal, Alessandro, but we can break it.' Not that she wanted to even now, God help her.

'We cannot!'

His hand slashed through the air, and, goaded, Meghan found herself replying, '*I* can.'

He came to her in two strides, his face lit with a primal ferocity as he grabbed her shoulders. 'You will not break it, Meghan. Swear to me!'

'Don't do this,' she whispered. Tears streaked down her face.

He released her. Then his hands slid down her arms, down her sides, and he fell to his knees, his head buried against her middle.

'I'm sorry,' he whispered, his voice jagged and broken. He drew in a shuddering breath and his arms wrapped around her waist, clinging to her as if she were his anchor. 'I never meant… What kind of man am I?' It came out as an anguished cry, a plea for mercy. '*What kind of man am I?*'

Meghan trembled with suppressed emotion, pain. The tears still streaked down her face as she buried her fingers in his hair. He lifted his head to gaze up at her. The bleak despair etched in harsh, unforgiving lines on Alessandro's face was nearly her undoing.

'The man you mean to be,' she whispered, and kissed him with all the tenderness she longed to give him. He knelt there, motionless, accepting her offering, before he pulled her down to him, turning the kiss into something deeper, something that hurt like a wound, deep inside.

His arms were around her, hard and desperate, the kiss plundering, plunging. Meghan kissed him back, desire fanning quickly, leaping into dangerous flames. She threw her head back to give him access to her throat, desire now pouring through her in a molten wave, burning her up. Their breathing was harsh, ragged.

He pulled her dress down, mindless of the delicate material. The sound of its tearing rent the air, and his voice came out in a sob as he buried his head between her breasts, touching her, suckling her, turning her to liquid fire even as the tears dried on her cheeks.

She pulled open his shirt, the buttons popping and scattering across the floor, let her hands touch and twist and tease, before wrapping her arms around the smooth, broad expanse of his back, pulling him closer.

She didn't know what was happening—why this moment of passion had sprung from pain and despair, sorrow and misery.

She only knew that she wanted to satisfy him—that she was his, she *would* be his.

It was what he needed.

And she needed it too; her body ached, demanding to be

quenched. She pulled him to her, her dress bunched around her waist, her thighs bare and splayed open.

Alessandro was poised above her, one hand on the waistband of his trousers, undoing his fly with urgent trembling fingers, when he suddenly stilled. Stopped.

The moment was endless. She looked up from the haze of her own need and desire and saw a terrible anguish on his face. He dropped his hand from his trousers, rolled off her onto his back on the floor, one arm covering his face.

'Alessandro…'

'Heaven help me,' he choked out. 'Look at us. Look at *me*.' He sounded disgusted, sickened.

'I'm sorry…' Meghan began hesitantly. She lay there, her dress in hopeless disarray, her body still open to him. Still wanting.

He didn't look at her as he shook his head. '*You* are sorry? *Gattina*, no. *No*.' It came out harshly. He dropped his arm from his face, sat up and raked a hand through his hair, his face still averted. 'Just go, Meghan,' he said in a low voice. 'Leave me. I'm no good to you now.'

Meghan sat up too, pulled her dress back on with trembling fingers. She wanted to touch him, wanted to put her arms around his hunched shoulders, stroke his bowed head. 'Yes, you are.'

He shook his head again, his hands fisted in his hair. '*Please*. Please leave me. For both our sakes.' His voice rose to a near roar. 'Go!'

Choking back the misery and confusion that threatened to rise up into an endless sob, Meghan went.

CHAPTER NINE

THE wedding was a blur.

Meghan understood the words, but the Italian washed over her in a soothing, melodious tide of language.

She wore the dress—Gabriella's timelessly elegant ivory gown—altered to fit her own more generous curves.

She saw the guests, a handful of discreet friends and business associates who watched the strange, sudden ceremony with carefully blank faces.

She had the bridesmaids—Alessandro's younger sister, Chiara, sleek and quiet, having flown in that morning from London. She was flying out immediately after the reception, and from the way she stood next to Meghan, her body tense and straining as the priest rambled on, Meghan guessed she couldn't get out of there fast enough.

Alessandro's best man, Stefano Lucrezi, was watchful and alert, his attention solely on the priest. Meghan had the sense that he was aware in some way of Chiara, though he never looked at her.

And Alessandro? He stood there, calm, urbane, implacable. In a few minutes—seconds, perhaps—he would be her husband.

He hadn't spoken one word to her since she'd entered the church, walked down the ancient stone aisle alone amidst a sea of frighteningly neutral faces.

This was her life now.

Now, *now* it was too late to back out.

And still she didn't want to.

Silly, naïve her.

After that shattered evening when they'd almost made love—passionate, desperate, on the floor—Alessandro had reverted to his old self: charming, urbane, amusing.

A fake.

Meghan saw it now—saw how the mask dropped into place, saw how he protected himself, kept anyone from guessing, knowing who he really was.

She still didn't.

And yet she was here, marrying him, because she wanted to know.

It wasn't just about the power any more.

It was about the need.

The priest stopped talking, and Meghan saw that the guests had all stood. Waiting.

She was married.

Alessandro took her cold hand in his, and together they walked out of the church into the pale sunshine of the early spring day.

Everyone else followed them out before either of them had exchanged a word. Stefano clapped Alessandro on the shoulder, and Meghan recognised the various phrases of congratulation, though she felt numb to the emotions.

Someone brought forward a beribboned box, gesturing excitedly for Meghan to open it.

She looked uncertainly from the box on the steps of the church to Alessandro, whose expression was inscrutable.

'They want you to open it,' he explained, with a slight smile, and Meghan moved forward. Was it a present? A custom? She wished Alessandro would explain, but he'd only folded his arms over his chest, his eyes glinting with cool amusement.

'You could help me a little,' she said under her breath, and Alessandro smiled.

'But I'm enjoying the view from here.'

Meghan gritted her teeth. Charming, aloof, distant. This was the man he chose to be now, and she would have to accept it.

She couldn't make him bare his true self. Wasn't sure she was ready for it. The glimpse she'd had so far had shot her to pieces.

She pulled on the ribbons and tentatively opened the lid of the box.

There was a loud cooing sound, the rushing of wings, and she stumbled back in surprise, her arms thrown over her face, as two doves soared into the sky amid many exclamations and cheers.

'An Italian tradition,' Alessandro informed her dryly as she lowered her arms and gazed upwards at the birds, now circling the church spire. 'To symbolise the happiness and unity of the married couple. My mother arranged it, no doubt. Reading things into this marriage that are not there.'

Meghan was struck to her soul, but she mustered enough spirit to reply in kind. 'What? You don't want happiness? Surely *that's* a reasonable expectation for both of us, Alessandro?'

'Is it?' There was no mistaking the sardonic doubt in his voice.

'Yes,' Meghan said firmly, daring him to believe, wanting to believe herself. 'It is.'

He gazed down at her, and a reluctant smile tugged at his mouth. 'As long as you realise what makes us happy.'

What made *him* happy. More warnings. Meghan was tired of it. 'Don't flatter yourself,' she hissed under her breath. 'I'm not in that much danger of falling in love with you!'

Alessandro's face relaxed and he gave a little chuckle. 'I'm glad to hear it. I like your claws, *gattina*. And perhaps we *shall* both be happy.'

He took her elbow, steering her through the crowd into the waiting limo that would take them to the reception.

'Who are all those people?' Meghan asked as she craned backwards to look at the milling crowd.

'Mostly business associates, friends of my mother's.' He shrugged in dismissal.

'What about your friends?'

He smiled, but his voice was hard. 'My friends were not invited.'

What on earth did that mean? Meghan leaned back against the seat and closed her eyes. 'But you have friends,' she said after a moment. 'Will I meet them?'

'No.'

End of discussion. Right now Meghan was too tired to press, too weary to hear his warnings, his rebukes.

'What a pair we are,' she said, trying to make her voice light. 'Friendless and alone.'

'That's why I married you, isn't it?' Alessandro returned silkily. 'Now we're not alone. Now we have each other.'

Somehow his lethal, mocking tone robbed the words of any comfort.

The reception was in a private room at the Principe di Savoia, one of Milan's most elegant hotels. Meghan sat down, ate the delicious food, drank the exquisite wine, and accepted the embraces and congratulations from a crowd that had become loosened and relaxed, ready to celebrate.

Alessandro sat in the middle of it all, dark and foreboding. When he greeted someone his voice was polished and smooth; he laughed at the jokes and participated in the customary dances, even La Tarantella, the circle dance that Meghan stumbled through, uncertain of the steps, distant from the jollity.

Yet there was no mistaking his dark preoccupation. Almost, Meghan thought sadly, as if he wanted to be somewhere else.

Be someone else.

Her stomach churned. Her heart twisted. Doubt washed over her, yet she couldn't regret. She'd made this decision. She'd wanted to be here.

Only she hadn't realised just how very hard it would be. How very hard *Alessandro* would be, his mouth a grim line, his eyes flinty, every taut line of his body making him guarded, unapproachable.

Unlovable.

How many secrets, dark and treacherous, churned and seethed in the space between them, creating an impossible chasm?

And they weren't even her secrets.

They were his.

When she was alone for a moment, scraping her sanity together as she stood by a pillar at the side of the dance floor, Stefano Lucrezi approached her.

'Congratulations, Signora di Agnio.' His voice was smooth and pleasant, yet the title jolted her.

'Thank you, Signor Lucrezi.'

'Please, call me Stefano. So, this was quite the love match?' He raised his eyebrows, smiling at her. 'I've never known Alessandro to move so quickly with a woman before.'

'Is that so?' Meghan's own smile turned brittle. 'He has taken care to warn me that he has moved quite quickly with plenty of women in the past.'

Stefano's gaze did not falter. 'Ah, so you know of his reputation?'

His reputation? It sounded bad. Still, if the secret that rode Alessandro, drove him to despair, was simply having had too many affairs, Meghan thought she could accept it. She didn't like it, but if it was the reality she would learn to deal with it.

'No one's told me much of anything,' she said frankly. She looked at Stefano. He seemed friendly, open, and she wanted answers. 'Do you know Alessandro well?'

'As well as anybody does. He keeps to himself.'

'Sometimes,' Meghan said quietly, her voice an ache, 'I think I know him quite well. And at other times not at all.'

'He is, perhaps, two different people,' Stefano said after a moment. 'The man he was, and the man he is now.'

And the man he meant to be. 'What do you mean, exactly? What happened to change him?'

Stefano shook his head. 'It is not for me to say.' He patted her hand gently. 'Perhaps he will tell you, *signora*, in time.'

Sketching a slight bow, Stefano left her.

Meghan sagged against the pillar behind her. She'd been given clues to this impossible, unfathomable man, but she didn't understand what they meant.

Didn't know if she could keep digging for answers.

Wasn't sure she wanted to find out.

Across the room Alessandro watched his bride with a cold detachment he was far from feeling. Encasing himself in ice was the only way to get through this event, when every pair of eyes watched him speculatively, hungrily, waiting for disaster, shame.

His own.

They all wanted him to fail—expected it. He'd lived with that for two years, and it should mean nothing to him now.

It *did* mean nothing to him—except for the one person in the room who didn't understand.

The one person he couldn't bear to see him fail.

And yet he would fail. Not with business, because he was good at that. He'd surprised everyone, especially himself, when he'd taken the reins of his father's company and found that he held them with natural ease.

He would fail *her*. He already had, in so many ways, and he saw it in the stark confusion in her eyes—the way she turned towards and away from him at the same time, because she didn't know what he would do, who he was.

What he was.

'I just spoke to your bride.' Stefano stood by Alessandro's chair, smiling faintly. 'She seems quite fond of you, my friend.'

'She'll learn better.'

'Do you love her?'

Alessandro laughed shortly. 'No. Of course not.'

Stefano nodded musingly, although his voice sounded regretful. 'It's easier that way, I suppose.'

Alessandro turned to him, raised one eyebrow in mocking incredulity. 'You're not going to tell me you believe in true love?'

'Of course not.' Stefano smiled tightly. 'You know as well as I do that such a thing is a fairytale. We're wise men, Alessandro.'

'Yes,' he replied flatly, his eyes fastened on Meghan's slight form. 'We are.'

It was time to end this torture. He could not take any more speculation, whispered gossip. He wanted to be alone. He wanted to be with Meghan.

It was time to claim his bride.

She felt someone's gaze on her, and before she turned, before she saw who it was, she knew.

The heat and the desire turned her limbs weak, her mind blank and yet flooded with feeling.

Alessandro.

Meghan turned, saw him watching her, a possessive smile quirking his lips.

He moved towards her, lithe and loose-limbed, an elegant stalking that she surrendered to completely.

'It is time to go.'

'Already?'

'The bride and groom must leave first. It is tradition.' His arm snaked around her waist and he pulled her to his side. 'And I can wait no longer. You look beautiful in that dress, *cara*.'

'It's your mother's. She was very generous to offer it.'

'Yes, I can see how she wants to make amends.' He brushed her hair with his lips. 'But I do not want to talk of her. There is a suite upstairs, waiting for us.'

Meghan's stomach plunged with nerves. She wanted this, she reminded herself. She wanted this so very much.

It didn't stop her from being scared.

'All right. Do we say goodbye?'

'Not unless you want lots of bawdy jokes and knowing looks.'

Meghan shuddered. 'I couldn't stand that.'

'Then we slip out now, quietly, when no one is looking.'

'What will people think?'

'That we can't wait to be alone with each other. And it's true…isn't it?'

She nodded shakily. 'Yes, it's true.'

Even if I'm terrified.

They were silent as they slipped from the reception, silent as they rode in the elevator to the top floor. Silent as Alessandro swiped the electronic key card and ushered her into a sumptuous suite of rooms.

Silent—yet the tension, the expectation, the desire, thrummed to life between them, more potent than any words or looks. It was a physical presence, a separate entity, and it filled the space with silent, urgent demand.

Meghan glanced around at the elegant chairs and sofas, the double doors that led into the bedroom. Her mind was blank and buzzing. 'This is very nice.'

'Do you want a bath? I've had your clothes brought from the town house.'

Meghan nodded numbly. 'Yes, fine.'

He walked over to her, skimmed his hands lightly over her bare shoulders. 'Don't be afraid, Meghan. There are no shadows here.'

But there were, she realised. There always would be. Because he didn't know. Didn't understand.

She couldn't make him tell her his secrets, but she could at least tell him her own. Banish her own shadows.

'I think,' she said jerkily, 'I'll have that bath.'

'*Buon*. I'll be waiting.'

Meghan sifted through her suitcase, found her toiletry bag, full of the new cosmetics, tubes and sprays and gels Gabriella had picked out for her, and the nightgown also selected by her mother-in-law—a sheath of ivory silk, held up with two tiny straps and scalloped with lace. She bunched the garment in her fist and, avoiding Alessandro's gaze, retreated into the bathroom.

The room was larger than her bedroom back at the hostel, a lifetime ago. Meghan turned the taps, added luxurious scented bath foam, carefully stripped off her wedding gown and slipped it on a hanger.

She stayed in the bath for half an hour, searching for her courage, clinging to what little she found.

Finally, reluctantly, her pulse thrumming—not just from the heat of the bath water—she rose from the tub and dried herself off, slipping on the bridal nightgown.

There was a thick terrycloth robe hanging on the door, provided by the hotel. Meghan slipped that on too.

Alessandro was stretched out on the bed, relaxed, his jacket and tie off, the top two buttons of his shirt undone. Just the sight of that little bit of clean, tanned skin caused Meghan's pulse to skitter higher.

He sat up when he saw her, taking in her bulky bathrobe with an ironic knowing look.

'You won't be needing that, will you?'

'No, but I want to talk to you first.'

A guarded expression came into his eyes, but he shrugged and patted the bed next to him. 'Of course. What about?'

'Me.' Meghan swallowed nervously and sat down. Her fingers fiddled with the sash of the robe. She couldn't look at him. 'Alessandro, I haven't told you everything about my past. About Stephen. I was too ashamed.'

'You want to tell me now?' His voice was carefully neutral.

'Yes. Because I don't want there to be secrets between us. My secrets.' Meghan forced herself to look up, meet his eyes. 'My shadows. And I want you to understand why I am…the way I am.'

He was quiet for a moment, his face blank. A mask. 'All right.'

Meghan took a deep, shuddering breath. This was so hard. Yet she knew she needed to do this.

Confession. Absolution.

'There was more to it than him just being married.'

Alessandro waited, silent. Meghan forced herself to continue. 'Stephen had always been handsome, charming. I knew he was a little racy, a little wild. I accepted it as part of him, and I loved him anyway. Or so I told myself. It's amazing the things you can convince yourself of when you're blind. In love.'

'Or naïve,' Alessandro added quietly.

Meghan nodded. 'I was all three. I accepted the sneaking around. I thought it was because he was a prominent business-man—a lawyer—and he didn't want to publicise his romantic re-lationships. I never thought that he thought…that he would…' She trailed off, staring down at her fingers still fiddling with the sash, her vision blurring.

'What did he think?' Alessandro asked, his voice soft, and yet with an underlying hardness that Meghan knew was not directed at her. 'What did he *do*?'

'The thing is,' she continued, her voice falsely bright, deter-mined, 'I should have known. I'm a modern, educated woman. Women like me don't get into situations where…'

Alessandro covered her hand with his own, stilling her nervous fidgeting. 'Where what?'

She squeezed his fingers, clutched them like a lifeline. 'Where you're controlled,' she explained quietly. 'First it was just how I was with him. I wanted to please him, to make him happy. He liked…certain things. Then it was what I wore, who I saw, what I said. He was jealous—horribly jealous, coldly jealous—and I thought it was love.'

Alessandro was silent for a moment, taking this in. 'He *did* abuse you,' he finally said flatly, still holding, stroking her fingers.

Meghan shook her head, denying the truth she'd suppressed for so long…the truth about Stephen, the truth about herself. 'But I *let* him. I should have known better. Everyone wondered what was happening to me—why I was so different, so distant. He didn't like my friends, my family, didn't like my life. I stopped going out… I lost my job because of it.' She closed her eyes briefly, recalling the pain, the shame. The obsession. The delusion. 'I told you Stanton Springs is a small town. Everybody watches out for everybody else. People *care*. They cared about me, and I just drove them all away. All that mattered to me was Stephen. I didn't know sometimes whether it was because of love or fear, but I couldn't leave him. I *couldn't*. How could I have been so blind? So *stupid*?'

'Our hearts are blind,' Alessandro said after a long moment. 'You thought he loved you.'

'If I'd had any self-respect—' Her voice caught jaggedly on a sob, then she choked it back. 'I would've walked out before it came to…before it brought me so low.'

Alessandro's eyes were gentle, but knowing. So knowing. 'What did he do to you?'

Meghan shook her head. She couldn't look at him. Didn't want to see disgust in his eyes, the disgust she'd felt herself, *at* herself. 'Nothing more than what he'd been doing before. Controlling me, humiliating me. He liked to see me under his thumb, catering to his whims, accepting his insults. Brought low. It gave him pleasure. I see that now, even though at the time I thought that was what you did when you loved someone. You just took it. You thought they'd stop. Change. I thought it was because I wasn't good enough, perfect enough. And then one night I'd had enough. I was so dispirited, so broken. I felt like I was dying inside—like all the good parts of me were gone. Used up. And I told him I'd had enough.'

'Did he let you go?' Alessandro asked quietly. Knowingly.

Meghan's hands clenched on the sash once more as memories assaulted her, battered her brain and heart. 'No. I should've realised he wouldn't. I told him I was sorry, that I loved him, and then…' She looked up now, met his gaze, faced the truth. 'He hit me. Across the face. I was so stunned I just lay there. I couldn't believe it. I was being *hit* by a man. The man I loved.'

'If I could get my hands on him…' Alessandro whispered savagely under his breath.

'He kept hitting me. I just took it. I was so surprised, so amazed it was happening. That I'd let it happen. It was my fault.'

'Meghan, it wasn't—'

She continued, determined to finish it to the end. 'He told me he was married then—said I must've known. He laughed about it. He said if I wondered why he treated me like a whore it was because I *was* one, and everyone knew it.' She closed her eyes briefly, shaking her head against the onslaught of memory. 'Of course, I knew he was lying. At least, my mind knew. My heart didn't. My heart believed every word he said.' She whispered the last, the confession echoing through her soul. She'd *believed*.

'What happened then?' Alessandro asked quietly, after a long moment when the only sound in the still room had been their breathing, ragged and uneven.

'I ran. He tried to grab me. I don't know what he would have done if— But I got away. And I kept on running. I ran right out of that town, that life, and I can't go back.'

'There are people there who would support you,' Alessandro said in a low voice. 'They would understand, Meghan.'

'But I'm so *ashamed*,' she confessed in a wretched whisper. 'It's my fault. I should have known. I should have known what kind of man he was. I should have stopped it.' Her voice broke, and Alessandro pulled her towards him, wrapped her in an embrace that was both tender and savage.

'No. How could you know? How could you expect…?'

He was silent, his arms around her, his chin resting on her head. Meghan tried to control her shuddering breaths, her pounding pulse.

'Did you press charges?' Alessandro asked after a long, ragged moment.

'No.' She was horrified at the thought. 'The last thing I wanted was people knowing what had happened, what I'd done. I told you—I ran. I didn't even explain where I was going. I sent a *postcard*. I know everyone is confused, hurt, even, but I couldn't live in that town knowing he was there. He wouldn't let me. And I couldn't bear people knowing.' She looked up at him, her eyes wide. 'I was afraid they would condemn me if they knew. I couldn't bear the shame.'

He stroked her face—light, feathering movements. 'No,' he said quietly, 'I don't suppose anyone could.'

He continued stroking her hair, her shoulders. Meghan never wanted him to let her go. She never wanted to feel alone, ashamed again.

'And for this you blame yourself?' he finally asked. 'You told me you thought you might have known deep down that he was married. I forced you to that confession.' Regret laced his words and roughened his tone. 'But this? Meghan, you could *never* blame yourself for this. That man—that Stephen—he was a monster. This was not your fault. None of it. You are not responsible for another's actions.'

'It's hard,' Meghan said after a moment, her voice no more than a thread of sound, 'not to blame yourself when someone else does. Someone you thought you loved. I stopped believing in myself, in who I *was*. I'm not sure if I even know any more.'

Alessandro was silent. Meghan heard their breathing, the ticking of a clock, the muted roar of traffic from Milan's busy streets below.

'Yes,' he agreed finally, softly. 'It is hard. Lord knows, it is very hard. But I am the man with you now, Meghan, *gattina*. I am the man who married you, and I believe in you.' He tilted her face up to meet his, wiped the traces of her tears with his thumbs. 'I *know* who you are, and I believe you.'

Meghan closed her eyes, felt the old shame slipping away. He knew. He knew, and he believed. 'Thank you,' she whispered. 'That's why I wanted to tell you.'

'I'm glad you did.' He cupped her face, slid his hand through the heavy mass of hair at the nape of her neck. 'Your trust in me is precious.' His voice was stilted, as if he was testing out new words, new emotions. 'I am humbled by it.'

Tears sparkled in her eyes. *Trust me.* She wanted to say it, to plead, but she knew now was not the time. She'd been ready to share, to confess.

Alessandro wasn't. Yet.

He gazed at her gently. 'And now? Are there shadows?'

Meghan smiled tremulously, glanced around the darkened room. 'No. There are no shadows for me.'

'Good.' He kissed her softly, the gesture a plea, a prayer. Not a demand. He would demand nothing of her tonight, Meghan knew.

Nothing that she didn't want.

She kissed him back, her hands sliding up the silkiness of his shirt, bunching the cloth between her restless seeking fingers.

He broke the kiss and glanced down at her with a faint frown between his brows. 'You are certain?'

'I am.' She felt drained, yet relieved. Empty, yet waiting to be filled.

'Good.' He kissed her again, this time his mouth sure and seeking, soft and warm.

Meghan felt him untie the bathrobe, felt it slip from her shoulders. She heard his indrawn breath as his gaze roamed over her, taking in the simplicity of the nightgown.

'You are so, so beautiful. *Bella.*' He kissed her shoulders, one first, then the other, and slipped the straps down. The material slid to her waist in a puddle of silk.

Meghan closed her eyes. She'd expected to feel exposed. Ashamed.

She felt neither.

She felt Alessandro's gaze on her—warm, admiring, gentle—and she smiled. He cupped her breasts in his hands, chuckling softly.

'As golden as the rest of you. You are like a sunbeam.'

She gave a little laugh, raised her eyes to meet his own heated gaze. 'I want to see you.' Fumbling just a little bit, she unbuttoned his shirt. He shrugged it off impatiently and she ran a hand down his chest, the smooth expanse of skin, sighing in satisfaction. 'I've wanted to do this.'

'I've wanted you to.' Alessandro's voice trembled as he laid her on the bed, stretching out beside her. 'This is how I've wanted it between us. Always.'

She nodded speechlessly, the feelings he was drawing from her filling her, spilling up to overflowing. She felt blessed.

He ran his hand over her breasts, across her navel, skimming over her hidden femininity.

Meghan moaned, arched helplessly. She wanted his touch. She craved it.

She lost herself to the exquisite feel of his hands on her, roaming, seeking, wanting. She was helpless, splayed beneath him, lost in sensation. Touch, taste, feel.

'Meghan, look at me.' There was amusement as well as tenderness in Alessandro's voice. 'Make love to me with your mind, not just your body. See the memory we're making together. See how I want you.'

Meghan opened her eyes, saw him braced on his forearms above her, the need and desire open in his face, his eyes, his languorous smile.

His hand moved down, deeper, slipping inside her with a gentle, knowing touch, to the very core of her womanhood, her self, stroking her to helpless flames.

She gasped, her eyes widening, fastened on his, as he smiled, his own eyes darkened with desire.

'Touch me.'

She touched his chest, let her hand slide down, her lips curving in an ancient, womanly smile of seductive power as she heard him gasp.

'Touch me…' His voice was ragged as he rolled on his back, taking her with him, giving her the power.

She straddled him, revelling in the feel of him underneath her, his hard thighs beneath hers, open, vulnerable to her, wanting her touch, her kiss, his entire body a supplication, a prayer.

She watched as his breathing hitched, his eyes glazed with

desire. He never stopped looking at her, even as he clasped her hips and she lowered herself onto him.

She gasped in shocked delight as she felt him fill her, felt the satisfaction deep in her core even as the hunger grew, wilder and deeper, needing to be met.

'You feel so good,' he said raggedly, 'so right.'

It did feel right, Meghan thought dizzily as she moved, rocking, adjusting to this new sensation, this wondrous flooding of feeling. Pleasure. Emotion. Joy. She threw her head back as they began to move in a beautiful dance, minds and bodies as one.

One.

One flesh.

She couldn't think any more, could only feel, her hands bunching on his arms, her thighs pressed against him as he reached up to cup her breasts in his hands, possess her in every way possible.

'Golden…' he whispered, chuckling softly, and Meghan gasped as he moved, clasping her to him, her legs wrapping around him so they were joined, fused, from shoulder to thigh. She buried her head in his neck, overwhelmed. Overcome.

'Look at me.'

I want you to see me when I make love to you. I want you to look in my eyes and see how I want you.

She saw it now as his eyes blazed into hers, filled with a desire that was elemental, consuming them both in its wondrous flames.

He never stopped looking at her, possessing with his eyes as well as his body, as the pressure and pleasure built to a glorious crescendo.

She cried out, and he captured her mouth with his own as she shattered, just as he had predicted she would, into a thousand sense-scattering pieces.

And then he put her back together again, cradling her as they lay there, still, sated, their breathing ragged.

I love you.

It came unbidden, helpless. Hopeless. Meghan closed her eyes, her cheek pressed against his chest, the tang of his sweat still on her lips.

I love you.

Why? When? How?

She didn't know when it had happened. Perhaps when she had first looked into his eyes at the trattoria, and her soul had recognised someone who knew her. Knew her completely and understood. Believed.

Perhaps it had happened later, when he'd opened her heart and mind to the possibility of trust, of desire without shame, need without fear.

Perhaps it had happened just now, when he'd undone her—known her—completely.

She just knew it was true.

She loved him—loved his tenderness, his teasing smile, his ability to give himself so completely. Loved him despite the darkness, the despair that he hid, the secrets she knew he kept, the pain she knew he would cause her.

She loved him.

And it was the last thing Alessandro wanted.

Alessandro listened as Meghan's breathing slowed, her breath feathering his chest. She was asleep.

He relaxed his arm around her, shifting to get more comfortable.

Except nothing could make him comfortable. Nothing could ease the guilt that ate at him, worse than any disease.

She doesn't know what kind of man I am.

He'd never realised how much she'd been through. Endured. His hand curled into a fist as he thought of what Meghan had been through, of the man who had abused her precious trust, her beautiful body.

He looked forward to going back to that hypocritical little town and wiping that man's face in the dirt.

Yet what help was that? *He* was the hypocrite; he was surely only going to cause her more suffering. He wouldn't be able to help it.

When she discovered his past…

When she learned who he really was…

What he was capable of. What he had done.

Then she would hate him. Affection would turn to disgust, love to hatred.

For he knew she would fall in love with him some time. It was in her nature, warm and generous.

No, he didn't want her to love him. Couldn't let it happen. He knew he wouldn't be able to bear it when it stopped.

And it would stop. Because he couldn't change. He couldn't be that man.

He couldn't be saved.

If only it were as simple as it had been for Meghan. Banishing the shadows and accepting forgiveness, love.

There was no such easy answer for him. People loved until you disappointed them. He'd seen it, lived it before. The moment you showed you were weak, needy, in pain or trouble, they left.

They fobbed you off on someone else. They turned away. They pretended they didn't know you.

And who could blame them?

He couldn't stand for that to happen to Meghan. Better for her not to love him at all.

The only way to keep her from falling in love with him, Alessandro knew, was to show her glimpses of the man he truly was.

Not enough to make her leave, but enough to make her wary.

He only prayed that he wouldn't hurt her too much…and that she would stay. It would be a fine line.

Because he didn't know what he would do if she left.

His arm tightened around her again instinctively, and she stirred in her sleep.

Glimpses, he reminded himself, his lips twisting in a savage smile. Glimpses would be enough.

CHAPTER TEN

MEGHAN awoke to an empty bed. For a moment she felt the familiar lurch of fear, then she forced herself to shrug it off.

There were no more shadows. For her.

Alessandro came into the room, showered, dressed, and bearing a tray with coffee and rolls.

'I thought you might be hungry.'

'Starving.'

His smile was knowing, seductive, and Meghan found herself grinning. She bit lustily into a roll as Alessandro took a cup of coffee and stretched out beside her.

'I thought today we could look for a place to live.'

'What about your flat?'

'It is a small place, sterile—a bachelor's pad, as they say. You would hate it.'

'I wouldn't,' Meghan protested. 'We could buy some flowers, some pictures—'

'No, no.' He was firm in his dismissal. 'It needs much more than that. It is simply not suitable. We can look for a place together—a home to start our new lives in?'

'If that's what you want,' Meghan said, a bit unsteadily. It sounded idyllic. Perfect. And far too good to be true. Like a dream they were weaving, something set apart. Unreal.

'That's what I want,' Alessandro replied. 'I need to make a few phone calls. I'll leave you to get dressed.'

He left the bedroom and Meghan leaned back against the

pillows, her mind buzzing happily with new thoughts, new dreams.

Half an hour later they were in Alessandro's car, cruising the streets of Milan.

Meghan gazed in wonder at the ancient buildings coupled with the modern glamour. This was Alessandro's city, she thought, as he navigated the traffic with expert and uncomplicated ease.

He belonged here, among the rich and powerful. And now she was part of that too. Yet somehow the prospect of power had lost its allure.

Wealth, security—even safety—they all seemed useless without love.

Meghan's mouth twisted grimly. Too bad, she thought. That was how it was. For now.

'Do you have a destination in mind?' she asked, and Alessandro gave her a fleeting smile.

'Wait and see…'

He turned the car into a narrow street which opened onto a square, not as impressive as at his mother's residence, but filled with sunlight.

Children played on the green, and the town houses that fronted it looked well cared for. Loved.

'This looks nice,' Meghan offered cautiously, for it wasn't the sort of place she'd imagined Alessandro in. It looked like a place for families—a place where happiness and joy were shared, simple pleasures enjoyed.

No glamour.

No power.

'Yes, it does,' he agreed. 'The agent gave me the key this morning.'

He led her up to one of the houses—a narrow stone building, with bright shutters and begonias spilling from the wrought-iron balconies.

Alessandro unlocked the door and ushered her inside.

Meghan walked slowly through the rooms. They were generously proportioned without being ostentatious, the wide windows thrown open to the spring sunshine.

She stood in the middle of the gleaming kitchen, the large pine table in its centre testifying to the fact that this was a family's house.

'It's semi-furnished,' Alessandro told her, reading the details from a brochure. 'We can pick up more bits and pieces as you like. Four bedrooms upstairs, another on the third floor if we want live-in help. The kitchen, lounge, and dining room on this floor. There is a small garden at the back, and of course the square out in front.' He looked up at her, eyes glinting. 'Do you like it?'

'It's perfect,' Meghan said simply. 'Perfect.'

He strode towards her, snatched her up and kissed her soundly. Meghan laughed in surprise.

'We'll have our children here. I'll teach our sons to play football in the square. It will be so good for us.'

His voice rang with certainty, and yet Meghan heard the desperation underneath, the ragged edges.

They were both trying so hard to believe. To make it real.

Yet it still smacked of a fairytale, a story that had to end— and perhaps not with a happily-ever-after.

They moved in the very next day. Alessandro had linens and towels brought from one of Milan's exclusive stores, and Meghan had fun shopping for food at the local *negozio*.

Alessandro came in from work as she made dinner, his gaze sweeping over the simple scene—from the food on the table to Meghan at the stove, a dishtowel tied around her waist.

'We forgot to buy an apron,' she said with a little smile, and he pulled her into a long, breathless kiss.

'I'd just want to take it off you anyway.' His hands roamed over her, leaving flames of need in their wake.

'Alessandro, the dinner…' Her protestation was so weak as to be laughable.

'We haven't christened this house,' Alessandro murmured against her mouth. 'I'd like to try every room—but we'll start with the bedroom. I like a soft bed…'

He pulled her upstairs, closing the bedroom door with a soft click, and laid her gently on the bed. Meghan lay there, happy, gazing up at him.

The look in his eyes—as if he were examining a priceless treasure—made her mouth dry. She held out her arms.

'Come to me.'

Pain slashed across his features so briefly she almost didn't notice it, but he shrugged off his clothes and fell upon her, and the moment of uncertainty was lost in passion, lost to the exquisite feeling of being touched, treasured.

'We've been invited to a party tomorrow,' Alessandro told her later, as they ate the reheated pasta, his voice suddenly turning alarmingly neutral. 'It's bound to happen as people hear about our wedding. They want to meet you.'

'A party could be fun,' Meghan said. She glanced at him uncertainly. 'You sound like you don't want me to meet them.'

'But of course not. I want to keep you all to myself. Any man would.'

'We can't hide for ever,' Meghan said teasingly, and knew immediately it had been the wrong thing to say.

A muscle bunched in his jaw and he set his wine glass down carefully. 'No,' he agreed flatly. 'We can't.'

What are you hiding? Meghan wanted to ask. Demand. *What secrets are you keeping?*

But of course she would demand nothing. Because Alessandro didn't want a wife who made demands.

A wife who loved him.

Too bad that was exactly what he had.

The next evening Meghan got dressed for the cocktail party with a mixture of anticipation and foreboding.

No matter what she'd said, she wanted to hide here with Alessandro for ever. Playing house and forgetting the world outside, the people who waited to meet them, to judge them.

Judge him.

'I have something for you.' Alessandro came in the bedroom, his black tuxedo setting off his ebony hair and navy eyes with stunning simplicity. He held a black velvet box in his hand.

Meghan turned, and he took in her evening gown—the amber silk she'd worn the other night, its tear discreetly mended—with an appreciative breath.

'My sunbeam,' he said softly. He handed her the box. 'This will match your gown and make your eyes sparkle.'

Intrigued, Meghan opened it. Nestled on the velvet was a necklace made up of pure topaz, the elegantly cut gems rimmed in gold, each piece daringly designed as if to fit a puzzle, sharp and brilliant.

'Alessandro, it's…amazing. Truly beautiful. Is it a Di Agnio piece?'

'As a matter of fact, yes. When I saw it I thought of you. May I?' She nodded, and he lifted the necklace from the box, slipping it around her throat.

It lay heavily against her collar-bone, each piece flat, shining. She touched it reverently. She'd never worn something so exquisite, so expensive.

Alessandro's appreciative smile hardened briefly. 'Now we must go. The party—and people—await.'

The cocktail party was in one of Milan's high-rises—a glittering needle of light that pierced the evening sky.

Meghan's nerves jangled as she thought of the people circulating above them, waiting for their arrival.

'We don't need to stay long,' Alessandro said, and she didn't know if he was reassuring her or himself. 'We're newlyweds, after all. People will understand.'

She nodded mutely, and a valet came to park the car.

Upstairs, guests mingled in a sumptuous penthouse apartment, the room filled with the murmur of voices and the clink of crystal.

Meghan searched the crowd for a familiar face and found none. She felt Alessandro tense beside her, though his urbane smile remained unchanged.

His whole body radiated tension. She wanted to reach out, to hold his hand, to tell him he could do this, *they* could do this, because she was at his side.

The idea was laughable. He would be furious that she saw his weakness, humiliated by her display. And she was too scared to do it anyway.

'Alessandro…and your lovely bride!' A man in his late forties, trim, with grey hair slicked back from a high forehead, came forward with a hard, bright smile. 'Who would ever have thought a man such as you would get married? It must be true love, eh?'

Alessandro inclined his head in cool acknowledgement. A muscle bunched in his jaw.

The man turned his crocodile smile on Meghan. She forced herself not to recoil from the way his gaze swept up and down her length. 'What is the trick, *bellissima*? To capture a man with such a—notorious—reputation with women?'

'I don't have any tricks,' Meghan replied with dignity. 'Perhaps that's why I have been successful where so many have not.'

'Ah, such a fair rose.' His smile verged on a sneer. 'Alessandro and I go way back, you know. We've shared many…experiences.' His voice caressed the last word with obvious lascivious intent.

'Experiences best forgotten,' Alessandro interjected lightly, although his eyes were like flint.

'I remember when you could have a woman on each arm and one in your lap, and be finished with all of them by midnight,' the man reminisced slyly. 'Good times, eh, Alessandro?'

'Things have changed.'

He raised one mocking eyebrow. 'Have they?'

Alessandro bunched his fist, flattened it. 'There are other people for us to greet, Bernardo.'

He turned his back on the man without another word.

'One of your friends?' Meghan asked in a low voice. She could feel the revulsion on her face, crawling along her skin, and she knew Alessandro could see it too.

He shrugged in reply. 'I told you—you don't know me.'

'I think I do know you,' Meghan replied. 'Even if I don't know who you were.'

He glanced at her sharply, the hunger in his eyes flaring quickly before dying out. 'No, Meghan,' he said softly. 'Don't make that mistake. I haven't changed. The man I was is the man I am. No matter what you think, what I do. No matter.' He squeezed her arm warningly. 'Let's enjoy what we have…and no more.'

Meghan was saved from a reply by another guest crossing to greet them, and the next hour passed in a blur of conversation—

some in Italian, some in English—with Meghan desperately trying to remember the faces and names.

She wouldn't forget the innuendoes.

They laced every sly word, drenched every speculative look. Hints about his past, his wild days, his many women. She heard the censure, the disapproval, sometimes the reluctant rakish admiration.

Everyone knew who Alessandro had been. Who he was.

Everyone but her.

After an hour she could take no more. She excused herself to the ladies' room, weaving among the guests in search of an escape, no matter how temporary.

'*Buona sera*, Signora di Agnio.'

Stefano Lucrezi lounged in a quiet corner, his wine glass cupped in one palm. He took in her bunched fists and desperate look with one sardonic sweep of his eyes. 'Are you trying to run away?'

'Yes,' Meghan replied, stung to honesty at last. 'These people are piranhas.'

'They scent an easy kill.'

She stopped, stared uncertainly. 'What do you mean?'

Stefano shrugged. 'No one ever expected Alessandro di Agnio to get married.'

'I've gathered that,' she replied, a bit tartly. 'I also understand he's had plenty of women, plenty of parties, and that he's probably been the most notorious playboy Milan—and Italy— have ever seen!'

She'd meant to be sarcastic, but Stefano just nodded slowly. 'Then you are starting to understand.'

Meghan was more shocked by Stefano's admission than she cared to admit, but she rallied her courage and spread her hands wide. 'So what? Lots of men—Italian men—have similar pasts. He's CEO of an important company. He's married now. What matters is *now*.' She so desperately wanted to believe that was true.

'Yes,' Stefano agreed quietly. 'But people don't want to forget. They can't. Alessandro least of all.'

Meghan shook her head, though she'd suspected as much. 'Then what can I do? I don't want the past to destroy us.'

'Has he told you about his brother?'

'He died. That's all I know.'

'Roberto was CEO of the company after their father died. He'd been groomed for the role since infancy, but he was hopeless at it. He was an artist, and he could not make good business decisions. When he died Alessandro took over, but there was not much to work with. People…' Stefano paused, his expression momentarily guarded. 'They doubted he could do it, but he has. He has brought the company back from the brink of ruin. He has proved many, many people wrong, *signora*. I hope he is proved right in you.'

'So do I,' Meghan whispered.

He nodded towards her necklace. 'One of his designs.'

'What?' Meghan touched the necklace, shocked. 'Alessandro designed this?'

'Yes—a hobby of his.' Stefano's face was shadowed for a moment. 'He doesn't like people to know…it's merely a pastime.'

Alessandro was quiet on the way home. Meghan watched him from under her lashes, saw the implacable lines of his face and knew he would not want to talk. He would certainly not want to answer questions.

Yet she had so many.

He needs love.

Did he? Meghan wondered achingly. She so wanted to be able to give it to him…if only he would accept her gift. If only he would dispel his own shadows…or let her help him do it.

'Did you have a good time tonight?' she finally asked, breaking the silence that hung like a pall of gloom over the car.

'No, but I didn't expect to,' Alessandro replied shortly. His eyes slid to Meghan, roamed over her. 'But I did enjoy seeing you in that dress, and picturing what you look like underneath.'

Meghan swallowed, smiled. Sex. That was what he was going to reduce it to now—what he wanted it to be.

She forced herself to smile. Knew she couldn't make him love her. The only power she had now was her love for him. It would have to be enough.

'I'm yours to command.'

Alessandro's eyes lit with a feral pleasure. 'Good.'

He came to her when she was in the bedroom, wiping her make-up off with a tissue.

He stood silently behind her, his hands resting on her shoulders, his face dangerously blank.

'Can you help me with the necklace?' Meghan asked lightly, though she trembled inwardly at the now-familiar mask he wore. A mask she didn't like. Didn't understand.

He obeyed, undoing the intricate clasp. He laid the necklace on the table and then looked at her. Their gazes met in the mirror, his face was still blank except for a cold, predatory smile.

'Take off your clothes.' It came out as a command, blunt and base, and Meghan stiffened, startled, uncertain.

'Take them off, Meghan,' he said silkily. 'I want to look at you.'

She hesitated, hating the cold smile he humiliated her with, yet seeing—wanting to see—desperation in his eyes. He was driven to this, and she didn't understand why.

'Scared?' he mocked softly.

She lifted her chin, met his chilling gaze, and obeyed.

Turning around slowly to face him, she slipped off the dress and it fell in a pool of silk around her feet. She took off her bra and panties and stood there naked, proud, unashamed.

Trembling.

His gaze swept her, raked her, inspecting and assessing.

Why was he doing this? Meghan didn't know. She wouldn't let herself feel the humiliation, the hurt. She'd felt it before, and that life was gone now. For ever. She came to him in love, even if he didn't know it. Even if he wouldn't accept it.

'Touch me.' His bold gaze challenged her, and simply, silently, she moved forward.

She stood before him while he watched her unbutton his shirt. She willed her hands not to shake. Meghan felt his muscles flex under her fingers, knew he was not unaffected by her, even though his still, stony stance made her think otherwise.

Her hands moved lower, hovered at his belt buckle.

'Touch me, Meghan. *Touch me.*' His voice was quiet, lethal, yet she could hear the need, the plea underneath the command. At least, she thought she could.

She hoped.

He was different. *This* was different.

She undid his buckle, slid his trousers down his legs, dropping down to her knees in front of him. He groaned softly, his hands fisted in her hair, pulling her to him.

She kissed him there softly, reverently, and with a shuddering gasp he pulled her up into his arms, burying his head in her hair, breathing in the scent of her as if it were air, as if it would save him.

'Why don't you stop?' he groaned against her hair, her eyes, her mouth. '*Why don't you stop?*'

'Stop?' she repeated uncertainly, accepting his kisses, his regrets.

'Stop loving me.'

Everything inside her stilled, became suspended and motionless. She touched his face with her hands, looked into his eyes, saw the anguish. 'You *know*?' She was shaken by his admission, by hers. By the truth they both knew.

'Don't, Meghan. Don't do it. Stop yourself. For your own sake, for mine, stop.' He was still kissing her, each touch a plea. 'I don't want to hurt you.'

But I will. The words hovered in the air, unspoken. Not needing to be said.

'I can't stop,' Meghan whispered. 'I don't want to.'

He shook his head in denial even as he laid her gently on the bed. 'No. No. You don't know…'

'Tell me.' She arched up, gasping as he touched her, his fingers slipping inside, so knowing, so tender, drawing her fevered response.

'No…Meghan.' His voice was ragged as he entered her warmth, filled her once again. Meghan moved beneath him, accepting his weight, the solid strength of him above and inside her.

He buried his face in her shoulder, his lips on her neck, gasping as they both moved, rocking, wanting, finding…and then shattering into pleasure. 'Meghan…I need you too much.'

Meghan clung to him, stroked his face, his hair. His words echoed in her mind with a flicker of hope.

He needed her. It wasn't love, but it was something.

It was all she had, and she clung to it fiercely.

* * *

Two days later Alessandro came home with two envelopes and a secretive smile.

Meghan was in the lounge, curled up with a book. Since that night of both pain and pleasure they had not talked of love—her love—again. Meghan had not wanted to mention it. She couldn't face the certain rebuff.

Alessandro had reverted—as he always did—into the charming, urbane man she'd once thought was his real self and now knew was not.

Even though she still wanted to find the truth she'd been grateful for the reprieve, a respite from the intensity. They talked, they ate, they made love. Life, on the surface, was simple. It wasn't real. It was a half-life, a life of pleasant pretence.

Meghan wondered how long it would last.

How long they could both keep it up. One of them was certain to break.

Shatter.

Now she took in his teasing, expectant smile with a little fizz of anticipation.

'What is it? What do you have?'

He handed her the first envelope. 'See for yourself.'

Meghan opened it, scanned the embossed paper. It was a letter from one of the American schools in Milan, offering her an interview.

'Alessandro!' she exclaimed. 'How did you arrange…?'

'I had your CV from Stanton Springs faxed to them. It was a matter of minutes.'

'And some ingenuity.'

He shrugged, the movement one of instinctive inherited male arrogance. 'That I have.'

'The interview is next week!' Meghan marvelled. 'I can't believe it!' She glanced at him over the letter, sincerity shining in her eyes. 'Thank you.'

Her gratitude bothered him; she saw it in his dismissive shrug, heard it in his brusque tone. 'It was easy. Open the other one.'

She opened the second envelope. A postcard fell out.

It was a vista of an aquamarine sea, a stunning white sand

beach. Meghan read the place name on the back of the card. 'Amorphos?'

'A Greek island, very small, very secluded. We leave tomorrow morning.'

Her eyes flew to his. 'Tomorrow?'

'I've arranged with my mother to buy the necessary things for you that you don't have already. Your bags are packed. There is nothing keeping us here.'

'Our honeymoon,' Meghan said in dawning delight, and he pulled her into an embrace, gave her a brief, hard kiss.

'Yes…where no one can find us.'

Meghan smiled, but she couldn't keep from thinking, *We can't run for ever.*

They took Alessandro's private jet to Amorphos, so there was just the two of them in the sumptuous interior, feasting on strawberries and chilled champagne.

Meghan glanced out at the Mediterranean below them, a blue blanket stretching to the horizon.

'I can't believe this is real,' she murmured, and Alessandro smiled.

'It's as real as we want it to be.'

She tensed slightly, aware that his remark was cryptic. Nothing so far had been very real.

This trip, just like their life in Milan, was a fantasy as manufactured as the Marmore Falls—a torrent one moment, a trickle the next.

It wouldn't be real until Alessandro confessed, shared the secrets that drove him to despair, that turned him into a desperate stranger.

Until he trusted her…loved her.

When would that happen? How could she make it happen?

Don't think you can save me.

The warning rang in Meghan's mind, echoed through her soul.

But you're worth saving.

She took a sip of champagne, determined to shrug such fears away, for now at least. The bubbles fizzed pleasantly through her.

'So, Di Agnio Enterprises can spare you for a few days?'

'They have to.' Alessandro stretched out in the seat opposite her. 'I am the CEO, after all. I make the rules.'

Meghan twirled her champagne flute in her fingers. 'Stefano mentioned that the company was on the brink of ruin. You saved it.'

Alessandro stilled. 'He exaggerates.'

Meghan felt her heart skip and then beat double-time at Alessandro's cold look, but she pressed on anyway.

'Does he? He seemed quite certain about his facts.'

'He was gossiping like a laundry woman, then,' Alessandro replied shortly. 'It's hardly like him.'

Meghan leaned forward. 'Don't blame him. He was trying to help me.'

'Help *you*?' Contemptuous disbelief delicately laced his words.

'Yes, as a matter of fact,' she replied with some spirit. 'Help me understand you, Alessandro, because you're hell to understand!'

He stared at her, eyes dark and cold as a lake in winter. Meghan held her breath, wondering if she'd pushed him too far. She hadn't meant to start this conversation, hadn't wanted to ask for answers. She just couldn't help herself. She wanted to know so much.

She wanted to understand.

'Maybe I am.' He smiled at her, coldly, and Meghan made herself press on.

'Stefano—he said your brother was an artist, that he didn't have a head for business. No one thought—'

'I know what people did and did not think,' Alessandro cut in shortly. 'And do not think to blame my brother. He did the best he could, and if he made any unwise business decisions it was because he was too naïve, too *trusting*, and people led him astray—' He broke off suddenly, his breathing ragged, and stared out of the window.

Meghan sat back, reeling from the bitterness that had twisted his voice, his features.

'Remember, Meghan, I married you because you don't know me. Don't understand me.' His eyes flashed dangerously. 'And I want to keep it that way.'

'What kind of marriage is that?' Meghan asked, a desperate edge to her voice. 'You can't—'

'The kind we agreed on,' Alessandro cut in with smooth, steely determination. 'Don't think to change it. I warn you, I will not allow it. You may think you love me, but you don't. You don't even know me. If you did—' He stopped, stared out of the window again, his face a mask.

'If I did…?' Meghan prompted softly.

'It hardly matters. Your love is worthless to me.'

The cold, casual dismissal sent stabbing pain through her. She blinked quickly. 'It's not worthless to me.'

'It should be. I warned you, Meghan. Don't forget that.' His mouth was a hard, unforgiving line. He reached forward and poured them both more champagne. 'Now,' he said with silky, lethal intent, 'let's try to enjoy the rest of our *honeymoon*, shall we?'

The rest of the trip passed in miserable silence, Meghan drowning in the fresh sorrow Alessandro had caused.

He did it on purpose. She knew that. He hurt her, drove her away intentionally, to keep her from loving him.

She could only blame herself; she'd known the terms when she'd agreed to the marriage.

It was her own fault now for trying to change them.

She'd just never expected to love so deeply, so purely, so hopelessly.

Was it hopeless? Would Alessandro never learn—perhaps never admit—that he loved her? Was she mad to think he might?

Meghan blinked back tears. The thought of years ahead in a loveless, soulless marriage made her wonder if she could stand it. Yet life without Alessandro at all was not even worth contemplating.

The plane landed on the resort's private airstrip, and Meghan and Alessandro stepped out into the hot, dry sunshine.

She rallied her numbed emotions, smiled at the Grecian paradise stretched out before them for their own pleasure, and said, 'This looks wonderful.'

Alessandro's eyes glinted approval at her change of mood. 'I'm sure we can make it so,' he murmured.

She smiled stiffly, wondered if she had the strength to act the affectionate wife—not loving, never that—when her heart was breaking. Not even breaking. A break would be clean. It was twisting with a torturous pain that Meghan wasn't sure would ever end.

The resort catered to a most exclusive crowd, and Meghan and Alessandro had their own villa, luxurious and intimate.

'Not bad,' Alessandro commented after the porter had left. Meghan took in the combination living and dining room, the tiled floor and simple yet sumptuous furniture, a sliding glass door leading directly to the beach and an aquamarine sea that sparkled like a jewel only metres away.

'Not bad?' she repeated with a little laugh. 'It's paradise.'

'I can hardly wait to enjoy it,' Alessandro murmured, and he moved towards her purposefully.

Meghan tried to return his kiss, tried to fan the flicker of desire in her core. Alessandro began to deftly unbutton her sundress and she stood there silently, her eyes closed, wishing this misery that consumed her heart, her soul, gone.

'Meghan?' Her dress was half off her shoulders when he looked up in perplexity. 'What is it—what is wrong?'

Meghan swallowed, choking down her sorrow. 'Nothing… I'm just tired.'

He paused, his eyes sweeping over her face, guessing at the truth. Meghan blinked, swallowed. Carefully he zipped her dress back up.

'Then you must rest.'

Taking her hand gently, he led her to the bed, tucked her in, and kissed her forehead.

'Rest. There will be plenty of time later.' He smiled softly, his eyes shadowed, and left the room.

Meghan lay in darkness and pressed her face into the pillow, willing the hot rush of tears back. They came anyway.

How could he be so kind, so tender, if he didn't love her? Was it an act? A deceit?

Who was the real Alessandro…? And did *that* man love her?

After a while she fell into an uneasy doze, awoke with her

tears spent. This was her honeymoon. It wasn't the time to demand answers, confessions. She wanted to enjoy it. She wanted Alessandro to enjoy it. The only way to ensure that was to work hard.

Scrubbing her cheeks, Meghan got out of bed.

Over the next week she worked hard to make sure they enjoyed themselves. They chatted rather than talked; joked rather than shared. Meghan kept her voice light. She didn't ask any questions. She wanted Alessandro happy, even if it hurt. She wanted to make him smile, laugh.

She wanted to heal him, but she didn't know how.

They swam and snorkelled, sunbathed and slept. They ate the delicious, plentiful Greek food, and drank the rich red wine. They made love—on the king-sized bed, in the kitchen, in the bath, on the cool white sand as the moon rose above the sea, turning it to silver.

Lying on the bed one evening, listening to the waves lap on the shore and to Alessandro's gentle breathing, Meghan wondered if she would ever be able to expect more. Hope for more.

For something real.

She didn't know how long she could last, how long her heart could last, living this loveless life.

I love him. I want him to love me.

She closed her eyes and sighed, willing herself to be content with what Alessandro offered.

Her only hope was that he would change, that he would come to love and trust her with time. She had nothing else.

On their last night they walked to a taverna in the village and sat outside. Fairylights were twined in the arbour that surrounded the tables, and the water lapped only metres from their feet, fishing boats knocking gently together as the moon cut a silver swath across the calm surface of the sea.

Meghan picked at her souvlaki, wondering what the future held for them, for their marriage. It was easy to pretend on a beautiful island. Real life back in Milan, with all of its shadows and memories, was something different altogether.

Alessandro covered her hand with his own. 'It has to end, *cara*. It always does.'

Meghan wondered if he meant the honeymoon, or something more. Another warning?

She bent her head, let her hair fall to obscure her face. Now was not the time to ask such questions, demand such answers. She knew instinctively Alessandro would recoil. Regret. Repulse.

When would the right time be?

'Alessandro?' They both jerked in surprise at the sensual female voice. A woman stood in front of their table, white-blonde hair framing a sharp, pixie face, her wide blue eyes darting speculatively between Alessandro and Meghan. She was dressed in an extremely skimpy and expensive sundress.

'Emilia.' Alessandro's voice was terse. He stood as a matter of form, of courtesy. 'It has been a while.'

'Hasn't it?' Although she spoke in rapid Italian, this one conversation Meghan was determined to follow. 'This isn't your usual type of place,' she said with a husky laugh. 'Too quiet by far. I came for a bit of rest and relaxation, but I'm already bored.'

'I'm sorry to hear that,' Alessandro replied with wintry politeness.

'Are you?' Her smile curled upwards, as sleek and sly as a cat's. 'Who's your friend?'

Alessandro's eyes narrowed. 'This is my wife—Meghan,' he said coldly. 'We're on our honeymoon.'

'Your *wife*?' Emilia let out a peal of incredulous laughter. 'You're joking! You? Married?'

'I assure you it is true, and a most pleasant truth at that.'

Emilia's gaze raked contemptuously over Meghan. 'This milky miss? Come on, Alessandro. She could amuse you for a day, a week, not much more. I know you…I know your pleasures.' Her smile was so intimate, so suggestive, that Meghan gave a little gasp of wounded surprise.

Alessandro's body was taut, his mouth a thin slash of anger. 'You are insulting me and my wife.'

Emilia's eyes narrowed. 'Her, perhaps,' she agreed, her voice lowered to a hiss. 'But you? That would be hard to do.'

Meghan saw the flash of acknowledgement in his eyes before he bit out, 'I will ask you to leave.'

Her lips tightened, and she turned to Meghan, speaking slowly now for her benefit. 'Forgive my rudeness. Alessandro and I go a long way back. I'd no idea he'd changed so very much.' She glanced back at him slyly. 'If indeed he needed changing.'

'You must have known he'd taken over Di Agnio Enterprises,' Meghan pointed out in what she hoped was a reasonable tone, though she felt like clawing the other woman's eyes out. 'It seems you are not such good friends with my husband as you thought.'

'Perhaps you're right,' Emilia acknowledged with an icy smile. 'I never would have imagined him latching on to a woman like you.' She turned to Alessandro, touched her fingers to her lips and boldly pressed them to Alessandro's mouth. '*Ciao, bello.*'

He stood still, a muscle ticking in his jaw, his eyes both blazing and cold.

Then she left.

Meghan stared down at her virtually untouched souvlaki. The silence stretched between them, thin and taut as a wire, oppressive as a leaden weight.

'I guess she's not too happy you're married,' she finally managed, trying to keep her voice light and amused and failing miserably.

Alessandro's eyes and voice were flat, cold. 'She wouldn't be. Emilia and I used to be lovers.'

Icy shock drenched her, left her near to trembling. It didn't surprise her—of course she'd guessed as much—but it still hurt.

And Alessandro's cold, calculating delivery of such a fact hurt even more.

'Used to be,' she finally repeated, lifting her chin. 'That's what's important now.'

Alessandro's mouth turned up in a mocking smile. 'How fortunate I am to have such an understanding wife,' he remarked lightly. 'And such sensitivity will surely come in useful, considering I'd slept with at least half the women at the cocktail party the other night.'

Meghan's vision blurred, whether from tears or shock she didn't know.

'That doesn't matter,' she whispered, though it felt as if it mattered very much.

'Oh, good,' Alessandro said musingly. 'Because it's probably more like two-thirds.'

'I know you were a playboy, a womaniser, Alessandro,' Meghan said through gritted teeth. 'It doesn't matter now. I know you'll be faithful.'

'Do you?' he mocked, and she gripped the edge of the table, struggling to hold onto her composure, her calm.

She wanted to break down completely.

'Why are you doing this?' she finally asked in a low voice. 'You're deliberately trying to provoke me. To hurt me.'

Alessandro leaned forward, his eyes glittering with malicious intent. 'But *gattina*,' he said softly, 'I'm showing you so you know not to be hurt. This is who I was—who I am. You can't change me. You can't save me.'

Right then Meghan didn't even want to try.

She barely remembered the rest of the meal. She must have eaten and drunk, because their plates were cleared away, her glass refilled. She lived in a shocked daze, wondering why Alessandro hurt her so much, why she let him.

Surely enough was enough?

She couldn't keep doing this.

It wasn't worth it.

But I love him.

Meghan had wanted power for herself this time, had married for it, but she'd become its victim instead. Again.

Alessandro's victim.

The pain of that realisaton sliced her soul in two—was worse than anything she'd known before.

And she didn't know what to do.

They walked back to their villa in silence, the air wrapping them in a warm, sultry blanket, so different from the shattered atmosphere that lay between them like a thousand splinters of hurt emotion, devastated feeling.

Back in the villa, Meghan walked on wooden legs to the bedroom. She undressed, slipped into her nightgown—another silky confection that made nonsense of what was between them now.

She lay still in bed, her eyes hot and dry.

She was past tears.

It was too late for them, anyway.

Alessandro came in after a little while. He peeled off his clothes and slipped between the cool sheets, his back, an expanse of indifference, towards her.

She wouldn't let it end this way tonight, Meghan thought.

She wouldn't be a victim.

She wouldn't run away.

She would take control. She would demand it.

She reached for him, found herself grabbing his shoulders, pulling him over to her. She cupped his face in her hands and kissed him hard, in demand.

A brand.

He didn't respond. She sensed rather than felt his surprise, and after a moment he rolled away from her.

'No, Meghan. Not like this.'

His rejection, on top of everything else, was too much.

She'd had enough.

'*Yes*, like this.' She pushed him onto his back, smiling as his eyes widened in surprise. She straddled him, her thighs pressed against his manhood, her own eyes blazing.

She felt the answering stir of his own desire, saw the flicker of admiration in his eyes as she sat above him, naked and bold.

She had him in her thrall, in her power. He was splayed beneath her, waiting, wanting.

Then Meghan smiled sadly.

'I'm not a whore,' she said softly. 'And I won't use a whore's tricks to bind you to me. I love you. I know you don't love me. You can run away from that, you can try to make me run, but you can't change the truth.'

He looked glorious, his chest bare and smooth and brown, his dark hair rumpled against the white linen pillow. His eyes were dark, fathomless, searching.

Then slowly he reached up, held her face in his hands, and brought her lips down to his.

Surrender.

'Make love to me, Meghan.' He smiled against her mouth, his hips rocking hers. 'Make love to me.'

With a small cry of acceptance, she did, letting him fill her, letting herself be filled to overflowing. Letting the physical joy and pleasure be enough—because right now it was all they had.

It was too much to bear. Alessandro lay on his side and watched Meghan sleep, curled up like a child, next to him.

It hurt too much.

He hadn't asked for her love, hadn't wanted it.

Hadn't ever expected it.

Yet now it was his.

Precious, rare, beautiful.

He rolled on his back and closed his eyes. What could he do with such a gift? He couldn't even begin to know its value, to understand its worth.

He only knew that it was a gift he would lose, utterly, hopelessly, when she discovered the truth.

Had he actually imagined that he could keep it from her? That the denizens of Milan, eager for his blood, his shame, would keep it from her? The few comments she'd heard so far, the innuendoes she'd figured out, were nothing, *nothing*, to the secrets that remained.

And when she discovered them he knew he'd see disgust instead of tenderness, revulsion instead of compassion. Then she would leave. Even if she didn't, even if some brand of honour kept her from going, she would leave in the ways that mattered.

Heart, mind, soul.

He couldn't bear that. It hurt as much as her love did, innocent and ignorant as it was.

So he kept hurting her. He couldn't help it; it was the only way he knew to protect her from more pain. To protect himself.

And he hated himself for it more than ever.

He hated himself more now than when he'd seen his photograph plastered on a thousand tasteless tabloids, than when he'd joked and drunk and slept his way through a worthless life, than when he'd killed his brother.

And he didn't see how it could ever get any better.

CHAPTER ELEVEN

'MAY I come in?'

Emilia Bentano stood at the doorway of the Milan town house, a heavy designer bag over one shoulder.

'I'd rather you didn't,' Meghan managed through stiff lips, after the shock of seeing this woman again—at her door—had eased.

'I know I didn't come off well in Greece,' Emilia said. 'I'm sorry about that.'

'Are you?' Meghan doubted it. So why was the woman here? To sow more discord between her and Alessandro?

That, she thought grimly, could hardly be done. In the week since they'd returned from Amorphos he'd been aloof, removed. The mask firmly in place. It happened every time their bodies—their souls, their hearts—joined, no matter how briefly.

He drew away; he grew cold. His charm was interspersed with careless mocking comments, a calculated indifference meant to drive her away.

Sometimes Meghan wondered if it would be enough to make her go.

She was so tired of the strain, the pretence. She wanted something real and warm and safe.

This was not part of our bargain.

Leaving him would tear her apart, heart and soul, mind and body. She would never be the same again. She would never be whole.

She didn't know what else to do.

This slow torture was accomplishing the same thing, only more slowly, more painfully.

And yet at night Alessandro reached for her. Their bodies merged with a desperate yearning that seemed at odds with the strained pleasantries exchanged each day.

They didn't speak, yet his eyes burned into hers as if memorising her features, as if sending forth a plea.

She just didn't know if she had the strength to believe any more. To fight for it.

'I wanted to talk to you,' Emilia said quietly, sensing Meghan's indecision, offering sincerity. 'I wanted to talk to you about Alessandro…perhaps explain why he is the way he is.'

Meghan's hand tightened on the door handle. A warm breeze caressed her face; she could smell the begonias that tumbled in a riot from their pots onto the steps.

'What do you mean?'

Emilia shrugged, smiled. 'Don't you have questions? Haven't you wondered? Everyone has seen what a transformation Alessandro has made in these last months…wondered if it will last. If it's real.'

'I know it's real,' Meghan said coldly, but her heart was hammering and there was a hollow ring to her words that even she heard.

Emilia raised her eyebrows, cool and knowing. 'Do you? Do you really, Meghan? Because if I were you in your place I'd wonder. I'd wonder very much.'

'But you're not in my place,' Meghan observed with a detachment she was far from feeling. 'As much as you may have once wanted to be.'

Emilia was unfazed. 'Did Alessandro tell you that? Yes, we were lovers. I once thought we might marry… After all, a man like Alessandro would expect to marry eventually, and we're very much alike.'

The thought that Alessandro was similar to this walking piranha made Meghan taste bile in her throat. Alessandro was nothing like this…not the Alessandro she knew.

The man she wanted him to be…the man she thought he wanted to be.

Yet was that really him? Or a façade?

A fake.

'I think,' Meghan said slowly, 'you're just trying to cause trouble. But I know you'll bother me until I let you have your say, so you might as well come in.'

Emilia's mouth curved up into a triumphant smile. Meghan stepped reluctantly aside, and the other woman sashayed into the house with such sultry confidence that Meghan wished she hadn't given in.

Yet she wanted to know.

No matter what the truth meant, what it revealed.

She wanted to know.

Then there would be no more secrets.

'What a quaint little home,' Emilia said with a gurgle of laughter. 'Does Alessandro spend much time here?'

Meghan heard the disbelief in her tone, as if she couldn't imagine Alessandro relaxing in such a boring, bourgeois place.

Maybe he was bored, she thought numbly. Maybe it was all getting too old, too familiar. And it had only been a few weeks.

She led the way into the friendly square lounge, with its squashy red sofas, its long windows spilling sunshine onto the wide pine boards of the floor.

Emilia looked around with an expression of mild distaste, wrinkling her nose as if she were too polite to mention how awful she found it all.

Meghan gritted her teeth. 'Sit down.'

'Thank you.' She perched elegantly on the edge of a sofa, her bag on her lap. She wore, Meghan saw, a tightly fitting red leather jacket and matching skirt, her legs long and bare, her toenails in open sandals painted scarlet.

Meghan sat across from her in an armchair.

'Now, what is it you want to say?'

'Ah, yes. Well…in fact…' Emilia smiled the smile of a sly cat, a cat with a mouse's tail dangling from its sleek jaws, and opened her bag. 'I thought these might tell the tale better than I ever could.' She took out a sheaf of newspaper clippings. Meghan's stomach dipped.

She held out her hand and took them silently, grateful that her hand didn't tremble. She leafed through them, one eyebrow raised, making her uninterest known though her mouth was dry.

Meghan handed them back, heart pounding, for the meaning was obvious enough. The clippings were plastered with photographs of Alessandro at parties, his arms around various scantily clad women, his expression somewhere between a rake's smile and a drunken leer.

He looked, Meghan thought with a sinking feeling, like someone she never wanted to know.

Emilia smiled and said sweetly, 'Look at this one.' She took the clippings, sifting through them until she came to the one she wanted and handed it back to Meghan, tapping the photo with one scarlet nail.

Meghan glanced down, recoiled slightly from the photograph of a smoking ruin of a car left on the side of the motorway. The one word in big block letters stood out in bold relief: OMICIDIO?

Murder.

She stared unseeingly, unthinkingly, down at the newspaper. She heard Emilia purr, 'Now do you want to know?'

'I think,' Meghan replied, barely keeping her voice above a whisper, 'that you're going to tell me.' She looked up, her eyes still dry, her heart weighing heavy like a stone. 'And then you're going to leave.'

'You know Alessandro was a bit of a playboy?' Emilia began, clearly relishing the telling.

'More than a bit, I believe,' Meghan replied, and Emilia looked slightly discomfited that she took this news so calmly.

'Did you know, then,' she continued in a harder voice, 'that he and his brother were involved in a car accident? A highly suspicious one, with Alessandro as the driver.'

'Suspicious?' Meghan repeated, trying to sound scornful and not quite succeeding. 'What's suspicious about a car accident?'

'A lot of things. They'd just had a very public argument—at one of Milan's fashionable parties. Alessandro was angry, and accused Roberto of something—no one heard exactly what this was, and no one would have believed him anyway, of course. Roberto was loved by everyone—kind, gentle, always turning a blind eye to Alessandro's antics. But this time he got upset. I was there and I saw it.' She leaned forward, eyes glittering, involved now in the story, the drama. Meghan, afraid now, could only watch and listen.

'Roberto looked terrible,' Emilia recalled. 'Pale, shaken, like he was going to be sick. Alessandro kept on at him, accusing him, so Roberto tried to leave. Alessandro wouldn't let him, though— he grabbed his arm and started shouting. They ended up leaving the party together—Alessandro threatening, Roberto looking terrified. The next thing we knew Alessandro had crashed the car, killing his brother while he walked away with barely a scratch.'

Meghan's mind and heart reeled from this information. It could explain so much…if she were able to understand it. Still she shook her head, managed to give a disdainful little laugh. 'Do you honestly expect me to believe that he engineered an accident where his brother was killed and he remained uninjured? That's ludicrous.'

Emilia inclined her head in acknowledgement. 'Perhaps. But the accident was on a stretch of smooth road—not a car in sight, no twists or turns. According to police reports, the car just veered off the road into a tree.'

'It's been known to happen before,' Meghan said.

The bands around her chest, her heart, eased—if only a little. An accident couldn't assign blame, no matter what the newspapers said.

'What did Alessandro say about it?' she asked now. 'He must have given some explanation.'

Emilia shrugged. 'Of course he was driving recklessly. But with the di Agnio name… The car had to have been going seventy miles an hour. It's a miracle he wasn't killed.'

'And the press twisted this into a case of murder?' Meghan shook her head.

'You have to admit it makes a certain amount of sense,' Emilia persisted in a silky purr. 'Think what Alessandro stood to gain from his brother's death—CEO of one of Italy's most important companies, prestige, respect…'

'Oh, has he got those?' Meghan queried sharply. 'Because it doesn't seem to me he has.'

Emilia was silent for a moment, watching Meghan with a sneering pity. 'You have no idea what he was like, do you? He may seem like a handsome knight in shining armour now, all set to rescue you, but in this country he was reviled. Pictures of him have been smeared across the tabloids for years, and I know from experience that rumours about him tend to be true.' Her mouth curved in a lasciviously knowing smile that made Meghan bite down on her lip, taste the metallic tang of blood. 'The public turned a blind eye to all his playboy antics, his women, but they couldn't stand what he did to his brother. They blamed him. They *wanted* to blame him. He destroyed the beloved Roberto di Agnio, Italy's golden boy.'

'I'm sure the press had a field-day with it,' Meghan said tightly, her control beginning to splinter. 'It still doesn't make it his fault.'

'Unless,' Emilia said, her voice little more than a whisper, a hiss, 'he *did* mean to crash the car…'

Meghan felt the blood drain from her face, her body turning icy and numb. Lifeless.

'He had nothing to lose,' Emilia continued with dangerous softness. 'He was a rake, a reprobate, his family had practically disowned him for the things he'd done, the shame he'd brought to them. In a moment of violent jealousy…' She shrugged delicately. 'Who knows what could have happened?'

Meghan sank unsteadily into a chair. Could Alessandro have been so desperate, so unhappy, so *murderous*, he'd tried to kill both himself and his brother?

Could he have been so vile?

'I want you to go,' she said in a thin voice. 'Now.'

Emilia chuckled softly. 'I've given you enough to think about, have I? Good. At least now you know what he's capable of. Alessandro was a desperate, dangerous man, Meghan. He still is. I'll leave the clippings here…just in case you want to look through them again. *Ciao.*'

The front door clicked softly shut behind her.

Meghan let out a shuddering breath and glanced down at the newspaper photograph of the smoking ruin of a convertible. He didn't drive those any more. *Now she knew why.*

She picked up the sheaf of clippings with numb fingers, a numb heart. She sifted through them, steeled herself against the images, glaring, garish, painful.

Alessandro with his arms wrapped around a blonde who was poured into a dress. Alessandro kissing another woman, one eye on the camera, giving a lascivious wink. Alessandro with a woman on each arm and a sardonic smile twisting his features, making him someone she could hate.

It was horrible.

It was wrong.

It was the truth.

She stared at the photographs until her eyes were gritty, forcing herself not to close them against the onslaught of images, realisations, shattered dreams.

This was Alessandro. This was the man he had been, the man he insisted he still was. As much as she'd suspected and feared what he'd done, this was worse. This was so much worse.

She believed he'd changed, but could a man actually change that much?

Was Alessandro even *trying* to change?

Her heart cried *yes*, he was; her mind ruthlessly reminded her of every cruel thing he'd said, every harsh warning he'd given.

He'd *told* her not to trust him, not to love him. He'd told her not to try to understand, to know.

Now she knew, and her ignorance—and innocence—were gone for ever.

How could he be at times so tender, so kind, so understanding, so *loving*? her heart cried out, and her mind replied dispassionately, *You always knew men abused power.*

Meghan stared at the photograph of the car, half-wrapped around a tree on a deserted road. It was charred, a wreck of a car, wrecking a life.

Two lives.

Three.

What had happened that night? Could Emilia possibly be right?

Meghan desperately wanted to believe she couldn't be, yet doubt had created a treacherous crack in her heart she couldn't ignore.

She was faced with the bleak reality that despite what her heart said her mind told her the truth.

She didn't *know* what kind of man Alessandro was.

She couldn't fathom what he was capable of.

So intent was Meghan on the clippings that she didn't register the click of the front door, the sound of soft footsteps. She didn't even notice the shadow that fell over her as Alessandro came into the room, didn't realise he was there until he spoke, ice coating every word.

'Ah. I see you've discovered my past.'

'Alessandro!' Meghan's stomach plunged with nerves; the clippings fell from her lap onto the floor.

His lips curving in a sardonic smile, Alessandro stooped to pick them up. 'Enjoying yourself?' he asked softly. 'Indulging in some vicarious pleasure? I have Emilia to thank for this, no doubt. Or did you manage to dig these up all on your own?' Menace turned his eyes dangerously indigo, his mouth a hard, thin line.

'It was Emilia,' Meghan whispered.

'Ah. She always liked to cause trouble.'

He riffled through the clippings with an uninterested air. 'Ah, yes. I think I remember this one. She was quite good in bed, if I recall. Daring.'

Meghan closed her eyes.

'And this one… Hmm, memory's a bit fuzzy there. Probably had too much to drink. I often did.'

'Don't do this.' She felt faint, dizzy, sick.

Alessandro glanced at her over the top of the clippings and smiled coolly. 'But why not, Meghan? Isn't this what you want to know? Isn't this why I found you here, staring at these photos?'

'I was trying,' Meghan replied as levelly as she could, 'to find out why you are the way you are.'

'Do not!' His voice came out sharp. 'Do *not* psychoanalyse me. I know who I am. These clippings prove it. And if you fell in love with me, Meghan, then you fell in love with a false image. What you wanted me to be, not what I am.'

It was what her own mind had been telling her, and it hurt. It hurt more than she'd ever thought it would to hear him say it, admit it.

'You were kind to me,' Meghan whispered, her eyes starting to pool with tears. The room, the clippings, Alessandro, were all a blur. 'You told me you would never hurt me.'

'*Da tutti i san*, by now you should've realised that wasn't true!'

Her vision swam; she clutched the arm of her chair like an anchor. 'Are you telling me you lied?'

'I got what I wanted,' Alessandro replied dispassionately. 'You.'

'I don't believe it.' She clung to one last hope that even now he would relent. Change. 'This isn't you.'

'Yes, it is. I warned you, Meghan.'

Alessandro's face was a mask, terrible in its blankness. It was as if the life had drained out of him, and Meghan didn't know if she could get it back. She dragged breath into her lungs. 'What about the car accident?'

He stilled, and for a tense moment Meghan wasn't sure what he would do next. What he was capable of. She stiffened, forced herself to remain still.

'Are you asking me if I killed my brother?' he asked, his voice indifferent. 'You saw the headlines. *Omicidio. Assassino.* They speak the truth.'

'It was an accident.'

'Was it?' He raised his eyebrows. 'I read the tabloid gossip, every word. Maybe I picked that stretch of road—crashed the car in a way that would only injure the passenger. Who knows?' He smiled mockingly, and Meghan shook her head, desperate now.

'Alessandro, that can't be true. Even if you were capable of such a thing, it would be an insane risk.'

He walked up to her, tilted her chin with cool fingers so Meghan was looking with anguish into his own blank eyes.

'But don't you know by now that I like to take risks? It's what makes me good at business. You were a risk, weren't you, *gattina*? Too bad that one hasn't worked out.'

She shook her head. 'No, it can't…' Her voice trailed off into desperate silence.

His fingers tightened on her chin. 'Tell me, Meghan,' he said softly, 'when you look at those clippings, what do you feel, think? What do you believe?'

Her mind spun, whirred hopelessly like a stalled engine. She thought of what she'd felt: the horror, the repulsion, the fear, and knew they were reflected in her eyes, her face. She tried to think of a word, an explanation, but nothing came out.

Something flickered to life in Alessandro's eyes and then deadened. Like ash, dust, ice. 'You see?' he said softly. 'You do believe it, don't you? I warned you before. I won't change.' He paused, his voice turning ragged. 'I can't.'

She stared. Her mind blanked. She couldn't speak.

He dropped his hand from her face and glanced down at the clippings; the photograph of the ruined car was on top. 'Damned by silence,' he mocked.

'Alessandro, don't…' she began, her voice a thread, but he ignored her.

'Never mind. It's just as well, you know. I was starting to get bored.'

'Bored?' she repeated faintly, and he smiled, a bitter twisting of his lips.

'Surely you saw in those papers that I'm a man of many tastes, pleasures? I'll get a few things,' he continued tonelessly, 'and move to my flat. You can continue to live here. I don't mind.'

Meghan felt as if she were plummeting through a cold, dark tunnel. She gazed at him in shock, her mind finally catching up, making sense of what was happening. 'What are you saying?'

'I'm saying,' Alessandro replied in clear, cutting tones, 'that I don't want to live with you any more. This marriage was a mistake, a bad risk, but unfortunately neither of us can undo it now. I won't bring shame to the di Agnio name again.' He held up one hand to still the wave of protests rising within her, unspoken. 'You'll still get what you want. I'll come with you to that godforsaken town in Iowa you once called home. I'll give you security. You, on the other hand, need give me nothing.'

'Alessandro…' Meghan was on her knees on the chair, tears streaking silently down her face. She felt as if her world had been torn apart in a matter of minutes and lay around her in bloody shreds. And she hadn't lifted a finger to stop it. She hadn't had the strength. 'This isn't what I want.'

He looked at her as if he didn't care. As if he'd already moved on, forgotten. 'Pity,' he remarked, 'because this is what you're going to get.'

Meghan remained half kneeling on the chair as Alessandro moved through the house. She knew he was gathering his things, preparing to leave her for ever.

And she didn't know what to do.

She hadn't expected this utter rejection—the man she loved turned into a stranger she couldn't even understand.

She should have spoken sooner—done something, thought something, acted. Shown him... But what? She'd still been reeling with shock, with disappointment, with sorrow.

And now it was too late.

It's never too late, her heart cried out, and Meghan forced herself to listen. Alessandro was her second chance at life, at love; she was his. She wouldn't let go of it lightly.

She couldn't let him leave.

Not like this. Never like this.

On weak, wobbling legs she walked up the stairs, her mind buzzing but blank. She wished she knew what to say, what to *think*. She only knew she had to act.

She turned the corner, came to the bedroom door. And saw him.

Alessandro sat on the bed, his head bowed, his hands fisted in his hair. Meghan's heart contracted, ached with a desperate longing that nearly made her stagger.

She recognised that stance, the bleak despair in every agonised line of his body. She'd felt it herself.

It was the look of a person who believed his own soul was damned because everyone had told him it was, even when his heart had cried out for belief, for love.

For salvation.

She'd felt it when one man had condemned her; Alessandro had suffered the judgement of an entire country.

This is the man I love.

This was the man. No matter what he'd thought, what he'd felt, what he'd done.

She loved Alessandro.

And she knew, had to believe, that he was the man she thought he was, knew he was.

The man he meant to be.

She must have made some sound, for he looked up, his face hardening into a mask once more.

'I'll be out of here in a few minutes,' he said coldly. 'Can't you wait?'

'No, I can't,' Meghan said. Her voice was a scratchy breath of sound but she forced it to come out stronger. 'And you won't.'

'I won't?' he repeated in a mocking tone. 'You should know by now there's little I *won't* do, *gattina*.' He stood up, grabbed the half-filled bag at his feet and slung it over one shoulder.

Meghan stood in the doorway, her arms flung out, blocking him. Alessandro walked towards her, one eyebrow raised in incredulous disdain.

'Get out of my way, Meghan.' He spoke softly, quietly, yet she still knew it was a threat.

'No.'

He paused, his eyes sweeping, assessing her, burning her, just as they had when he'd looked at her that first time in the restaurant.

Even then her body, her *heart*, had known this was the man—the man she needed.

And she wasn't going to let him walk away now.

'Haven't you had enough, Meghan? Or did you lose all of your self-respect when that man abused you?' He shook his head. 'Save us the shame of such a scene and let me walk out of here with head held high.'

'I don't think anyone's head is high right now,' Meghan replied in a low voice. 'Yours wasn't a moment ago, and mine isn't now. I'm ashamed—' her breath hitched '—that I didn't answer you downstairs. That I didn't tell you I believed.'

'But you did believe. You believed the truth. Now, enough of this!' His hand slashed through the air. 'Leave me alone. Let me go.'

Meghan's throat ached with unshed tears. She held them back, forced herself to be strong, if only for a moment. Trembling, she put one hand flat on Alessandro's chest, felt his sucked-in breath at the contact. The caress. 'But I can't let you go, Alessandro. I love you.'

He shrugged, determinedly unmoved. 'You love the man I pretended to be to make you marry me.'

'Why would you do that? You didn't have to marry me. I told you that myself. It could have been an affair.'

'You hold yourself rather cheaply,' he said coldly, his mouth twisting.

Meghan's eyes blazed for a second. She might be dying inside—her dreams, her hopes, her heart, all on their last breath, their last chance—but she was still going to fight. Fight for her own shattered hopes, for Alessandro's.

'*You* hold yourself cheaply, it seems,' she responded levelly. 'I don't know your secrets, Alessandro. I don't know all the things you did. I don't want to. But I know—*I know*—that you've been trying to overcome your past. To not be the man the tabloids painted you—the man you and everyone else believed you to be. I've seen you struggle with it. I've seen you lose, and I've seen you win. It's not an act.' Her voice broke into fragments of pain and sorrow, of hope too painful to bear, too precious to lose. 'I believe in you. I love you.'

Alessandro was silent, still. She could feel the energy thrumming through him, a raw, angry pulse.

'It doesn't matter. It's not real.'

'It *is* real,' Meghan flashed. 'You can't keep denying what I know! I don't care what you do, how many times you try to push me away. I know who you are and I love you!'

'No, you don't!' His voice came out in a savage roar, ripped from his body, his lungs, and Meghan jerked back, startled. His face twisted into a grimacing sneer as he dropped his bag on the floor, grabbed her arms. 'What do you want from me? What do I have to do to show you I'm not the man you think I am?' His fingers dug into her arms and Meghan forced herself to submit, to stare into his face, a beautiful face no longer blank, but tormented by pain and misery.

He felt. The mask had dropped, and she was glad.

'There's nothing you can do,' she said quietly. Her voice

shook only a little. 'You've already shown me, Alessandro. You've shown me with compassion, love and tenderness what kind of man you are. The man I love.'

He let out a low, rasping sound; Meghan thought it was a laugh. Then he pulled her to him, her breasts flattening against his chest, and kissed her with a hard desperation that felt like a bruise.

Meghan's hands crept up his chest, wound around his neck. She pulled him closer and gentled the kiss, turning it into something loving and warm.

He refused, breaking it off, coming up for air with a choked laugh of disbelief. 'Have you no self-respect?' he demanded, and though pain was slicing cleanly through her, Meghan answered steadily.

'I didn't. But you gave it back to me. You can't take it away again.'

'Can't I?' he jeered, and, pulling on her wrists, led her to the bed, tossing her carelessly down on it. Meghan lay there, her heart pounding so loudly it seemed to fill the room with its desperate beat. She was on her back, splayed, helpless.

She thought of the first time he'd touched her, what he'd said. *I'm not going to touch you. I'm not that kind of man.*

No, he wasn't. She still believed. Even now, when he was determined to show her differently, to prove her love was worthless.

Especially now.

The final test.

He looked down at her, his hands on his hips, his expression coldly mocking. 'Scared, Meghan?'

'No.' Her voice wavered, but she kept looking at him. Forced herself to meet the icy steel of his eyes.

'You should be.'

'What are you going to do, Alessandro? Try to make me stop loving you? Is that what this is about?'

'What this is about?' he mused, his smile a taunt. He dropped his hand down to her ankle, ran it slowly, temptingly up her bare leg—a deliberate, calculated caress. Meghan didn't move even when his hand travelled further upwards, under her skirt, teased her at the joining of her thighs, his eyes still on hers, still cold.

Even now she felt the flickerings of desire, unbearably sweet, piercing the anger.

'Do you want me,' he said in disbelief, 'even now?'

Unashamed, Meghan raised her head, looked at him. Offered herself to him. 'Yes. I love you.'

He jerked back his hand, scalded by her honesty. 'This isn't about love!'

'Yes, it is. I love you. And you love me.' She met his gaze, let her eyes blaze into his.

He shook his head, hunched his shoulders. After a moment of tense silence, he said, 'Meghan, I've never wanted to hurt you.'

'Then don't.'

'*You don't know me!*' He bit the words out, raking a frustrated hand through his hair.

'I don't know who you were,' Meghan corrected. 'But I know you now.'

He shook his head, his eyes blanking again. The mask was slipping down once more, and Meghan knew she couldn't let it return.

'Alessandro, don't.' She struggled up from the bed, pulled her skirt back down. 'Don't shut me out.' She stood before him, begging. 'What will it take to prove to you that you can't turn me away? That I won't desert you?'

'You've proved that to me, Meghan,' he snapped savagely. 'You're like a little beaten dog, accepting every careless kick. I can't *get* you to leave!'

Meghan blinked. She wanted to be strong. She *wanted* to be able to do this. She just didn't know if she had the strength.

'I was honest with you,' she said, after a long, taut moment, her voice barely audible. 'I told you my secrets. My shadows. I took the risk.'

'What risk?'

'The risk of having you not believe me. Of having you disgusted by me, by my past. Believing of me what Stephen did. It was a big risk.'

He was silent, arrested, his eyes narrowed. Meghan dragged a breath into her lungs, willed herself to continue.

'You told me you liked taking risks. *I* was a risk, you said. Well, sorry, Alessandro, but I don't see that from here. All I see is a man haunted by his past. A man afraid to tell the truth. A coward.'

'I am *not* a coward!' His eyes flashed flint and his hands balled into fists. Meghan lifted her chin.

'No? Then tell me the truth.'

'I told you the truth.'

'You told me the tabloid truth. I want to know what really happened the night of the car accident.'

'That has nothing—'

'Yes, it does,' she cut him off. She pressed her hands flat against his chest. He shrugged away, but she kept on holding him. Touching him. 'I think I'm smart enough to realise that even being the world's biggest playboy wouldn't drive you like this. Torture you like this. It has to be something else. So what else is there? It must be the car accident. Something happened that night—something that is consuming you with guilt. I know what guilt feels like, Alessandro. I know what it *tastes* like. It tastes like cold metal. It rides you, wakes you up in the night, drenched in sweat, in icy terror. *I know*. You said I had shadows, but you have them too, and I don't want them here any more.'

He looked down at her, curled his fingers around her hands as if to remove them, then stopped. His eyes weren't blank; they were shadowed with pain, darkened with sorrow.

'It's not that simple.'

Meghan felt the first tremulous thrill of victory. She leaned in, kissed the rapid pulse of his throat. 'It is.'

Alessandro shook his head, the barest of movements, his eyes closed, his face working into hard lines, harsh angles.

'What happened that night?' Meghan asked softly. 'You argued—you said something to Roberto and he didn't like it. He was shaken, frightened. What did you tell him?'

Alessandro was silent for a long moment. Meghan could hear the ragged rasp of their breathing; the pounding of their hearts. Outside a child laughed, a muted sound of joy from another world.

'I told him the truth.' Alessandro spoke through stiff lips, his eyes focused on a distant place, a remembered time. His voice was little more than a whisper.

'What was the truth?'

His hands curled tightly around hers; he was holding onto her now, Meghan realised. He didn't want her to let go.

She wouldn't. She never would.

'He'd made a mistake.' Alessandro stopped, and Meghan held her breath. She knew it would take time, and it would take pain, to bring the truth from him. She could wait. 'He had no head for business, Roberto,' he continued after a moment, his voice turning toneless. Meghan understood the need to distance himself from the telling. 'He was an artist, burdened by my parents' expectations. He never should have…' He let out a low breath, shook his head, then continued. 'After my father died, the company was Roberto's alone. He made all the decisions, and he couldn't handle the responsibility. He never should have been given it.'

It should have been you, Meghan thought. Alessandro was the one with the head for business; he'd designed the most stunning piece of jewellery she'd ever seen. Yet he'd been passed over since he was a child—perhaps a bit too high-spirited, his mischievous pranks turning wilder as he was continually overlooked. It was so easy to imagine. To understand.

'He made some bad business deals,' Alessandro finally said. 'Ran into debt, terrible debt, and he couldn't get out. He became desperate, but he was also stupid. He wanted to pay back the loan sharks without anyone noticing, so he started embezzling from the company. Our company.'

He looked down at her, regret etched on every line of his face. 'I found out. I wish I hadn't. Roberto would be alive today…'

Meghan doubted that, but she held her tongue. Alessandro's honesty—his confession—was too precious.

'I used to check the company's finances,' he explained, expressionless once more. 'I…I always had an interest. When I realised what was going on I was angry.' He closed his eyes briefly. 'I was very angry—unreasonably so, perhaps—and I went to find him immediately. He was at a party—Paula, his wife, was there. *Everyone* was there. I spoke to him—I tried to keep it private…' Now his voice turned urgent, almost pleading. 'But Roberto decided to brazen it out. He said he didn't know what I was talking about, asked why I was checking up on him, so I stated figures. Facts. Then the life drained out of him. I saw him then, defeated, hopeless, and I was glad.' He looked at her, his face twisted with torment. 'What sort of man does that make me, to feel that way towards my own brother? My own brother, who never did me a moment's harm?'

Meghan shrugged. She felt eerily calm. In control. At last. 'A natural one, to have such a reaction in the heat of the moment.'

'He left the party; I followed him.' He was determined to finish it now, to have the reckoning. 'We got in the car. Once we were alone Roberto became furious. I'd never seen him so angry, so…hateful. I knew he was afraid, but I didn't let him off. I didn't give him any mercy.'

'Did he ask for it?' Meghan asked.

'He told me that I should turn a blind eye to his doings, that he'd always turned a blind eye to mine. I said… I said…' Alessandro dragged in a shuddering breath. 'I said I'd see him rot in hell first.'

Meghan's fingers ached from where he was clenching them, clinging to her as his last hope for redemption. She held on.

'And then?'

'And then…' He drew in another breath. 'And then he said that's just what I'd do.'

Alessandro was silent, his lips pressed tightly together, unable to say any more. To finish the story.

Realisation dawned slowly, achingly. 'He was driving the car, wasn't he?' Meghan said softly. 'He tried to kill you both.'

Alessandro didn't answer. Couldn't. Tenderly Meghan reached up and stroked his face, let her fingers trail along his cheek.

'You took the blame,' she surmised. It all made sense now. It was all so horrifyingly clear. 'You didn't want to sully his perfect reputation, did you? His wife… Your mother…'

'He tried—'

'What did you do? Trade places in the car? Emilia said you walked away without a scratch, but you must have had some injuries.'

'A concussion,' Alessandro said tonelessly. 'I dragged him across to the passenger seat, managed to get myself behind the wheel before I blacked out. It was the only way,' he told her, urgency roughening his tone into a demand. 'Roberto was the kindest, gentlest person... He had a moment of terrible weakness, but one that would be remembered for ever. I knew they'd believe I was driving the car—maybe they'd even think I meant to do it. They'd believe anything of me. It hardly mattered. But Roberto never hurt anyone.'

Except you, she thought. *He hurt you.*

Meghan shook her head slowly; love swelled within her, hurting her with its beauty and joy. *This* was the man she loved. 'And for this you feel guilt? Shame?'

'I killed him,' Alessandro whispered. 'If I hadn't confronted him...if I hadn't said that...' His voice turned angry, savage in its recrimination. 'I knew he was weak. That he didn't have a head for business. I'd always known it. It didn't help matters that I was partying every night, acting the playboy to thumb my nose at my parents and the world. I was stupid and reckless, and no more so than the night I got into that car. If only *I'd* taken the keys...'

'He would have done it another day,' Meghan said calmly. 'Another way. He was desperate, Alessandro, forced into a corner. It's not your fault.'

'It is.' He spoke with such certainty that her heart plummeted; then she felt angry.

'You can't be responsible for someone else's actions! Didn't you show me that when I told you what happened to me? Was I responsible for Stephen's actions? For what he did to me?'

His face twisted in horror. 'Meghan, don't.'

'No—*you* don't,' Meghan snapped back. He looked startled, and she almost smiled. 'I see who you really are. The world even sees it—sees what you've done with Di Agnio Enterprises. Alessandro, you must forgive yourself. If not for your own sake, then for mine.' She paused, her voice turning into an ache as she repeated the words he'd once said to her, the words with which he'd healed her. 'I know, and I accept you. I believe you.' She paused, tears filling her eyes as her fingers skimmed his cheek. 'I love you.'

Alessandro was silent; his eyes were closed. Meghan's heart beat a steady, desperate staccato as she wondered what was going on in his tormented mind, what would happen now.

Then a single tear slipped down his cheek; it dampened her fingers. Alessandro's grief for his brother. Meghan's breath caught in her chest; her heart expanded and she could breathe again. She could believe again.

Alessandro opened his eyes. 'I love you.'

Meghan felt weak with relief, giddy with joy.

He shook his head, took her tear-dampened fingers and lifted them to his lips. 'I don't know why I have been so blessed to have a woman who believes in me enough to see me through this. To make me go through this.' He smiled, the sorrow sifting from his eyes, revealing a flicker of hope. 'You saved me, Meghan. *You saved me.*'

'And you saved me.'

'I need to ask you to forgive me,' he continued in a low voice, 'for hurting you so very much. I did it to drive you away. I thought it would be easier for both of us. Or at least for me. I couldn't bear seeing you walk away from me, *gattina.* Seeing you disgusted by who I was, by who I am.'

'No,' Meghan whispered, 'never that. I know who you are, Alessandro, and you are the man I love.'

He nodded in acceptance, in wonder. 'You knew even before I did. How can you know me so well when I was blind to myself?'

'We were both blind,' she said with a little laugh. 'And we needed each other to be healed. Forgiven.' *Loved.*

He pulled her towards him, kissed her with a gentle passion that had her swaying into him completely, surrendering everything. Her heart, her soul, her mind, her body. His. All his.

'I am a blessed, blessed man,' he said, and there was a ragged edge of incredulous gratitude in his voice.

'No more blessed than I am.'

He nodded, kissing her again, and as sunlight slanted through the windows, sifting patterns on the floor, Meghan realised the shadows were gone. All of them.

All that was left was her and Alessandro, and joy.

Only joy.

The Italian's Captive Virgin

INDIA GREY

To John.
Thank you for the Happy Ever After.

A self-confessed romance junkie, **India Grey** was just thirteen years old when she first sent off for the Mills & Boon Writers' Guidelines. She can still recall the thrill of getting the large brown envelope with its distinctive logo through the letterbox, and subsequently whiled away many a dull school-day staring out of the window and dreaming of the perfect hero. She kept these guidelines with her for the next ten years, tucking them carefully inside the cover of each new diary in January, and beginning every list of New Year's Resolutions with the words *Start Novel*. In the meantime she also gained a degree in English Literature and Language from Manchester University and, in a stroke of genius on the part of the Gods of Romance, met her gorgeous future husband on the very last night of their three years there. The last fifteen years have been spent blissfully buried in domesticity, and heaps of pink washing generated by three small daughters, but she has never really stopped daydreaming about romance. She's just profoundly grateful to have finally got an excuse to do it legitimately!

India Grey's special new novel should be available from Mills & Boon® Modern™ in the autumn.

PROLOGUE

THE dress was ivory satin, heavy and smooth. Once a nineteen-fifties cocktail dress belonging to Grandmère, Anna's mother had taken it in to fit Anna's skinny ten-year-old frame and added a narrow grosgrain ribbon around the waist, just above where the skirt flared out with wonderful fullness. An old piece of net curtain trimmed with tiny crystal beads and fixed down with a pleasingly authentic-looking plastic tiara completed the picture.

'It's beautiful.' Anna looked at herself in the mirror, her dark eyes shining with joy. 'Just like what a real bride would wear. It's the best birthday present ever. Thank you, Mama.'

Lisette smiled. 'Happy Birthday, *chérie. You're* beautiful. You look like a fairy princess.'

Anna frowned. She knew it wasn't true. Fairy princesses would be soft and blonde and blue-eyed like her mother, not olive-skinned and dark like she was. But she loved the dress all the same.

She was lucky that her birthday always fell in the summer holidays, when she and her mother were staying with Grandmère at Château Belle-Eden, and that summer she did nothing but play weddings. Gathering armfuls of flowers from the château's garden, she entwined garlands of jasmine and ivy around the banisters and tied heavy old-fashioned roses into spiky bouquets. In the hot, still afternoons the hallway was cool and the dim light filtering through the magnificent stained-glass dome above cast shimmering patterns on to the pale stone floor. While her mother played the piano in the salon Anna would drift down the stairs, shedding petals from her wilting rose bouquet, towards her imaginary waiting groom.

She pictured him standing at the bottom of the sweeping staircase, looking exactly like the prince in her book of fairy tales. Tall, blond, impossibly elegant in his morning coat, she imagined over and over again the moment when he would turn and look up at her.

The love that blazed in his blue eyes took her breath away every time.

CHAPTER ONE

'*C'EST tout, mademoiselle?*'

Anna cast a last look at her childhood, jumbled into the back of the auctioneer's van, and swallowed hard.

'Yes. That's all.'

The man slid up the tailgate and dusted off his big hands. '*Bien, mademoiselle.* There are just a few boxes left in the attic now; nothing that can go in a Paris saleroom, I'm afraid. Perhaps a local firm, a *brocante*?

Anna nodded, absent-mindedly scuffing the dusty gravel with the toe of her little green ballet pump, then stopping abruptly. She'd spent too long in tatty espadrilles hanging around with the GreenPlanet gang—she'd almost forgotten how to behave in proper clothes.

She straightened up and smiled apologetically at the removal man. His face softened. He'd worked for Paris's top auction house for a good many years now, so by rights nothing should surprise him any more. Aristocrats were an eccentric lot, and English aristocrats were the oddest of all, but Lady Roseanna Delafield was like no one he had ever come across before. With her silky black hair shot through with pink streaks and her quick, graceful ballerina's movements, she was like a pedigree kitten who had got lost and gone feral. Today her hair was caught back in a discreet knot at the nape of her neck, she was wearing a little black linen shift dress that made her skin glow like sun-kissed apricots and she looked for all the world like any other smart young lady of breeding, but nothing could quite disguise the vulnerability in those big dark eyes.

'*Bon chance, ma petite,*' he said kindly, climbing into the driver's seat of his lorry. 'Is sad to say goodbye to somewhere where we 'ave been 'appy, no?'

Anna shrugged sadly. 'Yes. But maybe it's not goodbye just yet. You never know…'

Leaning out of the window the man laughed. 'Miracles do 'appen, *chérie.* I 'ope you find one.' He started the engine and winked at her. 'You deserve it. *Au revoir.*'

Anna watched the van disappear round the bend in the drive, through the pine trees, then she turned and walked slowly back into the château. Inside the hot, late summer air was heavy with the smell of decay and her eyes travelled desolately around the once-splendid entrance hall. The duck-egg-blue silk that lined the walls was rotting and torn; pale squares were left where the men had taken down the paintings and darker patches showed the ravages of damp.

Her little low-heeled shoes echoed on the leaf-strewn floor as she walked slowly up the stairs. Above her, miraculously the stained glass dome was still intact and at that moment a shaft of afternoon sunlight sent shimmering pools of light on to the stairs. She smiled, remembering how she used to love trying to catch those rippling rainbows as a child, and how they used to fall in vivid splashes on the white bride's dress she'd got for her birthday that summer when she'd played the wedding game.

That last summer before her mother had died.

She jumped as her mobile phone rang, and slid it out of her bag.

'Fliss, I'm on my way. The auctioneer people just left, so I'm just going to lock up and leave.'

'OK, honey, I'll order you a very strong Martini.' Fliss's

voice was warm with compassion and understanding. 'Are you getting the bus?'

'No. One of the guys in the GreenPlanet camp has a bike I can borrow. It's only a few miles.'

From the other end of the phone Fliss gave a snort of laughter. 'You're joking, right? Anna, *no one* has ever arrived at the Hotel Paradis *by bike*. Are you going to get it valet parked?'

Stamping up a narrower flight of stairs to the attic, Anna scowled. 'Don't be silly. I don't see why I should pump carbon monoxide into the atmosphere just to keep the parking valets at the Paradis in tips.'

'OK, OK, spare me the environmental lecture.' The laughter died in Fliss's voice, leaving her sounding suddenly subdued. 'Talking of which, how's life in the GreenPlanet camp? Have you finished saving the world for the rest of us yet?'

Anna wandered over to the forlorn stack of boxes and old trunks the men had left piled in the middle of the dusty attic. 'We're still working on it,' she said stiffly, lifting the lid of a metal-banded trunk at her feet and finding herself looking down at a jumble of old clothes. 'Saving Château Belle-Eden from this…this vile property developer would be a good start, though.'

'Well, if word in our office is correct and the "vile property developer" in question *is* Angelo Emiliani you don't stand a cat in hell's chance of saving it,' Fliss retorted, then, hearing Anna's soft gasp, said, 'Anna? What's the matter?'

'Nothing. I've just found my old dressing-up box. All my ballet stuff is in here—my first pointe shoes.' Reverently she wound the trailing ribbons around the tattered slippers, then slowly pulled out a crushed tumble of heavy cream satin from the depths of the trunk. 'The wedding dress!'

Anna held the dress out at arm's length, gazing wonderingly at it. She'd thought it was so perfect, but now she could see how home-made it looked, how obvious that it had been inexpertly cut down from one of Grandmère's gowns and trimmed with mismatched bits salvaged from other garments. The fabric had yellowed with age and was spotted with mildew in places. Wedging the phone against her shoulder, she held the dress up against her and twirled slowly around.

'To think I truly believed *this* made me look like a real bride,' she said vaguely. 'A fairy princess… I must have been spectacularly naïve…'

That was an understatement.

Abruptly she tore the dress away from her body and dropped it back into the box. 'Anyway,' she continued briskly, 'like I said, there's nothing left for me to do here. I'm on my way.'

'Great. I'll be in the terrace bar, provided we can get a table. Don't forget it's Saskia Middleton's twenty-first tonight too, so wear something suitable. You *are* wearing something suitable, aren't you?' Fliss added, sounding worried. 'Only I haven't quite got over the puffball-skirt-and-biker-boots combo from Lucinda's party at Christmas. Her poor mother didn't know what to say.'

Anna glanced down at the subdued black dress. 'Don't panic, I'm looking deeply respectable,' she said ruefully. 'And it's entirely in your honour, as I have absolutely no intention of going to Saskia Middleton's party. I'd rather spend an evening with Lucretia Borgia and Hannibal Lecter. But go and grab a table on the terrace and get those Martinis ordered. I'll be there in fifteen minutes.'

Hanging up before Fliss could argue about the party, Anna turned back to the wedding dress, stroking her hand over the slippery satin.

How much had changed since that long ago summer, when she had thought that life was simple.

Nothing was simple. Nothing was what she'd thought it was. Herself included.

The château was just about all that was left of that old life. And that, she thought fiercely, standing up and walking quickly

across the room and down the stairs, was why she had no intention of letting it go without a fight. It was nothing whatsoever
to do with any lingering fantasies about white dresses and
wedding bells, but her mother was dead, her dreams were
broken, her own sense of who she was shaken to the core. *That*
was why she had to hang on to the last shreds of the person she
used to think she was.

A door slammed below.

Crossing the landing, Anna stopped dead. A little gust of air
seemed to shiver through the building, then everything sank back
into stillness. But the atmosphere had changed. There was a charge
in the air, like electricity before a storm, and with a pulse of horrified certainty Anna knew she was no longer alone in the house.

She froze and then, with agonizing caution, tiptoed to the top
of the stairs.

For a long moment there was no sound at all.

Then, with a mounting sense of panic, she heard footsteps
moving across the hall. Instinctively she recognized them as
male: slow, measured and sounding like the footsteps of the axe-
murderer in every horror film she'd ever seen.

The footsteps stopped.

Forcing herself to lean forward, she tentatively peered over
the banisters, then drew back with a sharp intake of breath.

She was right.

He was male. Very male. And very blond. Perhaps it was just
because she was looking down on him from directly above that
he seemed to have the broadest shoulders she'd ever seen.

'Hello?'

His voice was deep and faintly accented. He didn't sound like
a murderer. He sounded gorgeous. Anna swallowed. The ability
to speak had inexplicably deserted her, but the pounding of her
heart seemed to echo through the whole building, declaring her
presence with every beat.

'Who's there?'

She opened her mouth but the only sound that came out was a dry croak.

There was a muttered curse from below. 'All right then, I'll come up.'

Oh, God. She was being utterly ridiculous and in a moment he—whoever he was—was going to come up and see her cowering on the landing like some frightened animal. Drawing herself up to her full five foot three inches, she smoothed down the slightly creased linen of her dress. 'Don't bother,' she called, clenching her fists into balls of determination and desperately trying to assume an air of insouciance. She moved to the top of the stairs and began to descend.

Halfway down she steeled herself to glance down at him and had to grip the banister to stop herself from falling. There was a roaring of blood in her ears and a dizzying surge of adrenalin flooded her body.

The man who stood at the foot of the stairs was her fantasy made flesh. For a moment time seemed to stand still and the years melt away, until she could have easily believed that she was ten years old again, a ragged bouquet of forget-me-nots and roses clasped in her hands, sweeping down the stairs to meet her hero. He was there, just as she had imagined him so many times.

Only his silver-blue eyes weren't filled with adoration.

They were icy cold.

'*Gesù*, who the hell are you?'

Angelo Emiliani was aware of the hostility in his tone and didn't bother to try and disguise it.

Arundel-Ducasse may be one of the longest established estate agents in the business, with offices in all the major European cities, but in his dealings with them over the past couple of weeks they had hardly stunned him with their efficiency. Now it seemed they'd not only got the time of his appointment wrong, so thwarting his plan to look around the château on his own first, but they'd also sent some juvenile delinquent office girl.

And, unfortunately for her, patience was not his strong point.

She stopped on the third step from the bottom, where her eyes were just about level with his, looking both nervous and defiant. In spite of his irritation, Angelo felt a vague, instinctive stirring inside him.

'Maybe I should ask you the same question,' she snapped.

'Oh, dear.' His tone was languid and mocking as he turned and walked into the centre of the hallway, his eyes travelling speculatively around the room. 'Am I to assume that the entire Nice office of Arundel-Ducasse have been struck down with the Black Death or something equally debilitating? I cannot imagine any other circumstances in which it would be necessary to send the girl who does the photocopying on a major viewing such as this.'

Behind him she gave a little gasp.

'Angelo Emiliani.'

Something in her voice jolted him out of his preoccupied irritation and he glanced sharply at her, noticing her properly for the first time.

At first he had assumed that the rainbow streaks in her hair were caused by the light from the stained-glass dome above them, but now he could see that there were indeed jagged blazes of shocking pink beneath the dark silk that was drawn back from her delicate heart-shaped face. His gaze travelled over her slowly, taking in the smoky kohl-rimmed eyes and the short black dress, the oddly defiant set of her small chin. Realization slotted into his brain like a well-oiled bolt sliding home. Of course. He'd spotted the protesters' camp through the trees as he'd approached the château. He gave a slow smile.

'Correct, *signorina*. And your name is…?'

Her hesitation was almost unnoticeable, then, with a little jangle of silver bracelets, she thrust out a slender hand and spoke in confident cut-glass tones.

'Forgive me, Signor Emiliani, you caught me off guard. I'm Felicity from the London office of Arundel-Ducasse. I've been liaising with the Marquess of Ifford over the sale of the château. I'm on holiday in Cannes, so I thought I'd come and see it for myself.'

That was pretty quick thinking. He had to hand it to her—she was a vast improvement on the usual spotty, dreadlocked eco-warriors that picketed his development sites and protested outside his offices in Rome and London.

'I see.' He looked down at the grimy limestone floor and tried to suppress a smile. Protester-baiting was one of his favourite sports and this time there was an added piquancy thanks to the unprecedented lusciousness of the quarry. The urge to play along with her little charade was irresistible. 'Well, I'm very glad that you did, Felicity.' He took a step towards her and watched with satisfaction as a shadow passed across her extraordinary wide-set eyes. 'Very glad indeed. As you'll have gathered, your colleague from the far less efficient Nice office hasn't appeared and due to unwelcome…*developments*…I'm very keen to get this deal sorted out today.'

'Developments?'

He sighed. 'Our little group of campers in the woods. I saw them as I came up the drive and the sooner my name is on the deeds for this property, the sooner I can send them on their way to spend their time doing something worthwhile. I hate to see idealistic young people wasting their time on a lost cause.'

Anna clenched her fists so that the fingernails dug painfully into her palms. Until this moment she wouldn't honestly have been able to list 'self-control' as being one of her personal strong points, but it seemed she certainly had more of it than she thought. How else was she managing to restrain herself from throwing herself at Angelo hot-shot Emiliani and raking her nails down his arrogant, self-satisfied, obscenely handsome face?

He took a step towards her, his eyes fixed on hers. 'So it's your lucky day, Felicity. As you'll be the one to show me the property, you'll be the one who gets the commission on the sale.'

Anna felt the blood drain from her face. She felt like Judas taking his thirty pieces of silver. The thought of walking through each familiar room of her beloved château in the company of the man who intended to take it from her made her feel dizzy with horror.

He was still looking at her, his narrow blue eyes glittering with ice.

'That won't be a problem, will it, *signorina*? You *are* an employee of the estate agency that is supposed to be selling this property, are you not?'

'Yes, of course, as I said I…'

'Good. And you said you've been handling its marketing in the London office, in which case you should know your way around?'

She met his gaze with a steadiness that surprised him. 'Yes.'

'Then let's not waste any more time.' He smiled suddenly and it lit up his exquisite features and carved perfectly symmetrical brackets on each side of his generous mouth. 'I've scheduled the first of my contractors to be on site here next week, so as you can see I can't afford to hang around.'

'Isn't that a little presumptuous? Until the contracts are signed, nothing is certain.'

'Not presumptuous. Realistic. I always get what I want. Now, are you going to show me around or do I have to phone the Nice office and get someone out here who knows what they're doing?'

She looked up at him and gave him her sweetest smile.

'Where would you like to start?'

His eyes flickered downwards for a second, causing her stomach to tighten convulsively and a gasp to rise in her throat.

'How about the master bedroom?'

Breathe in… Hold… And out…

It was no good. The surge of white-hot tingling fury that was currently coursing through her veins wasn't going to be calmed down with yoga. She needed tranquillisers at the very least. Or a general anaesthetic.

The trouble was, she admitted disgustedly to herself, it wasn't just anger that was making her knees shake so much that she had to lean on the banisters for support. Waiting on the landing outside what used to be her grandmother's room, Anna cursed her own stupidity and the pathetic weakness that had made her hormones sing in response to his blatant flirting.

How could she have told such a ridiculous lie? Fliss would kill her when she found out she had 'borrowed' her identity. Oh, God—supposing Emiliani complained to her boss and she got into terrible trouble? Anna felt panic surge through her.

She'd just have to be very, very nice to the obnoxious Signor Emiliani and make sure that he had no cause to complain, but jeez, that wasn't going to be easy. How could he be so complacent—so sure of himself—to have already scheduled contractors to start destroying her beloved château when the sale was far from assured? She felt a fresh wave of indignation crash through her at the thought.

Thank goodness for GreenPlanet. It wasn't over yet.

She turned. Through the open doorway she could see him standing at the window. He was leaning against the sill, his arms stretched out on either side and his broad shoulders blocking out an unreasonable amount of daylight. No doubt he was planning which parts of the formal parterre would have to be flattened to make way for the helipad and all-weather tennis courts, she thought bitterly, trying not to notice the way his unruly blond hair curled on to the collar of his dark linen suit, or the length of the suntanned fingers resting so lightly on the window sill. Even with his back to her there was something about his slim-hipped, elegant figure that screamed self-assurance and power.

I always get what I want.

GreenPlanet was no match for him, she acknowledged with

a mixture of despair and awful, treacherous excitement. He had an aura of quiet, dangerous focus that made her shiver.

Levering himself upright, he turned to her and she experienced a momentary *frisson* of shock at the youthful beauty of his face. The skin over his elegant cheekbones was taut and bronzed, and his aura of restless energy was like that of an exotic animal in the absolute peak of physical condition. He couldn't be that much older than she was and yet he seemed as hard and cold and jaded as a man twice his age. What the hell had happened to turn him to stone?

'Well?'

'Well what?' she stuttered, suddenly jolted out of her thoughts and aware that she'd been staring. Although he was no doubt used to that.

He leaned his narrow hips against the window sill and folded his arms. 'Come on, Felicity, you can do better than that. This is the part where you're supposed to talk about location and square footage and security. You're an *estate agent*, remember?'

His voice was quiet, amused, slightly reproving. Anna gritted her teeth as she recognized that he was testing her, teasing her.

'Of course. And you're an internationally renowned property developer, *signor*,' she retorted, trying to keep her tone light. 'I wouldn't presume to tell you anything about this building or any other, since of the two of us you are so clearly the expert.'

'Wouldn't or couldn't?'

He spoke very softly, the words dropping into the silence like pebbles into a lake. Anna felt the ripples spreading through the still air between them and, despite the warmth of the afternoon, she shivered suddenly.

He was *so* on to her. And so enjoying it. For the sake of her own pride as well as Fliss's professional reputation, she had to do a bit better than this.

'What do you want to know?' Squaring her shoulders, she walked slowly towards him, slipping again into that clipped upper-crust drawl. 'As I'm sure you can see for yourself, Château Belle-Eden is a perfect example of the nineteenth century Anglo-Norman style, set in five acres of prime real estate in one of the world's most desirable locations.'

'Very impressive.'

'That was the intention.' She had reached the window now and stood beside him, unable to meet his eyes. 'It was built in 1897 for the owner of one of Paris's most exclusive department stores and no expense was spared on its construction or its furnishings. The walls were covered with silk from—'

'I wasn't actually talking about the property.'

'I beg your pardon?'

He was looking at her steadily. 'I was referring to your in-depth knowledge of Château Belle-Eden.'

'I told you, I've been responsible for the marketing of this property at the London end,' she said abruptly, staring straight ahead of her to where the driveway snaked through the pine trees towards the road and the cliffs beyond. 'As I was saying, this is one of the most sought after locations in the world. Cannes is a mere three kilometres away, the château has its own stretch of private beach, accessed through the pine forest—which you can see over there to your left.'

'Ah, yes.' Much to Anna's relief, he shifted his smoky, searching gaze and looked out of the window to where the GreenPlanet tents and guy-ropes of washing were just about visible above the pine trees. His eyes were narrowed and slightly menacing.

'Do you intend to keep the château as a private residence, Signor Emiliani?' she asked, trying to keep her tone casual.

Slowly he turned back to face her with a mocking smile. 'No. I thought I'd use it as a youth hostel. And maybe establish a permanent camp over there in the woods for hippies and drop-outs. That way maybe I'd be able to get on with my other projects at least without having them constantly on my case.'

She didn't flinch, he noticed. Not a flicker of emotion passed through those slanting, watchful eyes.

'It was a genuine enquiry, *signor.*'

'I'm sure it was. But if you think I'd be stupid enough to tell you honestly what I plan to do with this building then you're obviously underestimating me.'

She looked steadily at him. 'Have you finished here?'

There it was again. She was perfectly polite, perfectly correct, but he picked up that tiny spark of challenge which a man who was less in tune with his instincts would undoubtedly have missed. Angelo Emiliani had not come from an orphanage in Milan to take his place in the international rich lists by behaving as other men did. Instinct was his speciality.

'For the time being, yes.'

'Good. Follow me.'

'My pleasure.'

And it certainly was a pleasure, he thought idly, watching the way the short linen dress cast undulating shadows on to the backs of her slim brown thighs as she sauntered down corridors, opening the doors on an endless succession of vast empty rooms. Despite the perfect respectability of the dress, there was something oddly rebellious about the way she wore it. Maybe it was the way she had teamed it with those slim bangles which made a soft, silvery, musical sound as she moved, or maybe it was the contrast of her long golden legs beneath the sober black.

There was something about this girl that whispered *'toxic'*. She gave the impression that the lightest brush against her would result in chemical burns.

The fact that she was lying to him didn't disturb Angelo at all. The fact that she was doing it so convincingly bothered him a little more. Environmental protesters were a constant source of irritation and disruption in his business, but he had never considered them to be a serious threat to his plans before. But this girl knew more about this property than a hippy-dippy eco-warrior should do.

It didn't cross his mind for a second that he might be wrong about her. So what if she had the diction of a minor royal and the lithe movements of a dancer? She was no more some posh airhead office girl than he was. It wasn't just the pink streaks in her hair that gave her away, but the hostility that crackled around her like static. She might as well have had 'REBEL' tattooed on to her skin in inch-high letters.

Maybe she did. Somewhere.

Desire hit him like the lash of a whip, sudden and stinging.

'In here is a slightly smaller bedroom, but the view of the sea more than makes up for the less sizable proportions…' She spoke before she'd opened the door, he noticed, but, walking into the room, Angelo's eyes narrowed as he ascertained that what she had just said was completely spot on.

He felt a cold pulse of adrenalin rush through him along with the realization that the group she belonged to may have some rich benefactor who was planning to put in a rival bid for the château. It wasn't such a ridiculous idea. There were plenty of stratospherically wealthy Hollywood celebs who would be only too willing to toss a few million in the direction of an environmental charity—especially if it meant acquiring such a gem of a property at the same time as making them feel they were doing their bit to save the planet. With the exception of the charity involved, it wasn't so very different from what he planned to do with it. And the prospect of having those plans thwarted by a group of tree-huggers was unthinkable.

In the past he had bought properties out of boredom or for a challenge or simply to irritate the people who tried to stop him, but this one was different. Angelo Emiliani wasn't in the habit of analyzing his feelings—in fact his entire purpose in life was to keep busy enough to avoid having to have them at all—but he was prepared to acknowledge how much this project mattered to him. For old times' sake.

For Lucia.

'…south facing, meaning the light is particularly lovely in here.'

There was something wistful in her tone that jerked him back to the present. Thrusting his hands into his pockets, he took a steadying breath in before turning his attention back to her.

She was standing by the window, looking out across the treetops to where the sea lay in a glittering arc. And she was right about the light, he thought bitterly. The evening sun fell on to her face, outlining her profile in gold-dust, highlighting the sudden softness of her sulky mouth. Crushing down the anger that smouldered somewhere inside his chest, he managed a smile.

'You've been very helpful, Felicity. Really. I appreciate you showing me round.'

She looked up at him and blinked, clearly taken by surprise by the softness of his tone. Walking slowly towards her, he could see that she was trembling slightly, but bravado flashed in her dark eyes. The combination caused an odd sensation in the pit of his stomach, which he recognized as lust spiked with something more complicated.

'It's nothing. I shouldn't have been here really…'

He stopped a couple of feet away from her. 'I'm very glad you were. I'll be sure to tell your boss how impressed I am by your professional dedication.'

That shook her. He tried not to let the tiny leap of triumph in his chest show on his face as he watched the colour flood her cheeks.

'Please don't. I probably shouldn't have—'

The bare room was bathed in softest apricot, turning the pink in her hair to gleaming copper.

'OK—but let me make it up to you in some other way. You said you were staying in Cannes—please let me take you out for dinner tonight.'

'I can't,' she said hastily. 'I'm meeting a friend.' She glanced at her watch. 'In fact, I'm late. I really should go.'

He nodded. Her refusal didn't surprise him in the slightest—he hadn't expected anything else—but, looking at those slanting, wary, kohl-smudged eyes, he felt a sharp kick of disappointment which caught him completely unawares.

She was already walking to the door, casting a last look around the room before going out on to the landing.

He followed her. Her footsteps echoed on the wooden stairs as she ran down them.

'Where are you staying? I'll give you a lift.'

Smiling slightly, he wondered how she would get out of that one, but she tossed a nonchalant glance at him over her shoulder.

'Thanks. Hotel Paradis, if that's not out of your way?'

Watching her shut the front door of the château, Angelo felt himself frowning.

He was used to having all the answers, to being at least ten steps ahead of the game. But he had to admit it that right now this girl had him floundering in the dark.

Which was an intoxicating image. But a very disturbing feeling.

CHAPTER TWO

'NICE car.'

Anna made an effort to mask her contempt behind a façade of admiration as she glanced around the white leather interior of the ridiculously flashy sports car. But she couldn't quite stop herself from adding with a simper, 'I always think that cars say so much about their owners.'

This one was shouting, *I belong to a man with obscene amounts of cash and issues about his masculinity*, she thought with some satisfaction. Maybe Angelo Emiliani wasn't as cool as he came across.

'Do you?'

Admittedly his voice was infuriatingly cool, as was the way he seemed to lounge in the driver's seat, controlling the powerful car with one hand and easing it around hairpin bends on the narrow road at speeds which…

Anna swallowed and averted her eyes from the speedometer.

'So you've no doubt come to the conclusion that I'm an insecure misogynist with more money than taste?' She felt the colour leap to her cheeks at the accuracy of his guess. 'Well, I hate to spoil the theory, but the car is only hired. I simply asked for the fastest model available—which should tell you that I'm very impatient and I like to get everything done in the shortest possible time.'

'In that case, wouldn't it make more sense to have a chauffeur? So you don't need to lose a second of valuable working time?'

'Yes. But my impatience is perhaps only outweighed by my desire for control.' His mouth curved into the merest suggestion of an ironic smile, letting her know he'd picked up the minute sting of sarcasm in her tone, and his blue gaze flickered over her for a second. A blissful, spine-tingling second. 'I do have a chauffeur, of course. But wherever practical I prefer to drive myself. What about you, *signorina*? What sort of car do you drive?'

'I don't. Cars are—'

She was about to spring automatically into the standard GreenPlanet sermon about the evils wrought on the planet by the internal combustion engine, but managed to stop herself just in time. Not, however, before she noticed the smirk of satisfaction on Angelo Emiliani's face.

'A nuisance where I live, in Central London,' she finished lamely, looking out of the window. 'I take the tube everywhere.'

He'd very nearly caught her out. And, dammit, he knew it. He didn't reply, but his silence spoke more articulately than anything he could have said.

The traffic grew heavier as they came into Cannes, and Angelo guided the car effortlessly through the streams of expensive vehicles towards the hotel. He wondered what she would do when they got there. Wait until he had gone and hitch a lift back to the protesters' camp, he guessed. There was no way she could possibly be telling the truth about staying at the Paradis.

Was there?

'I don't think I got your full name,' he said casually. With this girl it was best not to take any chances.

'Hanson-Brooks'

'Felicity Hanson-Brooks,' he repeated, echoing her clipped upper-class pronunciation with a slight curl of his lip. That accent, with its suggestion of effortless privilege and complacency, never failed to set his teeth on edge and make his hackles rise. 'That's a very smart name.'

She glanced across at him and shrugged slightly. Defensively?

Out of the corner of his eye he watched her stretch out her long legs and shift slightly in her seat, arching her back away from the hot leather upholstery with the lissom grace of a cat stretching.

Angelo Emiliani had slept with so many women—from cocktail waitresses to *contessas*. Novelty, the ruthless pursuit of the new, which was what drove him in his work, was something he no longer expected to experience in the bedroom.

But he'd never had an eco-warrior.

Idly he wondered what lay beneath that perfectly simple, perfectly demure black linen dress. There was something raw about her, something earthy. He had grown tired of the neat, waxed sterility that turned every woman he undressed into a conveyor-belt Barbie—perfect and plastic. This girl looked as if she was liberatingly, excitingly beyond all of that. He breathed in deeply, savouring the thought, and was suddenly aware of the scent of her.

She smelled of dark things—bitter chocolate, black coffee, overlaid with woodsmoke.

Strong. Exotic. Delicious.

Benedetto Gesù. The very things he didn't trust about her were the things that turned him on.

He swung into the hotel's VIP forecourt more recklessly than he had intended and brought the car to a halt in a screech of brakes. For a moment neither of them moved and the interior of the small car suddenly seemed thick with swirling undercurrents of meaning.

His hand, still on the handbrake, was inches from her bare thigh. He flexed his fingers around the brake, and then was instantly, uncomfortably aware of the phallic symbolism of the gesture.

And so was she.

Slowly her eyes travelled upwards, until she was looking at him from beneath her lashes as shaming colour rushed to her cheeks. He must have guessed what she was thinking, he must be mocking her, she thought in miserable humiliation. How amusingly predictable that she should end up falling under his spell like every other woman. Groping for the door handle, she mustered what she hoped was a cool smile, but her attempt at nonchalance was totally ruined by the fact that she couldn't work out how to open the door.

He leaned across her and she flattened herself against the back of the seat to avoid coming into contact with the hard length of his body. But she could smell his cool, clean scent. He straightened up slowly and she scrambled out of the car.

'Thanks for the lift, Signor Emiliani.'

He nodded curtly, suddenly finding that the acerbic retort he would usually have found eluded him. For a fraction of a second there he had been out of control—of the car and of his ruthlessly contained emotions—and the realisation had left a very bitter taste in his mouth.

He should follow her, he thought savagely as he watched her run lightly up the steps to the hotel, but the tell-tale evidence of her effect on him made movement temporarily inadvisable. Slamming his fist down on the steering wheel, he waited a moment, then got stiffly out of the low driving seat and leaned against the roof of the car, watching her all the time.

At the top of the steps she paused and turned her head towards the long rows of little metal tables that spilled out from the hotel's ultra-fashionable bar on to a balcony overlooking the beach. At this hour of the early evening they were already crowded with those who were wealthy and well-connected enough to be able to afford to drink in one of the most exclusive watering holes on the Riviera, and beautiful enough to want to be seen there.

Angelo's eyes narrowed as he watched her wave frantically before hurrying inside. He straightened up, searching the crowd on the outdoor terrace for the person she could have been greeting, but in the crush of lithe, designer-clad bodies perched at tables and standing in groups it was impossible to distinguish anyone in particular.

Which, he thought savagely, tossing the car keys to a uniformed concierge, was exactly what she had calculated. It was all part of the game she was playing to try to persuade him that she genuinely was some harmless, well-bred English girl, holidaying on the Riviera with a similarly respectable friend.

He didn't intend to let her get away with it.

Ignoring the polite greeting of the doorman, he stalked angrily through the opulent lobby to the reception desk. While he waited his eyes roved restlessly over the shifting groups of people, but there was no sign of her.

The blonde receptionist batted thickly mascaraed eyelashes at him as he asked for Felicity Hanson-Brooks's room number.

'Well, *monsieur*, we're really not supposed to…'

'Please. She gave it to me last night and I arranged to pick her up, but I'm afraid I've forgotten it.' He gave her his most helpless smile and watched her melt. 'I can't stand her up.'

Blushing furiously under her heavy make-up, the girl gave it to him and was rewarded with a smile that would give her sleepless nights for the next month.

His face hardening as he turned away, Angelo took a seat on a Louis XIV-style sofa beneath a hideous golden palm tree and thoughtfully took out his phone. That hadn't been the outcome he had expected. He checked his watch. It was too late now to catch any of his contacts in the London office of Arundel-Ducasse, and he was starting to get a nasty feeling that he might just be in for a surprise there too.

Was his instinct about this girl completely wrong?

With fresh determination he speed-dialled his PA and asked

her to arrange for his chauffeur to bring his dinner suit down to the Paradis. He wasn't leaving tonight until he'd got some answers. In the meantime, he had a deal to finalise.

'OK, you have precisely thirty seconds to explain.'

Leaning over the little table, Anna gave Fliss a brief hug then sank down into one of the trendy aluminium chairs and took a long sip of the drink that was waiting for her.

''Splain wha'?' she queried innocently around the ridiculous straw and cocktail olive with which the Hotel Paradis saw fit to furnish their Martinis. The ice in hers had melted long ago so it was warm and watery, but it still had a very welcome alcoholic kick.

Leaning back in her seat, Fliss tapped her foot and tried to look cross, but her eyes sparkled with excitement. 'Let me think now… Who invented cellulite? Why men don't have a shopping gene? Or maybe why you've turned up forty minutes late in the company of a gorgeous bloke?'

Sullenly Anna took a long suck of Martini. 'Hmm, that's actually quite interesting. You see "gorgeous bloke" and I see "ruthless, vulgar billionaire property developer."'

Fliss's eyes widened and she let out a long, low whistle.

'*That* was Angelo Emiliani?'

As reactions went it was a pretty satisfying one, Anna reflected sulkily, so why did it irritate the life out of her?

Fliss's eyes skimmed the terrace, as if hungry to see him again. 'Now I understand why the girls in our office call him The Ice Prince and fight each other practically to the death to take his calls. He is quite *amazingly* lush…'

Anna affected extreme indifference and looked into the distance, to where the sun was dyeing the surface of the sea the same colour as her hair.

'So the gossip was spot on,' Fliss mused eagerly. 'He's the mystery buyer for the château.'

'Correction,' snapped Anna. 'He's the *would-be* mystery buyer for the château. The papers aren't signed yet.'

Fliss glanced at her sharply. 'But they will be, surely? As soon as his offer is made formally? I mean, the whole point is that you and your father need the money from the sale, isn't it?'

Viciously Anna stabbed the olive with the cocktail stick. 'Of course. But I don't want to let Château Belle-Eden go to someone who's going to rip it apart and turn it into some hideous show-piece of trendy architecture.'

Fliss was looking at her steadily. 'And what about your father? What does he say about that?'

'Why should he care? He hasn't been near the place in years. He wouldn't care if Emiliani wanted to paint it purple and turn it into a vice den, but luckily, thanks to French inheritance law, it's half mine, so whatever he says the sale can't go ahead until I've signed the papers.'

'Right,' said Fliss decisively. 'I'll come with you if you like. You can introduce me to the delicious Signor Emiliani.'

Anna paled at the thought. As far as Angelo Emiliani was concerned he'd already met Felicity Hanson-Brooks, but now wasn't the time to confess about that. Not when Fliss had that scary look on her face.

'You *are* going to sign them, aren't you, Anna?'

Anna's gaze swept over the packed terrace. The setting sun gave the beautiful tanned faces of the Riviera crowd a flattering rosy glow. The noise of excited conversation was underlaid by a faint but insistent bass beat as the nightclubs and parties swung into life. Edgy and restless, Anna felt its feverish pulse echoed inside her.

'Eventually. I—that is, GreenPlanet too—just want to try to find out what he has in mind for it before the sale is completed. Gavin—one of the GreenPlanet guys—has heard something about a connection with a pharmaceutical company, and apparently Emiliani is intending to cut down most of the pine forest for a landing strip, which of course we're very concerned about. If that's the case—'

Fliss shook her glossy, well-groomed head. 'You won't stop him. The guy's legendary for making things happen. It's what he *does*. And hell, Anna, it's what he does *beautifully*. He'll make Belle-Eden into something wonderful.'

Seeing the stricken look on Anna's face, she realised instantly that she'd said the wrong thing. 'It's wonderful as it is,' Anna snapped. 'He can only ruin it. And the environment. All those trees—'

Fliss was looking at her steadily, sadly. 'Oh, Anna, that's not really the issue here, is it? Look, honey, I know when you had to give up ballet it hit you hard. It was your life, and it's left a big empty space which no one can blame you for trying to fill. But all this eco-stuff? Are you sure you really care about it enough to take on someone like Angelo Emiliani?'

Leaning her elbows on the table, Anna dropped her head into her hands. Suddenly she felt very tired. In the darkness behind her fingers the image of Angelo Emiliani standing at the window in her grandmother's room came back to her—tall, broad-shouldered and utterly sure of the power he wielded. His confidence was daunting.

It was also horribly, irresistibly attractive.

She felt Fliss's hand on her arm. 'Are you sure you're not just grasping at something to fill that empty space, and maybe—just maybe—get back at your father?'

Anna sat up abruptly and tugged out the band that held her hair back, letting it fall around her face with a flash of vivid pink.

'Oh, God, Fliss. Maybe. I don't know; I'm still so angry with him for not being honest with me for all those years. And with Mum, but that's awful because she's not here and I still miss her so much too. And that's why I can't just let go of the château. It's my last…link with her. It meant everything to her. It was a part of her.'

'I think you're wrong. It's just a place. She'd understand why it had to be sold. *You* meant everything to her. *You* were a part of her.'

Anna got stiffly to her feet and Fliss almost gasped at the pain in her eyes, still raw after all these years. 'Ah, but that's the thing, isn't it? I wasn't.' Clumsily she hitched her bag over her shoulder and pushed her chair in, then looked at Fliss with a bright, false smile. 'Anyway, you'd better go and get ready for Saskia's gruesome party.'

'Why don't you come?' Fliss was standing up too now, but beneath the red glow cast over the table by the umbrella her face was lined with concern. 'I know you hate her, but the party's in the nightclub downstairs; it'll be pitch dark and she'll have invited so many people you probably won't even see her.'

Anna smiled ruefully and began making her way through the crowd back to the hotel lobby. 'The GreenPlanet guys are having a party on the beach later on. I think I fit in better there somehow, don't you?'

'Who cares? You can fit in wherever you want to, Anna. Stop worrying about who you are or what you are and just relax.' Fliss was almost having to run to keep up with her, but that just meant she talked louder, her exasperated voice rising above the general chatter. Anna clenched her teeth and walked faster.

In the lobby she stopped, leaning against the trunk of a giant golden ornamental palm tree while she waited for Fliss to catch up. But a voice behind her caught her attention.

She felt her throat constrict, her stomach tighten as she recognised that deep, smooth timbre with its faint Italian accent.

She didn't even have to look round to know where he was. She could tell simply from seeing the direction in which the eyes of every woman in the room were drawn. But still she couldn't resist.

He was leaning against one of the ornamental palm trees also, his mobile phone pressed to his ear, his broad shoulders stooped and his blond head bent. Utterly self-contained, he looked languid and somehow separate from the bustle of the busy hotel. Only the staccato tap of one long brown finger on the golden tree trunk hinted at the restless energy beneath the impassive exterior.

She darted back out of sight behind her own palm tree, biting her lip, wishing as she used to when she was a little girl that she could click her heels like Dorothy in *The Wizard of Oz* and find herself back at home. If she left now he'd see her, and then he'd know that her story about staying in the hotel was a big lie. He'd probably find out sooner or later, but she wasn't ready to give him the satisfaction yet.

Fliss appeared and was just about to launch into reproach, but Anna pressed a finger to her lips. 'Listen, I'll come to the party,' she hissed urgently as Fliss looked at her in bewilderment. 'Can you lend me something to wear?'

Fliss nodded.

'Great. Thanks, Fliss. Now, we're going to walk quickly across this lobby to the lifts *without looking round*. Do you understand?'

Fliss nodded again, looking as if she thought there was a very real possibility that Anna was in fact seriously mentally disturbed. 'Why?'

'I'll tell you later. Let's go.'

Slowly, with admirable cool, she left the safety of her palm tree and sauntered past him, managing to keep her gaze firmly fixed ahead. Fliss, however, was much less disciplined and by the time she stepped into the lift her eyes were virtually out on stalks.

'It was him, wasn't it? Angelo Emiliani? He is *glorious*. I wonder if he's staying here.' She giggled. 'I wonder if I could find out his room number.'

But Anna wasn't listening. She was too busy thinking about the two words she'd just overheard Angelo Emiliani saying.

Words that, it would seem, proved that GreenPlanet were on the right lines.

Grafton-Tarrant.

The name of one of the biggest pharmaceutical companies in the world.

CHAPTER THREE

'BETTER?' asked Fliss with a grin as Anna emerged, pink-cheeked and wrapped in a towel, from her *en suite* bathroom.

'Much. The facilities in the Belle-Eden pinewoods aren't exactly five star,' Anna replied, vigorously towelling her hair. 'I've spent the last week hallucinating about hot baths and scented oils.'

Fliss opened the mini-bar and took out a couple of tiny bottles of Chablis. 'I'm so glad you decided to come tonight,' she said, unscrewing the tops and handing one to Anna before raising hers and taking a swig. 'Here's to Angelo Emiliani and whatever he did to make you change your mind.' Picking up a paperback and a bathrobe, she headed towards the bathroom and waved a hand airily around the room before she disappeared. 'Help yourself. Make-up, clothes, whatever—although I do have a dress in mind for you. I bought it because it was so lovely I couldn't leave it in the shop, but in all honesty it makes my boobs look like over-inflated balloons.'

'That's a bad thing?'

'Yep. Believe me. On you it'll look sensational.' Blowing a kiss, she vanished into the steam and shut the door.

Left alone, Anna sank on to the enormous bed and thought about what Fliss had just said.

Here's to Angelo Emiliani and whatever he did to make you change your mind.

But that was just it. He hadn't had to do anything. Just his presence down there in the lobby had been enough, and she had to admit that even his absence was pretty potent too. Throwing herself backwards on to the bed with a hungry moan, she gave in to the thoughts that had flitted distractingly though her head all evening, conjuring his face in her mind's eye, hearing the low rasp of his voice. Her body, still hot and damp from the bath, throbbed, reminding her of her forbidden feelings with devastating honesty. Trailing trembling, hesitant fingers down over her midriff, she imagined his touch…

There was a knock at the door.

Guiltily she snatched her hand away. Leaping up, she ran across the room, re-wrapping the towel tightly around herself and dragging a shaking hand through her damp hair. Breathlessly, aware of the blush creeping up her throat, she pulled the door open.

'Yes? Oh! Oh. *You.*'

He was leaning against the door-frame, casually, menacingly. Smiling, but there was a dark glitter in his eyes that made her take a step backwards.

Dimly she heard Fliss's voice drifting out from behind the closed door of the bathroom. 'Who is it?'

'It's OK,' she called back shakily, 'I've got it.'

He made no move, but raised an eyebrow. 'Am I disturbing anything?'

Yes! How about my sanity and my sense of self-respect for a start?

'No. What do you want?'

Oh, God. Did that sound how she thought it sounded? As if she might as well have said, Would you like to have sex with me? He shifted position slightly, straightening up, dipping his head, looking at her from under his long eyelashes in a way that made her feel the towel had just dissolved.

'Well. There are a number of answers to that question. The politest would be "dinner".'

'I can't. I told you. I'm going out. How did you find me?'

'I asked for your room number at Reception.'

Anna felt her heart plummet. Oh, help. She had a lot of explaining to do to Fliss. Or to him. Should she just come clean now?

But he had already turned and, slinging his jacket over one shoulder, started walking away along the corridor. Spinning back to face her, he shrugged and gave her a half-smile.

'Oh, well. It was worth one more try.'

Don't go! she wanted to shout, as the blood sang in her veins and her hormones cried out for her to follow him. He didn't turn back. She watched him disappear around the corner and then, shutting the door, slumped against it.

He was the man who was supposed to get everything he wanted, she thought despairingly—so why hadn't he persisted?

She let out a small cry of frustration. Because he hadn't wanted her enough.

Rounding the corner Angelo felt his hands harden into fists at his sides.

It seemed she had been telling the truth after all, and his instincts had been wrong. She was Felicity Hanson-Brooks, and she was staying in one of the most over-priced hotels on the Riviera, which was hardly the kind of accommodation one would associate with a committed eco-warrior.

He gave a small shrug. At least he'd found out now rather than taking any further trouble over her. Now he could forget all about her and get on with the deal.

'It's just as well we've been best friends since the dawn of time.' Fliss sighed enviously. 'If not I'd hate you. I knew it would look great on you—I just didn't realize *how* great.'

Distractedly Anna fingered the gossamer-fine oyster-coloured silk. She had submitted to Fliss's ministrations without a murmur, but all the time her head had been elsewhere. With Angelo. Wondering what would have happened if she'd said *yes*...

Forcing herself reluctantly back to reality, she managed a dazed smile. 'It's a fabulous dress. Thanks, Fliss. I'll just have to try very hard not to think about the millions of silkworms that died to make it.'

Fliss gave her a warning look. 'Good, because I'm sure that each and every one of them is up in heaven now agreeing that it was worth the sacrifice. Just look at yourself.'

Slowly Anna met her reflection in the full-length mirror. Gone was the smoky-eyed wild child. In her place stood a sophisticated society girl. The dress was short, a sort of baby doll style that managed to look demure while also being almost indecently sexy. The pearly silk fell in softly gathered folds from a yoke that reached just to the top of her breasts, and everything about her gleamed, from the tiny clusters of beads and crystals on the short bodice at the top of the dress to the little sequinned slip of a scarf Fliss had wound around her throat.

How could she look so smooth, so polished while underneath she was on fire?

She breathed out slowly, wondering how long the dizzying cocktail of hormones was going to keep pumping through her body.

Her hair, newly washed and straightened, hung in a dark silken curtain over her shoulders with no sign of the pink streaks beneath. She gave her head a little shake to reassure herself that they were still there, and flicked up the dress to see her denim hotpants underneath.

'You can't wear those, Anna! They'll spoil the line of the dress!'

'They're fine. I might go to the beach party later on, and I can hardly wear this there. The GreenPlanet guys wouldn't recognize me. *I* don't recognize me.'

'Excellent. That was the general idea.' Going over to the wardrobe, Fliss selected a shoe box from the stack on the floor. 'Try these.'

Inside was a pair of high-heeled sandals consisting simply of two slim diamanté bands. The room seemed to go very still for a moment as Anna looked down at them. When she lifted her head again her face was bleak.

'I can't wear them, Fliss. They're too high.'

'Ah. Then we have a problem. You know me and shoes—I don't do flat. You couldn't manage just for one evening?'

Anna shook her head. 'My ankle won't hold up in that position. The surgeon who operated was pretty clear about that. But thanks anyway.'

For a moment the two of them looked at each other in mute sadness, then Anna managed a watery smile.

'Oh, well, I'll just have to go barefoot. It's exactly the kind of stupid thing people expect me to do. You know how I hate to disappoint.'

They could hear the thud of the music long before they reached the party. As the lift plummeted downwards towards the basement nightclub the hot evening air vibrated with rhythm and with sensual promise, until the lift doors opened and the full impact of the party atmosphere was unleashed.

'Come on!' yelled Fliss, dragging her into the mass of sweating bodies. 'Let's dance!'

A problem with the bones in her ankle may have put paid to Anna's ballet career but it hadn't stopped her from dancing. The music was loud and pulsating, a wailing cacophony of guitar and drum that seeped into her spine and turned her bones to jelly. Smiling into Fliss's eyes, she tried to lose herself in the noise and movement.

But it was as if he were there with her. Every time she raked her hands into her hair and lifted it from her hot neck, in her head she was inviting the touch of his lips; every thrust of her hips in time to the throb of the music was wishful fantasy...

'Anna! *Anna!*'

She opened her eyes, dazed by yearning. Fliss stood in front of her, grinning. 'I need a drink!'

Anna stumbled after her through the crush, out into the relative quiet of the bar. Fliss came to an abrupt halt and cursed quietly. 'Uh-oh,' she said in a low voice. 'Quick. Turn round.'

Too late.

Coming towards them was a blonde in a tiny silver dress with waist-length platinum hair.

'Hi, Saskia!' said Fliss. 'You look great!'

Saskia inclined her head in silent agreement, but said, 'Oh, I feel dreadful. I haven't had a full night's sleep since we've been down here—too many parties. But you look marvellous, darling.' Kissing the air beside Fliss's left cheek, Saskia's eyes slid round to Anna and swept over her coldly. 'And what's this? Roberto Cavalli?'

'You were never the sharpest tool in the box, Saskia, but I'd have thought that even you could remember my name after five years in the same class at school,' Anna muttered.

'The dress. It's Roberto Cavalli.' Anna remembered that sly, insinuating tone so well. 'How kind of Fliss to lend it to you.'

Anna's chin shot up. 'How do you know it isn't mine?'

Saskia laughed. 'A Cavalli? Out of your league, Delafield. I hear that Ifford Park is having to throw itself open to parties of schoolchildren again this year. Sad, really.'

Noticing the storm clouds gathering in Anna's eyes, Fliss stepped in quickly.

'*Love* the hair, Saskia! It looks astonishingly real.'

Saskia looked smug. 'It *is* real. Swedish, apparently. Feel. *The Sunday Tribune* paid for it. I heard that they asked you to do that article too, Anna. Pity they didn't devote a bit more of the budget to you. But then—' she paused, flicking one long, sugary-pink acrylic nail '—I suppose you should think yourself pretty lucky you were asked to do it at all as it's an article about the *daughters* of the aristocracy. Trade Descriptions Act, and all that.'

The colour drained from Anna's face and beside her Fliss gave a shocked gasp.

'Anyway, must go. So many eligible bachelors to dance with, so little time. Enjoy the party, darlings.' She gave a little smirk as she teetered off and then turned back, her long hair swishing out like a pale vampire's cloak.

'Isn't it your birthday any day soon, Anna? I think I remember that it was pretty close to mine.'

'Yes.'

'Are you having a party this year? Do let me know if you are—I'd love to come.'

'Oh, she is *such* a cow. Anna! Wait!'

Fliss's voice reached Anna over the heads of the crowd as she pushed her way through but she didn't slow down. She knew it was stupid to let Saskia's barbed comments upset her, but as usual they had flown with unerring accuracy right to her rawest nerve.

She had been stupid to come.

Flinging herself through an unmarked door, she found herself in the merciful quiet of a dimly lit corridor. Heart hammering, she leaned back against the scarlet damask-covered wall and closed her eyes, waiting for the demons that snapped at her heels to retreat.

A moment later Fliss appeared, her face creased with concern.

'I'm sorry, Anna. I'd forgotten how poisonous she is. Or how jealous of you.'

'Jealous?' Anna gave a harsh laugh. 'I doubt it. She's mummy and daddy's little princess, rich and spoiled and pampered. What on earth has she got to be jealous of me for? I'm nothing. Nobody. As she likes to remind me whenever we meet.'

Gently Fliss took her arm. 'Don't. Come on. Let's go and get that drink. We may as well get tipsy at her expense.'

'No.' Anna pulled away. 'I'd rather drink cyanide. And I'm not going back in there either. Sorry, Fliss. I'm going to head back to the château—but I really should go and change out of this dress first.'

Fliss shook her head. 'It's fine. Keep it—it was pretty much made for you. Are you sure you'll be all right?'

'Absolutely.' Anna looked around for a way out. Several doors led off the dingy corridor and she made for the nearest one. 'Get back to the party and I'll call you soon.'

Without looking back, Anna pushed open the door and slipped through.

The room she found herself standing in was dark and smelled of cigar smoke and maleness spiked with excitement. And danger.

She'd found the casino.

Recklessly she strode forward, any hesitancy driven away by the adrenalin rush of fury and the persistent, painful drumbeat of desire in the cradle of her pelvis.

The beat of the music from the party was just discernible, but in here all was hushed. At the tables men in dinner jackets eyed each other through clouds of cigar smoke and spoke only when necessary. Standing behind them, women in evening dresses looked on, mentally spending the money their partners were winning or watching their plans evaporate in a disappointing hand, a luckless spin of the wheel. Their mask-like painted faces gave nothing away.

The tension in the air matched Anna's own pent-up feelings. Taking a glass of champagne from the tray held out by a waiter, she walked slowly past the roulette tables, trailing a hand along the backs of the velvet-upholstered chairs. She paused. A croupier was swiftly and impassively raking piles of chips off the emerald baize and Anna watched, fascinated, as the men seated around the table replaced them with more. The numbing warmth of the champagne started to steal down inside her, obliterating the pain of Saskia's venom.

'Any more bets?'

There was a further flurry of activity. In the halo of light cast by the Tiffany lamp hanging low over the table Anna could see beads of sweat breaking out on foreheads as men moved innocuous-looking piles of chips around.

How much money was represented on that table? she wondered idly. Enough to secure the future of the château?

She felt horribly restless.

The glass of champagne in her hand was deliciously cool against her feverish skin and she pressed it to her cheek, but it couldn't damp the fire that seemed to smoulder somewhere deep inside her. The back of her neck fizzed and tingled, each hair seeming to respond to some invisible stimulus, and she turned round.

He was standing a few feet away from her, the bright pool of light from one of the low-hanging lamps over the roulette table falling on his mane of dark blond hair and turning it into a halo of gold. One hand was thrust into his pocket, the other was loosely around the slender waist of an obscenely elegant blonde in a scarlet dress. Completely at ease, squinting through the smoke with narrowed eyes, he looked like a particularly wicked fallen angel—beautiful, but menacing. And utterly compelling. The expensively groomed, formally dressed men around him seemed like shadows, or bit players in the presence of his raw, charismatic sexuality.

She heard her own unsteady breath, felt the panicky race of her heart and the searing wild-fire heat of desire scorching through her veins.

And then he looked up.

Angelo drained his glass of champagne and forced himself to focus on the game.

It was one of those nights when he could do no wrong, and the chips on his side of the table were amassing at a rate that had the other men around the table sweating with fear. But he was bored.

When winning came too easily it was time to look elsewhere for excitement.

The man at the head of the table held up his hands in defeat and moved away as the croupier moved his depleted pile of chips away from him. His departure caused a little ripple of unease to go around the table, and the space he had left was not filled.

Angelo looked down at the table. Everyone else was playing cautiously now, and he idly considered walking away and leaving them while they still had something. But the black dog of his old despair was shadowing him and he knew he would keep going. Keep playing. Keep pushing himself to feel something.

Anything.

'Place your bets now, gentlemen, please.'

There was a rush of last-minute activity around the table as everyone placed their chips.

The blonde pouted and placed a perfectly manicured hand on one silk lapel. '*Chéri?* Rouge, I think this time, don't you?'

A smile lifted one corner of Angelo's mouth, but his narrowed eyes were as blank and expressionless as ever. He looked down, moving a towering pile of chips across the baize, pausing as he reached the solitary green marker. Considering.

Green.

The stack of coloured counters represented several hundreds of thousands of pounds, but around them his hands were perfectly steady. Green. It would be like making a bet with himself that he hadn't been wrong about her or who she really was. The odds might be outrageously, overwhelmingly against him, but there was a spark in the dark, dark, self-destructive heart of him that urged him onwards. The money was easily dispensable, easily replaceable…

It wasn't about the money.

It was about the danger. It was about that girl.

For a brief second Angelo closed his eyes and allowed himself to imagine the adrenalin rush of taking such a wild gamble—like a shot of alcohol on an empty stomach—astringent, invigorating, intoxicating. Even to lose would be something. Would make him feel *something*.

A sting.

Pleasure-pain.

Anything.

Opening his eyes again, he caught a flash of movement at the corner of his eye.

In the space left by the departed player, a shadow had fallen across the table. Cast by the light from the low lamps, it showed a woman's silhouette—the sweep of her shoulder, the curve and swell of a breast that, even though it was only two-dimensional shades of grey made him want to brush it with his fingers.

Her perfume was infinitely subtle, but he picked it up instinctively, like an animal on the scent of its prey. Or its mate. That scent of darkness vibrated like a low note inside his head, drowning out the shriller, sweeter, more sickly perfume of the blonde girl beside him.

Slowly he lifted his head.

Like heat-seeking missiles his eyes found hers, his gaze searing through the space that separated them. His expression remained absolutely still as his eyes travelled over her, taking in her perfect poise, the elegance of the pearlescent dress, the dark silken fall of her hair, stripping them away to try to find traces of the trembling, rebellious girl he knew lay beneath.

And then he noticed her bare brown feet.

Sensation struck him like a punch in the solar plexus. Sharp, breathtaking. Surprising.

A ripple of impatience went around the table and vaguely he was aware of the other players waiting. The croupier hesitated. *'Monsieur?'*

'No. I'm out. Settle my account, please.'

The croupier nodded respectfully and Angelo felt the blonde at his elbow wilt with disappointment. He didn't care.

He was fed up with playing, fed up with winning. He wanted the next challenge.

But when he looked up she was gone.

CHAPTER FOUR

ANNA didn't stop running until she had reached the bottom of the hotel steps and there was a taxi right in front of her. Heart hammering, she wrenched the door open and flung herself inside.

'Château Belle-Eden, *s'il vous plaît*. The beach. *La plage*.'

She saw the taxi driver glance at her curiously in his rear-view mirror, no doubt wondering why a girl in an expensive designer dress wanted to go to the beach at this time of night, but Anna didn't care. Anything to put some distance between her and Angelo Emiliani.

Green. He had been going to bet on green. To taunt her with the fact that he recognized her and knew exactly what she was up to. And to show her exactly how wealthy he was, and how little a loss like that would affect him.

She could still picture his hands as they moved the chips across the table. God, they were beautiful: slim, long-fingered, artistic, the skin smooth and golden in the light from the lamp above. Hands that could handle huge sums of money without a tremble—what else could they do?

A small sound escaped her—something between a whimper and a groan—as she stared wildly and unseeingly out of the window into the street-lit dark. It was completely new to her, this maelstrom of yearning that turned every nerve in her body into a taut string, vibrating with sexual awareness. She realized that she was shivering, sitting bolt upright on the back seat of the car, and with a conscious effort leaned back, looking up at the stars through the back window. But it was impossible to relax while every cell in her body was screaming in protest at being torn away from Angelo Emiliani.

'Stop the car! *Arret!*'

'*Mademoiselle?* Are you OK? We are almost there—at the beach. You want me to stop now?'

Up ahead Anna could see the turning off the main road on to the private track that led down to Belle-Eden's beach. In desperation and despair she rubbed her fingers over her stinging eyes.

'No. Sorry. Carry on. The beach will be fine, thank you.'

Pulling up at the top of the track, the driver looked worried. '*Ici, mademoiselle?* You will be all right on your own out here?'

'Fine, thank you. I'm home now.'

Stepping out into the warm night air, she breathed in the salt wind and heard the bass beat of music from the beach below. Hurriedly she paid the driver, suddenly desperate to get back to the uncomplicated company of her GreenPlanet friends and drink beer and dance.

Her bare feet sank into the sand as she ran to the edge of the dune, from where she could see the camp fire on the beach and the writhing bodies of people dancing to the music that came from some unseen source. Stumbling down towards them, she hitched the silk dress into the denim hotpants and put both hands up to her head, burying them in her hair, messing it out of the silken sleekness achieved by Fliss. The warm salt breeze caressed her bare skin. Every nerve-ending seemed to have heightened sensitivity and to be crying out for more.

'Anna! You're back! Cool dress…'

She moved through the crowd, closer to the camp fire. Normally there were only about twenty GreenPlanet campers, but tonight there were maybe double that number as friends had joined them. Gavin, one of the group's founders, broke away from the people he'd been talking to and came over, holding out a beer.

'OK?'

She nodded. 'I met him.'

Behind his small wire-framed glasses Gavin looked momentarily bewildered. 'Who?'

Anna almost wanted to laugh. How bizarre that Gavin shouldn't know who she was talking about when Angelo's face, his voice, his scent was filling her head and blurring the rest of the world behind a haze of longing.

'Angelo Emiliani.'

Even saying his name set fireworks off in her pelvis. She took a mouthful of warm beer and continued slightly breathlessly, 'I think you might be right about the pharmaceutical connection. I overheard him on the phone mentioning Grafton-Tarrant.'

Gavin nodded slowly, thoughtfully. 'Wow. Righteous. I'll get a couple of animal rights mates on to that in the morning. They might have heard something.' He had started to drift away towards some more people who had just arrived, but turned back and called over his shoulder, 'Nice one, Anna.'

She closed her eyes, inhaling deeply, feeling the rhythm begin to steal down inside her. It was more mellow than the vibrating wall of sound in the nightclub, but no less insistent for that. All around her people were swaying, together or alone, their eyes closed, their voices muted, totally relaxed.

With a thud of misery Anna knew she didn't fit in here either. She had told Fliss this was where she belonged, but looking around at the peaceful, carefree faces in the firelight she knew that wasn't true. Maybe it was all that talk of karma and chi, but these people had an inner peace, a deep-down conviction that Anna completely lacked. They had a passion for their cause.

She had passion. Passion that before now she had never imagined. The difference was that hers wasn't going to be satisfied by saving the nesting sites of a few woodpeckers.

Her throaty moan was lost beneath the music. Snaking her arms above her, she let her head fall backwards and circled her hips as all the pent-up tension of the last few hours seeped out of her and the music took over.

Anna knew plenty of people who had sought the solution to their problems in drink and drugs, and had seen the fallout that followed. The cure for the frantic beating of her heart and the tingling adrenalin that was surging through her veins was not to be found in the bottom of a bottle or the contents of a syringe, but in music.

When she was dancing she forgot everything. The past blurred into insignificance beside the rhythmic immediacy of *now*. It was the closest she ever came to being simply herself.

Above her the sky was vast and dark indigo, studded with stars. Underfoot the sand was soft and caressing, and around her the low murmur of conversation gradually faded as everyone lost themselves in the dancing.

No one noticed that they were being watched.

Angelo got out of his chauffeur-driven car and leaned against it, looking down over the beach.

A slight breath of wind caught his hair, lifting it off his forehead, and carrying to him the salt tang of the sea and, beneath it, the more earthy scent of woodsmoke from the fire.

There were more of them than he'd thought. But he could still pick out Felicity Hanson-Brooks without even having to try. It would have been much harder to ignore her presence, as his eyes seemed to be irresistibly drawn to her as she swayed and writhed to the hypnotic beat of the music.

So his instinct *had* been right and his private bet had been a winner. She was a spoiled little society princess who stayed in one of the best rooms at the Paradis and came down here to play at eco-warriors between social engagements. The smile that curved his lips in the darkness was one of triumph mixed with disdain.

Her money and status no doubt made her more of a dangerous adversary, but in many ways it made his position much simpler. So much easier to bring her to heel now he had lost all respect for her.

Swiftly he bent and unlaced his shoes, then took them off and tossed them into the back of the car. His socks followed, joining the dinner jacket and black silk tie he had discarded on the journey here, as he had followed the taxi.

'You want me to wait, sir?' The chauffeur's voice was entirely expressionless. 'Will you be going back to the hotel tonight?'

Angelo considered for a moment. 'No. Ask Paulo to prepare the yacht and send the tender down to the far end of the beach in—' he glanced at his watch, calculating '—half an hour.'

'The far end of the beach, sir?'

'Yes. Down there, where the forest slopes down to the water.'

'Very good, sir.'

Slamming the door, Angelo rolled up his exquisitely tailored trousers and set off at a run.

The music was loud, pulsing, good.

Anna scooped her hair up from her hot neck and held it loosely on the top of her head while the breeze cooled her skin. She was hot, she was tired, but she didn't want to stop dancing. As long as she kept moving she could deal with the torrent of emotions that raged within her. The torrent of desire.

It hadn't subsided. If anything, the music had intensified it, so that with every flick of her hips, every snaky undulation of her spine she could almost feel invisible hands upon her, holding her as she longed to be held. Every so often one of the boys would sway against her and the sheer nearness of another human being was like a spark on the dry tinder of her longing. But none of them even came close to providing what she needed.

She felt as if she were burning from the inside, and threw her head back to gasp for air. The music slowed, seguing seamlessly into Nina Simone, singing 'I Put a Spell on You'.

Anna shuddered with need and frustration and longing, sliding her hands through the tangle of her hair and arching backwards as two hands slid around her waist.

Strong hands, slipping down to her hips. She felt them writhe sinuously beneath their touch. Eyes closed, she leaned back against him as an image of Angelo Emiliani's beautiful hands swam into her head. Helplessly she found herself imagining that the hands that were now resting on the flat of her belly were his hands, that it was his strong thumb which was slowly caressing her quivering flesh.

A shot of pure molten desire shuddered through her.

With a low groan of anguish she wrenched herself away, but those hands pulled her back. Her eyes flew open and for a second she found herself staring into the narrow gleaming eyes that had haunted her all evening.

Her overwhelming feeling was of relief. He had found her. He had picked up the desperate signals her body had been sending out to his and responded. Thank God. Thank God. He was here. There was nothing more to do than give in to it. *This* was her passion. The white-heat generated by the friction between their bodies as they danced, his chest hard against her shoulders, his hands moving across her midriff, spanning her ribs, cupping her breasts—*that* was what she lived for.

She couldn't have said how long they danced like that, his body curved around hers in a way that was simultaneously passionate and protective and possessive. It was everything she wanted, but at the same time it wasn't enough. Her hands were raised above her head, knotted around his neck, her fingers exploring the hardness at its nape and the little dip at the base of his skull, then matting themselves into his hair. She loved the feel of him, but she needed more. She needed to see him.

To taste him.

With a smooth flick of her hips, she spun round so she was facing him, her eyes level with the hollow at the base of his throat. Her hands were still locked loosely around his neck and despite the pain in her ankle she found herself rising up on her tiptoes so that her pelvis was level with his. For long moments they swayed together like that—their hips meeting and grinding together in mutual hunger as the music wrapped itself around them in the darkness. Their eyes met, and held. It was like looking into a furnace.

His hands were on her waist now, their warmth and strength radiating through the thin fabric of the dress. His fingers slid downwards and for a second she registered the question in his eyes as they encountered the heavy denim top of her tiny shorts, low on her hips.

Slowly, without taking her eyes off his face, she crossed her arms and, taking hold of the hem of the dress, peeled it upwards over her head. Tossing it aside, she looked defiantly up at him.

Angelo let his gaze travel slowly over her.

Madre di dio, she was glorious, he thought grimly as his eyes swept downwards over the perfect breasts, barely concealed beneath a small white bikini top, and flat, narrow stomach, in the centre of which glittered a diamond piercing.

He felt liquid fire lick through his veins.

In a split second she was transformed from high-maintenance It-girl to rebellious grunge-chick but, *Gesù*, he liked it. Reaching out, he trailed a finger from the valley between her breasts down to her midriff, gently circling the silver stud above her navel.

His physical response to the feel of her skin was instantaneous. And uncomfortably strong.

The music gathered pace and intensity. He felt the shiver that vibrated through her at his touch and watched her face intently as she let her head fall back, her half-closed eyes proclaiming her desire.

It had started as a cynical ploy to find out what she was up to, but Angelo realised his actions were no longer motivated by business. Sliding his hands around to the small of her back, he pulled her towards him, bending his head to brush his lips across the exposed column of her throat.

This was pleasure. Pure, wicked pleasure, he thought, trailing the tip of his tongue slowly upwards to her jaw before their mouths met in ferocious mutual hunger.

And then suddenly his long fingers were in her hair, his hands cupping her head, so that the sound of the music and the sea were drowned out by the roaring of the blood in Anna's ears. Their bodies didn't touch, but she was aware of his height as he bent his head to hers, the strength and power that radiated from him like a physical force. Their open mouths devoured each other, desperately seeking, exploring, plundering until their teeth clashed and Anna tasted the iron-tang of blood.

Breathlessly she pulled away, then, catching sight of the expression of dark arousal on his perfect face, helplessly reached for him again. This time their bodies met too, as the music swept them up in its hypnotic beat. She was aware of her fingers digging into the hard muscles of his arms but was powerless to let go.

It was as if a dam had burst inside her and all the frustration, the anger, the loneliness and longing of the last ten years had come bursting out in a boiling tide of all-consuming lust. Like a volcano. She had always been too scared of intimacy, too frightened of rejection to give herself to a man, but suddenly all of those fears were simply swept away by the strength and simplicity of her need.

It didn't matter any more who she was. *This* was who she was.

The music had changed, become more upbeat, and people were drifting apart, going in search of another drink, as the spell of sensuality that had captured them all dissipated. But in their midst Anna and Angelo remained oblivious, until someone started clapping, drawing attention to them.

'Hey, Anna! Get a room!'

Dazed, she opened her eyes. Angelo's face was very close to hers, his eyes glittering in the firelight.

'*Anna?*' he murmured sardonically. 'I think we have some talking to do, don't you? Smile nicely at your friends, sweetheart, and let's walk.'

His fingers were like steel bands around her upper arm, but she was grateful. Without him holding her up, she wasn't sure she would have been able to stand. Behind them there were a few scattered whoops and catcalls as they stumbled away from the group in the firelight and felt the velvet darkness envelop them. The rhythmic swish of the sea grew louder as the music receded slightly and for a few moments they walked side by side in silence.

When he eventually spoke his voice was soft, but edged with menace.

'So, *Anna*, don't tell me—that was a staff party for the London office of Arundel-Ducasse. A team-building exercise?'

She tugged her arm free of his grip and took a couple of stumbling steps away from him, raising her chin as she spoke. 'I'm not an estate agent. I made that up. But I'm not ashamed of what I am.'

He stopped, slipping his hands into his pockets and looking down, as if looking at her was somehow distasteful.

'And what is that, *Anna*?'

'A member of GreenPlanet. Someone who's prepared to stand up for what they believe in and fight what they know is wrong.'

He sighed deeply and started walking again. 'Yawn, yawn, yawn. And what is so very wrong about me buying Château Belle-Eden, may I ask?'

The GreenPlanet group was far behind now and the sand beneath their feet was no longer soft and shifting but firm and damp, indicating that they were being inexorably drawn down towards the water's edge. Ahead of them she watched unseeingly as a small motor boat skimmed over the waves and came to a halt near the shore.

'Apart from the fact that you intend to cause environmental havoc by destroying most of the pinewoods for a landing strip?'

'You have done your homework.' He gave a small snort of cynical laughter. 'Don't worry—I'll arrange a decent relocation package for every displaced squirrel in the area.'

'Don't be flippant,' she snapped, then paused, watching his face intently in the darkness. This was a long shot, but she had nothing to lose. 'We don't like the sound of Grafton-Tarrant's involvement.'

That had him worried, she thought with a flash of triumph. He was suddenly very still, but in the silvery moonlight she could just make out a muscle flickering in the taut plane of his cheek.

'You interest me, Anna—?'

She hesitated for a fraction of a second. 'Field. Anna Field.'

'You obviously have a great passion for your cause.' His voice was like a caress in the warm night air. He took a step closer to her and caught hold of the ends of her slender sequinned scarf. 'But, *Anna Field*, I think it's only fair to warn you that I have a great deal of passion for this project. Which means that one of us will end up being hurt. And—' he lifted his hand and stroked the backs of his fingers down her cheek '—I think it's only fair to warn you that I don't *do* failure.'

Oh, I do, thought Anna savagely as a shudder of pleasure ricocheted through her at his touch. *Failure and I are old friends.*

She took a step backwards and was caught off balance for a second as her foot sank into the wet sand. At that moment a bigger wave rolled in, lapping over her feet and making her gasp at the sudden chill.

He caught her before she fell, scooping her up in his arms as if she were no heavier than a child. On the dark beach the intimacy of his nearness stole her breath away and banished every rational thought from her head. The cold water had spread goosebumps over her quivering flesh.

He radiated warmth.

And strength.

And sex.

His smile stopped her heart and stole her soul—and along with it her powers of resistance. 'I've got you now.'

'Put me—' She tried to struggle but knew the movement her body made was a desperate wriggle of invitation. His lips came down on to hers, silencing her and concentrating all her thoughts on the sensation of being in his arms, clasped against his chest, while he waded powerfully through the water.

She should feel scared. Angry. Indignant. But she didn't.

She felt cherished.

And so aroused she couldn't think straight.

Dazedly she opened her eyes as he stopped. The boat she had seen from further down the beach was right in front of them, and the man inside it stood as they approached.

'Wh—what the—? What are you—?'

'Shh.'

Effortlessly he lifted her in and vaulted over the side to take his place on the seat beside her.

'*Grazie*, Gianni.'

Anna looked around her with wild eyes as the speedboat engine started up with a roar. Her hair whipped her cheeks as it spun round and accelerated away, seeming to fly across the water away from the shore. 'What are you doing? Where are we going? I didn't ask—'

Gently he placed a long brown finger on her lips, then, as her words died away, trailed it down her throat and into the deep V between the triangles of her bikini. His eyes burned into hers.

'Not in so many words, *carissima*, but you can't deny that you want this as much as I do.'

'What?'

'Privacy. I don't doubt your friends are all very open-minded and liberal, but I prefer not to have an audience.'

She gasped in outrage. 'You're very sure of yourself, aren't you?'

He slid his hand beneath one of the triangles of fabric. Lazily he moved his palm downwards so that he was cupping her breast, and with exquisite, agonizing gentleness brushed his thumb across her hard nipple.

She couldn't restrain the cry that escaped her.

'Yes.' He smiled wickedly. 'With good reason, I'd say.'

With a barely there touch like the whisper of a butterfly's wings, his lips brushed hers, then he dipped his head and murmured against her neck, 'If you want to go back to the shore say so now. Gianni will turn round. But—' he nuzzled her earlobe '—I can assure you, you're quite safe. I'm a property developer, not a mass murderer.'

The blood was pounding in her ears, matching beat for beat the pulse that throbbed between her legs. Closing her eyes, she shook her head, trying to clear it, but instead arching her neck backwards and offering it to the caress of his mouth.

'I don't know who you are. I don't know anything about you…' she groaned.

'Exactly. That's what I intend to remedy. Give me the chance to show you that I'm not the complete philistine you imagine.'

This was madness. His hand rested lightly on her shoulder, in the sensitive curve at the base of her neck, sending cascades of shooting stars through her, so she couldn't concentrate on anything beyond the growing need inside her.

'*Tesoro?* Do you want to go back to the shore?' he whispered, his thumb tracing delicate circles beneath her ear.

'No.'

CHAPTER FIVE

'MAKE yourself at home. I need to go and have a quick word with the captain, if you'll excuse me.'

Stepping out of the tender on to the deck of a yacht, Anna glanced round at her sleek surroundings and tried desperately to look as if she were the sort of person who had been making herself at home on luxury super-yachts all her life.

'No problem. Where do I go?'

He gestured up a flight of steel steps. 'Why don't you go up to the top deck? I'll join you there in a moment.'

So this was Angelo Emiliani's natural habitat, she thought dazedly as she reached the top of the stairs and emerged into a breathtaking space. The deck stretched away from her in both directions—one end housing a seating area with huge white cushions and a steel-topped bar, while at the other a softly lit spa pool glowed azure-blue in the darkness.

She wandered over to the pool and sat on its tiled edge, trailing her fingers in the water. She'd expected it to be cool, but it was warm. Blood-warm. She withdrew her hand sharply and stood up again, scared of the sudden image she had of herself and Angelo in its silky embrace.

God, her senses were on such high alert she'd be getting turned on by her own shadow in a minute. It was as if her brain had been rewired, so that every thought brought her back on to the same tormenting loop of desire. She looked out across the dark stretch of water to the shore. On the beach the party continued, the bass thud of the music drifting across to her, the glow of the fire illuminating the pine forests on the cliff top and throwing the silhouettes of the dancers into dark relief.

They seemed a million miles away, like strangers rather than the people she lived with and had come to regard as a substitute family.

She'd got to know Gavin and the rest of the group when they had camped on the edge of the parkland at Ifford while they'd carried out a protest against a proposed motorway extension nearby. She had been at home recovering from the operation on her ankle at the time, facing a future without dancing. But it was the truth she had found out just before the operation—when the doctors had been investigating a possible genetic cause of the bone weakness from which she suffered—that had shattered her the most. That was why she had been ready to rebel against everything she had been brought up to stand for. Because all of it had been based on a shameful lie.

GreenPlanet had offered her an escape, a purpose and a very convenient way to get back at her father. But she could see now that it had never offered her anything deeper. At the time that had been enough.

Angelo stood at the top of the stairs, watching her for a moment. She was leaning on the deck rail, her face turned towards the bright point on the beach where the party was still in full swing. In the soft glow cast by the discreet lighting on deck he could see a wistfulness in her expression.

Taking a bottle of champagne from the chiller, he walked quietly towards her.

'Are you wishing you were still at the party?'

Startled, she spun round, a hand pressed to her chest as a small cry escaped her. 'I didn't hear you!'

He smiled, tearing the foil off the bottle. 'I know. You looked...' he paused, choosing the word carefully '...sad. I wondered if you were wishing you were back on the shore with your friends.'

She met his gaze steadily. 'No. I'm not. I'm glad I'm here.'

Her honesty surprised him. And excited him. He'd expected more of a show of resistance, though from the white-heat that had almost devoured them both back there on the beach he had known it would only be token. That was what most of the girls he knew would have done—made a great show of being uncertain or shy, and then stormed off in high drama when he wasn't interested enough to play along with persuading them.

'It was a good party,' he said gravely, easing the cork out of the bottle with his thumbs. Feeling the release of pressure as it came free and a plume of froth spilled over his hand. Coveting it.

'Yes.' It was little more than a harsh whisper.

He paused.

'Great dancing.'

He watched her close her eyes. Heard her drag in a ragged breath.

'Yes.'

Benedetto Gesù, this thing could easily spin out of control if he wasn't careful. His hand was perfectly steady as he poured the champagne into two slim flutes, but he was all too aware of the painful ache in his groin and cursed himself for it. Last night he'd had an actress in his bed whose blonde perfection had earned her the tabloid title 'cinematic icon' and had found himself struggling to go through the motions. So why, when faced with this rebellious stranger, was he suddenly like a walking advertisement for Viagra?

He handed the glass to her. For a moment neither of them spoke. She held his gaze bravely, though he could see that she was shaking violently.

'You're cold.'

Her chin lifted a fraction but her gaze didn't waver. 'No, I'm not cold.' She drew in a desperate breath.

I'm burning.

How could he stand there looking so bloody relaxed? she thought in anguish. What was it that Fliss had called him? *The Ice Prince.* It was a singularly appropriate name—obviously thought up by someone who had felt the polar chill of his detachment in the same way she was feeling it now. The passion that had threatened to engulf them both on the beach still raged within her, but he had obviously had second thoughts.

And then she felt him gently take the glass from her hand and put it down on a low table.

Her heart leapt and her stomach tightened.

'Bedtime, I think.'

His hand stroked down the length of her arm, sending an explosion of tiny sparks along her nerve-endings. Lacing his fingers though hers, he turned and she had no choice but to follow him, back down the steps up which she had come, down on to a lower deck with a huge dining table set out before a wide sliding glass screen. In the doorway he hesitated, looking down at her. The amusement and mockery that she had come to recognize in his blue eyes had gone, leaving in its place a brooding darkness that made her want to scream with longing.

'This way.'

His long brown fingers were still loosely entwined with hers and, looking hazily down at them, she allowed herself a dizzying moment of fantasy about the pleasure they were about to bring her. He stopped outside a polished wooden door in a discreetly lit corridor and held it open for her.

Walking over to the bed, she felt a lifetime of anticipation flutter like a cloud of butterflies in her stomach. This was what she had longed for. *This*, had she but known it at the time, was the logical conclusion of all those girlhood wedding fantasies.

She sat primly on the edge of the huge bed—or as primly as she could, given that she was wearing only the briefest bikini top, behind which her nipples were all too clearly visible—and forced herself to look up at Angelo. It was a little like looking into the sun.

He was dazzling.

Tall, broad, effortlessly and stomach-meltingly gorgeous, he stood in front of her, towering over her. But his face was emotionless. With a thrill of dark excitement she wondered if he was going to ask her to strip.

'You should have everything you need. The bathroom is through there. Just pick up the phone if you need anything and one of the crew will bring it to you.'

Anna felt as if the world were tilting beneath her as the full horror of his words hit her. A whimper of shame and panic rose in her throat and she concentrated every ounce of self-control she possessed on swallowing it.

How could I have got it so wrong? How could I have made such a pitiful fool of myself?

It was pride that enabled her to raise her head and look him in the eye. Muster a small brittle smile. Say a polite, hollow thank you.

But when the door finally shut behind him she threw herself on to the bed and, seizing a pillow, howled out her fury and humiliation into the muffling layers of finest Siberian goose down.

Walking away wasn't easy, but returning to the upper deck, Angelo grimly congratulated himself.

Whatever he had felt on the beach, she *was* business, not pleasure.

He wasn't a man who was overly troubled by conscience. Life had not showered a steady stream of blessings upon him, so he worked on the principle that if he wanted something he had to get it himself. That had made him ruthless.

Reckless.

With money. With rules. With people.

And tonight he had wanted her, but something had stopped him. Some sort of hitherto undiscovered sense of chivalry, which had prevented him from taking her just because he could.

Sometimes he wondered if the nuns in the orphanage still prayed for his immortal soul. Maybe, finally, their prayers were being heard. Maybe there was a glimmer of hope that he wouldn't be consigned to eternal damnation after all.

He gave a short bitter laugh.

Or maybe he just wanted to make her wait. Who knew how long it might take to get the sale of the château completed? It wouldn't do to rush things. The longer he kept her on a slow-burn, the better.

And the more satisfying.

In Anna's dream she was a child again, sitting on her mother's knee and being rocked.

She looked up into her mother's eyes, those blue-green eyes she remembered so well, and then a really odd thing happened. They were her mother's eyes, but they were also Angelo Emiliani's eyes, and something about that bothered her. She felt safe, protected, loved, but unaccountably uneasy.

When she woke up the rocking continued. For a moment she lay there, as fragments of the events of yesterday and last night came back to her. She sat up with a start.

The boat was moving.

Throwing herself out of bed, she stood up and looked wildly around her. The view through the window showed nothing but sea and sky. She made a sharp exhalation of fury and had reached the door of the cabin before she stopped.

She was still stark naked.

She was in the middle of the ocean and the only items of clothing she had with her were a bikini and a pair of hotpants.

Oh, and a sequinned evening scarf—which would no doubt make all the difference should formal dress be required. Collapsing back on to the bed, she pulled the covers up over her head and let out a howl of rage and frustration.

'Ah, so you're awake.'

In the darkness beneath the covers she felt her eyes widen in horror and for a second she froze, hoping she'd imagined that dry, mocking voice. But then the covers were drawn back and she found herself staring up into those wicked eyes.

In the clear light of morning his beauty came as a fresh shock. Naked to the waist and wearing only a pair of long shorts, his blond hair was tousled and untidy. He looked more like a carefree golden surfer-boy than a billionaire businessman.

Which was horribly unfair.

Snatching the covers up to cover her breasts, she sat up and glared at him. 'What the hell is going on?'

That cool, unruffled smile. 'I brought you coffee.'

'I don't want coffee!'

'I believe the polite response is "thank you very much". I can assure you, you're very privileged. I don't usually do this sort of thing, but I looked in on you earlier and you were rather…exposed. My crew can cope with most things, but a naked eco-warrior might just prove too much, even for them.'

It almost had for him. Lying on top of the cream sheets with her pink hair tumbling over her face and the diamond stud in her navel rising and falling with every sleepy breath, she had looked wild but unbelievably sweet. Like a panther cub. He had to keep reminding himself that if he wasn't careful she could do real damage.

Anna took a deep steadying breath and pulled the sheet more tightly around her. Making a huge effort to keep her voice level, she looked up at him.

'Look, Angelo… Last night was…' *Oh, God, don't blush. Don't behave like a pathetic, inexperienced kid. Don't give it away.* 'A huge mistake. I shouldn't have come here.'

'So why did you?'

He had set the coffee down on the bedside table and was looking at the newspaper he'd had tucked beneath his arm. He looked totally absorbed, as if what she was saying was a minor distraction.

'I didn't have much choice,' she hissed, thoroughly nettled by his obvious unconcern.

He looked up at her with a slight puzzled inclination of his eyebrows. It was almost as though he'd forgotten she was there for a second. 'Sorry? That wasn't how I remember it. I think I asked you if you wanted to go back to your "friends" on the beach—' he looked back down at the newspaper with a faint smile '—and you said no.'

'I didn't know then that a cruise around the Med was on the itinerary.'

'I see. A quick screw. That's all you had in mind, was it?' He glanced back up at her. 'I'm hurt.'

He didn't look hurt. He look supremely unconcerned, hugely pleased with himself. And immensely bloody gorgeous.

Anna gritted her teeth. 'We didn't have sex.'

'No. But you wanted to.'

Oh, God, the bastard.

Tugging the sheet, she wound it around herself and got up. Sitting in bed she felt at far too much of a disadvantage to be having this conversation. Standing up, she raked a hand through her hair and made a huge effort to keep the hysteria out of her voice.

'Look, I didn't have anything in mind. I wasn't exactly thinking straight. I don't know—maybe I drank more than I thought. I was upset and—'

'Upset about what?'

She shook her head. 'Doesn't matter,' she said hastily. 'What matters now is that I have to get back. I have stuff that I need to do.'

Rubbing a hand through his already dishevelled hair, he strode towards the door. Anna squeezed her eyes shut as he passed within a few feet of her, unable to trust herself not to reach out and touch the body that had haunted her dreams all night. At the door he paused and looked at her with great seriousness.

'How good are you at swimming?'

'Very good.'

He nodded gravely. 'It's probably about ten kilometres back to shore. Just as well you brought your bikini.'

Anna gave a howl of rage, picked up a book and hurled it in the direction of his head. It missed and she reached for another, but he was too quick for her. The next thing she knew, he was beside her and had caught her wrist in a steely grip.

'Enough.'

She let herself relax completely for a moment, until she felt his fingers slacken slightly, then seized her chance and gave an almighty lunge to break free.

'*Not* enough. Not nearly enough.'

Her only thought was to put as much distance between them as possible, but the bed was in the way. Clasping the sheet to her, she leapt on to it and stood, legs apart, chest heaving, looking down at him.

He raised an eyebrow. 'Well, now you come to mention it…'

In one swift movement he had reached out and swept her legs from beneath her so that she tumbled down on to the soft cushion of pillows. High on adrenalin, she struggled upright, but he was already on top of her, pinning her arms above her head with one strong hand as easily as if she had been a child. Above her, only inches away from her face, his chest curved. If she lifted her head she could probably brush his nipple with her lips. Her breath was coming in huge, shaky gasps, but the rise and fall of his chest was as steady as ever.

Frantically she thrashed beneath him, desperately trying to ignore the treacherous, tell-tale stickiness at the top of her thighs, praying he wouldn't notice that she was virtually at the point of orgasm.

Their eyes met and locked. Neither of them spoke and the only sound was the ragged gasp of Anna's breathing.

His eyes glittered down into hers, narrow and knowing. Slowly, lazily he reached out with his free hand and trailed a leisurely finger along her collar-bone. She was no longer holding the sheet—all it would take would be one flick of his wrist and she'd be naked and exposed to his glittering gaze.

'If you were hoping to persuade me to take you back to shore, this is hardly the best way to go about it.'

Her eyes flashed fire and fury at him.

'Why? Would you prefer it if I *begged*?' she spat.

He laughed huskily and released her wrists. '*Amore mio*, that would be equally alluring, and therefore equally counter-productive.'

She rolled out from beneath him, not trusting herself to spend one more second in such close proximity with his long golden body. 'I'm not hoping to *persuade* you of anything. I'm demanding that you take me back. Today.'

'Or else?'

'Or else I'll call the police.'

'You have your mobile?'

'You know I haven't'

She had nothing, and he knew it. Not a change of clothes, not a toothbrush, and certainly not a mobile. Furiously she swung her legs out of the bed and stood up, yanking the sheet from under him and wrapping it around herself again.

He sighed and stood up.

'So I guess you'll be wanting me to lend you my satellite phone, which is a bit much considering you intend to use it to have me arrested for…well, what? Kidnapping you? Forcing myself upon you against your will?'

She blushed. 'No.'

If only.

Unhurriedly he ran a hand through his hair, making it stand up in spiky golden tufts that only served to accentuate his perfect bone structure. Turning towards the door, he said, 'In that case, may I just suggest you come along for the ride? You never know, you might learn something.'

She tossed her head and threw him a disdainful look. 'What could I possibly learn from you?'

He paused and half turned back, studying her silently for a moment with his head tilted to one side.

'We're heading for a property I finished work on last year. It's been bought by a certain celebrity with a bit of an environmental conscience and developed to be as environmentally friendly as possible. I'd like to show it to you. Maybe you'll learn not to believe everything that's been written about me. Maybe you'll find I'm not the devil incarnate after all.'

'I doubt it,' she spat. But he had already gone and she was speaking to a closed door.

CHAPTER SIX

Two hours later Anna had to admit that, whatever Angelo Emiliani was, life aboard his yacht wasn't at all bad. She had idled away some time in the spa pool, until the steward, Paulo, had brought her a delicious brunch of fresh fruit and warm, sweet brioche and coffee, and now she was lounging on the soft white cushions feeling heavy and replete.

There was something very liberating about being out in the middle of the ocean. Something therapeutic about literally sailing away from your problems. Last night, and Saskia's malice, seemed light years ago. Here there was no need to apologise for who she was.

Who she wasn't.

She had spent her early life feeling torn between England and France—Ifford Park and Château Belle-Eden—but, closing her eyes and letting her head fall back against the cushioned lounger, she realised she'd missed the obvious solution. Somewhere in between.

'Anna.'

Her eyes opened slowly and she stretched luxuriously. 'Hmm?'

'I don't know what you do for a real job, but you certainly could sleep on a professional basis. It's time to wake up. We're here.'

Anna stumbled to her feet quickly. Too quickly. There was a roaring in her ears and she almost lost her balance.

Angelo's hand shot out to steady her and when the fog cleared from behind her eyes she found herself staring at the bronzed plane of his chest. She shook him off and took a step backwards.

'I don't usually sleep like that. I don't know what came over me. Maybe it's the sea air.'

He was looking at her with unconcealed amusement. 'It certainly can't be the exercise—although not for want of trying.'

Why could he make her blush so easily?

His gaze swept down over her, taking in the skimpy bikini top and minute denim hotpants. 'Before we go ashore, would you like to get changed into something a little more…discreet?'

'Oh, yes. Silly me. I'll just go and choose something from the selection of cruisewear I packed in preparation for this trip, shall I?'

'I'm sure I can find something that would fit.'

'Why, Angelo, how fascinating. Do you have a large selection of ladies' clothes in your wardrobe?'

'No, but I have a number of visitors to the yacht who've left things.'

'Oh, puh-leese. If you think I'm going to wear something belonging to one of your harem of mistresses, you can think again.'

'I don't know why you find the thought so unpleasant, *tesoro*. I recall that last night you were pretty keen to join them. Anyway, if you're going to be stubborn…'

She looked at him for a moment, speechless with humiliation and loathing.

'Let's just go, shall we?'

Arriving at the private landing stage of Villa Santa Domitilla, Angelo held out his hand to help Anna from the tender. She ignored it.

'Where are we?'

Angelo was already halfway along the boarded walkway and spoke over his shoulder. 'Let's just say it's one of Italy's undiscovered islands. The celebrity who's bought this property would be extremely unhappy about having its location given away. Especially to known troublemakers.'

'I thought you said it was very environmentally friendly?'

He nodded.

'Well, in that case, they have nothing to fear from us. It's only projects that put personal profit before responsibility to the planet that we campaign against.'

Why do I bother? He's not even listening, she thought furiously as she trailed after him up a set of steep steps cut into the rock. Despite the fact that it was scorching hot, Anna was annoyed to see how cool Angelo looked in a pair of long cotton surf shorts and a white linen shirt.

Why hadn't she taken up his offer of borrowing something to wear? Despite her olive skin, she could already feel the sun burning on to her shoulders and she felt uncomfortably exposed in the tiny bikini top and hotpants.

Exposed and—when she saw the magnificent honey-coloured house in front of them—entirely underdressed.

'It used to be an old convent,' Angelo explained, keying a number into the security pad beside the huge wrought iron gates. 'The thickness of the stone walls made it ideal from an energy-saving point of view.' The gates swung open and he sauntered through, while she hung back.

'What's the matter? I thought you'd be desperate to see all your principles in practice.'

Folding her arms, Anna looked up at the building. 'I'm not going in.'

'I see. Why not?'

'I don't need the whole marketing and PR package, Angelo. I'm sure you're very good at talking the talk. It won't change anything.'

He'd stopped and now began to stroll slowly back towards her. His long limbs moved like liquid. Pure animal grace.

She swallowed.

He shrugged. 'So, just enjoy the trip. Soon enough it'll get out who's bought this place and you'll be able to tell all your friends that you've been here.' He carried on walking up the narrow path to the front of the villa.

She stamped her foot and followed him up the path. 'I wouldn't stoop to celebrity *name-dropping*,' she said scornfully. 'I couldn't care less who this house belongs to, it doesn't alter the fact that what you're planning to do at Château Belle-Eden is wrong!'

Smiling to himself, Angelo resisted the temptation to turn round and look at her.

Perhaps it wasn't fair to tease her, but he couldn't help it. She was so quick to rise to the bait and so funny when she was angry. And she was such a bloody cliché, with her tired old environmental platitudes.

He frowned.

A cliché, but a mystery too. He still wasn't entirely sure who she was. His PA in London was right now trying to find information on Anna Field, but when he'd spoken to her just before setting out had come up with nothing. It was possible that she was a runaway, of no fixed address, which would explain why she had fallen in with those appalling campaigners. They probably had some sort of group squat.

The thought horrified him.

Reaching the front door of the villa, he stopped and waited for her. She was a little way behind him and he watched her trail slowly up the path, between the artfully planted 'wildflower' borders which his celebrity client had commissioned at a cost of thousands from Italy's top garden designer. The shadows played across her glistening amber-coloured skin, the sunlight glinting off the diamond in her navel. A bumblebee, heavy and clumsy with pollen, blundered through the flowers and came to land on her arm. She stopped, her tongue darting out between moist pink lips as, with an expression of rapt concentration, she carefully scooped it into her hand and placed it on a leaf. It was the first time he'd seen her give in to the softness he sensed beneath that rebellious veneer, and he felt an unexpected twist in his gut.

Anna looked up at the building in front of her. It was solid and square, a cloistered walkway running the length of the ground floor and providing a sheltered position for olive and citrus trees in huge terracotta pots. The golden stone was mellow with age, and the overall impression was of timeless peace and spirituality.

The front door was open, Angelo having gone in ahead of her. She walked into the centre of the hallway and turned slowly around, taking in the acres of polished wooden floor and the galleried landing above, from which were suspended vast modern canvases depicting images that reminded Anna of photographs in her biology textbook at school.

'It's…' She hesitated, gazing up at the massive twisted metal chandelier that hung above them, which on closer inspection seemed to be constructed from used car parts. The contrast of the stark interior with the gracious exterior of the building was like a slap in the face.

'It's utterly *hideous*.'

She'd intended to hurt him, she realized, but she was completely unsuccessful. He smiled and, with his hands in his pockets, walked casually across the hallway. 'I'm inclined to agree. However, that's not the point.'

'Not the point? How can you say that? This was a convent— an ancient place of worship and contemplation and devoutness— and you've made it look like some soulless New York loft apartment. It's totally disgusting!'

He'd reached one of the doorways that opened off the hall and paused, leaning nonchalantly against it. 'There you go again.'

'What?'

'Making assumptions.' His voice was very quiet. 'Firstly, *I* didn't make it look like anything. My brief stopped with the building itself. The interior was entirely the work of the client and her team of lifestyle gurus, interior designers, feng shui experts and spiritual analysts. Secondly, you're assuming I don't agree with you. And, thirdly, don't ever make the mistake of thinking that convents are all places of *devoutness*.'

There was a savagery in his tone that made her look at him sharply. But his face gave nothing away. 'I thought you'd be thrilled that the floor is reclaimed hardwood, that all the artwork was commissioned from a local women's co-operative and shows magnified images of the plant-life on the estate, and the chandelier was made out of recycled industrial parts.' He smiled sardonically. 'Come up and I'll show you the rest.'

He was almost at the top of the stairs now and she had to choose between following him or remaining alone in the hallway. Mutinously she stared up at him, her arms crossed.

'No, thanks. I think I've seen enough.'

'Suit yourself. But, if you'll excuse me, I've got a couple of things to attend to. I may be a while, so make yourself comfortable.'

'I think that's pretty unlikely in this—' she said contemptuously, but was interrupted by the ringing of his mobile phone.

He answered impassively, striding away from her along the corridor, out of earshot. Left alone, Anna shivered, hugging her arms around her all too exposed flesh.

She was just about to leave the house and wait for him outside when, with a flash of defiant insight, she realised that by doing so she would be playing right into his hands. The call was obviously one he didn't want her to overhear, and was maybe information about the château or something to do with Grafton-Tarrant.

She was wasting a golden opportunity with her immaturity

and her pathetic inability to rise above his physical attributes. It was stupid and embarrassing. He was beautiful, but he was also the person who was about to rob her of the only place that tied her to a happier past.

Swiftly she made for the stairs and took them two at a time. Up on the galleried landing she paused, listening intently, but there was no sound. The silence played on her senses, making her both nervous and full of anticipation as she strained to hear the deep rumble of his voice.

All she could hear was her own heartbeat.

Fast.

Excited.

Rows of closed doors stretched away from her. Tentatively approaching one, she pressed her ear to the wood—reclaimed, no doubt—not that she could have cared less—and listened.

Nothing.

She slid along to the next door and listened again.

Silence.

In frustration she opened the door and looked inside. It was a bedroom, dominated by the biggest bed she'd ever seen. Sulkily she wandered in, her bare feet practically disappearing into the thick white carpet. It was decorated in the same aggressively modernist style, the huge canvases on the walls depicting unintelligible blobs and shapes which looked vaguely erotic. Anna stopped in front of one that seemed to show the curve of a woman's breast against the sweep of a male buttock.

Or was she imagining that?

She tried to imagine it hanging in the château, and felt a shiver of distaste ripple down her spine.

Of course it was distaste.

She tore her gaze away abruptly and pushed open the door into an *en suite* bathroom. Or shower room, she mentally amended, looking round the spartan cell derisively. There was nothing so luxurious and water-wasteful as a bath tub in there.

In fact, maybe it wasn't finished, she thought, taking a step forward. The room was lined in tiny glowing green glass tiles like the scales on a mermaid's tail, but apart from that it was empty.

Suddenly jets of water exploded on to her bare skin from all sides, soaking her. She screamed and tried to dart out of the way, but the whole room was filled with tiny water outlets and she had moved directly into the firing line for freezing cold jets.

She screamed again. Louder.

Just as suddenly and unexpectedly as it had begun, the water stopped. Dripping, shivering, incoherent with shock and fury, she pushed back her streaming hair from her face and looked up to find Angelo lounging in the doorway.

Laughing.

CHAPTER SEVEN

'I SEE you discovered the wet room.'

Anna tried to frame a coherent sentence but found herself able to do nothing more than mouth impotently. The only words that came to mind were too offensive for her to even utter.

'Pretty impressive, no? Designed to use as little water as possible. All the shower jets incorporate tiny vacuum pumps to aerate the water as it comes out and so increase the pressure.' He'd been lounging against the door-frame, but now he levered himself upright. 'That way, you get a very powerful shower while using a minimum amount of water, and the whole thing is operated by sensors.'

'Thank you,' she spat. 'I think I'd just about worked that bit out for myself.'

The second part of the sentence came out as a dry croak as she watched him unbuttoning his shirt. She took a step backwards, unable to take her eyes off the rippling golden chest that was gradually being revealed.

'What are you doing?'

He looked up and grinned as he slipped his shirt off. For a fleeting moment she thought she might pass out.

He held out the shirt to her.

'Here. Put this on.'

'No, thanks. I'm fine.'

She made to walk past him, but as she did so he caught hold of the tie at the back of her sodden bikini. And pulled.

She breathed in sharply, making a small shivering sound.

In an instant he was behind her and, with swift, capable hands, had drawn the tiny triangles of fabric over her head, in the same seamless movement wrapping his shirt around her. She was aware of nothing but the warm scent of him, imprinted into the whisper-soft linen, the firm pressure of his hands.

'Now, take off those wet shorts.'

She spun round to face him. 'No! No—I—'

He took a single step towards her and reached out. She had to bite her lip against the gasp that sprang from her, the flicker of fiery arousal that licked up her belly in anticipation of his touch. But he only took hold of the shirt and started to do up the buttons. Through a mist of agonizing desire, she glanced up at his face.

His eyes gave nothing away.

He had moved upwards and was now buttoning the shirt over her bare breasts. She was aware of the painful thrust of her nipples against the fabric and closed her eyes for a second in blissful submission.

'There. Perfectly respectable. It almost comes down to your knees, so you're perfectly safe to take off your shorts. I won't look.'

Her eyes fluttered open and she swung blindly away from him, fumbling with the stiff button of the wet denim. But her hands were slow and clumsy with confusion. 'I—can't.'

'Then allow me.'

Gently he drew her towards him. Unable to raise her eyes to meet his, she watched, mesmerized, as his long elegant fingers undid the button of her shorts, aware of the flat plane of his tanned stomach only inches from her own. His thumb brushed the quivering flesh of her midriff, sending a cascade of shooting stars up her spine, almost making her knees give way beneath her.

Slowly, he tugged down the short zip and, slowly, deliberately slid the wet denim downwards. Helplessly she felt her hips wriggle beneath his hands, as if they had a mind of their own and were desperate to free themselves of the layers that separated her from him.

He dropped to his knees in front of her and she let her head fall backwards, lifting her hands and instinctively winding them into her wet hair as she fought to keep control of the murmurs of pleasure his touch aroused in her. His warm hand slid down one leg, then the other, stopping at her foot, his fingers tracing a swift arc of fire across her instep before gently picking it up and making her step out of the shorts. Looking down, she saw him bent before her, his tousled dark blond hair contrasting with the paler gold of the skin of his bare shoulders, beneath which the muscles flexed and rippled. Dimly she was aware of her own fingers twisting her hair into knots of desire, and she opened her eyes as he straightened up before her.

His thumb kneaded her parted lips, his fingertips caressing the hollow beneath her jaw, then trailing down the long, exposed column of her throat as she arched her back and pressed her hips to him.

She ached.

His fingers crept into the damp tangle of her hair, supporting the heavy weight of her head as she waited for his lips to meet hers. He brought his head down to brush his mouth against the side of her neck, where the pulse beat frenziedly beneath her damp skin.

'Time to go,' he murmured dryly. 'A-list celebrities can be very touchy about complete strangers having sex in their bedrooms.'

Her eyes flew open as he drew away and bent to scoop her discarded shorts up off the floor. Without looking back, he walked perfectly steadily across the room to the door.

Anna dragged a hand across her burning lips and swore softly.

Striding after him, she caught up with him in the doorway and snatched her clothes from him. Then she ran ahead of him down the stairs and out into the sunlight.

Closing the front door behind him, Angelo paused briefly and rubbed the frown from his forehead.

Careful, he warned himself, but his knuckles were white on the large iron door handle. He needed to get this deal completed and return Anna to the safety of dry land, because if this carried on much longer he knew his resolve wouldn't hold and he'd have to bed her.

He wanted to, but he'd glimpsed a vulnerability in her that scared him. It was that moment when he'd done the buttons up on the shirt. It had made him think of Lucia.

He shook his head and gave the door a last little push to check that it was closed properly and turned to go down the steps. He could see her walking ahead of him down the path back to the gate that led to the jetty, the tails of his shirt reaching just above her knees. She was sexy as hell, he thought, and she had walked into this situation with her eyes wide open—she must be pretty sure of herself to have done that. As he watched, she dragged a hand through her hair, making the pink streaks flash in the sun. A sardonic smile spread across his face.

She was nothing like that other little girl he had let down all those years ago in the orphanage. Lucia had been a child—a vulnerable child—who had relied on him as her only source of support in a harsh, loveless world, and he would never forgive himself for what had happened to her. But this was different. Anna was strong and spiky and rebellious—she could look after herself. He was just imagining the trembling little girl beneath the surface.

His expression was stony as he set off down the path after her.

He'd ring his PA as soon as they were back on the yacht and see if she'd had any word from Ifford's people about what the hell was going on at their end. The sooner those papers were signed the better. For his sanity.

Storming back into her cabin, Anna slammed the door behind her and threw herself on to the bed.

She wanted to scream, she wanted to tear things up, she wanted to smash Angelo Emiliani's perfect face to a pulp.

But mostly, she admitted to herself with a low moan, she wanted to have sex with him. Wild, uninhibited, magical, mind-altering sex.

For about twenty-four hours.

She rolled over and buried her face in her arms. The situation was unbearable. She was in the middle of nowhere with the most beautiful man she could imagine and he was playing some kind of sadistic game with her. She remembered her conversation with Fliss—how she'd said that he had a reputation for being icy cool. She hated men like that—the kind who messed with your head—and, Lord knew, there were plenty of them around. Always the best-looking ones, of course, the ones who would pursue you and flatter and flirt until you succumbed and slept with them, and then you wouldn't see them for dust. Until you spotted them again across a crowded bar, doing exactly the same with someone else.

Roseanna Delafield wasn't going to be a notch on anyone's bedpost.

She'd kept herself well clear of all that; packed her heart on ice and buried her desires beneath a thick layer of cynicism and denial. But here she was, stranded at sea with nowhere to run. Nowhere to hide from the feelings he'd unleashed in her.

Bastard.

She sat up, suddenly blindingly, furiously angry. How dared he put her through this, with no concern whatsoever for her feelings? No—worse than that. He wasn't unconcerned about her feelings—he was actively *enjoying* watching her squirm.

Roughly she shrugged off his shirt and slipped back into her bikini. So what if it was still damp? At least it didn't carry his scent on it, tantalizing her.

Restlessly she paced the length of her small cabin, her mind racing, trying to think up a plan to get away from him. With no contact with the outside world, she could hardly claim a sudden death in the family or some similar crisis. Besides, she doubted whether Angelo Emiliani would be human enough to let a little thing like that change his plans. Business, maybe, but a personal matter…

She stopped dead.

That was it.

She groaned out loud, cursing her own stupidity. Of course— why hadn't she realized? He hadn't brought her here to try to change her mind. He'd brought her to keep her out of the way until the sale had gone through. What he didn't know was that that wasn't going to happen without her going to Nice to sign the papers.

That changed everything. She was in no hurry to leave now. Suddenly, unexpectedly, she found she was holding all the aces and the game had started to get a lot more interesting.

At seven o'clock precisely there was a knock at her door. Despising the treacherous leap of excitement in the pit of her stomach, Anna yanked it open.

It was Paulo, the steward.

'Dinner is served in the saloon, *signorina*.'

'Oh. Thank you, Paulo, but I'm not dressed. I don't have anything else to wear…'

'It would be no trouble to find something, if you would be more comfortable, *signorina*?'

'No,' she said curtly, 'I don't mind, but I thought that maybe Signor Emiliani might object.'

Walking down the corridor in the direction of the saloon,

Paulo turned and grinned. 'I don't think so, *signorina*. Here on *Lucia* we have a pretty laid-back dress code, and the evening is still beautifully warm.'

The sliding doors of the saloon were open and soft orchestral music was pouring out of the sound system into the warm air. Anna could see the table beyond, softly lit against the pastel-hued evening. It was beautiful, but as she approached her heart sank.

'There's only one place set, Paulo… Is Signor Emiliani not dining?'

Paulo didn't quite meet her eye. 'I'm sorry, Signorina Field, but he has a lot of work to do. He's very busy taking calls right now, but he might be able to join you later. In the meantime, please take a seat. Would you like some champagne or is there anything else I can get you? A cocktail?'

'Champagne is fine, thank you.'

It was irritation that was hardening like cement in her chest, she thought grimly. Not disappointment. Not hurt. She was annoyed by his rudeness, that was all. Yet again he had managed to make her feel about two feet tall, and about as sophisticated as a school kid. There was no way she was sitting down at that ridiculously big table to eat on her own, she thought mutinously, wandering over to the deck rail and looking out over the darkening ocean as uniformed crew brought out numerous dishes and plates arranged with food.

She wasn't hungry. Or not in a way that could be satisfied by eating.

The evening was a cliché of romantic perfection—the flaming sun just dipping down into the sea, spreading shimmering trails of rose pink across the glassy surface, but its beauty only intensified the yearning inside her. Finishing the glass of champagne, she trailed restlessly back into the saloon, where a nineteen-fifties style jukebox stood against the wall.

She surveyed the selection with a measure of disdain, which

quickly turned to grudging respect. Angelo Emiliani had better taste than the average billionaire property tycoon, she thought sourly. Or maybe when you were as rich as he was you had 'people' to choose your music for you? She programmed in a few songs she liked, upped the volume and drifted back outside again.

The table stood under a sort of canopy created by the mezzanine floor of the deck above which projected outwards, supported by slim chrome pillars. Passing it, she pulled off an artichoke leaf and trailed it in warm hollandaise before lasciviously sucking it.

Oh, God. Why did everything have to bring her back to the same agonizing place?

The lights from the saloon spilled out over the deck, casting long shadows in the hazy evening. The sun had disappeared now and the stars were beginning to come out in little glittering groups, like celebrities at happy hour, but there was nothing else to see. She felt all alone—a beacon of burning desire adrift on a darkling ocean.

There was a whirr and click from the jukebox as one track ended and another one began. She moaned softly as she recognized it. Nina Simone—'I Put a Spell on You'.

The music was like a match to a petrol-soaked rag and the longing she had been trying to extinguish inside her burst instantly into flame. Slowly, languorously she reached out and grasped the chrome pole at the front of the deck and leaned outwards, swinging lazily around it, automatically hooking her legs up and snaking around in a sinuous arc.

She hadn't practised all summer. But she hadn't forgotten the moves.

Walking around the pole, she grasped it high up and stretched her legs out wide, twisting her body around and spinning gracefully to the ground. She repeated the move, this time curling around the pole in a foetal position, her knees tucked up. The music informed her movements—slow, indolent, but ripe with sensuality. Shinning to the top of the pole, she wrapped her thighs tightly around it, gasping in exquisite pain at the pressure of the cool chrome on her burning flesh. The memory of Angelo's hands on her waist as they danced last night filled her head, driving her to the brink of oblivion. Eyes closed, head tipped back in an agony of remembrance she spread her legs wide and swivelled down before climbing up again.

Her body pulsed with longing for his touch, the warmth of his breath on her neck. The music held her in thrall, throbbing through her as she let her body twist and curve almost of its own volition, every move an expression of desperate need. Dropping backwards in a sinuous arc, she gripped the pole near the floor and cartwheeled back to her feet as the music finished.

For a second there was silence.

Then Angelo's voice, cold and steel-edged.

'What the hell do you think you're doing?'

He was on the deck above, waiting for another call from London, when he heard the music. Recognizing it, he gave a wry smile as remembered sensations from last night crowded into his mind, driving out all thoughts of business.

He got up and walked over to the railing, leaning his back against it, reliving the dance. How long had they swayed together like that, oblivious to the rest of the world? Minutes? Hours? He didn't have a clue, he realised, and in his rigidly timetabled, efficiency-driven world that was unheard of. He'd let go of everything, in a way that was completely alien to him. He'd felt young. Carefree.

And Angelo Emiliani had never done young or carefree.

He couldn't afford to do them now either, he reflected ruefully, trying to re-focus his brain on the matters in hand. Countless phone calls to just about every contact in his address book had failed to come up with anything concrete on an Anna Field, and Ifford's solicitors were being extremely vague about when the contract on the château could be signed. French law dictated that the signatures of all interested parties had to be obtained, and it was taking some time to make the necessary arrangements. Angelo sneeringly assumed that the English aristocracy didn't work to the same imperatives as the rest of the business world.

Rubbing a hand over his eyes, he turned to look out over the serene ocean, and that was when the light from below caught his attention.

Or not the light, exactly. The shadow.

The lamps from the saloon spilled out on to the deck below, throwing a perfect silhouette of Anna on to the smooth boards, like a screen projection.

She was dancing.

Not just dancing… She was…

Dio mio…

It should have been sleazy, but it wasn't. Watching her, he was astonished by her graceful strength, by the smooth, elegant precision of her moves. She snaked around the pole with catlike neatness. Like a ballerina.

She'd surprised him again, he thought bleakly as the music came to an end. Surprised him and intrigued him, while all the time evading him. The girl was like a nuclear explosion in the centre of his well-ordered life.

'What the hell do you think you're doing?'

She scrambled to her feet, her chest rising and falling quickly, a thin sheen of sweat on her skin. Angelo crossed the deck with swift, savage strides. His face was as impassive as always—glacial in its calm—but she could see a muscle flicker in the lean plane of his jaw.

He stopped in front of her.

She tilted her chin defiantly, but behind her back her hands gripped the pole to stop her knees from giving way beneath her. The look in his eyes was blistering.

'I was bored.'

He gave an incredulous rasp of laughter and ran a hand through his unruly mane of gold.

'Bored?'

And then their mouths met and his hands were on the pole above her head, trapping her in a cage of his body. Her fists flew to his rock-hard chest, beating against the solid wall of muscle, while their tongues fought and meshed in the hot cavern of their mouths. She felt her hands slide round his back, her fingers helplessly kneading his silken flesh, her nails convulsively digging themselves into his skin.

Still he held on. Apart from his mouth, he wasn't touching her at all, his arms braced against the metal pole, his head bent to hers. But his kiss was hot, savage and full of hunger.

Suddenly she ducked under his arm, stooping low and swinging out from the pole as he had seen her do as she had danced. Straightening up on the other side, she looked at him with naked desire.

'Yes. *Bored.* You're always working.'

He took a step backwards and gave her a hard, appraising smile. His eyes glittered with lust.

'I have to try to stay one step ahead of you and your friends.'

Idly, slowly, lazily she shinned up the pole and swung around at the top, arching herself down towards him.

'You're wasting your time.'

'Am I?'

He reached out a hand and traced a languorous finger around her belly button, flicking the silver bar there, never taking his eyes off her face. He saw her eyes darken and her eyelids flutter at his touch and was ready for her as she shivered and faltered. Snaking an arm around her waist, he lifted her down. Her legs closed around his waist as tightly as they had gripped the pole, her strong dancer's muscles squeezing him.

'Well, maybe I shouldn't wast any more time, then,' he said harshly, carrying her through the saloon. His mouth was set in a grim line, his fingers hard on her ribs. She felt a delicious flutter of fear and anticipation as he kicked open the door to her cabin. He looked down at her for a moment, his expression dark and savage.

'I might not know who you are, Anna Field, but I know what you want.'

She whimpered. And then, almost without knowing how, her hands were in his hair, her mouth crashed and ground against his as he dropped her on the bed and tore at the fastening of his shorts. Her fingers closed around the back of his neck and she pulled him down beside her. Holding his face in both hands, she looked into his eyes with an expression that threatened to tip him over the edge of desire into total abandonment.

Her mouth closed over his again while her hands slid down the length of his arms to his wrists. Her fingers circled them in a steely grip as she hauled herself up so she was sitting on top of him. Without tearing her mouth from his, she edged her hips upwards until her knees rested on his outspread arms. The kiss deepened. They were tearing at each other's face with their mouths, grinding, rasping, devouring.

Then suddenly she threw her head backwards, gasping triumphantly. Her knees pinioned his arms to the bed on either side of him. Eyes glittering, she looked down on him.

'Got you' she whispered throatily.

He gazed up at her as a slow smile curved his bruised lips, making those little brackets at each corner of his mouth. Sinuously he edged downwards beneath her, so that her crotch was centimetres from his mouth.

He breathed out. Heavily.

She moaned as the heat of his breath fanned the fire raging through her pelvis and caressed her more intimately, more delicately, more thoroughly than she had thought possible. Her eyes closed in blissful submission, then flew open again as she felt the first stroke of his tongue.

'Oh, God. Oh—oh, Angelo—'

He felt the shudder that shook her whole body.

'Take them off,' he breathed.

Her hands went to her bikini bottoms and she rose up on her knees as she frantically tugged them downwards. He watched her, waiting for the moment when she would have to lift her knees to remove the tiny scrap of white fabric, and as she did so he flipped her over so she rolled on to the bed beneath him.

In one fluid movement he was astride her.

'Got *you*.'

She jerked and bucked under his thighs, half rising up on her elbows, wanting to fight, but wanting to surrender more. He inserted a knee between her hot, writhing thighs, separating her legs and spreading them wide open. Growling, snarling, she pushed her hips upwards, questing for the hardness of him that she could see but not touch, almost deranged with the need to feel him inside her.

Watching him slide on a condom was almost more than she could bear.

With one slow thrust he entered her, and felt a sudden shock, like lightning through his veins at the momentary look of vulnerability that passed across her face, the soft gasp that sprang from her sweet mouth. Surely she couldn't be...?

'Anna?'

He withdrew, and she let out a cry of pure desperation, arching her hips up towards him again. Her eyes locked into his, any trace of hesitation vanished in the blistering heat of her need. Sensing his uncertainty she pressed her fists against his chest, clawing, beating, every blow an expression of her longing. He thrust slowly into her again.

'Who are you?' he whispered harshly, almost despairingly.

Her eyes were a dark abyss from which she looked at him with hopeless desire.

'I don't know. I'm—oh, God—' He thrust into her again. 'I'm whatever...you want me...to be.'

He leaned forward, low over her face, brushing her lips with his as he withdrew again.

'Or everything I *don't* want you to be.'

He thrust into her again. Through a haze of ecstasy she looked up at him.

'That's…' she breathed out, closed her eyes and slid a hand around his neck, pulling his head down to hers so that her lips caressed his ear '…that's what you *like*. That's why I'm here.'

With a primitive growl he gathered her to his chest and then they were rolling and fighting and writhing together in a tangle of limbs and hands and mouths, until finally Anna arched her back and let out a shout of rapture that drifted across the dark ocean. In silent joy Angelo held her shuddering body and let go, feeling his own release like a triumph.

Her hair fanned out on the pillow, black and pink. He looked down at her, at her heart-shaped face, her flushed cheeks, her swollen mouth with its perfect Cupid's-bow lips smudged and reddened. Silently she looked back. Defiant, but defeated by her own need.

She must have slept, or at least fallen into that deeply relaxed state of total, contented submission. The next thing she knew Angelo was gently easing his arm out from beneath her head and tugging the sheet over her naked body.

'Hmm? What are you doing? Where are you going?'

He leaned over her, his perfect face as blank and pale as marble in the moonlight.

'I'm going back to my cabin.'

'No! Stay! You can't just leave like that, after we…after *that*.' She stretched out a hand towards him, suddenly bereft. He captured it and kissed her fingertips, then placed her hand softly down on the bed.

He stood upright, looking terrifyingly remote and heartbreakingly gorgeous.

She struggled into a sitting position, clutching the sheet to her breasts as she watched him walk towards the door.

'Angelo—' she called out, unable to stop herself.

He turned.

'Did I do something wrong?'

He shook his head, unsmiling.

'Sex is for sharing. But I sleep alone.'

And with that he was gone.

CHAPTER EIGHT

OPENING her eyes, Anna found the cabin flooded with sunlight. She stretched luxuriously, feeling the pleasurable ache in her thighs, the delicious throb at their apex, then she frowned.

In spite of the brightness of the day, a shadow lurked at the edge of her mind. Her thoughts roved over the events of last night, to the point where Angelo had left her, and she felt a little flip in her stomach as she remembered his distance, his beauty.

God, he was amazing…

But that wasn't what was bothering her. If anything, his remoteness intrigued her. She respected it.

No, something else…

She got up and padded over the thick carpet into her *en suite* bathroom. In the mirror her face looked hopelessly young, but that vagueness, that vacuum that she often felt when she looked at herself was absent.

Who are you…? he had asked.

She closed her eyes and tipped her head back as the remembered words shivered through her consciousness. She had found somewhere where she felt she belonged. Here. Out in the middle of nowhere with this man who called up feelings and responses in her that she had never had before. That she had never even suspected she was capable of.

It felt as if this was what she had been born for.

Her eyes snapped open.

Oh, God, that was it. The shadow at the back of her thoughts. It was her birthday today.

Resolutely she stared at herself in the glass, holding tightly on to the edge of the basin. Her birthday, and the anniversary of her mother's death, when Lisette had been killed as she'd sped through the countryside, bringing back the cake she had ordered from the caterers for Anna's party. It had been the first summer they hadn't been at the château, as Lisette had decided that Anna should be at home and have a proper party for the girls from her school.

She'd been at St Catherine's for a term by then and had hated every minute of it. The lessons had bored her, the rules had horrified and confounded her and the other girls had teased her—delighting in provoking her fiery temper. Used to being an only child and perfectly happy in her own company, Anna had found the enforced proximity of the dormitories suffocating. She had been small and way behind the other girls, some of whom had already started wearing bras and talking about boys. Scared of showing her naiveté Anna had kept herself aloof from them, earning herself a reputation for being 'stuck-up'.

It hadn't been a good start.

Keen to improve matters before term started again in September, Lisette had planned a lavish party at Ifford, which Anna had been ferociously against. The thought of all her hated classmates coming to Ifford had filled her with utter horror. Ifford was huge and had once been extremely grand, but it had long since fallen into shabbiness. There had never been enough money to keep the rain out and the furnishings up to date and her parents were of the bohemian artistic persuasion that considered wall-to-wall carpets and videos and CD players to be completely irrelevant. Anna had known that her friends would find it all deeply pitiful, and had prayed fervently in the weeks leading up to the party for some surprise deliverance from the dreaded event.

She had got it.

Snatching up her toothbrush, she began to brush her teeth with savage thoroughness. Ten years ago. Of course she was old enough now not to blame herself, and to realize that she hadn't brought about the accident herself. Of course she was.

She stopped brushing.

But if only they had gone to the château as normal that year...

She thought of the wedding dress, still lying in the dusty attic, and felt tears prickle at the back of her eyes. It was almost as if a part of her refused to believe that Lisette was really gone, for ever, and that by hanging on to the château she might, somehow, find some way of turning the clock back and reversing that decision. Persuading Lisette out of the idea of the party. Spending another carefree summer swimming and dancing and inventing more games...

Keeping up the pretence that they were a normal family.

She spat toothpaste into the sink and rinsed out her mouth with water.

Twenty-one today, she thought desolately, and still dreaming of the impossible.

'I've found one.'

Angelo squinted into the sun and pressed the phone a little closer to his ear so he didn't miss what his PA was about to say.

'Go on, Helen.'

'Anna Field. Arrested in October 2003 for animal rights activities in Oxford, released with a caution.'

Angelo was very still. 'That sounds likely.'

'Lives in London,' Helen continued, 'works in a vegetarian café, aged forty-five, divorced—'

Angelo let out a single Italian expletive, which stopped Helen in her tracks. 'I'm sorry, Signor Emiliani, should I continue?'

The image of Anna's lithe, petite body winding itself around the pole last night swam in front of his eyes.

Again.

'No,' he snapped. 'It's not her. Not unless she's the most youthful forty-five-year-old on the planet. You're sure about the age?'

'Yes, *signor*. It's on her police records.'

'OK, well, keep looking. The solicitors in Nice are still waiting for Ifford to send someone to sign the papers, and the longer it takes the more chance these bloody eco-warriors have of complicating the whole process immeasurably.' He couldn't keep Anna on board indefinitely, however tempting that prospect seemed after her performance last night.

Precisely because of her performance last night… Who knew what might happen if he spent much longer with her?

Angelo switched the phone off and threw it down on to the cushioned deck couch beside him. He picked up the plain brown folder that was lying there and leaned back on one elbow to leaf through it.

Last night when he'd left Anna's cabin he'd come out here, as he often did, to work. He slept little, and badly, which he guessed went back to his days of sharing a room with twenty other children. Twenty other abandoned children, each with their own personal demons who visited nightly and made sure the hours of darkness were never peaceful.

Angelo had his own demons too, of course. Which was why he never slept with any of the women he bedded. As far as most people were concerned, sex would be the most intimate act two people could share, but to him, curling another person's body into his own and slipping into the oblivion of sleep was far, far more intimate and required a degree of trust that he didn't possess.

He couldn't leave himself so vulnerable in front of another human being. Lucia was the only person he had ever fallen asleep with—tiny, three-year-old Lucia, who'd been plagued by night terrors and asthma attacks. When she had first come to the orphanage she hadn't spoken for months and the only time anyone ever heard her voice was when she'd screamed in the night. Gradually, it had been Angelo who had won her trust— probably because he had been the one who had tried the least. When she used to creep into his bed in the night he had at first taken her back to her own little cot with its single rough blanket. But eventually he had relented and kept her with him—wrapping his own blanket around her, sitting with her propped up against him to ease her breathing, hardly slipping into sleep at all so that he would be able to lift her back into her own bed before the nuns rang the morning bell.

He realised he had been leafing through the sketches he had done last night without seeing them. Rubbing a hand over his stinging eyes, he looked again.

They were of the château, but they weren't businesslike architectural drawings showing proposed floor layouts and extension plans. They were impressions, memories of the building from when Anna had shown him round. Letting them come to rest on his chest, he lay back and sighed.

He wanted this property. Badly.

He'd wanted Anna too but, far from satisfying that need, possessing her had only made it stronger. *Gesù*, he thought bitterly, his first impression of her had been absolutely right. Whoever she was, she was toxic. She was fiery and surprising and addictive and contradictory—an eco-warrior who stayed on one of the Riviera's most opulent hotels, a pole dancer who was also a virgin. All of this might make her as intriguing as hell, but as far as he was concerned it also meant she was one hundred per cent bad news.

He needed her out of his life and out of his head so he could concentrate properly on this deal.

Anna trailed slowly up the steps to the sun deck. She was beginning to get very happily accustomed to life at sea, having been introduced to the hallowed sanctuary of the below-deck gym. Paulo had taken her there, saying with a slight smile, 'Signor Emiliani thought you might find this a more suitable place for a work-out, Signorina Field.'

Once her initial indignation had subsided, she had enjoyed herself hugely. She was no regular gym-bunny on land, but this was different. Gleaming white, totally secluded, there was a purity about the place that appealed to her and, selecting a soothing new-age soundtrack, she had lost herself in the simple release of physical exercise, emerging later feeling purged.

Her limbs felt as if they were filled with warm honey and her mind was pleasantly numb.

Rounding the corner at the front of the boat, she stopped sharply and, swearing curtly beneath her breath, took a step backwards again. For there, stretched out on the wide cushioned area that surrounded the hot tub, was Angelo.

She half turned, muttering, 'Sorry.' Then turned back.

He was asleep.

She hesitated, not wanting to approach him, not able to stop herself. Hardly breathing, she found herself stepping towards him on tiptoe, until she stood looking down on to his face.

She felt her breath escape in a long, awestruck exhalation. His hair fell back from his golden forehead, showing the darker layer underneath where the sun had not bleached it to white-goldness. His nose was so perfectly straight, his cheekbones hard and high, his mouth utterly composed and still.

But he looked different. With those startling, penetrating eyes closed, his face had lost its cold, amused air and looked simply young and heartbreakingly beautiful. Tilting her head to one side, she smiled, remembering her surprise at how young he was when she'd first met him at the château. He was surely barely older than the boys she knew in London who shared squalid bachelor flats with each other and got drunk and groped girls on Friday nights.

She laughed softly.

This man…this man…was in a different league.

Her eyes travelled downwards slowly, as her throat constricted with desire. He was like a Renaissance sculpture cast in gold—perfectly proportioned, utterly flawless. Biting her lip, she let her gaze skim over the lean planes of his stomach, frustratingly obscured by the sheaf of papers he held against him. Gently she reached out, telling herself she was only acting in his best interests. He'd be furious if he woke up to find his tan was marred by a large A4-shaped paler patch… Carefully, so as not to wake him, she extracted them from his loose grip and looked round for somewhere to put them.

She glanced down at them and felt a tiny *frisson* of shock as she recognized the familiar outline of Château Belle-Eden, sensitively brought to life in a few masterful strokes of black ink. Quickly she leafed though the sketches—the front elevation, with its familiar gables and turrets, the French windows from the salon which led down a flight of stone steps into the rose garden—all of it drawn with such skill and clarity that it brought tears to her eyes. She almost felt she could peer more closely into the picture and see her mother's piano through the French windows, and beyond it the staircase with her ten-year-old self descending in that tattered white dress…

Oh, Mama, if only…

The next moment she was falling as an arm snaked around her waist and pulled her down on to the cushioned deck, scattering the papers. In one lithe movement Angelo rolled over and got up, towering above her as she lay, winded and shocked.

'Bad luck, Anna,' he said huskily. 'They're just sketches. No information. No plans. No details. You don't think I'd be stupid enough to leave anything significant lying around while you're here, do you?'

'I could see what they were,' she snapped, sitting up. 'I wasn't looking for anything. I was trying to—' His coldness and lack of trust stung her, so she couldn't think straight. 'Oh, never mind,' she muttered miserably, getting to her feet. 'As a matter of fact, I was just thinking how lovely they were.' She bent and picked up the picture of the French windows, looking down at it for a moment, before thrusting it at him. 'But then it is an exceptionally lovely building, which is precisely why we intend to protect it from the same fate as that house you showed me yesterday.'

'*Protect* it?' Angelo walked away from her, speaking slowly, his voice dripping with scorn. He hadn't slept for long, but during that brief spell of unconsciousness he had dreamed disjointedly of Lucia and his earlier frustration had hardened into a smouldering anger. He shook his head disbelievingly at Anna's careless words. 'And can you explain to me exactly why a *building* needs protection? Anna, the world is full of suffering and injustice and you choose to devote your time to *protecting* a *building*.'

She looked at him, hurt and pride welling in her wide eyes.

'Yes, well, at least I'm doing something worthwhile instead of just accumulating indecent sums of money by committing acts of hideous vandalism on national architectural treasures. Buildings need protecting for posterity, for future generations to enjoy.'

He had turned away from her, but she could see the tension in his broad brown shoulders as he thrust a hand through his hair. Her heart lurched uncomfortably in her chest, but whether it was out of fear for what he was about to say or the persistent nagging undercurrent of sickening desire she felt when she looked at him she couldn't tell.

'Future generations? I see. That would be future generations of the wealthy, idle, privileged families who have already enjoyed them for hundreds of years, would it?'

Families who put land, titles, a name, *for pity's sake, before the welfare of their own children.*

'Maybe. What does that matter if they're being looked after by people who care about them and the land that surrounds them? This isn't just about bricks and mortar, it's about land and how it's managed and maintained in the same way as it's been for centuries—without bulldozing woodland to make way for executives to land their Learjets!'

He spun round slowly. His narrow eyes were penetratingly blue, his mouth eloquently communicating his utter scorn. '*Land?* You environmentalists are just as bad as the nuns in the convent where I grew up. You genuinely believe that you're acting for some sort of higher authority, for the common good, but you're so blinkered by your own piety, so *blinded* by your own virtue that you can't see what's really going on around you. You feel so passionately about this building, Anna, and about its *land…* You really think you and your scruffy, irresponsible friends are striking some huge blow for democracy and perpetuity, but you couldn't be more pitifully misguided.'

He had taken a step towards her and was standing very close. His tone was lazy, but that just made the venom of his words all the more powerful. Anna felt the blood drain from her face.

'How…how dare you…?'

'Because it's the truth. You'd like everything to stay the same, would you? For *posterity*? Lovely idea, Marie-Antoinette, but may I suggest you wake up and take a long hard look at the real world. It's not all picture-book castles and fairy-tale princesses, it's poverty and disease and injustice. It's about ruthless self-interest. About people sacrificing other, more vulnerable people for their own purposes. You can't see past the romantic ideal that the château symbolizes, but the reality is that the history of buildings like that represents a whole lot of misery and exploitation. Of the lower orders. Of women and…and *children*, for God's sake, of people forced into rigid roles and restricted and repressed. I *free* buildings from all that. I don't protect them, I make them *relevant*. You're just too immature to see that.'

Ouch.

She looked down. Anything to avoid the chilling contempt on his face, but he had already moved away and was putting the sketches back into their folder.

Tears prickled dangerously at the back of her eyes, but she was determined not to let them fall. Desperately attempting to sound utterly unemotional, she said, 'If you've quite finished, I'd like to go. I want you to take me back to shore.'

'Of course. We're headed back to Cannes now.'

'Good. It was stupid of me to come. I don't know what I was thinking of.'

That's good. Make it all sound like nothing more than a tedious interlude. An unfortunate error of judgement. Nothing personal.

'I don't think you were thinking at all. But, if you were, I imagine it was about what you could gain from coming.'

Her cool façade cracked. 'What's that supposed to mean?'

'Information about what I intend to do with the château,' he said reasonably, coming back towards her. 'But, more immediately, sex.'

'You…*you bastard.* You wanted it as much as I did!'

He looked at her thoughtfully and slid a finger down her midriff, circling the diamond bar. 'I wanted it, that's true. But you wanted it more.'

There was a second's silence. Then the sharp crack of her hand as it made stinging contact with his cheek.

He hardly moved. Had it not been for the bright blossoming of colour that spread across his cheekbone, she would have thought she had barely touched him, but his eyes burned with icy rage. It seemed like an eternity that they held her. Anna's breath came in ragged gasps as she looked defiantly back up at him, every vein pulsing with adrenalin and fury.

And then he simply turned and walked away, without looking back. And Anna found that all her anger disappeared with him, leaving her feeling a miserable, churning desire and a sickening sense of self-loathing and shame.

Going back to her cabin, she started shivering so hard her teeth chattered as the full impact of the encounter hit her like a series of hammer-blows to her heart and her pride. Underneath the awfulness of feeling his anger and contempt like that, the worst thing was that she knew he was right.

She had wanted him more than she had ever wanted anyone before. Perhaps more than she had ever wanted anything too.

Apart from the château, she told herself fiercely. Her priority when she had come aboard the yacht had been finding out anything that would help GreenPlanet oppose his plans. Hadn't it?

But, as she lay curled up on the bed, shaking with shock and misery, she relived that searing lust she had felt when she'd danced with him on the beach and knew that she wasn't being honest with herself.

Oh, God, he was right about everything.

GreenPlanet was a way of life and when she'd met Gavin and the rest of the group she'd been desperately seeking an escape from a home in which she felt she no longer belonged, and revenge on a family who had tried to pretend she was someone she wasn't.

She'd lost her future when she'd had to give up dancing, and she'd lost her past when she'd found out about her birth, and GreenPlanet had offered a perfect escape—a complete lifestyle package, where all the thinking was done for her. It *was* like a religion. It told her who to believe and what to do—even what to eat and what to wear. She had been so grateful for its direction that she'd never bothered to question the legitimacy of its creed, until now. And it scared her.

But Angelo's words scared her more. He had put his elegant finger exactly on the place in her heart where the hurt still welled and throbbed.

Hadn't her family sacrificed her, in a way, for the title? The Delafield bloodline? They'd tried to keep the truth hidden to preserve her father's pride and the purity of their oh-so-important heritage and family honour, but in doing so had left her with a deep, abiding sense of shame and self-loathing.

She was supposed to suffer the pain in silence, keep her scars hidden, play her part with nobility and grace. Mix with the right people, marry the right man and fill Ifford Park with children to perpetuate the name and continue the miserable charade. History would forget her own accident of birth.

Her own feelings were unimportant.

No!

Angelo was right. Her belief in the sanctity of the past was pathetically naïve, just as her wholehearted acceptance of the GreenPlanet ideology was spectacularly misguided. But what did that leave her with? Without a family identity, without dancing, without GreenPlanet, who was she?

She had been so busy rejecting all her father's values that she'd forgotten to get any of her own. So imprisoned in the past she'd forgotten to think about the future. So ashamed of who she wasn't she'd forgotten to find out who she really was. She even tried to deny she had a birthday.

From now on, she thought, pulling the duvet back and crawling beneath it like a wounded animal, this is my *re*-birthday. The day I learned enough about myself to realize I had to make a new start. For that, at least, she had Angelo to thank, and every birthday she would remember him.

Yeah right. And the other three hundred and sixty-four days of the year as well.

Much later, when the room was filled with violet shadow, there was a discreet knock at the door and Paulo appeared.

'Signor Emiliani asked me to tell you we'll be mooring in about an hour. I'll come and get you when he's ready to go ashore, *signorina*. In the meantime, is there anything I can get you?'

'No. No, thank you.'

So this was it. Time to say goodbye.

CHAPTER NINE

TWENTY minutes later Anna stepped out of the bath and reached for one of the vast thick towels to wrap around herself.

She had washed her hair and soaped every inch of herself thoroughly, partly to fill the time and partly in an attempt to be practical. If she was going to spend the next few days travelling she didn't know when she would next get the chance of a hot bath.

And a hot bath like this? Never.

Bending to wrap her hair in another towel, she straightened up and looked around her. The oval bath was sunk into a raised marble platform and surrounded by dark polished wood that Anna was certain was neither reclaimed nor from a sustainable source. The room, like the rest of the yacht, gave an impression of devil-may-care luxury, as if its designer could have required the very last trees in the forest for some minor embellishment and wouldn't have cared. Out of sheer habit, she found herself wondering what Gavin would make of it, and stopped herself.

She was going to learn to form her own judgements.

She loved it. And the contrast with the ancient clanking plumbing and draughty bathrooms at Ifford Park could hardly have been greater.

Padding back into the bedroom, she dismally surveyed her wardrobe choices and sighed. She was beginning to hate the sight of the denim hotpants and that damned white bikini. If only she hadn't been so quick to discard Fliss's dress at the beach party…

Memories rushed in and she smiled ruefully to herself. If she hadn't, maybe she wouldn't be here. She could have spared herself the heartache, but would also have missed out on the most significant thing to happen to her in years. The last two days had taught her so much. About sex for a start. But also about herself. Things she hadn't even begun to know before.

Her capacity for arousal, for enjoyment. And self-delusion.

Giving herself a mental shake, she dragged her attention back to the matter in hand. Clothes. Maybe she should have taken up Angelo's offer of something left behind by one of his previous visitors to the yacht. She imagined a closet full of gossamer wisps of designer fabric, scented with the perfume of other women, each one with its own memories and associations of which she would be oblivious but Angelo would be all too aware.

No, she couldn't have done that. Her time with him was all too brief as it was. At the very least she could know that he had been thinking of her while they had been together, not one of his many other women.

Dropping the towel to the floor, she slipped on the wretched bikini bottoms and picked up Angelo's shirt. Pressing the soft linen against her face, she could still discern the faintest trace of his scent.

That would soon fade, like she would from his memory.

Briskly she did up the buttons and regarded herself dismally in the mirror. She wanted to make an impression on him as she left, make him admire her poise and sophistication and maturity. Instead she looked like a schoolgirl. Her hair, tangle free and straight, fell down past her shoulders in a dark silky waterfall, obscuring the streaks of pink. The sun had tanned her skin to a deep olive brown and her eyes, without their usual dark smudging of kohl, looked wide and vulnerable.

She was hardly going to attract more than a cursory glance from him like this.

Looking around, she caught sight of Fliss's little sequinned evening scarf on the back of a chair and tied it round her hips in a desperate attempt to make it look as if she wasn't dressed for bed. It made the shirt rather shorter, displaying a little bit more of her long tanned thighs than she was comfortable with, but she pushed her doubts away.

She was hardly dressed to kill. She'd be lucky to inflict even minor injury. But it was the best she could do. She jumped at the knock on her cabin door.

'Signor Emiliani is waiting, *signorina*. If you'd like to follow me?'

Now she had to go out there and hold her head high while she said goodbye to the man who had changed her life.

The sky had darkened to a quiet indigo-rose. Stepping out on to the deck, Anna felt the caress of the warm sea-scented air on her bare legs and blinked.

It was so quiet.

She looked around in confusion, searching for some familiar landmark from which she could get her bearings. Instead she found her gaze coming to rest on Angelo.

He was leaning against the deck rail, dressed in faded jeans and a dark blue T-shirt, and he straightened up as she approached. Across the darkening space between them, his eyes met hers and held them.

She felt her pulse surge and her stomach tighten. Desperate not to show him how much she wanted him, she frowned.

'Where are we? This isn't Cannes...'

He took a step towards her, sliding his hands into the pockets of his jeans, dipping his head and looking at her from under his hair. Newly washed, it was white-gold and tousled. Her fingers itched with the longing to touch it.

'No. We're not far away—St Honorat.' She recognized the name of the tiny island just off the coast. 'I wanted to apologize for this afternoon before you left. I said some harsh things.'

Anna straightened her spine and lifted her head to meet his gaze squarely. 'There's no need. You were absolutely right,' she said stiffly. Unable to look at him any longer, she turned her face to the sea, letting the warm breeze whip her hair across her cheeks, giving her a welcome curtain to hide behind. 'Please don't feel you have to waste any more of your precious time on me. You've lost two days already.'

'I don't think they could be called entirely wasted,' he drawled softly, reaching out his hand. She closed her eyes. *Please don't touch me. Please don't be nice or I won't be able to stop myself from crying, or kissing you, or telling you I—*'

She felt his fingers close around her chin, turning her head towards him with infinite gentleness. She kept her eyes fixed on the floor as she spoke, desperately trying to keep the tremor out of her voice. 'It's been...fun,' she finished lamely, as misery washed over her.

'Fun? You have a very odd idea of fun, Anna Field. But it's not over yet.'

She glanced sharply up at him. Eyes glittering with amusement, he stood aside and swept an arm in the direction of the shore behind him.

'Dinner?'

She gasped. A crescent of deserted beach stretched out on both sides, and in the mauve twilight she could see candles glittering around a blanket spread out on the silver sand. 'Wh—what do you mean? I can't—I mean, I shouldn't. I have to get back to Cannes, I—'

He sighed, taking her hand and lacing his long fingers though hers.

'You really are the most contrary, difficult, rebellious girl I've ever met. Do you realize how idiotic I'm going to look in front of my crew if I have to ask them to pack all that away and sail on to Cannes now? Not to mention the irresponsibility of letting all that food go to waste.'

His tone was light and mocking, but the touch of his hand was sending X-rated messages right to the core of her. Trying to control the dizzying waves of desire that lapped through her, she pulled her hand away. Blushing, she mumbled, 'I probably can't eat it anyway. I'm vegetarian.'

'Do you think I hadn't worked that out?'

'I'm not dressed…'

'What's new?'

'I—'

'Stop arguing. Come on.'

The long wooden jetty that stretched from the beach to the yacht tender was too narrow to walk along side by side, so Angelo let Anna go in front of him. A mistake, he thought wryly, unable to take his eyes off her long bare legs. She looked sensational—relaxed and soft and almost unrecognizable from the wary, aggressive girl he had met at the château. She seemed different too, he mused silently. Quieter, more subdued. More grown up somehow. Maybe removing her from the influence of those hippy wasters had done her a favour.

Their bare feet sank into the soft sand as they reached the end of the jetty and she hesitated, looking round at him. A light sea breeze caught her hair so it streamed back from her face, showing the streaks of pink.

'It's beautiful.'

He smiled. 'I was just thinking the same thing,' he said lightly, taking her hand. She was trembling, he realized with a slight lurch inside his chest. All of a sudden she seemed very young and vulnerable.

Dammit.

This was his last chance, he reminded himself as he led her

across the uneven sand towards the cashmere rug his crew had laid out and weighed down with heavy stones. All around they'd set hurricane lanterns containing thick church candles, and had left a basket containing the picnic and a silver bucket containing a bottle of vintage champagne and one of local *rosé* nestling in ice.

They'd done well.

He'd spent the last two days exploring all the avenues he could think of, trying to find out exactly who this girl was and what she was up to, and he'd come up against dead end after dead end. It had been partly frustration that had made him lose it so spectacularly this afternoon. Afterwards he'd realized he had missed the very thing that had been right under his nose all this time.

Her.

He'd been so busy fighting with her it hadn't occurred to him to get the answers to everything he wanted to know straight, as it were, from the horse's mouth.

He handed her a couple of glasses and slid the bottle out of the ice bucket. Easing the cork out with his thumbs, he held it aloft as a plume of foam cascaded out and splashed over her feet, making her gasp.

He looked directly into her eyes, noticing the blush that spread across her cheeks in the soft evening light. Easy. This was going to be easy.

She held out the glasses and, without taking his eyes from hers, he splashed champagne into them. It spilled over, running down her arms.

He took one of the glasses from her and with his other hand picked up her wrist and held it to his mouth, running his tongue along the rivulet of champagne, to her elbow.

'To getting to know each other,' he said softly.

The champagne bubbles sparkled against her tongue, but that was nothing to the rocket-bursts of shooting stars that exploded in the pit of her stomach as his warm mouth moved down the inside of her arm. She gritted her teeth against the ecstasy that threatened to erupt from her in a whimper of pleasure.

'What's the point of getting to know each other?' she rasped. 'We're about to say goodbye.'

He lifted his head and gave her a smile that went straight to her knees.

'Ah, come on, Anna. You're not making this easy. I've behaved like a pig, and this is my way of making amends. We've become pretty well acquainted in some ways over the last couple of days, but I'm aware I don't really know the first thing about you.'

'But that was never part of the deal, was it, Angelo?' Anna took a few steps away from him and turned to look out over the sea so he couldn't see the pain in her eyes. The lights of the yacht reflected on the flat silky water and it was almost impossible to tell where the sky began and the sea ended. 'You took me on to the yacht because you wanted to *change* my mind, not become intimately acquainted with it. Anyway—' she sighed '—I don't know why you're suddenly suffering an attack of conscience. I bet you hardly bother to ask the names of most of the women you sleep with. There's absolutely no need to make an exception for me.'

For a long moment all that could be heard was the soft sigh of the ocean. And then he spoke and in the warm twilight his voice was rough and low.

'It was your first time. I think that makes it exceptional. And did it occur to you that I might just want to make an exception for you?'

She turned slowly round. The candlelight turned his skin to burnished gold and emphasized the deep hollows beneath his hard, high cheekbones. He was looking at her steadily, his face for once not showing any signs of mockery or amusement. Her blood seemed suddenly to have been replaced with warm syrup.

She tore her eyes away from him and shook her head.

'No. I don't believe you. You hate everything I stand for. You hate everything about me.'

Very gently she felt the glass being taken from her hand. He put them both down, then took her hands in his. 'Anna, Anna, Anna, does the word paranoid mean anything to you? I confess, on paper we're hardly soul mates—'

'That has to be the understatement of the century. I'm a member of the environmental action group that intends to put a stop to your development of the château, Angelo. Let's not pretend we can be friends.'

'We've been lovers.'

'No. We've had sex. I think there's a difference.'

He laughed, but it was tinged with irony 'You're right, of course, but maybe I'd like to make up for that. I should have shown a little more restraint last night, but I must confess I had no idea you were a virgin.' He tucked a strand of pink hair behind her ear and smiled ruefully. 'Which just goes to prove my point—we need to get to know each other a little better. Look, I confess that environmental activists aren't amongst my favourite people, but it could be worse… When I saw you at the hotel I had a sudden horrible thought that you might be some spoilt little rich girl with a title and a trust fund.'

She felt the blood freeze in her veins. 'That would be worse?' she said flatly.

'Much worse. Now…' He put a finger under her chin and tilted her face up to his. 'Either you relax and stop behaving as if you're being force fed toads, or I'll…' he hesitated, his mouth curving into a wicked half-smile '…I'll have to do something about it.'

'You could try,' she said coldly, tugging her hands from his. 'But I don't like being told what to do, Angelo. Look, I really think we should just go—oh!'

In one deft movement he had swept her up into his arms and

was holding her against his chest. 'Angelo, what are you doing? Let me go! Put me down, *now*!'

'No. Not until you accept my apology and stop sulking. Otherwise—' he had begun to walk towards the sea, crossing the soft sand with long, loping strides '—you may just find yourself taking another dip.'

'No!' she squealed. 'No, Angelo, please! I haven't any more clothes!'

He stopped, and she felt the deep rumble of laughter within his chest. 'Is that supposed to put me off?'

Looking up, she could see the lean outline of his jaw, the hollow at the base of his throat. Her mouth suddenly felt very dry.

'Put me down,' she croaked.

He looked down into her face. 'Are you going to be a good girl?'

God. The look in his eyes sent a tidal wave of lust smashing through her, breaking down every flimsy defence and barrier and inhibition.

'No,' she whispered hoarsely, with a gasp that was meant to have been a laugh.

He whirled around, making her shriek and thrash in his arms as the world spun and only the hardness of his chest was real and solid.

'Stop! Stop, Angelo!' She felt dizzy and breathless with laughter.

He stopped, looking down at her with a deliberately deadpan expression. 'Are you going to be nice and polite now, Anna, or shall I…?'

'No!' she squealed. 'Don't you dare…!'

'Are you going to be good?' His mouth was inches from her own. Gradually she stopped thrashing in his arms and in the sudden stillness felt the torment of a desire that needed to be sated. Soon.

'No,' she breathed. 'I don't want to be a good girl. I want to be very, very naughty.'

His mouth came down on hers and the breaking of the waves was drowned out by the sound of the blood crashing through her veins. He was still holding her against him, so she could feel the heat of his skin through their clothes, the hardness of his body. Dimly she was aware that he was walking back up the beach with her, but she was lost in a world of flesh and fire, where the undulation of his stomach against her hip-bone spoke of something far more intimate. She felt him stoop, felt the softness of the rug beneath her, then he was standing over her, his eyes dark and unreadable.

She writhed, arching her back upwards, pulled towards him by invisible cords of instinctive longing. 'Angelo…you can't just stop…'

He laughed softly and lowered himself on to the rug beside her, languidly leaning over to the picnic basket beside them. 'Now, listen here, Anna Field or whoever you are. I can do what I like because I'm the host of this party and you're the guest, and you're supposed to be behaving yourself.'

He pulled out boxes and began to open them. Anna lay back and gazed up at the sky. Dark lilac and velvety and scattered with a million brilliant stars, it was as beautiful and opulent as a designer dress.

'Do you eat fish?'

She was about to say no—like all the other GreenPlanet members she'd been a strict, label-reading, nothing-with-a-face-on vegetarian. But suddenly she didn't care. She loved fish.

'Yes. I think tonight I eat just about anything.'

'Good. Close your eyes.'

Rolling over on to her side and propping herself up on one elbow, she looked at him. In the soft flickering light he looked like a young prince from one of the fairy-tale books she used to adore as a child.

'Anna,' he said with mock warning, 'do as you're told or I swear I'll…'

'OK! They're closed!'

She waited, her senses on high alert, her breathing fast and shallow, a giggle rising irrepressibly in her chest.

Something brushed against her lips. She opened them, questing, wanting, and bit down on something soft and delicious. Langoustine.

'Mmm…more.'

'Good girl.' His voice was very close to her ear, his breath caressing her neck. She opened her mouth again and was rewarded with another bite of fragrant langoustine, this time dipped in cool, creamy mayonnaise.

She groaned, lost in deep, greedy, sensuous pleasure.

'Good girl, that's better.'

She let her eyes drift open. His head was bent and the sun-bleached gold of his hair looked almost white in the candlelight. She slowly levered herself up into a sitting position and reached for her champagne. Taking a long mouthful, she leaned over and pressed her lips to his, filling his mouth with cool liquid silk.

A drop ran down her chin as they pulled apart.

'This isn't supposed to be happening like this,' he said hoarsely. 'We're supposed to be getting to know each other.'

'We are.'

'Not like this. We've introduced ourselves this way already.'

'So ask me a question.'

Who are you?

Angelo pushed the thought away. *Slowly. Don't rush her. Don't scare her.* Picking up another delicate curled langoustine, he dipped it into the mayonnaise and offered it to her quivering lips.

'What's your favourite colour?'

She leaned back on her elbows and looked at him consideringly. 'I don't know. Black.'

He rolled his eyes and gave her a stern look. 'You have to be sensible. Honest answers only. Or you have to do a forfeit.'

She laughed, and it was such a sweet, happy, musical sound that it took him by surprise.

'How will you know if I'm being honest?'

'You forget, *tesoro*,' he growled, 'that I have carved out a business and an extremely large fortune on instinct alone. I can tell when you're lying. Now, what's your favourite colour?'

'Pink'

'Good girl.' He held out another prawn, watching with satisfaction as her plump pink lips closed around its soft flesh. 'Middle name.'

She groaned. 'Josephine. After my French grandmother.'

Angelo felt a tiny dart of triumph. *Good. Carefully now. Keep going.*

'Best subject at school?'

She wiped mayonnaise off her lip. 'None of them. I hated school with a passion. I suppose I hated games marginally less than everything else. Look, shouldn't I be asking you some questions as well?'

'Go on, then.'

She hesitated, suddenly shy. 'Where are you from?'

'Milan.' He spoke abruptly.

'And did you...' She faltered and started again. 'You said something this afternoon about being brought up by nuns. What did you mean?'

'I was brought up in a convent orphanage.'

'I see.' She kept her head down and didn't look at him or attempt to touch him. *Interesting*, thought Angelo wryly. He could count on the fingers of one hand the number of women he had told about his childhood, but all of them had reacted in the same way—with suffocating affection, as if their kisses could somehow make up for those years.

'Your turn, I think.' She was looking at him over the rim of her champagne glass. He reached over for the bottle and topped it up, more to distract him from his unsettling thoughts than because she needed it.

'Where did you learn to dance like that?'

She slanted him a wicked glance from under sooty eyelashes.
'Like what?'

'Like you danced last night,' he replied gruffly, not wanting
to let his mind take him back there. *Focus.*

She sighed, suddenly sad. 'I was training to be a ballet dancer,
but I had a problem with the bones in my ankle. There was a
weakness—the doctors didn't know why. I had an operation,
which was successful enough, but I had to give up ballet. Pole
dancing was a substitute. It uses lots of the same skills, the same
muscles and strength in the legs but doesn't involve too much
pressure on the feet.'

He leaned over and picked up her foot, tracing his thumb over
the inch-long scar on the inside of her ankle, frowning in the
gathering dusk as he steeled himself to ask the question that was
forming on his lips. This could be the key.

It was *business.*

'Where did you do your ballet training?'

'Uh-uh.' She shook her head seriously. 'My turn. Favourite
food.'

'Hmm…' he said, wondering why he felt a tingle of relief.
'Difficult. Food is wonderful. *Can* be wonderful,' he corrected
himself. 'The food when I was growing up was appalling. But
now I love dark, bitter chocolate, and figs, and really good bread,
and Parma ham, and these…' He picked up a langoustine and
put it in his mouth. 'I can't choose just one.'

'And, let me guess, you feel the same about your women too?'
she said lightly, taking a sip of champagne.

'Absolutely. Now, my question. How old are you?'

'Twenty. No—twenty-one.'

Topping up his own glass, he paused and raised an eyebrow.
'You're not sure?'

'It's my birthday. Today,' she said quietly.

Contrition sliced through him like a razor. *Benedetto Gesù,*
here he was playing mind games with her when she should be

with her friends, having a party, celebrating. Twenty-one. *Bloody, bloody hell.*

'I'm sorry.' He got up stiffly and packed away the box that had contained the prawns and the mayonnaise.

'Why?' Her voice was leaden.

'I've kept you from your friends. That was wrong. You should have said; I would never have suggested—'

'It's all right. I hadn't planned to do anything. I don't like birthdays much. So this…' she looked around at the beach, the candles, him… 'this is…nice. Now,' she added hastily, desperately trying to rekindle the relaxed mood, 'my question. Do you have any brothers or sisters?'

He stopped what he was doing and suddenly went very still.

'No. Not that I know of. Except that I—Sort of.'

He rubbed a hand over his eyes. Great. Very articulate. What the hell was wrong with him all of a sudden? He had started this stupid thing for completely practical reasons. This was work. *Just answer her questions and choose your own very carefully*, he berated himself. *Concentrate.*

'Angelo?'

She was standing behind him, a little distance away. He turned. In the dim light her small heart-shaped face was full of anxiety. 'Tell me…'

'There's nothing to tell,' he said harshly, taking out a package of fragrant bread and a covered dish containing artichoke hearts, sun-dried tomatoes and olives glistening in oil. 'I don't know who my parents are. I was handed in at a convent somewhere in the South of France when I was a few hours old. From there I was taken to the foundling orphanage in Milan. They called me Angelo because I had blond hair, like an angel—' his voice was heavy with sarcasm, thinly disguising the hurt '—and gave me the surname Emiliani because St Jerome Emiliani is the patron saint of abandoned children.'

There was a small silence, filled by the silky rustle of the sea.

'You have no idea who your parents were?'

He hesitated, thinking of the ruby and diamond earring he kept in a box in his safe. The Paris jeweller he had shown it to had been able to tell him it was made by Cartier in 1922 and was almost certainly unique. From that information it would probably have been possible to discover the name of the original purchaser, but he hadn't done so. It would tell him either that his mother was some rich aristocrat who valued her family name above the welfare of her child, or that she was a common thief. Of the two, he would definitely have chosen the latter.

'No. I was wrapped in a shawl made of cashmere and there was a pretty expensive piece of jewellery tucked inside, so I assume my mother wasn't pushed for money,' he said acidly. 'My guess is she was from one of those backgrounds where an illegitimate child would have meant exclusion from all the best parties of the season.'

He waited for her to say what people always said. *I'm sorry.* Stupid, inadequate words that would mean he would have to smile and say, *It's fine.* But the silence stretched and deepened.

'Children live such terrible lives,' she whispered. 'I think we forget, as adults, how awful it can be to be helpless, and alone, and at the mercy of things you can't control.'

'Was your life awful?'

'No. No.'

'But?'

'But…nothing. You said you had "sort of" brothers and sisters. The other children in the orphanage?'

He gritted his teeth. *Gesù.* How the hell had he come to find himself talking about this? Never, not once in the last twelve years, had he uttered a single word about Lucia to anybody. But to deny her now would be an intolerable betrayal.

'One in particular,' he said curtly. 'A little girl called Lucia.'

Anna said nothing, just waited quietly for him to go on. God, he thought bleakly, why couldn't she just make it easier for him and fill the gap with inane chatter like any other woman would? He swallowed.

'She wasn't my real sister, of course, but she got very attached to me. I was sixteen, and she used to ask if she could come and live with me when I was old enough to leave, and if I could adopt her as my sister. I promised I would. It was what first motivated me to earn money—so I could get her out of there.'

He balled his hands into fists and with iron self-control held back the emotion that threatened to choke him. Glancing up, he could see the shimmer of tears in her dark eyes and almost succumbed. He stood up and, picking up a pebble from the sand, hurled it down towards the incoming tide.

'Anyway. She died. She had an asthma attack in the night. I wasn't there at the time and no one else heard. She was only three.'

For a long moment he stood, his back towards her, his shoulders tense. Then he turned and sat back down beside her, his emotions tightly reined in again, and managed a grim smile. 'So. My question, I think. Which do you prefer? Strawberries or grapes?'

Lying back on the rug, Anna sighed with contentment as Angelo packed the boxes back into the picnic basket.

If only she could freeze time, right here, for ever.

They had shared the food, taking it from each other's fingers, until there was nothing left but a few strawberries, and she felt replete.

Leaving only the more primeval hunger at the top of her thighs to be satisfied.

Her eyelids fluttered open a little; she wondered where Angelo was. Through the soft darkness she could just make out the outline of his broad shoulders down by the water's edge, and she felt her heart lurch as she watched him.

Tonight had been heaven. But tomorrow would be hell.

No. Don't think about it. Don't do what you always do and spoil it, don't push him away to try to defend yourself from getting hurt. This is your one chance, your one night. Savour every moment.

She got up and stretched, then began to walk down the beach towards him. The champagne and food had made her sleepy and languid, but there was a slow-burning need within her to be near him, to feel and taste and smell the scent of him.

'What are you doing?'

'Washing the oil off my hands. I don't want to leave finger-marks all over you.' He straightened up. 'Look what I found.'

He held out his hand and uncurled his fingers. Lying on his palm was a small pale shell, hinged in the middle, the two halves making a perfect heart shape.

'Oh,' she breathed, 'it's so pretty, so delicate.'

His eyes burned into hers as he took the shell and slipped it into the breast pocket of the shirt she was wearing. His hands were wet with salt water and icy drops fell on to the thin fabric, soaking through and making her gasp. Instantly she felt her nipple harden and as he took his hand away it brushed against his hot skin.

His face, inches from hers, was unreadable in the darkness, but above the whisper of the waves she thought she heard him moan quietly. The tiny sound tipped her over the edge into the yawning chasm of her desire. She was aware of her fingers, twisting themselves into the soft fabric of his T-shirt, pulling him to her, her lips seeking his, a soft pleading sound escaping her as they found his, and parted.

'No.'

The word brought her up short.

Angelo pulled away.

'Not like that. Not this time…' With something that felt like tenderness, he scooped her up in his arms and started to carry her back up the beach. His breathing was laboured, his voice low and grave as he set her gently down.

'No fighting this time. This time I want you to relax, to take it slowly…'

'God, Angelo…' her words were like a sob '…I don't know if I can… I want you so…'

He stopped her by planting a gossamer-light kiss on her lips.

'Shh…just relax…trust me…'

And with wonderful, agonizing, exquisite care he began to undo the buttons of her shirt. Looking upwards, Anna gazed in silent rapture at the infinite heavens, the vast, complicated miracle of the constellations, until, quivering with ecstasy and violent longing, her eyes slid out of focus and she was aware of nothing but her own private paradise.

CHAPTER TEN

IT WAS in the violet hour before dawn that Anna awoke.

Opening her eyes slowly, she saw the stars fading above her in a lavender sky and heard the distant sigh of the sea. Her cheeks felt cold, but beneath the blanket Angelo's body was wrapped around hers, warming her, shielding her from the chill morning air. For a second she closed her eyes and savoured the feeling of his arms around her, his long thighs tucked beneath her knees, his chest, reassuringly solid, rising and falling steadily against the curve of her back.

He had slept with her.

A tiny glow of joy flickered somewhere in the darkness of her heart. When she had gone, in the bleak days and nights—the bleak years—that lay ahead, she would always have that. It wasn't much, but it was something that she had shared with him that he had given no one else.

She half regretted that she had slept at all, but in the afterglow of their lovemaking she had been exhausted. And it was a final giving, one last intimacy after all that their bodies had shared with each other.

She looked down. His hand lay, fingers loosely curled across one of her bare breasts. She let her gaze linger on his long fingers, the well-shaped nails with their narrow crescent moons at the base, the fine gold-tinged skin. There was a tiny scar between his index and middle fingers, a fine line of white against the sun-bronzed flesh, and she wondered how he'd got it.

Her throat ached with unshed tears.

All the things she would never know about him. How many nights like last night would it take to have all those questions answered?

Closing her eyes, she steeled herself to inch her body away from his. It went against every instinct she possessed, but then she remembered what he had said last night.

It could be worse… You might be some spoilt little rich girl with a title and a trust fund.

She stood up unsteadily, clenching her hands into fists and pressing them to her temples as the tears spilled down her cheeks. She had no alternative but to leave. He would find out about her sooner or later, and she couldn't face the contempt in his face when he did. This might feel as if she were cutting out her own heart with a pair of nail scissors, but at least she would walk away with the memory of something perfect.

She shivered and, not trusting herself to look down on his sleeping face, gathered up the clothes they had discarded last night. She put on the shirt again, and bit her lip. If she was going to make her own way to the ferry terminal on the island she was going to need something a bit less revealing to wear.

Hesitantly she picked up his jeans. They were well-washed and soft and, although they dwarfed her slim hips, she quickly threaded the sequinned scarf through the belt loops and pulled them in to her waist, turning up the legs to mid-calf.

His mobile phone was in the back pocket. She took it out and placed it gently on top of the picnic basket where he would see it.

It was getting lighter. Soon the air would lose its haze of purple secrecy and become tinged with the soft pink of the new day. Hugging her arms around her, Anna looked out to sea, where Angelo's yacht slept serenely on the smooth water, its glass surfaces reflecting the rosy glow of the sky to the east. There was no reason for her to go back there; she had left nothing behind. Except her heart, and that didn't belong to her any more anyway.

A few metres beyond where they had slept the soft white sand gave way to the hard, smooth, tide-washed beach. Impulsively she walked towards it and, picking up a shell, bent to write a message for him. Tears splashed from her eyes and disappeared into the sand, leaving no mark.

She couldn't help herself from walking back to the rug and looking down on him. He looked young, not so very much different from that lonely boy in the orphanage, his blond hair tousled, his beautiful mouth slightly open, his dark lashes sweeping down over his cheeks.

Inhaling brokenly, she tried to stifle the sobs that tore through her and turned away to stumble blindly across the sand.

At the top of the dune she looked back, but the view was veiled behind a mist of tears.

The island was tiny and Anna knew she wouldn't have far to walk before she reached the little ferry port back to the mainland. It had been inhabited solely by the monks who had lived there since the fifth century; she felt no fear walking on her own through the shadowy forests of pine and eucalyptus in the hazy mist of the early morning.

In fact she felt nothing. She simply concentrated on putting one bare foot in front of the other, and the details of what she would do next. Arrive at Cannes. Go back to the GreenPlanet camp to pick up the few things she had left there. Take a bus to Nice. Book a flight home.

The feeling would come later.

Angelo woke with a start and sat up, instantly alert.

The beach was empty in the clear grey early morning light,

the slight indentation in the sand where she had slept beside him cold. Anna was gone.

Swiftly he pulled on his boxer shorts and looked around for the rest of his clothes. The T-shirt he had worn was lying on the sand a little way off where Anna had thrown it last night, but there was no sign of his jeans. Swearing savagely, he stood up and, seeing the writing in the sand, swore again.

THANK YOU

Gesù, she had taken his clothes and slipped away in the night, leaving a message saying *thank you*? She may as well have left a 'with compliments' slip and a mint on the pillow, the cold-hearted bitch. The shell that she had used to write in the sand was lying where she had dropped it, and beside it he noticed the prints left by her small feet.

With another muffled curse, he picked up the shell and hurled it along the beach, then stood motionless for a moment.

He had had the best night's sleep he could remember having for years. But he had broken his own golden rule and had ended up paying the price.

He had left himself vulnerable, and she had exploited that.

Bitch.

It had taken less than half an hour to reach the little ferry port, but by the time she got there Anna was exhausted with the effort of not thinking about Angelo. It had taken every ounce of will-power she had to keep her mind focused on the practical details of the day ahead, and a ruthlessness she didn't know she had to banish the images that kept flickering in front of her mind's eye like some masochistic internal slide-show. Angelo laughing, Angelo's broad bare shoulders as she'd looked down on them in the villa, Angelo sleeping.

It was that last image that was the most haunting.

Her bare feet were sore from the rough unmade island roads, bloodied where pine needles had pierced them. She didn't feel it, but when she arrived at the port and discovered that the first ferry back to the mainland didn't leave until midday, that was when she almost gave way to tears. The thought of waiting there, of Angelo coming to find her and confronting her, filled her with panic.

But the thought of waiting there and him not coming to find her was even worse.

In the end she was spared the torment. Salvation came in the form of two monks from the monastery, arriving in a battered old pick-up truck with crates of wine and honey in the back. These were the products which the monastery produced for sale, and were to be transported in their boat over to the mainland. Seeing Anna's ill-fitting clothes and tear-stained face, they agreed to take her across with them without hesitation.

'Est-ce que vous bien, ma petite?' one of them asked quietly and looking into his kindly, serene face she was filled with resolve.

'Yes,' she replied with fierce determination. 'I'm going to be fine.'

Catching the bus that went along the coast road past the château was worse. She had arrived at the same time as the first of the day's tourists, pristine in fresh summer dresses and neatly pressed shorts, and was aware of their eyes on her obviously borrowed clothes. It was a relief to disembark at the gates of the château and escape their curious glances and whispered speculation.

The GreenPlanet camp was still sleeping. Wincing at the noise, Anna unzipped the entrance to her tent. Her belongings were pretty much as she had left them, and she was relieved to see that someone had brought her things back from the beach the other night. Fliss's dress was there, folded on her rucksack in a slither of silk, alongside her little Indian bag. Rummaging in it, she found her mobile phone and squinted at the screen in the unearthly green light filtering through the canvas.

42 missed calls.

She scrolled through them. There were a couple from Fliss, but the vast majority were from the solicitors and the estate agents. She activated her voice mail and listened.

The initially impassive tone of various secretaries grew increasingly desperate, until eventually messages were being left by senior partners at the solicitors and Monsieur Ducasse himself at the estate agents. Their client was *most keen*, he stressed in his impeccable, formal English, to complete the purchase *with the utmost urgency…*

Of course he was, thought Anna dully. *He wanted to get those papers signed and the sale completed while he had me on board. No wonder he wanted to keep me another night.*

In the final message, left at about six p.m. yesterday, Monsieur Ducasse stated that the sale was in jeopardy if she didn't make contact before ten a.m. this morning. That must have been Angelo's last-ditch attempt to get things signed and sealed because he had known he would be returning her this morning.

She looked at her watch. Still only nine o'clock.

Hurriedly she rifled through her rucksack for some clean clothes, remembering with a groan that she'd left her only decent dress in Fliss's hotel room. None of the rest of her tattered and tie-dyed clothes seemed remotely suitable or appealing. *Have I changed that much in just two days?* she thought, pulling out a long tiered gypsy skirt and a midriff-skimming white cotton top. It felt like dressing up as someone else, putting on a costume to act a role in a play.

Outside the tent she could hear sleepy voices and the familiar sound of the camp waking up. With one last look around, she picked up her bag and started to walk in the direction of the road.

She hadn't gone very far when there was a shout behind her.

'Anna! Bloody hell, you're back! Where did you get to?'

'Hi, Gavin.' She smiled wearily, setting down her rucksack. 'It's a long story.'

'OK, well, let me tell you this first, then. I've found out what Emiliani has in mind for the château, and the good news is that I'm pretty sure we can stop him. He wants to turn it into a research centre for childhood respiratory diseases—asthma, tuberculosis, that sort of thing—which is why Grafton-Tarrant are on board, and we're pretty sure the plans will include some sort of residential or clinical type facility. I think that once the word *tuberculosis* gets out there our work is done…'

'No.'

'It's almost *too* easy. We won't even have to bother dredging up all the animal rights scandals attached to Grafton-Tarrant…'

'No, Gavin. I'm signing the papers. Today.'

Gavin blinked. '*What?* What about the pine forest…the landing strip…the château being stripped of its features and made into a *clinic*?'

She looked at him steadily, her new-found confidence surging through her. 'I'm sorry, Gavin. Château Belle-Eden is just a building…an empty old building with a lot of memories and ghosts, and it's probably high time it was put to some good use. A research centre for childhood respiratory diseases sounds like a wonderful idea. I'm letting it go. Sorry, I know you've worked hard.'

Gavin's small, short-sighted eyes looked peculiarly naked without his glasses. He ran a shaking hand over his matted hair.

'Why, Anna?'

She picked up her rucksack. 'Because buildings don't need protecting. People do.'

'My God.' He shook his head disbelievingly, his voice suddenly very cold. 'You've changed.'

'I know.' She smiled sadly at him. 'Goodbye, Gavin.'

Walking back towards the road, Anna took out her phone and dialled.

'Monsieur Ducasse? It's Roseanna Delafield. I'm on my way to Nice now to sign the sale contract.'

Dropping her phone back into her bag, she turned around. Behind her, above the trees, she could just make out the pinnacled tip of one turret.

'Goodbye,' she whispered, feeling a lone tear slide down her cheek.

Walking on, she dashed it away impatiently. She knew it wasn't the loss of the château she was crying for. It was the loss of Angelo.

Later that afternoon Angelo arrived at the Nice office of the Marquess of Ifford's solicitors for what should have been his moment of triumph. His PA had called mid-morning to let him know that his legal team had just had confirmation that the papers had been signed agreeing the sale of the château.

He had won.

Standing in the extremely upmarket waiting area, he wondered why he didn't feel like the victor.

This was the realization of a long-held ambition, the culmination of twelve years of private planning. He had hoped that funding a designated research centre for childhood asthma, and combining it with a state-of-the-art treatment centre for respiratory illness, would bring him just a tiny bit closer to the inner peace that had always eluded him.

He sighed, tipping his head back and gazing up at the impossibly ornate chandelier above in black despair.

It was the same old story.

Once his goal was in sight, achieving it ceased to bring him any sense of satisfaction at all. This was supposed to lay the ghost of Lucia to rest, make him feel that he had done something for her.

It didn't.

He felt colder and emptier inside than ever.

'Signor Emiliani? Monsieur Clermont will see you now.'

Angelo stood up and followed the petite blonde secretary into the solicitor's office, noticing her narrow back and long legs automatically and completely without interest.

Where was Anna now?

The thought took him by surprise, causing an odd pain somewhere in his gut. Her face swum in front of his eyes until he wondered what was the matter with him.

'Are you all right, *monsieur*?'

He looked distractedly across the desk. Monsieur Clermont's face was creased into a frown of concern and Angelo realised he hadn't heard a word that he'd said.

'Yes. Sorry, I'm just tired. It's been a difficult deal to finalise.'

Anna's mutinous face and defiant eyes flashed into his mind.

Monsieur Clermont smiled. 'I'm sorry. Lady Delafield was most apologetic when she arrived this morning to sign the papers. Hopefully now everything should proceed smoothly. Please—if you could sign in the places I've indicated...?'

'Sure.'

Angelo's eyes skimmed the document, swiftly checking and double checking the details.

He swore softly as he read the name printed on the contract again. Checked the spiky black signature.

Roseanna Josephine Delafield.

So that was the real identity of the mysterious Anna Field.

CHAPTER ELEVEN

England. One month later.

THE cold wind cut through the stable yard, sending a hail of fallen leaves scurrying across the ancient cobbles. Autumn had come early this year in a succession of cold damp days that perfectly matched Anna's mood.

It was difficult to get through them.

Locking up the dairy with stiff fingers, she sighed and leaned her head briefly against the door. She had spent the afternoon with a party of eager seven-year-olds from a local primary school, showing them how to churn butter and make bread, and the cold had seeped through the thin cotton of her Victorian dairy maid's dress into her bones, wrapping itself around the icy lump of her heart. The children's enthusiasm had been sweet and touching but, like everything else since she'd returned from France, she observed it rather than felt it.

She used to hate the days when Ifford was opened to the public, and remembered the scorn and derision with which she had regarded the steady stream of visitors who had toured the chilly staterooms and echoing marble halls with their painted ranks of scowling Delafield ancestors.

Times had changed. She had changed. She was ashamed of her former arrogance. She had thought she was so liberal, rejecting everything her family stood for, but she had just been cowardly. And in denial about her own snobbishness.

Well, Angelo would have been proud if he had seen her this afternoon. She smiled, remembering how one little girl had stroked a hand down the crisp sprigged cotton of her dress and said, 'I like your dress, miss. It's beautiful. I wish I was a dairy maid.'

Anna had knelt in front of her, and fixed her firmly in the eye. 'What's your name?'

'Emma, miss.'

'Well, Emma, I'm going to let you into a secret. If you were alive one hundred years ago, you would have considered yourself quite lucky to be a dairy maid. You would have had to get up very early in the morning—about five o'clock, in the cold with no heating and no light, and you would have had to work all day, hard, for very little money and hardly any time off. And your hands would have hurt from the cold and the damp. And choice and freedom and relaxation would have been things that you couldn't ever really hope to have, but you wouldn't worry about that because you'd be so glad to have a roof over your head and some money coming in. And you'd need the money because you would have to send it home to your mother because you've got five brothers and sisters at home who need food, and the baby's sick and the medicine she needs is expensive.'

'Why do I have to pay for it out of *my* money? That's not fair!' Emma had wailed indignantly.

Anna had paused and smiled sadly. 'Exactly.' She'd stood up, brushing a hand down her white apron. 'Life isn't fair. *Wasn't* fair. It was full of misery and exploitation. Of people forced into rigid roles and restricted and repressed.'

How easily his words came back to her. If only she could forget them.

Forget him.

'Are there any questions?' The children had stared up at her, enraptured. Then one of the boys had asked shyly, 'Are you really a real Lady?'

No.

'It's just a name,' Anna had said briskly. 'Anyone else? No, well, I think it's time for you to get your things and get back to the coach. Mrs Harris?'

The teacher had smiled at her in admiration. 'Yes, yes, thank you, Lady Delafield, it's been fascinating. Very informative, hasn't it, children?'

A chorus of enthusiastic agreement had risen from twenty-three small mouths, followed by a babble of excited chatter. Anna had shouted her goodbyes above the din and turned and left the dairy.

But, stepping out into the thin afternoon sunshine, the smile faded from her face. That was the busy part of the day finished, the part where she was saved from her own thoughts, and now the quiet hours of the late afternoon beckoned, where there was nothing to do but make dinner for her father's increasingly weak appetite and steel herself for another long, dark night.

Of course, it was the nights that were the worst.

During the interminable dark hours it was impossible to stop her thoughts from straying to Angelo. Wondering where he was and, agonisingly, who he was with. Sometimes, driven to distraction by hour upon hour of tossing and turning, worn out and defeated by the hopelessness of trying to focus her thoughts on something else, she would get up and sit on the window-seat in her bedroom and confront her fears. *He was on the yacht, he was with a beautiful blonde woman, they were laughing, drinking champagne, collapsing into bed. He was undressing her, tracing his long fingers over her perfect body...*

And then the masochistic fantasy would slip inexorably into blissful memory.

He was dancing with her on the beach at the château, he was hauling her off the pole on the yacht and throwing her on the bed, he was laying her down on the sand at St Honorat and making her weep with ecstasy...

Hugging herself in the darkness, she would look up at the serene face of the moon, hanging low over the horse chestnut trees at the edge of the parkland, and wonder if he was looking at it too. And it was in those moments that she wondered if she'd ever be happy again.

The answer seemed horrifyingly obvious.

She straightened up abruptly, pushing back the hair that was blowing across her face with a nervous flick of her hand and walking briskly towards the tack room. The really grim thing about being totally desolate, Anna had discovered, was that the world kept spinning. Days kept coming, with hours that needed to be filled with other stuff besides crying and watching black and white movies in the afternoon.

Other stuff besides dwelling on the humiliation. The sadness. On Angelo.

Grabbing a saddle and bridle, she looked down doubtfully at the ridiculous dairy maid costume for a second. She should get changed, obviously, but that would mean going back into the house and getting caught up in conversation and probably making tea for her father. An awkward peace had settled between them and she was doing her best to make amends for the years of pain she had given him, but it wasn't easy. Not when she was also carrying around the heavy burden of her broken heart.

She couldn't face it.

Speaking soothingly, softly, she unbolted the stable door of her father's chestnut hunter. Since she'd been back she'd taken to riding him round the parkland often, and the exercise was beginning to tell in the improved condition of his glossy coat. He tossed his head as she slid the saddle swiftly on to his back, eager to be off.

It wasn't until she had led him out into the stable yard that she realised she hadn't got her hard hat.

So what? she thought despairingly, springing into the saddle in a billow of skirts. My heart's already in pieces. I'm not sure that anything much worse could happen.

Setting her chin determinedly, she kicked the horse on and clattered out of the yard.

Angelo brought the helicopter in lower, letting his gaze drift over the picture-perfect patchwork of fields and hedges below him. There was something peculiarly beautiful about autumn in England. This was Anna's landscape, he thought grimly—peculiarly magnificent, but somehow sad. The trees wore their autumn colours with great bravado, but already one could see the bare branches beneath the red and gold—naked, vulnerable, just like Anna.

The thought needled him and his knuckles were white on the gear lever as he circled and banked, looking for the house. Whether she was sad or happy or bloody over-the-moon was of absolutely no interest to him whatsoever, he reminded himself tersely. He was only here on a completely practical matter.

That was all.

The last month had been non-stop and he'd hardly had time to draw breath, never mind dwell on Anna. He had two more projects on the go—exciting ones, in Corsica and Ibiza. Of course he was too busy to wonder how she was and what she was doing. He probably would have forgotten her altogether had it not been for a call from the building manager on site at the château, asking him what to do with all the stuff in the attic.

His automatic response had been, 'Dispose of it.' Ending the call curtly, he had tried to get back to the other business of his meeting with the financial team, but had found it impossible to concentrate on profit margin and potential growth. Excusing himself abruptly, he had left the meeting and phoned back.

'What is there in the attic?'

'Nothing of value. You're right, *signor*, it should be disposed of. I'll see to—'

'I asked what there is.'

'A few boxes. Photographs and letters. Some kids' stuff—dressing-up clothes and a dolls' house.'

'Keep it.'

'Signor?'

'I said keep it. I'll be down later.'

Late that evening, after a day in the Rome office, he'd flown the helicopter back to the château and gone up to the attic. The light had been fading, casting hazy rainbows on the majestic staircase as he'd run up it, two steps at a time, trying not to think of her as he had first seen her there.

He'd seen the dress straight away, draped over an old wash-stand as if she had taken it off and dropped it there only minutes ago. Picking it up, he'd held it out in front of him.

A miniature wedding dress.

Ragged. Mildewed. Fit only for disposal.

The sharp noise of self-disgust he made now was drowned out by the noise of the helicopter. It wasn't his to throw away, he rationalized impatiently, which was why it was currently in the back, wrapped in tissue paper and folded carefully into a box.

Below him he could see the rolling parkland and lush woodland of Ifford Park and the sight sent a shot of adrenalin-fuelled indignation through his veins that made him bring the helicopter into a steep upwards climb. The sulky, vulnerable, sensitive girl he was remembering from the yacht was an act. That was Anna Field, and she didn't exist.

The person he was about to meet was Lady Roseanna Delafield. Heiress, aristo-party girl, deceiving bitch.

It would be good to confront her with some of that.

Swooping low over the trees, he looked for somewhere suitable to land. To the right he could see the imposing house, with its stone frontage and pillared portico, its outbuildings arranged around a courtyard to one side. The wide sweep of lawn to the front of the house was flanked by huge sycamore trees, making it impossible to land there, so he banked away again, going out and beyond the trees to more open ground, and coming down lower again.

As he did so he noticed a dark shape break from the cover of the trees, moving at breakneck speed into the open. Cursing violently in Italian, he saw that it was a horse and rider and swung the helicopter almost vertically back into the sky.

Righting it again, he swung round in a circle, banking around the fixed point of the house, frantically scanning the ground below for any sign of them. On the controls his hands were perfectly steady but his jaw was set in a tight line of tension, which softened slightly as he spotted the horse for a moment as it galloped beneath the trees some distance away. It was another split second before he realised with a sickening lurch of his stomach that the rider was no longer astride.

With ice-cold precision he brought the helicopter in to land and, without waiting for the blades to stop spinning, leapt down, running across the uneven grass to the horribly still figure on the ground. As he grew nearer he felt the colour drain from his face and the acid rise to his throat.

No. God, no. Please don't let it be—

He knelt on the damp grass and reached out a shaking hand to the slender neck beneath the tumble of dark hair, with its fading streaks of pink.

It was Anna.

But the faint flutter of a pulse told him she was alive.

Thank God.

CHAPTER TWELVE

ANGELO pressed his fists to his temples in a despairing attempt to stop himself from snatching Anna up and pressing her to him. Somewhere in the recesses of his frozen brain he was still thinking rationally enough to know that he mustn't move her in case her spine was damaged.

Why, *per l'amore di dio*, hadn't she been wearing a hard hat?

Ruthlessly suppressing the panic that was swelling inside him, he moved around to the other side of her, so he could see her face.

He gritted his teeth and forced himself to stand back, not to touch her. Dark lashes swept over cheeks that were deathly pale but, other than that, her face was exactly…the same. The same face that had drifted in and out of his broken dreams and restless nights for the last month.

He let out a desolate moan and sank to his knees beside her, feeling in the pocket of his jacket for his mobile and jabbing the emergency service number with shaking fingers.

'Wh—what—?'

Her eyes opened just a crack, but enough for her to see the face that swam hazily in front of her like some fierce guardian angel. It looked like Angelo's face, but it couldn't be, because Angelo was in Italy—or was it France?—and he was making love to beautiful blonde women and, anyway, his eyes were cold, cold, cold, and these eyes burned with…

'*No!*'

Anna struggled to sit up. She knew what this meant. When you saw angels and felt surrounded by love—that meant you were dying. And she wasn't ready to die now.

'*No! no!*'

Strong arms went round her, a hard body covered her own, easing her gently back on to the ground, cushioning her, cradling her with infinite tenderness. And it was Angelo's voice she heard, murmuring, Angelo's scent that filled her nostrils, Angelo's warmth against her cold cheek.

Oh, please…yes…don't make this stop. If this is death, I'll take it…

She felt the tears squeeze from beneath her closed eyelids as she stopped fighting and surrendered, going limp and pliant in his arms.

'Anna. *Gesù—Anna?*'

His hands cupped her face and then, miraculously, his lips brushed against hers. With a moan of longing, she tilted her face upwards and caught his mouth with hers, kissing him hungrily, with all the pent-up despair and hopeless longing of the past empty month. Helplessly she felt her arms snake around his neck until she was clinging to him, kissing the life out of him. Kissing the life back into herself.

'Anna, stop!' His voice was like ground glass. 'You might be hurt.'

He disentangled himself, holding her away from him at arm's length so he could look into her face. Apart from the pallor and two faint crescents of blue beneath her eyes she looked OK, but he couldn't take any chances.

'I need to call an ambulance. Please, until they get here, lie still.'

'What are you doing here?'

He tried to keep his tone light, not let her see the panic that was pulsing through his veins. 'I came to see you, which under the circumstances was just as well. What the hell do you think you're playing at, riding like a madwoman, without a hat? You could have been killed.'

'Only because of you,' she said faintly. 'It was the helicopter that scared the horse.' She sank back on to the grass, waiting for the pounding in her head to subside. It didn't.

'*Dio*, Anna, I didn't come here to argue with you,' he muttered through gritted teeth. 'I think we both had enough of that last time. Just do as you're told for once in your life and lie still, please.'

'I'm fine.' Suddenly she realized that the top of her ridiculously low-cut and inauthentic dairy maid costume had slipped down off one shoulder and her breasts were spilling over the top. Ineffectually she tugged at it, grateful that at least she still had the vestiges of her Riviera tan. She giggled weakly. She could hardly be at death's door if all she could think about was her cleavage.

She struggled into an upright position and began to tentatively flex her arms and legs. 'Look. No damage done.' She frowned up at him as the darkness seemed to gather behind his blond head, concentrating the light around him like a halo. She felt suddenly very, very tired.

'Angelo, you are here, aren't you? I haven't imagined you, have I? Am I going to wake up and find this is just another wonderful, cruel dream? Because, if I do, I can't bear it, I—'

He just managed to catch her as she blacked out.

'Concussion.'

Angelo stood up as the doctor came into the sitting room. He'd been trying to make a fire out of the meagre amount of damp kindling and logs and had finally achieved a small but promising blaze. However, the temperature still felt lower in there than it was outside.

'It's nothing too serious,' the young doctor continued, 'but I want you to keep a close eye on her for the next twenty-four hours. If she shows any sign of losing consciousness again, or she's sick or confused or you're at all worried, please don't hesitate to call, Mr er…'

'I'm worried now,' Angelo growled, ignoring the courtesy. 'I think she should go to hospital.'

Dr Adams adjusted his glasses nervously. 'I can assure you, they won't be able to do anything more for her than let her rest, which she can do better here. I can understand your concern— she's had a nasty fall, but she's really been very lucky. There's absolutely no sign of any internal bleed—I've checked her over very thoroughly.'

Angelo's eyes narrowed dangerously. That was an image he didn't want to dwell on.

'She's pretty sleepy now, but make sure you wake her every hour or so, just to check she's all right. While I'm here I'll pop in on Sir William, make sure he's doing OK and fill him in on the situation, if that's all right with you?'

Angelo nodded curtly, turning towards the fire and stretching out his cold hands to the weak flames.

The doctor opened the door and was just about to leave, but hesitated and looked back at the imposing blond stranger. He was intimidatingly good-looking and exuded power and wealth, but there was something touching about the anxiety in his narrow blue eyes.

'She'll be fine, you know,' he said.

Walking down the gloomy corridor towards the library where he knew Sir William would be found, Dr Adams allowed himself a rueful smile. Whoever this guy was, he was obviously utterly besotted with Roseanna Delafield, but he'd have his hands full with her.

Lucky, lucky bloke.

Angelo knocked gently on the heavy oak door to Anna's room and, hearing no sound, pushed it open.

Madre di dio, it was even colder up here. That was why he was shivering so violently.

Lying in the enormous four-poster bed with its dark red curtains of moth-eaten velvet, Anna looked about twelve years old. Angelo felt his heart miss a beat at the sight of her porcelain-pale face, her dark hair falling back on to the pillow. For a moment he gazed helplessly down on her. Since the summer the pink had begun to grow out of her hair and she'd lost weight, so that her face had a new angularity. She had lost some of that childlike softness he remembered and, devouring her with his eyes, he noticed her arms were thinner. Stifling a groan of physical pain, he remembered the sinuous grace with which she'd swung around the pole on the yacht. God, she didn't look strong enough to lift a spoon now.

His throat tightened and he felt as if a lead weight were crushing his chest. The hour that had passed since he had carried her in here after the fall felt like a week. She'd drifted back to consciousness pretty quickly, but had been drowsy and confused, and he had had to hold her against his chest as he'd undone the little hooks at the back of the odd Victorian-style dress she was wearing. At one point her head had rolled sideways, off his shoulder, and he had caught her, cradling her cheek against his hand, finding himself unable to stop shaking as he'd felt her fragility.

That was the point when he'd found himself right up against the wall, facing the black shadow of his own private nemesis. There was nowhere else to run. He had nothing with which to defend himself against the emotion which rampaged through him.

Easing the bodice down off her shoulders, he had lain her down on the bed and searched around for something in which to dress her. Reaching under the pillows, he had grasped what he'd assumed was her nightdress and pulled it out.

It was his shirt—the one he had put on her in the Villa Santa Domitilla.

He pulled a ridiculously low, threadbare chair over to Anna's bedside and settled himself into it. Up until now he had automatically dealt with emotion by ruthlessly blanking it out—by distracting himself with the next project, the next hand of cards, the next blonde. He'd thought that by now his heart had simply shrivelled and died.

Discovering that it hadn't, that in fact he was as susceptible, as fallible, as capable of falling headlong in love with someone should have come as a huge relief. *Would* have done. If only it hadn't been so bloody excruciatingly painful.

For numberless hours he sat beside her, watching her face as the afternoon shadows deepened and he couldn't see her properly any more. Not that it mattered. Every curve of lip and cheekbone, every eyelash was imprinted on his mind like a photograph.

But it was cold. Like the cold of the orphanage, he thought bleakly, getting up and stretching his cramped limbs. And to think he had scathingly condemned her for her privileged upbringing. This place was straight out of Dickens.

'Anna?' He shook her gently, using every ounce of self-control he possessed to keep his hand on her shoulder and not slide it into the thick tangle of her hair. She moved her head slightly, but didn't open her eyes. He bent down to her, feeling the whisper of her breath against his cheek and pressed his lips to her forehead.

'Anna, *dolce amore*, open your eyes for me, please.'

She murmured and stirred, her dark lashes fluttering like the wings of some exotic butterfly against her blue-shadowed skin. Beneath them he caught the glint of her dark eyes and felt his breathing steady again. She was all right.

'I'm going to make you a cup of tea.'

A frown creased her smooth forehead and she lifted a hand to her temple. Angelo took it in his, trying to keep the anguish from showing on his face as he felt the bones beneath the skin.

'Go back to sleep.'

'But…my father. I have to…'

'Don't worry about anything. Leave it to me.' He was aware that his voice sounded harsh and cold, but was terrified of letting her see how scared he was.

How raw.

She turned her head away from him as a tear trickled down her cheek and into her hair. 'I'm sorry, Angelo.'

He sighed. 'Don't be silly. Now, tell me where to find your father and go back to sleep.'

'Library.'

'Good girl.' He crossed the room, fists clenched, wondering if she was thinking, as he was, of that night on the beach when he had teased her with those words, but, glancing back at the bed, she seemed to have drifted back into sleep.

'Sir William?'

The old man was sitting in the evening gloom, staring out of the window, the embers of a dead fire glowing feebly in the grate, but he looked up when Angelo entered the room. Striding across to where he sat, Angelo extended a hand. 'I'm Angelo Emiliani. Please don't stand.'

Sir William sank back into his chair gratefully. His hand was thin but surprisingly strong and the eyes that met Angelo's were sharp.

'So you're the chap who bought the château. Hope you didn't come here to tell me you want your money back. Too late, I'm afraid—all gone to the blasted taxman already. Have you seen Rose?'

For a moment Angelo was confused. 'Rose?'

'Yes. Doctor said she'd had a fall.'

'Oh, Anna! She's asleep.'

Sir William laughed wheezily. 'Ever the chameleon. D'you know, one summer she kept two boyfriends on the go by pretending she had a sister. So one of them always asked for Rose and the other one for Anna. One was terribly respectable, took her to the ballet and all that carry-on, while the other was a tearaway with a motorbike.' He shook his head. 'I could never keep up with her.'

Angelo smiled bleakly. 'I'm afraid that makes two of us.'

The old man's face looked suddenly sad. 'Lisette understood her. Damn tragedy that she died. For Roseanna and for me.' He looked up at the portrait of an incredibly beautiful blonde woman which was over the fireplace. She was dressed in a clinging scarlet evening dress; the painter had captured exactly the glow of her golden skin, so that in the darkling gloom of the dank room it seemed to give out light. Angelo thrust his hands in his pockets and looked up at the picture. Something bothered him about it.

'Anna's mother?'

She wasn't at all like Anna. Ice-cool, elegant, her beauty had a look-but-don't-touch air that made him shiver. Anna's heat and vitality seemed suddenly even braver and more special by comparison.

'Anyway, you didn't come here to hear ancient family history. What can I do for you?'

'I came to return some things that got left behind in the château. In the attics there were some photos and letters and clothes.'

Sir William snorted. 'Jolly decent of you, but you could have saved yourself the trouble. Nothing there that I want. Never liked the place. Avoided it.' He looked suddenly agitated. 'Letters, you say? Photographs? Best just get rid of it all. Don't want to rake over old wounds now.'

'Of course,' Angelo replied with impeccable courtesy. There was something odd about the other man's reaction. 'Do you think Anna would like to keep any of it, if it belonged to her mother…?'

Sir William's head jerked upwards, his eyes blazing. '*No!* I don't want you showing any of it to her, d'you hear me? It's private. Personal. It all happened a long time ago. She's been upset enough—finding out about all that would just hurt her more.'

'Finding out about what?'

For a moment Angelo thought the old man hadn't heard him, or had chosen not to answer, but then he spoke. 'The baby. Lisette…' His voice was harsh with remembered pain. 'It was the summer we got engaged. She was too young, really—too young by far for an old bachelor like me, but her parents wanted it. The title, you see? Anyway, that summer she went back to Belle-Eden to plan the wedding and met some chap.' He gave a short, bitter laugh. 'Of course her parents were having none of it. Forbade her to see him. But the damage was already done, d'you see?'

Angelo looked up at the golden girl in the picture. 'She got pregnant?'

Sir William gave an almost imperceptible nod. 'But Roseanna doesn't know. When Lisette was alive she was too young to understand, and now… Well, it could only make things worse. She mustn't see those letters, d'you understand?'

Angelo saw the old man's distress and felt a twinge of pity. 'I understand. Now, if you'll excuse me, I came to make a cup of tea for Anna. Could I bring one for you too?'

'What?' The old man was lost in a world of his own. 'Oh, yes. Yes. Kitchen's across the hall and along the passage to the left. Bit of a mess, I'm afraid. Mrs Haskett's in again tomorrow.'

Reaching the door, Angelo paused and turned back. 'If you don't mind me asking, what happened to the baby?'

Sir William looked at him vaguely, as if struggling to remember. 'Hmm? The baby? Adopted, I suppose.'

Angelo nodded thoughtfully and opened the door. Instantly the draught from the passageway outside curled around him like the caress of a ghost and followed him along the dim hallway towards the kitchen.

'Bit of a mess' had been something of an understatement. Washing-up was piled in the sink and assorted cats lay about on surfaces and along the length of the huge scrubbed pine table in the centre of the room. Putting the large kettle on to the hotplate of an old, chipped Aga, Angelo found himself fighting the temptation to go upstairs, gather Anna up in his arms and fly her somewhere where he could make her warm and comfortable and take care of her properly.

Leaning against the rail of the Aga while he waited for the kettle to boil, he dropped his head briefly into his hands in an agony of despair and frustration. The reality was that he could do nothing. He was utterly powerless. The feeling was as unpleasant as it was unfamiliar.

He rubbed his cold fingers over his forehead and thought about the conversation he'd just had with Anna's father.

Adopted, I suppose... He had made it sound so insignificant, and Angelo felt his lip curl into a sneer of contempt.

To his sort it probably was. It only reinforced what Angelo had suspected about the aristocracy all along. A baby with a blemished bloodline was worth nothing.

Clumsily, feeling dizzy and disorientated, Anna made her way slowly down the stairs. Dr Adams had given her something to take the edge off the pain in her head and the gathering ache in her shoulders and ribs, but it had also made everything else feel slightly fuzzy.

Like the fact that Angelo Emiliani was downstairs in the kitchen making tea.

The image was so unlikely that she wondered if she'd dreamt it. Maybe the fall had made her hallucinate? Which would also mean she'd imagined the bit where he'd carried her upstairs and held her against him as he'd taken off her dress. She felt the blood flood into her cheeks as she remembered how he had pulled back the cover on her bed and looked beneath her pillow for a nightdress, eventually unearthing the garment she'd been sleeping in since she'd left him in St Honorat.

His shirt.

Pausing to steady herself against the wall of the kitchen passageway, she bit her lip. Oh, God, how deeply, desperately embarrassing. Nothing could have made her feelings more obvious really, which he would either find amusing or just tedious and awkward. She took a deep breath and walked down the passageway to the kitchen, stopping in the doorway. He was standing against the Aga, his head in his hands in an attitude of utter despair.

An icy chill crept into her heart. So that answered that, then.

Glancing around the kitchen she could suddenly see it as he must see it. Compared to the sleek perfection of the yacht, this must seem like the armpit of the universe.

She was about to flee back upstairs when he looked up.

'Anna, you shouldn't be out of bed. I'm bringing you some tea.'

'I'm fine, honestly,' she said, doing her best impression of bright and cheerful. 'I'll make the tea. I should take some in to my father. He'll be wondering what's happened to me.'

'It's all in hand. Stop worrying.'

She spun round. 'You've seen my father?'

'Yes, and I found the number for Mrs Haskett and I've arranged for her to come down first thing tomorrow—and bring some groceries.' His voice was harsh and impatient, filling her with black despair. Perhaps he noticed that because, with a heroic effort, he softened it and said, 'Really, there's nothing for you to worry about.'

Yeah, right. The tidying up was in hand. Shopping was being delivered. That would just leave the embarrassing detail that she was head-over-heels in love with him, then.

Awkwardly she nodded and looked down. 'Thanks,' she whispered. 'It's all such a mess.'

She heard him expel a heavy breath, then felt the delicious warmth and strength of his hands on her shoulders. 'Go back to bed. I'll bring the tea. And is there anything to eat in this place, apart from cat food?'

Anna reddened. 'I've been so busy with the schools, I haven't really had the time to shop.' Or the inclination. She'd lost all interest in food since she'd been back, which was possibly one of the up sides of unrequited love. She'd lived mainly on breakfast cereal and the awful instant soups favoured by her father. The langoustines and olives of St Honorat seemed to belong in another lifetime.

'Schools? Am I right in thinking that would explain your rather unusual outfit this afternoon?'

She nodded, then was struck by a thought. 'The bread! We made bread—and butter! It's out in the dairy—I'll just go and get it.'

'No! You'll go back to bed. *I'll* go and get it and if you're not in bed when I come up there'll be trouble.'

Going back upstairs, Anna's heart felt like lead in her chest.

He was here and he was being so wonderful. This was everything she'd dreamed of, so why wasn't she swinging from the chandeliers with joy?

Because she had trapped him. He felt guilty, obviously, for the accident, and he couldn't leave until he was sure she was OK. The doctor had probably even told him as much, so he was stuck here until she was deemed to be well enough to leave on her own. Twenty-four hours?

Twenty-four hours.

It wasn't much, but it was all she had to keep her going—maybe for a lifetime.

He was back in twenty minutes, balancing a tray on one hand as he kicked the door to her room shut to keep out the draught that curled through the passages of the old house.

Sitting up in bed, Anna smiled bravely. No tears, no neediness, but as she watched him walk towards her she felt her heart give a painful kick.

The late September light was failing outside and the sky in the west over the parkland was streaked with fire. In the gloom and shabbiness of the room he seemed more golden and perfect than ever. In some strange way he suddenly reminded her of her mother. Maybe it was his beauty. Maybe it was the fact that, for however briefly, he was looking after her.

'So,' he said gravely, setting the tray down on the end of the bed and coming to sit beside her, 'I have to admit that you're the first pole-dancing, aristocratic eco-warrior I've ever met who can also bake a great loaf of bread. You're full of surprises, Lady Delafield.'

Anna grinned weakly. 'I try. I'd hate to be the same as all the other pole-dancing, aristocratic eco-warriors out there.'

He laughed briefly. *Oh, God*, Anna thought, *he's bored out of his brain, he can't wait to get away.*

'I found some soup. God knows what it'll taste like, but I want you to eat something. You've got far too thin.' He held up a spoon to her lips and she parted them, looking into his eyes.

The room fell silent, apart from the hammering of her heart. It was so dark now that it was impossible to make out the expression on his face.

'Why didn't you tell me who you were, when we were on the yacht?' he asked, tearing off a mouthful of bread with those long poetic fingers and offering it to her.

She leaned back on the pillows, sighing softly.

'Do you remember you accused me of making assumptions?'

He nodded, his face in shadow.

'Well, you were right. I did do that. But I think that's because I've had a lifetime of people doing it to me. Lady Roseanna Delafield—daughter of a Marquess. Spoiled, rich, brought up in the lap of luxury with an army of servants. That's what people always assume. And, as you've seen, that's not how it is.' She hesitated and bit her lip, struggling to find the words to confront her old demon. Her secret shame.

'No,' he said dryly. 'Go on.'

'It's also not who I am. I don't belong here. I found—' She faltered. She could see his profile silhouetted against the window. He was so unreachable, so remote, and all of a sudden she was reminded of that lonely boy in the orphanage. The words died on her lips. She would not start whining about her own sense of isolation and lack of identity. Not to this man who had had none of the blessings she had been given—parents who had loved her and had been willing to look after her as their own.

'I don't know,' she finished lamely. 'I guess I've never been someone who wanted to be labelled. I've spent my life trying to avoid that.'

'Running away?'

There was a small pause as Anna digested his words.

'Maybe. Running away sometimes, but also hiding. Behind different roles. Rebel. Disciplined dancer. Activist. All of them designed to distract people from the simple fact that, underneath, I don't know who I am, and that I'm ashamed of that.'

That was the nearest she was going to get to saying it. Their eyes locked and she looked at him imploringly, silently willing him to understand.

'Don't be.'

Electricity seemed to be buzzing and crackling through her veins and the throbbing in her head had been drowned out by the more persistent drum-beat of the pulse between her thighs. She was trembling, so that as Angelo held the spoon to her lips again it clattered against her teeth.

Two fat tears slid down her bruised cheeks.

Turning away, he replaced the spoon in the bowl, then slowly, slowly brought his face back round to look into hers. Reaching out one hand, he cupped her jaw, brushing away the tears with his thumb. His chest felt it might implode with the effort it was taking not to crush her mouth with his and rip that bloody shirt off her. Again.

Mustering every shred of self-control he possessed, he slid an arm around her heaving shoulders and cradled her against his chest, where her hot tears soaked through his shirt.

Gradually her sobs subsided under the soothing stroke of his hand and the murmur of his lips against her hair. He didn't know how long he held her like that, but the moon had risen above the trees by the time her breathing steadied and deepened and he felt her grow heavy in his arms. He lay staring into the silvery dark, testing out his new-found emotional depth.

Not since Lucia had he allowed himself to get this close to someone without ravishing them. For him, closeness had involved nothing more than considerate foreplay, but here he was, holding this girl, kissing her hair.

He pressed a final kiss against her head, settled her more comfortably against him and lay back on the pillows.

Slipping into sleep, he felt a tiny flicker of hope glowing in the ashes of his heart.

'Angelo?'

His eyes snapped open. It was still dark, he realised, struggling into a sitting position and rubbing a hand over his face. It must be the middle of the night.

'I'm here. What is it? Are you all right?' his voice was harsh with anxiety. He'd dreamed of Lucia and had awoken with that old familiar feeling of panic.

'I'm fine. It's OK…' He felt her slim arms slip around his waist, her cheek come to rest on his back so that he could feel the warmth of her breath through his thin shirt. Then she moved so that she was kneeling in front of him. Her eyes were like liquid in the darkness, then the lashes swept down over their rich gleam.

'You were talking,' she said softly. 'About Lucia.'

He sighed and swore quietly. 'Sorry. It's a dream I have often.'

'I know what you said on the yacht, that you never sleep with…anyone…and I thought that may be why and…I didn't want to trap you into something you didn't want to…' She took a deep breath. 'I just wanted you to know that you can sleep in a guest room, if you want.'

'Do you want me to?'

For a moment he could neither see nor hear anything in the velvet blackness. Then he felt the blissful softness of her mouth on his, felt her shake her head.

'But please, if you're staying, would you get undressed?'

Her hands were already undoing the buttons of his shirt. He caught them in his, held them.

'I can't, Anna. You've got concussion, for God's sake, and I'm not such a cold-blooded bastard that I'm going to make love to you tonight.'

She sighed and pulled him down beside her, flipping on to her back. In the dull light he could just make out the outline of her breasts. His body thrummed and pulsed with raw desire.

It was a baptism of fire. Every nerve screamed to touch her, but he lay still.

His life for the last twelve years had been about instant gratification—in business and in pleasure, about taking and not keeping. But, as the cold grey light of morning filtered through the grimy window, he allowed himself a small smile of triumph. For the first time in his life he had managed to hold out. He had felt the need, experienced the longing, and resisted it.

That, he thought, was love.

CHAPTER THIRTEEN

WHEN Angelo opened his eyes again it was properly light and the bed beside him was cold and empty. This time he felt no panic but lay on his back, his hands behind his head, staring up at the faded velvet canopy over the bed. He had slept deeply and, judging by the bright, cold light falling through the grimy window, for a long time.

And he had awoken feeling at peace with himself. Today, for the first time ever that he could remember, his head was not immediately full of targets and imperatives for the day ahead. There was no buzzy need to achieve something, to score the first business advantage of the day, to better an adversary or get ahead on a deal driving him to get out of bed.

In fact, if Anna was feeling better, absolutely nothing was going to drive him out of bed today.

Right on cue the door opened and she appeared.

He felt his body harden, the jeans he had slept in, like armour, tighten. *Gesù*, he thought wryly. This was another stage of youth he'd missed out on. From the moment he'd lost his virginity at the age of sixteen to the bored thirty-something wife of a shipping magnate, he'd screwed women artfully, effortlessly, emotionlessly. But this, this heart-flipping arousal, was something he'd never experienced before.

She was wearing jeans and an enormous, thick polo-neck

sweater that highlighted the delicacy of her face and in her hands she carried two steaming mugs of coffee.

'Is it sacrilege to offer instant coffee to an Italian?'

'I suspect you could get away with offering ice cream to an Eskimo,' he said dryly, accepting one of the mugs and shifting over on the bed so she could sit down beside him. 'How are you feeling this morning?'

She smiled wickedly into his eyes, but there was a hint of uncertainty there. A question. 'Frustrated.'

He took a sip of the watery coffee, relying on the caffeine rush to counteract the far more powerful testosterone hit her words had just initiated. 'Anna, I'm being serious. How's your head?'

She reached out and took the mug from his hand, putting it on to the dusty bedside table, then swung one leg over him.

'My head's OK,' she said slowly. 'However…' she took one of his hands and slid it under her sweater '…I'm a bit concerned about my heart, doctor.'

Angelo sucked in a sharp breath as his hand encountered the soft warmth of her bare breast. He could feel her heart, beating fast beneath his palm. Slowly he sat upright and tipped her off his chest so that she was lying on the bed beside him. Carefully keeping his face perfectly blank, he pulled the curtains on one side of the bed closed in a shower of dust.

'In that case, I'd better examine you. Take your clothes off, please.'

On the bed, Anna writhed out of her jeans as Angelo viciously tugged the curtains at the end of the bed closed. In the sudden shadowy darkness she saw his throat move as he swallowed. She sat up, raising her arms to pull the sweater over her head, and as the soft wool enveloped her face she felt his hands on her ribs, sliding upwards, along her arms, easing her out of the tangle of her clothes.

'You're beautiful.'

Her hair crackled with static, but that was nothing to the

passion that snapped and fizzed in her dark, dark eyes. His gaze travelled downwards and he forced himself to go slowly, taking her in, inch by inch: the delicate outline of her collar-bone above the luscious breasts that he knew just fitted perfectly into his hands. The narrowness of her ribs, the decadent sparkle of the jewelled bar in her midriff, the pale line on her flawless skin that showed where her bikini had been…

He made a low guttural sound, caught between wanting that moment to last for ever and the need to have her, to be inside her right now, to possess her and never let her go.

She stood up on the bed and, reaching round him, unhooked the curtains on the last side of the four poster, pulling them together to enclose them in secret darkness. He could see nothing, could only feel her hands on his waist, unfastening the button on his jeans, gently working them down over his hips. He let his head fall backwards as her fingers swept across the skin beneath the top of his boxer shorts, easing them over the hard jut of his painful arousal.

He was lost, throbbing with longing. Feeling every touch as if for the first time.

Aching.

Anna let her palms linger on the hard flatness of his stomach, adoring the way she could feel his flesh quiver as her hands inched downwards. Sitting on the edge of the bed, she leaned her forehead against his chest, knowing that her mouth was only inches from his straining erection, exhaling heavily so that her breath caressed his skin. The darkness wreathed them completely, but her mind was full of images of him. She jumped as she felt his fingertips on her shoulders, then relaxed against him as they began to move in caressing, languid circles down her back.

There was no hurry, no sense of urgency in their dark paradise. Every move, every touch was filled with the pleasure of the moment. Gently he pushed her back on to the bed, leaning over her to bring his mouth down to hers and plundering it softly, lovingly before moving downwards to her neck, her breast. Only as his lips brushed her dew-drenched thigh did she cry out, at last driven to the very edges of self-control and she felt him pull away from her.

'Angelo, please…'

'Wait,' he rasped, stooping swiftly to where he'd kicked his jeans and fumbling in the pockets for a condom. 'Damn.'

'I don't care. Please…'

Her hands gripped his hips, pulling him down on to her, and the next moment a deep shudder of total surrender ricocheted through him as he felt her fingers close around the very core of his desire, guiding him into her. And then she was wrapping her slender legs around him and arching her pelvis up to take all of him inside her, and the past, the future and everything was obliterated in the pure perfection of *now*.

She was in his arms, underneath him, beside him, her hair on his face, her lips on his skin, her dark, delicious scent all around him. He was lost, but he was also home. The bliss stretched and quivered until convulsively he grasped her closer, cupping her bottom and driving deeply into her as desire spilled over into fulfilment. At the moment of his own explosion into ecstasy her soft, high gasp in his ear was like a gift.

Afterwards they lay locked together and he thought about the consequences and implications of what he'd just done. Never before, *ever*, had he had sex without protection. To him it was automatic—part of the ritual, to guard himself against disease and paternity, and maybe just to guard himself against closeness. Anna had removed that barrier as she had removed so many of the others he had built between himself and the rest of the world.

She shifted a little in his arms and he twitched the curtain aside so that a thin shaft of sunlight penetrated their warm cave.

'No-o-o!' She rolled over and buried her face in his chest. 'Too bright!'

'I want to see you.' He frowned and stroked the hair back from her face. 'Are you all right—does your head hurt?'

'No, thank you, doctor.' She smiled teasingly up at him. 'But I'm suddenly hugely hungry.'

'Is Mrs Haskett downstairs? Did she bring groceries?'

Anna moaned. 'I can't believe you can even mention the word "groceries" at a moment like this. Angelo Emiliani, there is no romance in your soul whatsoever.' Scrambling up on to her knees, he was treated to the glorious sight of her naked body as she reached up to the carved wooden headboard of the bed.

'What are you doing? Not that I'm not enjoying the view, whatever it is…'

'Aha…' She flopped down beside him again with a look of pure triumph and produced a packet of biscuits.

'Where did those come from?' He looked at her suspiciously. 'And how old are they? Anna, have those been there since you had your last sleepover party when you were about fifteen?'

'I never had sleepover parties. You're my first one.'

'Are you having a nice time?'

'Yep.' Her face was alight with happiness and it seemed to warm him from the inside, melting the ice that had slowed the passage of blood through his veins for the last eternity.

'So where did the biscuits come from?'

'Secret cupboard. Look.' She kneeled up again and he watched as she slid across one of the carved panels in the headboard. 'This is a Victorian reproduction, but during the sixteenth century Catholics used to hide their bibles and rosary beads in them.'

He quirked an eyebrow at her. 'Interesting. Do you bring parties of schoolchildren on educational visits in here too?'

'Only the very good-looking sixth-formers from the boys' school.'

'I'm sure they learn a lot,' he said dryly. 'So what do you keep in your secret cupboard, apart from biscuits?'

She shrugged, suddenly shy. 'Special things.' Taking down a small box, she shut the little cupboard again and settled herself back on the pillows, the box on her knee. 'There's the first merit award I won for ballet, and the programme from *The Nutcracker*, which my mother took me to see at Covent Garden.' She laid them out on the bed and, leaning on one elbow, he watched her face as she looked into the little box. 'That used to be lavender from the garden of the château, but look, it's shed all its flowers.' She held out the box, tipping it so that the dead flower-heads fell into her hand, along with a couple of other things.

Glancing into the palm of her hand just before her fingers closed, Angelo felt his heart stop for a second, then begin again, pumping ice through his veins.

Benedetto Gesù, it couldn't be…Please, God, let his eyes and his mind be playing tricks on him…

'What have you got there?' His throat suddenly felt as if it were made of sandpaper.

'Ah—the most precious thing of all.' Smiling softly, she uncurled her fingers. There, cupped in her hand beside the shell he had given her on St Honorat, was a ruby and diamond earring. The exact match to the one that had been tucked into the shawl he had been wrapped in when he had been found by the nuns.

'It's an incredibly rare, incredibly valuable piece,' she was saying teasingly, 'traditionally given by emotionally inarticulate Italian males to their women and meaning *I love you…*'

'I'm not talking about the shell. I mean the earring.'

To his own ears his voice sounded hollow and very far away, but if she noticed she gave nothing away.

'Oh, that. It's not an earring, it's a pendant.'

Relief flooded through him.

'Although…' Anna was holding it between her fingers, looking at the back '…oddly enough, it was an earring once, but the other one was lost so my mother had it made into a pendant for me. She inherited them from her grandmother and there was big trouble when the other one went missing. It's worth a lot, I know that much.'

Cartier. 1922.

'This, however,' Anna continued, stroking a finger over the pearly pink surface of the shell, '*this* is actually priceless…'

Angelo stood up, waiting for the nausea to subside and the fog to clear from his head, then strode across to the door. He didn't know where he was going, just that he had to put some distance between himself and Anna. There was a burning feeling in his chest.

'Angelo?'

Her voice was full of fear and it felt like tiny barbs in his heart. Gritting his teeth, he forced himself to turn back towards her, but, not trusting himself to speak, he simply looked at her, desperately trying to keep his expression blank.

'What's wrong?'

He shook his head, then left the room, closing the door very quietly behind him.

The plumbing at Ifford was as Dickensian as the rest of the God-forsaken place, thought Angelo savagely, towelling himself with a scrap of fabric that felt like sandpaper. But the freezing temperature of the pitiful shower had only matched the ice in his blood, and in his heart.

Deep down, this was what he had always dreaded, what every person who didn't know their parents must secretly dread—that they would inadvertently fall in love with a blood relative. He looked at his reflection in the small square of mirror above the basin and hardly recognised himself.

His skin was ashen, his eyes like dark hollows, but suddenly in every line and plane of his face he could see the woman in the portrait downstairs laughing back at him. His mother.

Anna's mother.

Dio, it all slotted horribly, sickeningly into place. Snatches of his conversation with Sir William yesterday echoed around his head.

'...*the damage was already done...*'

Gripping the sides of the basin with both hands, Angelo braced his arms and bent his head, waiting for the wave of nausea to pass, wondering what to tell Anna. *Gesù*, he was blighted. Jinxed.

Cursed.

And now he had brought his poison into her life, infecting her with the blackness that had always shadowed him, like an indelible stain on his soul.

He couldn't tell her. This was a burden he would bear alone.

Anna stood at the window, looking down at the familiar view without seeing it. Her head throbbed with dull pain as self-reproach and recrimination chased themselves around her brain in sickening circles.

She had said the L-word.

How could she have been so bloody, bloody *stupid*?

Right from the beginning she had thrown herself at him in one humiliating episode after another, and he had never given her any reason to think the tumult of emotions he aroused in her was in any way reciprocated.

Well, maybe in *one* way, she thought, remembering the ferocity of his passion when he had caught her pole-dancing. But he had also never made any bones about the fact that sex was one of the many currencies he dealt in. He had many women.

But he didn't sleep *with them!* she thought in anguish. *That was what had made her reckless. The intimacy they had shared last night in the long dark hours he had lain beside her was what had deluded her!*

In her desolation she pressed her palms against the window-panes, the reflection of her own dark, haunted eyes staring back at her from the pale blur of her face. Behind her, she heard the door open and whirled round to see Angelo. He was dressed and there was something about him that told her he was leaving. Something final that said that in every way that mattered he was already gone.

'You're going?'

He hardly glanced at her as he spoke and his voice was cool and impersonal.

'Yes. I've got meetings this afternoon. I should have left last night really.'

'I'm sorry.' Her voice was very small. 'That was my fault.'

He gave an impatient sigh. 'Don't be silly; you couldn't help it.' He was looking around the room restlessly, as if he was just dying to be off. Anna felt her heart wither and die, her pride along with it as everything in her demanded that she throw herself at his feet and beg him not to go.

'Angelo—' she began desperately as tears surged into her eyes. 'I'm sorry, I'm so sorry. I was stupid to say that, but I wasn't being serious. I know I shouldn't have—'

He stopped her with a dismissive wave of his hand. 'Look, Anna, it doesn't really matter what you said. This was never going to come to anything, was it?' He gave a short, mirthless laugh, as if trying to emphasise the outrageousness of the idea that they could be together. 'I guess I just realised that it's all going a bit too far now. I shouldn't lead you on like this. I'm not right for you—'

'That's not true!' She was wringing her hands in a classic, clichéd gesture of distress but couldn't stop her cold fingers from twisting around each other, squeezing until the bones ached.

'Just *listen*!' It was almost a roar and she felt the blood drain from her face until she thought she might faint. '*You're* not right for me. It's not going to happen, Anna. I have a…a life and other…commitments, and I was wrong to stay here last night…'

His voice almost cracked. *Gesù, Gesù*, he had to stay strong.

'Other commitments?' she whispered, her face a mask of pain. He couldn't look at her. 'You mean you have someone else?'

'I'm sorry,' he said tonelessly and shrugged, thrusting his hands deep into his pockets as a physical restraint against the need to go to her and hold her. 'It's better that I leave now. Please don't come down.'

He didn't look back.

Downstairs, he strode along the passageway to the library where he had talked to Anna's father last night. The room was empty this morning, the fire cold, but the portrait above it was as warm and glowing as he remembered.

So that was the thing that had snagged in his brain. The earrings. In the picture they were little more than a smudge of crimson and blue-white oil, not easily identifiable, but now he knew he could recognize them all too clearly. Just as he could recognize his own eyes smiling back at him from Lisette Delafield's portrait.

He stood before it for just a few seconds, then turned on his heel and strode back towards the door.

He could hardly think straight to do the necessary pre-flight checks on the helicopter, he was so distracted by the idea of Anna looking out of one of the many blank windows that lined the front of the great barren house. He had a sudden vision of her like a princess abandoned in a tower, left to her fate. Cursed.

Cursed by me, he thought despairingly.

All the peace he had felt in the dark hours of the night had deserted him. There was no hope for him now—she had been his only chance of salvation, and now there was nothing standing between him and an eternity of aloneness.

The fires of hell seemed positively inviting by comparison.

CHAPTER FOURTEEN

LEAVING the warmth of Fliss's plush office at Arundel-Ducasse, Anna pulled her long black coat more tightly around her and put her head down against the wind. London in October was particularly bleak. But then, she thought, walking quickly along the crowded pavement towards the tube, she could have been lying on a beach in the Bahamas and it wouldn't have made any difference. Everywhere felt bleak when your heart had been hacked to bits with a pickaxe.

People said that time was supposed to be a great healer. Well, in Anna's opinion, time was doing a pretty rubbish job. It had been five interminably hideous weeks since Angelo had left, and her heart was definitely still on the critical list and showing no sign of recovery. She still cried herself to sleep every night, she still cried herself awake every morning, she still cried over songs on the radio and langoustines in the window of the fishmongers near Fliss's flat.

Fliss was making a very brave and very noble attempt at trying to remind her that her life wasn't over but, despite her best efforts, Anna wasn't convinced. Tired of leaving messages on Anna's voicemail, Fliss had appeared at Ifford one Saturday, two weeks after Angelo had gone, and found a pale, thin ghost of her former friend. Persuading Anna to take off Angelo's shirt and get dressed into some proper clothes had been the biggest hurdle:

after that, getting her to agree to come and stay in Fliss's flat in London, helping her find a part-time job in one of the trendy delis nearby and even getting her to eat occasionally had been relatively easy. Anna had simply submitted.

But recently even that numb submission had been shattered by two letters, forwarded from Ifford, from Angelo's firm of solicitors.

It had been the cold, impersonal tone that had upset her more than anything—until she thought of the implications behind it, and then that made the cold, impersonal tone seem like the least of her worries.

> Our client regrets the breakdown of the relationship between himself and Lady Roseanna Delafield, but requires confirmation from a medical professional that Lady Delafield has not conceived a child as a result of the relationship. We regret the personal and sensitive nature of this request, but would appreciate your co-operation.

The excessive courtesy veiled the lethal, steel-tipped message. Really, she would rather he had just sent a scrawled note saying, *I'm really desperate never to have anything to do with you again, so please help me out by letting me know you have no further hold on me.* She would have respected him more.

Bloody hell, she thought bitterly, stumbling a little as her vision was blurred by another deluge of tears. Even thinking about it was enough to push her back into the swamp of her own misery. One day she'd simply sink without trace beneath the murky waters, like Alice in Wonderland, and—

Head down, she didn't see the face of the person she bumped into, only his elegant handmade shoes.

'Sorry, I wasn't—'

'What the—? *Gesù*, Anna!'

White-faced, she backed off, slightly winded by the force of her collision with the tall blond stranger in the dark suit, and shocked to the core by the realization it was no stranger. The crowd eddied around and between them, forcing them apart for a moment. He reached out to grab her arm, but she was too quick for him.

'Don't touch me!'

For a moment she thought she saw a flicker of emotion in the narrow blue eyes she remembered so perfectly, but when she looked again she realised she'd imagined it. They were as hard and cold as icebergs.

'I need to talk to you,' he said through gritted teeth, as if he was only hanging on to his temper by a thread, 'so don't even think of running away.'

'What? Like *you* did at Ifford?' she retorted, her eyes blazing at him.

He steadied himself, managed to produce a sardonic smile. 'I apologized for that at the time. And explained. I'm sure we can both be grown-up about it now.'

Anna looked down at the damp, leaf-strewn pavement and shook her head in disbelief. 'Oh, right,' she said sadly. 'That's what the solicitor's letters are about, is it? That's how *grown-ups* behave. Silly me. I'm just so immature.'

'You haven't replied.'

She looked up at him, feeling the wrenching pain in her poor, wounded heart as she did so. A little of the golden beach-boy glow he had had on the yacht had faded and he looked harder. Older. But still lethally handsome.

'No, Angelo, I haven't,' she said slowly. 'And I suppose it's only fair to warn you that I have no intention of doing so. You're a businessman, after all, so you might like to consider whether it's worth accumulating further legal fees when—ouch!'

He managed to get hold of her arm this time, his fingers burning her flesh through the layers of her clothes.

'I need an answer, Anna.'

'Why?' she spat, wrenching herself free of his grasp and backing away from him. 'Because you need to be in control? Well, you forfeited your right to control me when you left that morning. End of story. Goodbye, Angelo.'

She swung round and strode blindly down the busy street, grateful for the press of bodies around her, separating her from him and preventing her from rushing back and throwing her arms around him. She reached the tube station and was carried along in the flow of people going down the stairs when she was suddenly aware of a commotion behind her as someone pushed their way through.

She didn't have to turn round to know who it was. Of course he wouldn't be able to let her have the last word. The next moment he was standing in front of her, blocking her way, his broad shoulders like a sea wall against the tide of people.

'Nice try. But when I say I want to talk to you, I mean it.' He gave her a wintry smile. 'End of story.'

She looked at him, taking in the faultless tailoring of his dark wool suit, the snowy perfection of his white shirt, all of which emphasised his chilling beauty. In the dingy light of the underground tunnel his magnificence was utterly incongruous. She gave a slightly hysterical laugh.

'You really get to see how the other half lives when you're with me, don't you, Angelo? Hippy beach parties, squalid country houses, and now the sordid reality of the public transport system. Stick around—who knows what might be next on the itinerary?'

His face was like ice. 'Don't forget where I came from, Anna. I've slept in underground stations before now, so having a conversation here is no problem, I can assure you. Especially as it won't take long.'

'No. It won't. Because I have nothing to say.'

She looked up at him defiantly, her jaw set against the sob that was rising in her throat. He straightened up, half-turning away from her, and for a moment, just for a fraction of a second, caught a look of haunting despair in his face.

'Please. Anna. Just tell me. There's a risk, we both know that. Tell me you're not pregnant!'

She sighed, feeling the fight go out of her, and looked up at him with huge, troubled eyes. 'Why, Angelo? What would it matter to you? I'd never ask anything of you. I don't want your money.'

Angelo felt the barbed wire band around his heart twist and tighten and braced himself against the familiar pain. 'I just need to know. For personal reasons.'

She bent her head. Her voice was so quiet that he had to lean towards her to hear it, which meant he could smell her wonderful dark scent.

'You said you had…other commitments. Are you getting married? Is that it?'

The crowd were pushing past them to the platform and in the midst of all the people she looked so fragile that he wanted to push everyone else back from her and make a space for her in the circle of his arms. Instead he tipped his head back and breathed in deeply.

Forgive me.

'Yes,' he said curtly. 'Yes, that's it. I'd like everything…sorted…first. I think it's only fair that there's no danger of anything that happened in my past interfering with…our…future.'

He saw the top of her dark head move up and down as she nodded. Sliding her hands into the pockets of her long black coat, she hunched her shoulders and started to move forwards. He fell into step beside her and, glancing down, saw that tears were coursing down her cheeks.

Gesù. Benedetto Gesù. Each tear was like the lash of the torturer's whip. And he absorbed the blows without complaint because he knew he deserved them.

'I'm sorry, Anna.' Pitifully inadequate. But better than nothing.

She gave a bleak smile. 'The thing is, it doesn't really make any difference if I am pregnant or not. Because, you see, Angelo, I'm afraid that I would never, ever in a million years consider terminating a baby because it wasn't convenient or it didn't fit in with your plans. I'm surprised you'd even want me to, considering your past.' They had reached the platform and her face in the harsh fluorescent strip lighting was pale grey. A gust of air lifted her hair from her face and he could see the last traces of pink, like the fading rays of sunset. He felt the darkness closing in around him, sealing him off from the rest of humanity with his guilt and his shame and his bitterness.

'What do you mean, my "past"?'

Her voice was oddly apologetic. 'Your mother. She must have been alone, terrified, *devastated*, to do what she did with you, but she still gave you the opportunity of a life. I hope that in the same situation I'd be brave enough to do the same thing.'

He stared straight ahead at the grimy tiled wall, his jaw clenched, not trusting himself to blink.

Anna couldn't stop herself from gazing up at him. He looked like a tortured angel. Fliss kept telling her that anger was the only way to get through the pain, but as she looked at him she could find nothing inside her but love.

There was another gust of warm stale air and a surge of bodies signalling the arrival of the train. Pressed into him in the crush, she said fiercely, 'If I was pregnant, nothing would stop me having the baby. Keeping it. And loving it like I love you.'

And then, head down, she slipped past him into the crowd. He spun round, searching for her, feeling that he'd been kicked brutally in the guts. He saw her standing by the doors of the train and strode towards her.

'*Dio*, Anna! You don't understand...' His voice was harsh. Raw. 'You don't *know*!'

'I do. I'm adopted too.' She stepped into the carriage and looked back at him, smiling wanly through her tears. 'And, believe me, at the moment it doesn't feel like it, but generally I'm glad I'm alive.'

She stood back as the doors started to close, her eyes searching his face. He looked ashen. Stunned.

'I'm not pregnant. So—there you are. Go and be happy.'

And in just a few seconds the platform had become quiet and almost empty as the train disappeared into the darkness of the tunnel. Angelo stumbled backwards, leaning against the wall for support, fighting for breath.

I'm adopted too.

The implications filled his brain, too big, too wonderful to be easily comprehended. That was what she'd said, wasn't it? Meaning that Lisette Delafield wasn't her natural mother? That there was no blood tie between them?

Incredulously he rubbed his hands over his face, then stood up and began to walk quickly in the direction of the exit, back up towards the light. His mind raced. He felt like a prisoner who, having been kept for five long weeks in solitary confinement in the pitch blackness, was suddenly thrust back out into the open and had no idea which way to go.

He didn't know where Anna had gone, where she was living, how to find her. Pushing both hands into his hair, he gritted his teeth and tried to focus. It was possible that her father would help him, but he had no telephone number for Ifford Park and his jet was waiting to fly him back to France tonight.

And then, with a flash of hope, he remembered Arundel-Ducasse. He had been on his way to a meeting there when he had bumped into her, and since they had dealt with the sale of the château they would surely have a contact number.

His pace quickened until he was almost running, trying to suppress the terrible weight of hope that was crushing his chest. He could have misheard. Misunderstood.

He had spent the last five weeks in a state of frozen numbness. As a small boy in the orphanage, he used to dream of the day when he would find his natural mother, but as he had grown older he had ruthlessly repressed his curiosity. How cruel then that he should discover Lisette—unsought, unwanted—and have to give up Anna as a consequence. Part of him had railed against the injustice, wishing he could not have seen the earring, wishing she had not chosen to leave the other half of the pair with him, wishing he had never known…

But then the consequences could have been dire, the curse of his own blighted life visited on the children he and Anna might have.

And that was when the real torment had begun. Night after harrowing night of lying awake, wondering…torturing himself. Instructing his solicitors to contact her had been the least personal, most brutal way of trying to extract an answer from her, but he had known the hurt it would cause her. From the depths of his own pain he'd ached for her, but had recognized that making her hate him was the best possible course of action, the one most likely to encourage her to end the pregnancy, should that be necessary.

He had, of course, not reckoned on her courage, her sensitivity, her capacity for love.

Or her own experience of adoption.

Racing up the steps to the Arundel-Ducasse office, he paused at the top with his hand on the door, breathing fast, and then pushed it open.

'Can I help you, sir?' enquired the girl at the desk at the front of the office, looking up at him with a polite smile. The smile faded slightly as she added, with a barely distinguishable acid tone, 'Oh. Signor Emiliani.'

His gaze flickered over the little sign on her desk, on which her name was printed, and his face broke into a grim smile.

'Yes, Ms Hanson-Brooks, I think you can. Or may I call you Felicity?'

* * *

Fliss left the office early and hailed a taxi on the street outside. She had actually made a resolution to be less extravagant and had given up taxis, lunch-hour trips to Bond Street and champagne on weekdays, but hell, this had to qualify as Exceptional Circumstances.

Thrusting two twenty pound notes at the driver as he pulled up outside her flat, she slammed the door and ran up the path without waiting for the change. Throwing open the front door into the communal hallway, she clattered up the stairs as fast as her office heels would allow, unable to stop a huge giveaway grin from spreading across her face.

Finally she flung open the door to her own flat.

'Anna! Anna, just guess what? *Guess* who I've spent the afternoon with?'

But her voice echoed around the dark flat, dissolving into the thick silence. She didn't have to read the note on the kitchen worktop to know that Anna had left.

Darling Fliss
Am taking my misery away for a while. Sorry for being
such awful company for the last few weeks and thanks for
everything.
Anna. xx

Fliss swore succinctly. She wasn't going to enjoy breaking the news to Angelo.

CHAPTER FIFTEEN

'*AND so the prince and the princess were married, and they all lived happily ever after...*'

Anna shut the book and looked down at the small head nestled against her. 'And now it's time to go to sleep. Did you like that story, Suzette?' she asked, lifting the little girl into her narrow bed and tucking the covers around her.

Suzette nodded, her dark eyes shining. '*Oui*. I love the bit where they get married. Her dress is so beautiful. I'll have a dress like that when I get married.'

Anna smiled, feeling the familiar lump in her throat. 'I'm sure you will, *chérie*. And you'll have flowers in your hair and a big bouquet of roses and lilies... And you'll look even more beautiful than the princess in the picture.'

'*Oui.*' Slipping her thumb contentedly into her mouth, the little girl settled down beneath the covers and Anna bent to kiss the top of her head. The delicate sense of peace she had found during the last month at the convent and as a volunteer helper in its children's home had come as a surprise to her. In the early days when she had first arrived there she had wondered how she would survive, but she had. And slowly she had begun to feel ready to face the rest of her life again.

But it was time to leave now. In her one hurried, panicked phone call to Fliss on the night she'd arrived she had told her she was taking one month away. One month in which she couldn't be contacted, couldn't be tempted to make any contact with home. She remembered how Fliss had tried to stop her, had tried to interrupt, but she knew that if she listened she would give in, and sobbing, she had apologized and cut the call. The kindly nun who had taken her in had simply sat in benevolent silence as she'd cried.

So now that month had come to an end. In the outside world it was nearly Christmas, and Anna tried to picture crowds of shoppers and hot, frantic department stores. The thought filled her with horror and she would have liked to stay where she was—safe in the quiet and simple routines of the convent. But she was growing too fond of the children, and for their sakes that wasn't a good idea.

She stopped in the doorway, looking back at Suzette. 'Sweet dreams.'

'Anna?' Suzette murmured. 'Tomorrow can we have that story again?'

Anna smiled sadly. 'I'm sure you can, darling. Maybe Lily will read it to you.'

'*Non.* Want you.'

'I'm leaving tomorrow, sweetheart, remember?' she said with infinite gentleness.

There was a little pause. 'Oh. Yes,' Suzette said in a very small voice. And then she turned over and faced the wall.

Anna's scarred heart turned over too. She longed to go back and hold the little girl, who had already learned that no one in life was to be relied on. But what comfort could she offer?

After all, it was pretty much the truth.

Later, sitting at the window in her bare, cell-like room, she looked out over the tree-tops towards the château as she had done every night since she had been here.

When she had first left Fliss's flat she had no idea where she was going, only that she had to get away. Seeing Angelo like that, finding out that he was to be married, had been agony almost beyond endurance. She had tried to believe in the time after he had left her so suddenly at Ifford Park that the scars from his difficult past ran too deep and that he was simply incapable of love, but to find out that he was in love with someone else was unbearable. And she had found herself drawn back to the place where she had always felt safest.

The château.

It had been easy to get a seat on a flight for Nice that evening, and it was only as she'd stepped out of the familiar airport building and got into a taxi that she'd realised how stupid she was being. The château was sold—she knew that, but it would also be exactly where Fliss would think to look for her, and then she might contact Angelo, and…

She had pictured him pulling up in front of the château and getting out of the car. Leaning back in to say to the woman who waited in the passenger seat, *Sorry about this,* tesoro. *She's a bit unhinged…*

'Where to, *mademoiselle*?' the taxi driver had asked.

'The convent near to Belle-Eden.'

'Sacre Coeur? *Bon.*'

And that was how she had ended up coming home—to her first and unremembered home: the place where she had lived as a tiny baby before Sir William and Lisette had taken her. Until then it was the last place she could have imagined coming to, but something had changed that afternoon on that dingy station platform. From the wreckage of her future she had managed at least to salvage something worthwhile about her past, which, she reflected sadly, was completely the wrong way round to do things. But fairly typical of her.

She'd said it. *I'm adopted.*

No one had laughed. No one had sneered. No one had moved away from her in the carriage, even though most of them must have heard. To be perfectly honest, there hadn't been much room to move away, but no one had tried. Somehow saying it like that had been a relief, and had planted in her head the seed of the idea which had brought her here.

She had used to come with her mother when she was very small, she remembered, no more than five or six. Looking back, she thought her mother had probably brought her back to maintain contact with the nuns who had looked after her as a baby and arranged her adoption, and then the visits had stopped when she had grown old enough to ask questions.

The shame. That was where the shame had begun.

But it was over now. For the first time ever, she felt at peace with herself.

OK, so everything else about her life was like the aftermath of an earthquake and her heart was lost in the rubble, but at least she knew who she was.

Roseanna Delafield, Spinster of this Parish.

Great. Just great.

The nuns did not encourage emotional goodbyes. People came and went, and Anna had been just one of a constant trickle of the lost and the lonely and the broken-hearted through the small number of guest rooms at the convent. They had accepted her departure with the same serene impassivity as they had accepted her arrival, giving her a bunch of late flowering roses and anemones from the walled garden and wishing her well.

Getting into the waiting taxi, she took the mobile out of her bag for the first time in a month and turned it on. Without even checking her messages, she dialled Fliss's work number.

'Good morning, Arundel-Ducasse, Felicity speaking. How may—'

'Fliss. It's me.'

'Anna. *Anna!* Where are you? *How* are you? Oh, my God—where have you been?'

'I'm OK. I'm just outside Cannes, but I'm coming home. But first I'm going to stop off at the château. I want to put some flowers on mum's grave and then—'

'You're going to the château? Now? Oh, God. OK, Anna, I have to go. Call me soon, d'you promise? Soon.'

The phone went dead and Anna was left staring out of the window as the car sped along the last familiar miles to the château. The landscape that she knew so well in its green, high summer glory looked different now, stripped of its lusciousness. It was stark, uncompromising, but somehow more honest.

To her surprise, the tall wrought iron gates of the château were open—she had expected them to be shut and locked—but even so she asked the taxi driver to stop at the foot of the drive so that she could approach on foot. She wasn't sure what she would find. A busy building site perhaps, crawling with earth-movers and men in hard hats? A brand-new, pristine-looking clinic, built around the old château, obscuring it so that it was barely recognizable?

Rounding the last corner of the drive, she felt her footsteps falter and a gasp of disbelief spring to her lips.

It was like stepping back in time.

The château looked the same as she remembered it when she was a child, when it had been clean and cared for and scrupulously maintained under Grandmère's watchful eye. The rotting woodwork had been repaired and repainted, broken pipes and missing slates replaced, clumps of moss and weeds removed from gutters and cracks in the masonry. The place gleamed.

Still carrying the flowers she had come to put on her mother's grave, she hesitated, wanting so much to go in, but hardly daring to hope…

With shaking hands, she took her keys from her bag and, stepping up to the front door, tried the largest and oldest one in the polished lock. He would have changed them…surely… He wouldn't risk…

It slid in. And turned.

And then she was standing in the hall and it was just as it must have been over a century before when her great-grandfather had first brought his new bride to the home he had built for her. The limestone floor had been cleaned and buffed to a soft sheen and the walls painted a soft duck-egg blue that exactly matched the colour of the silk that had rotted and decayed. And the whole space was imbued with that magical light from the dome above, like the shadows of birds of paradise flitting through sunlight.

Walking in a daze up the stairs, Anna trailed her fingers up the newly stripped and polished wooden banister. Any minute now she expected to wake up in her hard little bed at the convent and find she had dreamed all this—it was almost too wonderful to take in. Wandering into Grandmère's room a second later, she gave a gasp and had to grip the door-frame for support.

The furniture that had been sent to the auction house that day was back—the grand bed with its delicately gilded wicker headboard was made up with piles of pristine white linen pillows and bolsters, covered in a chalky pink silk eiderdown, just as if Grandmère were expected to come and slip between its sheets at any moment. The dressing table stood in its old position beneath the window, and the vast heavy mahogany wardrobe had been replaced against the wall beside the doorway.

But then the dream slipped inexorably into a nightmare and Anna's blood ran cold.

There, hanging up on the wardrobe, swathed in layers of protective tissue and polythene, was a dress. A long ivory dress.

A wedding dress.

She heard her own cry of anguish as it was wrenched from her throat, felt her hands fly to her mouth to stop the sobs that spilled out of her as the truth dawned.

Angelo's plans had changed. The château was not to be used as a clinic, but as his own home, the place where he and his bride would live together and raise their family.

They would get married from here. Just as she had always wanted to do.

For a moment she couldn't move. It was as if her brain, unable to deal with the horror of the situation, had simply shut down for a moment, leaving her immobilized in the centre of the room, unable to think what to do next. Outside, she was faintly aware of noises—of a car door slamming and feet crunching on gravel—and that broke the spell. Looking wildly around her, she made a run for the stairs as below the front door burst open.

Reaching the top of the staircase, she froze, her heart smashing against her ribs. Angelo was there, standing below in the hallway, just as she had first seen him. Just as she had remembered him a million times since, just as she had imagined him a thousand times before, as a little girl in her homemade wedding dress.

He looked up at her, his eyes blazing.

'Anna!'

'I know,' she whispered hoarsely. 'I'm sorry, I shouldn't be here. I'm going.'

'No!' he roared, racing up the stairs towards her. She shrank back, trembling violently, and, seeing her horrified reaction, he stopped abruptly.

'Please, Angelo—don't say anything. I'm getting myself together. The last month has been…good. Anything you say will only make it worse again. Please.'

She was pleading with him. Standing close, he could see the dark shadows of anguish beneath her beautiful dark eyes and it took all his self-restraint not to grab her and kiss them away. Instead he shoved his hands into his pockets.

'We have to talk, Anna. There's so much you don't know about.'

'No!' She almost shouted the word and her voice echoed around the walls and into the high dome above them, reproaching him with the hollow sound of her despair. 'Angelo—I've seen the wedding dress! I don't need to hear anything more!'

He gave a groan and raised his hands to his head. 'You saw it. I'm sorry—I wanted to speak to you first.'

'There's no need.' With a terrible gasping sob, she pushed past him and clattered down the stairs. 'You told me in London you were getting married, remember? It's not like I haven't had time to get used to the idea, but—' She stopped, grabbing hold of the banister for support and turning slowly back to look up at him. Her face was wet with tears. 'That doesn't mean I've got over it.'

Dizzying hope crashed through him. In his desperation to get things straight between them he'd forgotten he'd made up the line about getting married. She'd seen the dress and assumed it was for someone else... Oh, *Dio*...

'No,' he moaned. 'Oh, Anna, no... The dress... Did you not look at it properly?'

She let out a high, slightly hysterical laugh. 'Why? So I would be able to picture properly just how very beautiful your bride will be on your wedding day, Angelo? I think not. I think I'd prefer blissful ignorance and a bottle of vodka, if you don't mind.'

'Anna, come here.' His voice was heartbreakingly gentle.

'I can't.' Her mouth was quivering.

He sighed. 'OK, I'll come down to you.'

'No!' she cried. 'Don't, Angelo. Don't make it worse.'

She was like a frightened animal, he thought. One false move on his part and she would disappear into the undergrowth and he would have lost her for ever. Tension knotted in his chest, making it difficult to breathe properly. Maybe she was right. Maybe it was best that he said what he had to say now, while he wasn't distracted by her closeness. He had no idea how she would take it. When she found out he was Lisette's son she might never want to see him again.

'There's something I have to tell you, Anna. It might not be easy for you to hear.'

Oh, God, he's going to say she's pregnant! Anna's hands went to her ears. 'Angelo, please! I don't need to hear any more!'

His self-control snapped. 'Yes! Yes, you do! Just bloody listen to me, Anna!'

'*Why?* You've destroyed me already! Isn't that enough?'

He sat down heavily on to the stairs, dropping his head into his hands. 'Look, Anna, I left you at Ifford that day, not because of anything you did or said, but because of this.' He took a small, square box from his pocket and held it out to her. She closed her eyes.

'You were going to ask whoever she is to marry you,' she whispered brokenly.

'No!' He ground the word out through clenched teeth. 'Here.' He tossed the box down to her. 'Look at it.'

Warily she snapped it open and looked up at him uncomprehendingly. 'My pendant. I don't understand…'

'*Not* your pendant. The missing earring. Lisette's missing earring. I was left at a convent when I was a few hours old, wrapped in a cashmere shawl with *that* tucked into it.'

Her eyes were very wide, filled with alarm. 'My mother…?'

'Was my mother,' he said tonelessly. 'Apparently she had a brief relationship with someone else the summer she got engaged to your father and it seems I was the unwelcome result. I thought you were my sister. I couldn't believe what I'd done to you, and I just had to get away before I dragged you down into hell with me.

Silence settled in the majestic hallway as Anna looked down at the small arrangement of rubies and diamonds against the dark velvet. Disjointed thoughts swirled around her head as fragments of the last harrowing months came back to her, fitting together to give a picture of Angelo's suffering.

'That was why you wanted to know if I was pregnant,' she whispered.

'Yes.'

She caught the break in his voice. And looked up at him.

He wore the same expression of fierce determination she'd

seen on his face that day at the station, only this time, as she gazed at him, she caught the minute tremble of his beautiful mouth and understood its meaning. Her heart turned over.

'Oh, Angelo,' she breathed. 'I'm sorry…'

He stood up quickly and turned away from her, walking up the stairs out of view. Anna shut the box and slowly climbed the stairs after him, her mind dazed with a million thoughts and questions, all of which came back to one thought, one question.

She found him in her grandmother's room, standing at the window as he had on the day she had first met him. Outside, the winter's day was grey and misty and against it his blond head was like burnished gold. Hesitantly she walked towards him, still holding the flowers limply in one hand.

'Angelo? Why didn't you tell me?'

He didn't turn his head, but shook it slowly, hopelessly. 'And see you look at me with disgust? How could I?' In the darkness of the window-pane, she thought she saw the glimmer of tears on his face and she wanted so much to slide her arms around his waist and press her face against his back and hold him tightly.

But, of course, she couldn't. He wasn't hers to hold.

'It was my fault,' she said with a moan of anguish. 'If only I'd been more honest about myself instead of trying to hide who I was—that I was…adopted…none of this would ever have happened. It seems so *stupid*, but my parents had hidden it from me for so many years and it was as if it was something to be ashamed of. My father…it was so difficult for him, so humiliating, with the weight of all that family responsibility, to find he couldn't have children, and I guess I just took on *his* shame. *I* felt ashamed too, that I was the one who had broken that Delafield bloodline that stretched all the way back to the Norman sodding Conquest. I felt like an impostor, a fake. And then, that day at the station, I realised *none of that matters*. I *am* lucky…But—' Sobs choked her and for a moment she couldn't continue. Swallowing, taking deep gulps of air, she controlled herself enough to smile painfully through the tears and say, 'Typical me, I guess. I realized too late.'

Slowly he turned to face her. His face was brutally blank.

'Why?' he asked in a voice like gravel. 'Why too late?'

'The dress,' she said hopelessly, gesturing to where it hung on the wardrobe, swathed in protective layers. 'The wedding dress.'

'Look at it.'

Haltingly, hesitantly, she crossed the room. Placing the flowers carefully on the silk counterpane, she stood in front of the dress and, with shaking hands, she lifted the polythene, folding it back over the hanger. And then she stepped back.

Her hands flew to her mouth as more tears slid down her cheeks, unchecked. There, in exquisite thick ivory satin was a perfect recreation of the small ragged dress her mother had made for her. The details were all there—from the tight fitted bodice with the grosgrain ribbon across the bust, to the flared ballerina-length skirt with its delicious layers of net beneath, all expertly made in the most sumptuous fabric.

She couldn't speak.

In the mirrored door of the wardrobe she saw him watching her and the expression of tortured love on his face stole her breath and stopped her heart. The next moment he was standing in front of her, gently peeling her fingers from across her mouth and brushing her quivering lips with his thumbs as he cupped her face in his hands.

'It's yours. Everything's yours. The château, the furniture, the dress, everything.'

'You?'

'Oh, Anna…' he moaned softly. 'It goes without saying but, just to avoid any more confusion, I'm going to say it anyway. I'm yours. Everything I have is yours. I love you. And maybe you're too free-spirited to do anything as conventional and boring as getting married, and if you don't want to it won't matter, because

I'll go on loving you whatever, and you can wear that dress with your bare feet and dance on the beach in it for all I care…' He kissed her mouth, very intently. 'Just as long as I can be there. Always.'

'And what if I *want* to get married?'

'Then, please, marry me.' He smiled wearily. 'Marry me as soon as possible and put your poor friend Felicity out of her misery. She's been looking at bridesmaids' dresses ever since you went away and she's desperate to know what colour you'll let her have.'

And then she was laughing and crying and then his lips caught hers again and she was oblivious to everything else. It was a few moments before either of them realized that his mobile was ringing, and a few more before he tore his mouth from hers and answered it.

'Fliss. Yes, I'm with her now…' Smiling, his eyes flickered to Anna's, the clear blue smoky with love. 'Yes, I have asked her, actually,' he said dryly, and then frowned. 'Do you know, I don't think she's actually given me an answer yet…'

'Yes,' Anna whispered, looking into his eyes. Then she tipped back her head and yelled, 'Yes, yes, *yes!*'

Angelo raised an eyebrow. 'Did you get that? She said *yes…*'

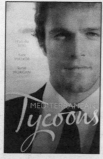